She's Gone Santa Fe

by

Maida Tilchen

To Louise and Faye,
I look forward to our
friendship!
Maida T.

Savvy Press

Salem, New York

Published by: Savvy Press, P.O. Box 63, Salem, NY 12865
http://www.savvypress.com

ISBN: 978-1-939113-20-7

LCCN: 2013917601

Printed in the United States of America

Cataloguing Data:
Tilchen, Maida
She's gone Santa Fe/by Maida Tilchen

p. 334 cm. 15x23

Summary: Historical fiction novel of the brief life of a Jewish sweatshop worker from Brooklyn who in 1925 drops out of the anthropology department at Columbia University, where she studied with Ruth Benedict and a fellow student was Margaret Mead. Hoping to live with the Indians, Ree goes to New Mexico where she works at a dude ranch for single women; assists Mary Cabot Wheelwright's research with Navajo medicine man Hosteen Klah; travels in a sheepherder's wagon; and works in a trading post. Inspired by the life and death of Henrietta Schmerler (1908-1931), one of the few anthropologists murdered during field work, and emphasizing lesbian history.

ISBN: 978-1-939113-20-7

1. Henrietta Schmerler – Fiction. 2. Lesbians – Southwestern states – Fiction. 3. Southwestern states – Fiction.

First printing, First Edition

Cover photograph by Edward Kemp

"Guest on horseback, San Gabriel Dude Ranch, Alcalde, New Mexico" ca. 1925

Courtesy Palace of the Governors Photo Archives (NMHM/DCA] Negative #LS.1433

View and order additional images online at http://www.palaceofthegovernors.org/photoarchives.html.

"Santa Fe had become a mecca for women who wanted to live openly with other women -- and it was not uncommon to see women paired with women there. During the 1920s and 1930s, Santa Fe and Taos were to American lesbians what Capri was to British homosexuals at the same time -- a place away from the constraints of organized society, which discouraged homosexual unions. ..In Broadway crowds at this time a woman who had switched her sexual preference was said to have "gone Santa Fe."

- *O'Keeffe: The Life of an American Legend* by Jeffrey Hogrefe (1994, p. 164).

"...Nobody can paint the sun, or sunlight. He [the artist] can only paint the tricks that shadows play with it, or what it does to forms. He cannot even paint those relations of light and shade -- he can only paint some emotions they give him, some man-made arrangement of them that happens to give him personal delight...No art can do anything at all with great natural forces or great elemental conditions. No poet can write of love, hate, jealousy. He can only touch these things as they affect the people in his drama and his story, and unless he is more interested in his own little story and his foolish little people than in the Preservation of the Indian or Sex or Tuberculosis, then he ought to be working in a laboratory or bureau."

- "Light on Adobe Walls" in *Willa Cather On Writing* (1988, pp. 123-125).

Prologue

"It's a telegram from Boas," Margaret Mead called to Ruth as she closed the door behind the delivery boy. She held the envelope up toward the bed where Ruth Benedict's face barely peeked out from a thick pile of blankets and quilts.

"Go ahead, you open it," Ruth said.

"Henrietta's father dropped suit. STOP. Leaving for Palestine to join Zionists. STOP."

Ruth started to answer but instead held up one hand while she blew her nose with a handkerchief held in the other.

"Columbia is off the hook!" Margaret squealed. He's admitting she brought it on herself. Where'd you put the champagne? Now there's nothing to stop me from going to Samoa. The department won't be afraid to send women into the field."

"He lost his daughter," Ruth gasped out through her stuffed nose. "He needed to blame someone."

"You can't say you didn't warn her. She broke every rule. She spit in all our faces. We were so right about her. She was never one of us. Did you hear what Sylvester Baxter just figured out about the time he spoke at the Brooklyn Museum?"

Part 1

From the moment she opened the moldy old magazine and saw the photograph, thirteen-year old Henrietta escaped the smelly tenement forever. She never again felt trapped in that world, because she saw a new one in the eyes of a fearless man, his arms crossed on his chest, daring the world to laugh at his strange outfit. Although clearly a white man, he wore leather trousers with a line of big white beads up the sides of his tall body, a bundle of beaded belts at his thin waist, a velvet shirt, necklaces piled around his throat, and, most defiantly, a cloth sash tied around his head. There was nothing feminine about him, but he was nothing like any man she had ever seen on the streets of Brooklyn. She saw a person with purpose, calm and assured, as far from her own life as could be.

She soon read as much as she could find about this man, Frank Hamilton Cushing, starting with that first article in the 1882 issue of *Harper's Magazine*. It was Sylvester's Baxter's account of visiting Cushing at the Zuni Indian pueblo where he had been living for two years. She giggled as she wondered if the meal Frank cooked for Baxter—roasted locusts—would be kosher. When Baxter described Frank's living space in a cozy corner of the humble Zuni home, consisting of a pile of brightly colored blankets, a sleeping hammock, and a makeshift writing table and bookshelves warmed by a corner oven against the softly rounded adobe walls and earthen floor, it was everything her tiny closet room in the crowded, noisy tenement was not.

She often called him Frank in her head and her dreams. He had died young, like that Latin movie star that all the other girls at school loved so much—Valentino, the Sheik. The Sheik was just an actor, but Frank was the real thing, the first white man to report on his life among the Indians. While Frank was living at Zuni pueblo, the Indians were still fighting with other tribes and with the U.S. Cavalry.

When she wasn't at school or trying to study in the noise and dank air at home, Henrietta worked in the steaming dark hallway of a sixth-floor coat factory, hunched over a sewing machine so close to the next girl that their elbows bumped too often to be friendly about it. For hours she faced an endless pile of flat cloth that she sewed into sleeves. Further down the assembly line, these were sewn onto tunics by another girl or pregnant wife or old woman. Wool, cotton, velveteen, Persian lamb, and leather passed through her fingers to make coats far nicer than any she could afford. She made it through the endless days thinking of the sunny courtyard of the pueblo, which was what the Zuni people called their little village of sun-dried adobe brick homes. Such beautiful words: adobe, pueblo, Zuni. She loved to say them to herself over the banging of all the sewing machines.

One day, as the needle stuck and almost broke in an especially thick fabric, she muttered Yiddish curses to herself. Across the room, an old woman did the same, and Henrietta saw herself decades in the future becoming that old woman. She had thought many times of running out of the room, but at the door of the factory there was always a line of women desperate to get a job like hers. As her father reminded her only too often, she was a lucky girl to be able to go to high school and only work after school and on Sundays.

As she freed the needle, grateful it didn't break and cause a deduction from her wages, she looked at the piece of soft brown leather and pictured the leather trousers that Frank Hamilton Cushing wore in the photo. She thought about the maroon velveteen sleeves she had just sewn and pictured Frank's shirt. As she bent back to her work, she put the next piece of leather under her hand and began to inch it up her own sleeve until it was tightly packed between her elbow and her cuff. When the shift finally ended, she put her thin cotton coat on quickly and walked past the foreman waving as naturally as she could. Did he see the bulge? But he merely shrugged and checked off her time.

The next day she snuck some velveteen, keeping her head low and her machine and hands moving as normally as possible. The hours passed slowly as she thought about how scary it would be to walk out with the stolen cloth. She considered slipping it back out again. Perhaps the first time had been a charm, beginner's luck, that she shouldn't test again. But she was soon walking away from the factory, trying not to touch the lump of cloth. Through the babble of women's voices, she expected the foreman to call her back. As she turned the corner to safety, a hand grabbed her shoulder. Her heart banged against her chest and she gasped. There was a hot breath on her ear, then the raspy voice of an old lady, in Yiddish, "Are you meshugana? Crazy? They'll put you in the jail with the goyim! You don't want to know what those shiksas will do to you! I know, I was there from a strike. Go to jail for a reason, not as a thief!" The pinching fingers let her go with a shove. She never saw the woman's face.

But she couldn't stop herself. One Saturday a few weeks later, she finished her studying and took out her contraband. She had hidden it in her book bag, not that her father would have intruded into the closet which served as her bedroom. The closet was just big enough for the child's bed she was outgrowing. It opened into the bedroom where her father slept beneath a photo of her mother, who had died when Henrietta was nine. She sat on the edge of his bed to work at the radiator she used as a desk. The window behind it faced a courtyard. Clotheslines of flapping sheets and underwear criss-crossed the space below and above their fourth floor home. Her fingers were cold from the wind rattling through the loose windows.

None of the smuggled pieces were larger than unsewn sleeves, but they were of the best fabrics. She leaned the photograph of Frank against her thickest school book and studied it carefully as she laid each remnant out into the shape of trousers and tunic like Frank's. She resented each minute of sewing at the factory and had never enjoyed sewing by hand, but for this she grinned as she worked. When she held up the finished pants, she considered asking for a transfer at work so she could steal big white buttons to run up the sides of the legs and to use like beads to imitate the necklaces.

Never rushing her studying to the point where it might affect her good grades, for the next weeks she worked faster to leave time to sew the suit. If her father asked, she would say she was sewing a dress, but he paid little attention to what she did. While she worked in the bedroom, he went out to Zionist meetings or sat in the living room, ignoring the tumult of their landlord's children, reading the books of his own hero, Theodore Herzl. He thought of America as a stopping place on his way from the pogroms of Belarus to the sheltering walls of Jerusalem, his City of Gold. She dreamed of Zuni Pueblo, of adobe walls, and of distant mountains. She saw Brooklyn as her launching point to a golden America she hadn't found yet. If they talked at all, their conversation would soon end in his disappointment that once again she did not want to be a pioneer in the Jewish homeland. She didn't even try to interest him in her passion.

When the suit was done, she locked herself in the bathroom and put it on, straining up on her tiptoes to try to see as much as she could, but the small mirror over the sink only showed her face with the sash tied around her head. She saved her lunch money, and on a Shabbat when her father thought she was studying at the library, she went to the movie palace, where the bathroom walls were floor to ceiling mirrors. While the movie was on and the bathroom empty, she paraded around in the outfit. She had expected to look imposing and fierce like tall, thin Frank Hamilton Cushing, but the clothes only made her look shorter and rounder. She tried crossing her arms and looking defiantly at the world as Frank did in the photo, but only to rush back into the stall when she heard the attendant coming.

As her teen years passed, she added more pieces to the outfit and read all she could about Frank. On a rare school trip, she discovered the Brooklyn Museum, which had a whole hall devoted to the Southwest and Zuni Pueblo. Any time she could sneak out of school or Shabbat responsibilities, she walked there, getting past the ticket booth by blending in with a group of schoolchildren. A sign explained that Frank Hamilton Cushing himself had helped design the exhibit, which opened in 1905, five years after his death. The hall was dominated by a huge Thomas Eakins' painting of Frank, in the same pose as his photograph. As she walked through the hall, examining the cases of clay pots, silver and turquoise jewelry, grotesque kachina masks, and little stone animal fetishes, she was always aware of the giant portrait behind her, as if Frank were with her, looking over her shoulder, puzzling out the mysteries of their Indian makers with her.

When she saw a poster saying Sylvester Baxter would be speaking at the Brooklyn Museum, sixteen-year old Henrietta was beside herself with excitement. To actually see Sylvester Baxter in person, the man who had visited Frank Hamilton Cushing at Zuni Pueblo! If Baxter had never written the magazine articles, she probably would never have heard of Frank. She had so much to tell Baxter about what Frank meant to her. She barely slept for days, running in her head the conversations they would have. Every day she changed her mind about whether to bring the suit with her, feeling she would never have the nerve to show it to him. In the end, she stuffed it into her satchel, just for good luck. It just felt right that the suit should go with her on this special day. She had to go see him speak, even if she risked losing her job by sending word that she was sick.

When the day came, she arrived early at the Southwest hall. The portrait of Frank Hamilton Cushing looked down at people wandering restlessly among the exhibits, waiting for Baxter. Their chatter and movement in the usually silent hall distracted her. Looking intently at the diorama of Zuni dancers, pretending she was there among them, she walked right into a man so big and broadshouldered that the softness of his stomach surprised her. Other than a rare hug from her father, she had never touched a man so closely in her life. He laughed as they both apologized.

"Hello down there," he said. He looked about her age, too young for his thick mustache and beard, a boy who had grown too fast. "I'm sorry. But isn't this wonderful? Did you know that Frank Hamilton Cushing himself is said to have posed as a dancer for the artist who did the diorama?"

"What!" Henrietta swung around to stare more closely at the carved wooden doll figures. "How did you know that?"

"I get around. Do you just happen to be here today, or did you come for Baxter's speech? By the way, my name's Sack Sackmann. Glad to meet you." He reached out a huge hand, reminding her of the overfriendly cemetery plot salesmen who visited the tenement regularly.

"Of course I do. I know everything about Frank—about Frank Hamilton Cushing."

"Not more than me, I'll bet you. You didn't know about the dancers."

"You think so? Well, look at what I have," Henrietta said, opening her satchel and pulling out the leggings of her Frank suit. She had never shown it to anyone before, and for an instant she was shocked at herself, but the boy immediately grabbed the fabric and held it up, comparing it to the painting.

"Where'd you get this? Wow, did you steal it?" He looked at the guard at the end of the room, crumpling it to hand back to her.

"No, I made it. I work as a seamstress. I've got the whole outfit." She pulled out the tunic, the headband, and the moccasins.

He held each piece up to compare it to the painting.

"This is amazing. Hey, put it on, show it to Baxter."

"I couldn't do that."

"I bet he'd love to see it." Sack ran his fingers on the fabric. "This is beautifully made. You should be proud to show it."

"Well, maybe I could show it to him."

"No, you've got to put it on. I heard that the director of the museum once wore Frank Cushing's real outfit to a party. You won't be the first."

Just then, the room quieted. The crowd formed a circle as a group of men entered.

"Our esteemed speaker, Mr. Sylvester Baxter," said one of the men.

Henrietta was thrilled from the moment Baxter walked into the room. Frank no longer existed only in her imagination and on paper, because here was a man who had met him in the flesh, although nineteen years had passed since Frank's sudden death. Of course Baxter was now an old man, but he still had a stocky body and thick mustache, and she could see in him the young adventurer who had first gone to Zuni pueblo in 1882. He was almost as much an explorer of the Indian lands as Frank had been. He had been on the Hemenway expedition, one of the first scholarly attempts to explore the Southwest. It had ended abruptly, leaving much gossip and rumor about conflicts and money problems. People had laughed it off as a product of Harvard arrogance. Little had been published from it. Frank had stayed on at Zuni after the rest of the explorers had left.

Standing under the portrait of Frank, with the audience clustered around him, Baxter spoke with a hearty voice, summarizing Frank Hamilton Cushing's life. Henrietta had read his articles so many times that she almost mouthed Baxter's words along with him. After the speech, it was announced that he needed to rest briefly and then would return to take questions. Her head filling with what she would say, she was startled when the young man poked her shoulder.

"Here's your chance! You can change right now."

"I can't do that."

"Sure you can. I know where the bathrooms are. I'll come with you—well, as far as I can."

Henrietta was shocked that he would refer to such a private matter. But he linked his elbow around hers and guided her down the corridor.

"I'll be right outside. Can't wait to see it!"

It didn't feel right, but Henrietta was used to men telling her what to do. When she came out, he stood back, tipped his hat and bowed to her. He took her arm and they walked together back to the Southwest Hall. She felt safe, escorted, and special. People stared at her but Sack's proud smile gave her confidence.

Many people crowded around Baxter, holding books for him to autograph. She was afraid Sack would push them right through the crowd, but he hesitated at the edge. A few people turned to stare. Sack let go of her arm and moved a step back. Suddenly she felt alone and conspicuous, her face steaming and her stomach knotted. The museum director who had introduced Baxter waved his hand and a guard ran up and blocked her. The chatter of the crowd stopped as everyone watched the guard look her over carefully. The guard looked back at the museum director, shrugging uncertainly.

"Come here, young lady," demanded the museum director. The crowd gasped. As she moved, her mocassins thudded on the hard marble floor. Sack did not come with her. The museum director looked her up and down.

"Just an amateurish copy," he said to Baxter. "Young lady, you've given us a scare. This is how forgers sneak things out of museums. Please don't do this again."

He turned away from her. "Go on, Mr. Baxter," he said. "Who else would like to speak to our esteemed guest?" he called out to the crowd.

Baxter smiled at her with curiosity. "Perhaps the young lady has a book for me to sign." Henrietta's heart started beating again, but she couldn't speak.

"Hello, do you have a book for me?" Baxter asked again.

She held up her empty hands. Everything she had read had been borrowed from the library.

"That's all right," Baxter said. As he turned away, she found her voice.

"Mr. Baxter," she squeaked. "I just wanted to tell you how much your writing has meant to me. Frank Frank-- " she stuttered

"Why thank you," Baxter said. "Fortunately for me, you're not alone." The group around them laughed self-consciously.

"Frank Hamilton---" she started again.

"Mr. Baxter," said a man the crowd with an armful of books. "What will you be writing in the future?"

Baxter turned toward the man, and Henrietta was left with her mouth open. If she didn't tell Baxter how she felt about Frank, then it would be as if she hadn't told Frank. At that moment, it was as if Baxter was Frank, the man she had thought about and dreamed of for so many years. She threw her arms around Baxter in an awkward hug, her face falling against his ear. He jerked out of her arms. The crowd gasped.

"What are you doing!" snapped a woman as the guard ran back to Henrietta.

"I, I—I'm sorry," Henrietta said. "I just, I just wanted to tell him how much he means to me."

"Me?" said Baxter. "I've never seen this girl before," he stated to the group.

"She must be mad," said the woman. The crowd moved in, protecting Baxter.

"I'm not mad," Henrietta's voice broke. "I just want to tell Frank how much he's meant to me. Frank—"she said and then realized what she had said.

"Frank! I'm not Frank," said Baxter.

"I mean, Frank Hamilton—"

"She's mad," the woman, more loudly. "She thinks you're Frank Hamilton Cushing."

"Frank's been dead a long time. I just write about him, I'm not him," said Baxter. His voice was more kindly than the others in the crowd.

"If Cushing was alive, he'd have a lot to answer for," said a man from the edge of the crowd.

"Don't say that!" said a woman with an armload of books.

"It's true," said the first man. "I teach at the University of Denver, and let me tell you, our students are still trying to reconstruct the field work he didn't write up. He took on projects and didn't finish them. His notes are unreadable. He pushed his way in with the Indians and created bad feelings towards all anthropologists who came after. We use him as an example of what not to do, in our classrooms today."

Henrietta wasn't the only one in the crowd who gasped as his outspokenness.

"There's some truth to that," said Baxter to the professor. "But it isn't everything about Frank Hamilton Cushing. He was my friend, and I looked up to him. We all have our faults." Baxter's voice choked. "And he died so suddenly, too soon to finish his work."

Henrietta almost hugged Baxter again. This was what she had wanted, to feel the connection and love that Baxter had to her hero. She wanted to tell Baxter but she was afraid to speak. The group was silent, respecting Baxter's grief. Too soon, Baxter straightened up.

"Well, does anyone else have a book for me to sign?"

The crowd turned back to Baxter, Henrietta forgotten. There was so much more she wanted to ask Baxter, and now it was impossible. She stepped back from the group. Without looking Sack in the eyes, she grabbed her satchel and slipped out of the hall, trying to capture in her memory what Baxter had said about Frank and to forget the humiliation.

Although she never wanted to see anyone again who had been at the museum that day, she couldn't stay away from the Southwest Hall. But not long after that, as she stood by the diorama of the kachina dance, she saw the young man, Sack, watching her. Before she could run from the room, he was at her side. She kept her eyes on the glass case, unable to look at him.

"Henrietta, here you are! I've been hoping to see you again." He winced slightly as he waved to her.

"Sure," she said as uninvitingly as she could.

"Guess what?" he said. "I've started Columbia, in the anthropology department." He threw back his shoulders proudly, then winced again, as if unable to straighten up, his back hunched. He saw her looking and said "Hurt myself working on the docks. But it doesn't matter. I'm a student now. And guess what? People from Columbia go to Zuni pueblo all the time. You could go, too."

"To Zuni pueblo?"

"You could go to Columbia and from there to Zuni. it didn't end with Frank Hamilton Cushing. Those people that were at Baxter's talk? A lot of them go to Columbia. After you left, I got to talking with one of the students. I was planning to go to City, but he told me what to do."

"Maybe you can go there," said Henrietta bitterly, backing away.

"Do I look like a rich boy to you? Or sound like one? I'm working and I'm going to school. You can do it."

Henrietta stared at the floor.

"If I can, you can. You'll love it. I'll tell you something, some of the rich kids there don't know what they have. Someone like us comes along who knows what hard work is and we can do ok. They even have scholarship money. And you know what else?" He didn't wait for an answer. "Being around those rich kids, all that money? Money breeds money. I'm going to come out of this a rich man. You can do it too. I've been looking for you, to tell you."

"My father says 'my smart daughter's going to go to City College for free.'" She spoke in her father's authoritarian tone. "I don't even want to go there. He just wants me to be a teacher. I hate children!"

"That's it! Columbia Teachers College. Tell him you want to go there. Then you can start taking anthropology courses. You can change departments, he won't know."

"You don't know my father. Look, thanks for thinking of me, but--"

"Let me talk to him. I'm a salesman, can't you tell? People say I can sell ice to the Eskimos."

"That's really funny," Henrietta said. "You have no idea how funny that is. Let's see, a big goy tells my father what he should let his daughter do. Hey, you want to see an old Jewish guy try to kill you with his rolled up copy of the *Jewish Daily Forward*?"

"The what?"

"No, probably he'd just try to throw you down the stairs or push you out the window."

"What are you talking about? Listen I can even offer to take him over to Columbia, show him around."

"Oh my God. Don't you understand? I shouldn't even be talking to a non-Jew. Especially a big Polack like you. My father would call you a Cossack."

"That's not fair. I'm a nice guy. And I'm not a Polack."

"Goy. That's all he would see. What would your folks say if they heard you were seeing a Jewish girl?"

"They're dead. I've been on my own since grade school."

"I'm sorry, but you know what I mean, what would they say? A good Catholic boy? What about the priest?"

"All right. But that's what I like about anthropology. Cultures are different, but people aren't that different. Underneath the clothes and the masks and the face painting, we all want the same things. I know what I want--"

"Wait a minute. I don't believe that. I don't believe the Zuni people are anything like the Jews. That's why I want to go there."

"You want to go there and find out? Go to Columbia. That's the fastest train to Zuni pueblo for a girl from Brooklyn. The subway to City College doesn't stop at Zuni pueblo."

Part 2

That September, Henrietta walked into her first class at Columbia. She had been so busy earning every cent she could that she had barely noticed high school graduation. Her father had agreed to Columbia Teacher's College, but what he didn't know was that she hadn't registered only for teacher's courses. She had snuck in one anthropology class, because Professor Ruth Benedict studied the Zuni Indians. It was the only class she was excited about.

Finally she was walking into the lecture hall, twisting to fit into the small chair with the desk attachment. On a little stage with velvet curtains stood a dark wood podium. It felt like a play was about to begin. As Henrietta waited for the curtains to part, the room filled with students talking and making friends, but all she wanted to do was to see the woman who had actually been to Zuni pueblo.

A small woman in a silk dress crossed the room and went up the stage stairs to the podium. She tapped a microphone and it clicked with static.

"Anthropology 101 will begin now," she said in a soft voice.

"Louder!" called someone way in the back.

"Is this all right?" she said in a too loud voice. The microphone shrieked.

"Too loud!" the woman near Henrietta called out.

"How's this?" she said, her voice somewhere in the middle. No one answered so she continued. "I am Professor Benedict. This semester we will be using the following textbooks…"

Henrietta was so shocked she barely listened. She hadn't thought about what she expected Professor Benedict, anthropological heir to Frank Hamilton Cushing and friend of the Zuni people, to look like. But now she realized that she had expected Frank himself to appear from behind the velvet curtains in his buckskin outfit, with his Navajo silver and turquoise necklaces and bracelets, his fringed leggings, his beaded moccasin boots, his long yellow hair, and his thin, doomed face. Not Professor Benedict, in her silk dress and pointy heeled shoes! She was old too, almost her father's age, probably around forty. How could she have gone to Zuni pueblo? How could she have climbed those rocky paths or crawled through the low doorways of their adobe houses? What had the Indians thought of her in city clothes fit for an opera? How could she be the scholarly progeny of Frank Hamilton Cushing?

"So, this semester we will examine methods for ethnographic fieldwork," Professor Benedict was saying. "Three cultures will be studied, including Dr. Boas work among the Trobriand Islanders, Dr. Sapir's study of language, and my work among the Zuni people."

Franz Boas, thought Henrietta. He was the chairman of the department and Sack had told her he was Jewish. That would be ammunition when she explained to her father why she had changed her major. But should she change her major? What could this frail woman teach her? Certainly not how to live among the Indians.

Had Benedict just said something about the Zuni people? Henrietta gripped her pen and stared at the professor.

"We will be studying the matrilineal and the matrilocal" said Benedict, and Henrietta 's pen raced across the page. Benedict was talking about the importance of anthropology, and how it had changed over the decades to incorporate more modern scientific methods. Henrietta realized that all her reading had been only of Frank's articles about Zuni pueblo in the 1880s. He hadn't gone back there after 1890. Things had changed so much that delicate Professor Benedict, with her large, luminous eyes and soft voice, had been able to take the place of Frank Hamilton Cushing, who not only hunted buffalo with the Zuni men, but went out on horseback with their warriors and had claimed to have taken a scalp. Henrietta pictured Benedict in her silk dress, the points of her high heels grabbing the stirrups of a horse galloping across the Plains, her face covered with war paint, her hair long and loose and blowing behind her in the wind, screaming and waving her spear.

Two girls whispered behind her, and a boy to her side shuffled pages. How could they not pay attention? She wanted to shush them.

At that moment, Benedict looked directly at Henrietta and stopped speaking. Henrietta's face heated. Was everyone in the room staring at her? But she heard their pens going, trying to catch up with what Benedict had said while Henrietta was daydreaming of their professor on a horse. Benedict was looking at her intently. Her eyes were huge and deep and Henrietta felt as if she were looking into a pale blue magnifying glass.

Time stopped as if they were alone in the room. Henrietta felt as if Benedict had looked at all the students and concluded that Henrietta was the only one truly paying attention, who understood her, who loved anthropology, who was chosen to carry on the work of Frank Hamilton Cushing and of Benedict herself. Henrietta felt chosen.

Just then a student in the front row dropped a book and stood up to get it. Benedict shook her head slightly as if to clear it, bent down to her notes, and continued.

Henrietta wanted to be looked at that way again. No one had ever looked at her like that. She had felt in that instant that she was the most special, unique, and interesting person in Benedict's world. For the rest of the class, she tried to catch Benedict's eye again, but the professor kept her nose to her notes. Henrietta was sure Benedict was embarrassed, thinking of little else but Henrietta, but trying desperately to keep her mind on her work. She decided that when the class ended, she would stay in her seat, and Benedict would come to her when the room emptied out. They would talk, but it would hardly take words, because Benedict understood her, knew her, even without words. She didn't need to call her Benedict anymore. It would be Ruth, her Ruth, her dear Ruth. She rehearsed the stories she would tell Ruth about how she had come to love Frank and the Zuni people so much, and how she dreamt only of going to the Southwest.

Maybe Ruth would even like to hear about her life, her father, their apartment. She had never told anyone about that or brought anyone home. But with Ruth it would be different. Ruth would want to know everything about her. Ruth's moist blue eyes would look at her, full of interest, and maybe this is what other people meant when they said love. She had come here for an anthropology class, she had come to hear about the Indians, but she had felt something she hadn't known she wanted: love. The severe clock that hung over the door showed that in only a few minutes the class period would end and then love would begin for Henrietta.

Ruth was answering questions now. Students wanted to know about the papers, the tests, the grades. It didn't matter to Henrietta. From this moment on, all her school work would be for this class, to please Ruth. She was sure to do well, and she would do much more than what was asked. Nothing would be too much for Ruth.

When the class ended, a crowd of students collected in front of the stage, blocking Henrietta's view of Ruth. She stayed in her chair so Ruth could find her. But when the students cleared out, the stage was empty. Henrietta grabbed her coat and frantically pushed her way through a logjam at the door. Her shoes slipped on the slick floor of the hall, polished for the new school year, and a cluster of girls giggled at her. Henrietta looked up and down the hall for sight of Ruth.

"Say, weren't you in Benedict's class?" a woman tapped her on the shoulder. Her curly brown hair was unsuccessfully held back by a huge barrette. "Did you get the dates for the tests? My pen ran out of ink. I can't believe she wants three research papers for a piddly 3-credit course."

"I've got to find someone," Henrietta said, and walked off. How could anyone complain about having to do work for Ruth? She headed past the crowded entrance to the stairwell and turned the corner into an empty corridor. Her heels clicked on the marble floor. Each door had a name on it in elaborate gold letters: Dr. E. M. Taylor; Dr. R. Bunzel; Dr. I. Goldquist. She walked faster, eager to read the next door, waiting to see those suddenly magic words, "Dr. R. Benedict."

Almost at the end of the hall, a door was open, and a sturdy woman with short dark hair blocked the name. She was talking to someone inside the room. Henrietta stood back, waiting for her to move.

"So, I'll be back for your office hours tomorrow morning, and you'll look at my research plans then. That'll be great. Thanks."

"Wait," said a soft voice in the office, which Henrietta recognized with a slight gasp. "We can talk right now if you'd like to, Margaret."

"That's even better! I can't wait to get started."

"Come on in and close the door. I'd love to hear all about your--." and that was the last thing Henrietta heard as the door closed, revealing the words "Dr. R. Benedict." Through the translucent glass she saw the shadows of the two heads bent together. How had that woman got here first? How could Ruth not have kept her door open for her? She hated the woman in the doorway.

Running from home to work to school and back again, it was a rare day when Henrietta and Sack had lunch at the cafeteria at Columbia and caught up with each other.

"When I met you at the museum and told you about Columbia, I never thought you really would come. I don't know any other girls like you."

"Oh come on," said Henrietta.

"They're ok, but their biggest dream is like a movie, that a rich man will come into the sweatshop or the grocery and fall in love at first sight. And they end up marrying guys with little dreams, too. Guys who think if they marry a beautiful woman, then all the other men will envy them and their lives will be wonderful, even if they are poor. Not me, I want more. And you want more. That's why we're here. We have dreams beyond this city."

"That's why I work so hard on Benedict's class and everything else. I'll get fieldwork and live like Frank Hamilton Cushing. Benedict will notice me." As soon as she said that, she stared away, embarrassed.

"I notice you." That made her blush even more. She couldn't look at him. "I've got to get to the library, I don't have time for lunch like this."

"Hey, don't you want to know what I want?"

"OK. Why do you study anthropology? Do you have someone like Frank you want to be like?"

"No, I just want to be rich."

Henrietta laughed. "But anthropologists don't get rich."

"I know, they come here rich already, the princes and the princesses of their father's Fifth Avenue mansions. But down at the docks, I've seen some of those fathers, and I've seen the bodies they dropped into the harbor to get rich. I don't want to get rich that way. But I go to school here just like the rich men's sons, so I'm studying them."

"So that's why you changed your beard. And your hair? You're starting to look like them."

"The way to get rich without killing people is to get to know the rich people, get to be their friends, be like them. This is a good place to do it."

"But why anthropology? You can find them in every department."

"I guess because I learned about it hanging around the Brooklyn Museum when I was supposed to be in school. Just like you I guess, I learned about a world beyond New York there. And those other things men study here – business and law – it's too much sitting around for me. I don't want to be working like a horse like I am now, but I also can't sit all day. Anthropologists get out and see places and do things. I think I'd like that. I'd be good at it. I already know how to work hard. But knowing how to act like a rich man's son, I'm learning that here."

Henrietta nodded as she stood and began to gather up her books.

"Wait—," Sack said. "We could do this together."

"I don't want to be like them. I just want to be like Frank Hamilton Cushing."

"And Ruth Benedict. Your darling Ruth." There was a snarl in his voice that Henrietta didn't like.

"Huh?" said Henrietta. "I have to get to class."

To get to Ruth's class on time took a frantic subway ride from her job downtown in the garment district, then a run through the campus. No matter how fast she went, the seat she wanted was always already occupied by none other than Margaret Mead. It was front row and over to the left. Henrietta had noticed that Ruth was deaf in her right ear. The professor always faced to the left as she spoke in her somewhat soft voice, and she never noticed a raised hand on her right because she didn't want to struggle to hear. Apparently she didn't want people to know, but Henrietta figured it out by careful observation. As Ruth had explained an anthropologist must do, Henrietta had watched carefully and discerned a secret. Clearly, she had the makings of a field anthropologist. She pictured herself walking in the footsteps of Ruth and of Frank Hamilton Cushing.

Henrietta liked figuring secrets out, but she didn't always know what to do with them. It wasn't always as simple as sitting where Ruth could hear her. Sometimes she berated herself because she could pick up the clues, but not act on them. Too often, she misjudged and misread and embarrassed herself.

That wasn't the case with Margaret. Henrietta first wondered how she had known where to sit, but by the end of the second class session, she knew it wasn't just random choice. During the question session, Margaret's hand was up, her mouth ran with impressive questions, and she would engage Ruth in discussion. Ruth never again looked at Henrietta with the curious stare of that first class, which Henrietta saw now when Ruth and Margaret's eyes locked while their mouths went on and on. Sitting next to Margaret, Henrietta felt the heat in the way that rays of sun burst out the edges of a window shade. What Henrietta hated most was the assured way Margaret took it in, never doubting that she was the star. When Ruth looked her way, it was only because she overshot looking at Margaret. Henrietta wanted to push Margaret out of her chair.

In the cafeteria, she heard talk of last year's golden boy, who had been the envy of all the first year students until final papers were turned in. The golden boy didn't come back the next semester, and the rumor was that his poorly written work was found so funny by the faculty that it had been read aloud for laughs at their Christmas party. Perhaps Margaret was a similar flash in the pan and Ruth would look Henrietta's way again.

But as the weeks passed, hope faded. Margaret Mead was invariably outstanding in class. Not just Ruth, but the other students began to face toward her. Henrietta changed seats, because she felt like she sat in blackness beside the bright full moon that was Margaret's round face.

If Henrietta hadn't resented Margaret so much, she might have idolized her, copied her, and wanted to be like her. Women had been among the first anthropologists, such as Matilda Coxe Stephenson and Elsie Clews Parsons. But as the field had taken on more respect in academic circles, and the departments had grown larger and richer, men had become the leaders and women their subordinates. But when Margaret went through the halls with her almost manly stride, some of the meeker men stepped aside. Some of the women students said that Margaret would take the field back for women. Henrietta would have championed her if her stomach hadn't wrenched every time she saw Margaret and Ruth heads together, as they often were now.

The more she saw them together, the more Henrietta cringed at her own feelings, ashamed at her inability to get what she wanted. She pictured herself telling Ruth how she felt, knowing she would never do it, because there was no chance Ruth might love her back as long as Margaret stood there first. She was also terrified that Ruth might tell Margaret. She would use her love for Ruth as a source of inspiration and motivation. Whenever she saw Ruth, she would draw her shoulders back and straighten up like a soldier, ready to continue her march toward anthropological glory.

For months, Henrietta's passion had been the major term paper for Ruth's "Zuni linguistics" course. She read every published work by Ruth and Ruth's previous graduate students. Throughout the semester she pictured the day her paper would be returned. The grade was a given, but she could hardly wait to see the comments in the margin and Ruth's admiring look during the conversation they would finally have. It would be the first of many, leading to the day that she pictured of them in a cozy adobe just outside Zuni pueblo, sitting by their glowing kiva fireplace, discussing their observations for the day, planning for the next week, perhaps going over a letter from their publisher for the book they would do together.

Henrietta stepped into the departmental office to pick up her mail. It was December, and classes were not in session. She hadn't seen Ruth since before Thanksgiving. Ruth's husband didn't live in New York, and the gossip was that their marriage was not good.

There was a large envelope with Ruth's home address. Her paper back, already! Henrietta hadn't expected it so soon. Ruth must have been eager to read it. There were other students in the office, and Henrietta wanted to be alone when she opened it, so she headed out to the corridor and sat on the cover of the radiator by the big windows looking out over the quad. The heat made a nice contrast to the snowy scene outside.

She began to open the envelope carefully, so as not to tear the return address, which she wanted to glue into her diary. Just then June, a second year student who had already been on a dig with Dr. Morris, sat down next to her so hard that Henrietta's leg bounced against the hot radiator.

"Let's just see what old Benedict has to say this time," said June. June wasn't much for desk work like linguistics, as she made clear quite often. She was always bragging about the mud and dust and problems with the Navajo laborers that archaeologists suffered.

Henrietta turned away with her paper. She knew she had done better than June and didn't want to get into a discussion about it. She pulled back the flap.

June ripped open her own envelope.

"Damn B minus!" said June. "You'd think she'd be nicer to us."

Henrietta wondered what June meant, but couldn't wait any longer to see her own grade. She slid the paper all the way out to see all the comments on the first page. But there was nothing but her own typing. She flipped to the back. In tiny blue ink it said "B" and "you should look into the writings of Whorf on the syllabic issue." She flipped through the pages desperately. That was it. That was all Ruth had written.

"Boy, she sure doesn't want to make us look good. Afraid someone will figure out about her and her husband," said June, who was looking over Henrietta's shoulder.

"What are you talking about?" Henrietta realized her tone was angrier than she had meant it to be.

"Oh," said June, jumping down from the radiator and putting her paper back in its envelope as she backed away. "Oh, nothing. Just she doesn't help her own, that's all."

June disappeared back into the departmental office while Henrietta stared at the floor. Maybe June meant it was like the shaman/apprentice relationships she had studied, leading her to feel that she was the apprentice and Ruth was her shaman. The shaman could never show satisfaction. She always had to demand more to make the apprentice good enough. It wasn't about Henrietta's present work. It was about pushing her harder for the future. Already Henrietta was feeling better. Someday she would have that A-plus, and they would talk about her work. For now, Ruth's role as her mentor meant that she had to keep a distance. The conversations could continue in her head. There was even more reason now to work harder. The B was the proof. Ruth expected more, and she would give her best.

After the disappointing grade on her Zuni linguistics paper, Henrietta lowered her expectations, but since then she had done well. Every paper she wrote focused on topics related to Ruth's work. She took every class of Ruth's and went to every presentation by Ruth's advisees, especially those returning from the field. Her heart rose the day she learned that Ruth had been assigned as her advisor, but their meetings were brief and formal and always left her angry at herself, sure she had disappointed Ruth. But by the time she was back on the subway or at her job or home, cringing at her bleak life outside of school, she was soon hopeful again.

She felt that fieldwork would change everything. Other students saw fieldwork as a steppingstone in their academic career, but Henrietta knew she would love it. It had been her life's dream since reading about Frank Hamilton Cushing, and now she added the dream of Ruth. She imagined the first few years of ingratiating herself into the community, guided by Ruth's letters and occasional supervisory visits. Eventually, Ruth would join her and they would work together. Side by side, they would write their journal articles, her name beneath Ruth's.

"So when are you going to stop kidding yourself?" Sack asked as he plopped down next to her on a bench in the quadrangle. It was an unusually warm and sunny day in early spring, and she was relieved to get out of the steam heat of the college halls. Sack was struggling to light a long pipe. When Henrietta stared he said, "the rich boys have these. I can't have everything they have just yet, but I can afford this."

"Kidding myself about what?" Henrietta asked.

"Your darling Benedict," he said. "and her darling Margaret."

"What are you talking about?"

"Don't play innocent. It's no secret. Everyone can see how you feel about her."

"What!" Henrietta's scream made him drop the match, burning his finger.

"Well, maybe not everyone. But I notice things, that's all. You're always in the front row, hanging on her every word, and anytime you pass Mead in the hall, I can almost hear the hissing."

"I don't know what you're talking about."

"Oh come on. You haven't noticed how Benedict and Mead are?" He held up two fingers, tight against each other.

"So Margaret's found a mentor. I'd like one myself."

"I'm sure you'd like Benedict," laughed Sack.

"She works at Zuni pueblo. You know why I'm here. She's the most obvious advisor for me."

"Sure," said Sack, "and exactly what advice do you need?"

"What do you mean by that?"

"Mead looks well advised. But she's probably taught Benedict even more."

Ree stood, grabbing her books. "I have studying to do," she said as she walked away.

As her years at Columbia passed, filled with tests, research papers, and menial jobs, Henrietta kept her mind on her field placement. Students back from the field talked about what went wrong and how they suffered far from home. The words she heard so often were "uncomfortable, miserable, unsanitary, too cold, too hot, repulsive." People in other cultures slaughtered animals cruelly and ate their offal. Children played marbles with little balls of sheep dung. Her fellow students were asked to examine cow piles to see if they were dry enough to be burnt for fuel. Breakfast was sheep intestines they had emptied the day before. They told the students who hadn't gone yet, "You think you won't mind, but it gets to you really fast. When you're tired and cold and hungry, you mind a lot." Few other students even had a preference for where they would do field work. "As long as I can work with a big name who can advance my career, I'll be happy," she heard often. She wanted to yell at them that they were mere careerists and that she was the real thing.

But Henrietta only wanted to get to the Southwest before it was all gone. The culture was changing so quickly. The Indians were buying trucks, visiting cities, and bringing back all the comforts they could afford. The fire holes in the hogans were not being replaced with wood stoves, but with kerosene ones. Frank, in his homemade outfit of furs and skins, would be as much a freak to the current-day Indians as to the other anthropologists.

Only a few years earlier, anthropologists had come back from summer trips to New Mexico and Arizona with tales of runaway packhorses and long stretches without water. Now in the cafeteria, the talk was of how to fix a broken fan belt on a Model T truck or how long it took to get from Zuni pueblo to Albuquerque for the weekend. There were so many anthropologists wanting to do fieldwork on the Southwest Indians that Henrietta heard jokes comparing it to the recent phenomenon of auto traffic jams that were happening on the newly built highways entering New York City from Long Island. The more Henrietta heard this, the harder and faster she worked. To get to the field sooner, she stayed up later, woke up earlier, and studied on the trolley, hanging onto the strap and swaying with the curves. She always had a book handy for coffee breaks at work. On days she could go to the library, she was there when the doors opened in the crisp morning air and didn't leave until the last warning bell rang, the lights flashed, and she was expelled into the night. If she stayed at this pace, she could qualify for fieldwork by the coming summer. She readied her proposal.

In more than one class, the professor said that Frank Hamilton Cushing had forced his way into Zuni pueblo, and that what he had seen as acceptance was just the Indians' way of accommodating and humoring an arrogant white man. Perhaps she admired Frank because the Zuni people did not want him there, yet he stayed. Was he right? Was his intrusion justified by the history he preserved at a time when the Zuni people did not understand how much of their culture they were about to lose? These questions troubled Henrietta, but her dream of living like Frank overwhelmed the questions. She had imagined herself living as Frank had, although now she didn't want to go to Zuni pueblo itself, because it was so crowded with anthropologists and tourists that it had become a joke for the field. She wanted to be the first to study a new, unknown group, as Frank had. She didn't care how uncomfortable it might be or how bad the food, as long as she was first and she had it to herself. She didn't want any of her annoying fellow students around disagreeing with her methods or not taking it seriously, whining about the need to get back to civilization.

Henrietta dreaded what she would have to do if she were assigned to go to New Guinea or the Yucatan. The only place she wanted to go, the only people she wanted to study, were the Indians of the Southwest. They would have to give her the Southwest. It was a done deal.

As a condition of their student financial aid, Henrietta and Sack were in a room off the department office, collating and stapling.

"New students always coming in, welcomed gladly. Old students always going out, to be immediately forgotten," said Sack.

"They won't forget me," snapped Henrietta.

"Why's that? Oh, I don't need to ask, you have your publications, your legendary work in the field—"

"Stop!"

"Ah, I forgot, your fame far and wide. Frank Hamilton Cushing will be pushed aside for your glory."

"I will stand beside him."

"In the field."

"Right."

"So, where is that field going to be?"

"You know. I told you from the first."

"Just because you want it doesn't mean you'll get it."

"How can you say that? There can't be anyone here who doesn't know how I feel about the Southwest. Plus that's Benedict's area and I'm her student."

"I'd call her your advisor. But I think her student is someone else."

Henrietta wrinkled her lip and shook her head at him. "I heard Margaret say she could care less about the Southwest, she wants a Pacific island assignment. Good, she can't get far enough away to make me happy. Anyway, I don't care about her. I know just what I want. And I have to get there before it's all gone."

"So, what if you don't get the Southwest?" Sack asked.

"That's not a possibility!"

"That's just what I mean. You've made it clear to everyone that it's only the Southwest for you. They feel bullied."

"Professors scared of me?" Henrietta's voice squeaked as she said it.

"They like to think they're the powerful ones. Like that New Guinea tribe where the most powerful men carry the biggest sticks."

"You think they're headhunters?" Henrietta giggled, but Sack didn't.

"In a sense. But what's the point of studying anthropology if you can't look at your own culture? They have the power. You better act like you know it or they'll have your head. Stop telling them what they should decide."

"They want the best students out there. No one could be doing better than I am in Benedict's class."

"I'm not so sure they want the best students doing field work. What about Greenberg?" Greenberg had been notorious for ruining the grading curve with his inevitably outstanding papers, but had done his field work in Connecticut.

"Greenberg didn't want to leave his mama in the Bronx, and everybody knew it."

"Anyway," Sack continued, "the best placements will go to those girls with the four names." This was Sack's term for their Social Register classmates. It usually made Henrietta smile, but this time she didn't find it funny.

"They barely do their homework. Of course I'll get a good placement. No one's worked harder than me."

Sack started to speak, looked away and then turned back.

"Stop kidding yourself. You've got to be realistic about the ways of the world. You and I, we're last on the list."

"I can't believe that," said Henrietta. "You can think all the negative thoughts you want, but don't poison me. I'm working harder than anyone and my field placement will be waiting for me."

"All right," said Sack. "Don't say I didn't warn you."

"Well, if you think that way, what's your plan?"

"The Wild West is where I'll make my fortune. The Gold Rush is still there for me." Like Henrietta, Sack didn't fit in at Columbia. His clothes, his strong ways of moving his body from years of chopping and hauling on the docks, and even his curly beard stood out against the elegant combed whiskers of the boarding school princes, as he had dubbed Joseph Campbell and the other rich boy students.

"Seen the latest crop back from the fields?" he said. "Falling all over each other bragging who had the toughest fieldwork, the wildest horses, the stupidest mules, the steepest trail, the hottest desert. They think that's hard? Let's see them spend a day at the docks unloading ships. They think rattlesnakes are scary? Let's have them try to cross the guys who boss the yards. You think they could stand up to your boss at the sweatshop?" He grinned at Henrietta. "But it doesn't matter. Let the rich boys build up their puny muscles digging up pots. My hands will be soft and clean."

"How?" Henrietta mumbled as she chewed her bagel.

"I'm taking it to the next step. Let them dig for the museums, I'll buy low from the treasure hunters and sell high to the treasure hoarders, the rich collectors who never get their jewel-covered hands dirty. They'll trust me because Columbia's going to give me credibility and expertise. I'll throw around names like Boas and Hewett."

"You didn't used to talk like this."

"I learned a lot in school. Why didn't you?"

"What about the Indians? Don't you want to help them preserve their culture?" Henrietta asked.

"They'd rather be rich, too. I'll buy from anyone. I'll do a lot more for the Indians than any museum that puts their precious stuff on display and won't even let them in to look at it."

Henrietta never listened to the endless chatter around her. The other students could afford time for stupid talk, she could not. In the student lunchroom, or when the weather forced her to share the steamy lounge with them, she would read while eating, then run to the library if she had time. But one day the talk grew loud, then oddly quiet. Ruth's name caught her attention.

"I hear Benedict goes to this dude ranch in New Mexico that's only women. No men at all!"

"How do you know?"

"I bet Mead goes with her," said another girl.

"That's not it. Not exactly. There's plenty of men," said the first girl.

"Toss it down! What do you know?"

"Well, that's not exactly what San Gabriel Dude Ranch is. The thing is--." the girl paused, tightening her lips and deciding what to say. Henrietta cocked her ear and even closed her eyes to hear better. She wanted to scream at everyone else in the room to shut up. She wished she knew these girls well enough to move to their table, but that would have ended the story for sure as they would focus on making her feel uncomfortable, if not outright unwelcome.

"Come on, out with it," one of the other girls said. "Do they go there to marry a handsome cowboy? I've heard that's why single girls go to those dude ranches."

"I can't picture Benedict with a cowboy," laughed another girl. "Anyway, isn't she married?"

"I can see Margaret with one," giggled the third. "But he'd be scared of her. She'd be roping him like a cow."

"Well, that's kind of it," said the purveyor of the story. "That's kind of what goes on there. My aunt told me all about it, she goes there sometimes. It's a scandal in Boston. You know the Stanleys from Beacon Hill? Caroline Stanley went there a few years ago, for her asthma. It's true, it's mostly women there. But most go for the cowboys. And she did, she went for a cowboy in a big way. Ended up marrying one, and she bought the ranch for him. Turns out he's quite the drinker and not much of a businessman, so she runs the place. Her family is having fits--a Stanley girl running a business, and a cowboy ranch at that! They say she came home for Christmas wearing cowboy boots. And her husband didn't know how to behave in public, and got drunk, and now she won't come home at all. But that's not all that goes on there." This time she hesitated not as if unsure what to say, but to build maximum attention.

Henrietta grabbed her pencil and scribbled as sincerely as she could just in case the girl looked her way.

"Some of the ones who go there aren't looking for cowboys at all," the girl said so quietly Henrietta strained to hear.

"What are they looking for, cows?" said a listener. She snorted on the last word and they all laughed but the principal speaker.

"No, *cowgirls*," the speaker said emphatically and loudly, trying to get the attention back. The laughter stopped abruptly and the speaker's voice dropped so low Henrietta could only catch a few words.

"Women and women...special friendships...you know..."

"But Benedict," said the second girl.

"There's something about Margaret I can't put my finger on," said the third girl.

"I can't believe you're saying this," said the second girl. She stood up, scraping her chair back. "I have to go. I don't care for this talk at all." She glared at the speaker and walked away, knocking a book off the corner of the table and not even stopping to pick it up.

"Wow, she's not as sophisticated as I thought," said the first girl to the third. "My aunt's got a friend who's that way-"

"It was nothing at Vassar," said the third girl. "Everyone had a crush. But after college--that's unnatural, don't you think?"

"What I don't understand is that Benedict is married. And Margaret's engaged, she shows off her ring. He's going to be a minister even."

"How does your aunt know all this?"

"She just likes it there. She says most dude ranches are for families and children, but that one's for single women. I don't think they even allow children."

"Women who don't like children! I think that's unnatural."

"Well, my aunt really likes to go on pack trips. They go on horses into the woods and sleep in tents."

"Ugh, I'd hate that. Think of the snakes and flies. And horses are so smelly!"

"My aunt says that at the family dude ranches, the kids get all the attention from the cowboys. The cowboys are the teachers for how to ride the horse and all. So she likes San Gabriel because she doesn't have to compete for the cowboys' attention. I guess that explains why some of the women go there. They get more than riding lessons from the cowboys!" she finished with a laugh.

"Sounds like your aunt is one of them."

"That's rude. Just because someone goes there? It may be because they aren't going with a family. It doesn't have to be anything else."

"So what about Benedict and Margaret? Maybe they just hate children."

"There's women who like the cowboys and women who just like having no children around. That's probably why Benedict likes it. It must be so sad to be so old and not have children."

"She's got her darling Margaret," said the third girl. They both laughed, then quieted self-consciously.

"I guess," the first girl said softly.

"Well, I've got to get going." The third girl picked up her tray. The first girl caught Henrietta watching her and they both blushed.

"You're in my class with Benedict, aren't you?" asked the girl. Henrietta nodded uncertainly.

Sliding her tray closer, the girl asked, "Did you understand what she was saying about kinship circles the other day?"

"Sure," said Henrietta confidently, then realized that wasn't a good way to get the girl to open up. "Sort of. Did you have a hard time, too?"

"Maybe you could explain the part about the matrilocal to me?" said the girl. "I just didn't get it. You always look so intent in class. You really work hard at it."

Surprised she had even been noticed, Henrietta explained the issue quickly to get through it fast before the other girls joined them. Maybe there would be a chance to ask her question. But how could she ask without admitting she eavesdropped?

"By the way, I'm Elizabeth."

"Henrietta."

"You must like Benedict a lot," said Elizabeth. "You're always sitting in front. You and Mead!" She blushed again.

"I hope to do fieldwork in the Southwest, like Professor Benedict," Henrietta said with as much dignity as she could, feeling caught in her fantasy world.

"Not me," said Elizabeth. "I'm going to work in a museum. No muddy old fieldwork with Indians for me!"

"That's nice."

"Uncle practically runs the Museum of Natural History. I have an internship for the summer. I'll be working with the gemstones and porcelain, not those old Indian pots. Oh, I'm sorry, maybe you like that stuff."

"I do." Sack was right, these people already had all the jobs lined up for themselves and folks like them never had a chance.

"Some women really like the Southwest. Are you going to go to San Gabriel?" She said it as if Henrietta hadn't been eavesdropping.

"Maybe. Where is it?"

"Someplace near Santa Fe. You should go there and spy on old Benedict and her pet." She picked up her tray. "I've got to get going, let me know what you find out."

Henrietta couldn't believe her good luck. She ran to the library to find out where San Gabriel was. Already the name had rung a bell. She was sure she had seen it in the latest issue of *El Palacio*, a magazine about Southwest anthropology. She leafed through a copy and there was the ad for "San Gabriel Ranch in Alcalde, New Mexico, near Old Santa Fe."

She wrote for information and soon received a lovely brochure titled "The Call of the Southwest," with woodcuts of horses and rock cliffs and women by campfires. It told of tours to Indian villages and pack trips to spectacular forests and mountains, all with delicious food and comfortable beds. The pictures showed big pines and trout streams and wild turkey cooked in a "Dutch oven." Henrietta's imagination spun as fast as when she first read about Frank Hamilton Cushing. Spanish villages with Fiesta days, Indian dances, and bronco-busting! It was a world as far from the pushcart-filled streets of Brooklyn as could be. As much as she had wanted to go west all these years, now she wanted to go even more.

The cost was also as far from her world as could be. But she resolved that when she got to the Southwest on her field assignment, she would visit San Gabriel. She would pretend she had the money to stay there and only wanted to take a look and consider it. She put the brochure on the shelf with her books, taking it out when her mind wandered from studying to remind herself why she was working so hard. It always got her back to work, except when it got her thinking back to the girls' conversation in the lunchroom.

Henrietta had never before had feelings like the ones she had for Ruth. She looked around the classroom and wondered if any of the other girls felt the same way about Ruth. Surely, Margaret felt the same way.

But was there anything wrong with her feelings? She had never even heard of this before, but now she was running into it everywhere. At the library, looking through magazines for articles about Frank Hamilton Cushing, her eyes were drawn to a story in the October, 1919 issue of *The Ladies Home Journal*. There among the articles about Halloween decorations was a drawing of two college girls smiling at each other. In the story, one girl wanted to be friends with another so much that she faked illness to be sent to the infirmary to be near her. But by the end of the story, she had dedicated herself to her future career in science.Henrietta sat up straighter, coming out of the world of a hidden-away women's college so different from her own city school. Like those girls, once she started her career, the passions and anxieties of these college days would be behind her. How she felt about Ruth was just stronger than how she had felt about any teacher. Ruth was a model of the anthropologist that she was going to be, if she stopped wasting time. She threw the magazine back on the pile and picked up another, searching the table of contents for anything about Frank, Zuni, or the Southwest.

But in her psychology class the teacher assigned a new and very controversial book, *Bi-Sexual Love* by Wilhelm Stekel. She had never heard this word before, nor the word within it, "homosexual." The book was filled with stories of depraved, insane, and criminal men who caused the worst problems of society. These topics were so unspoken of and the discussion in class was so delicate she would never had understood what it was about if she hadn't had the book to read. The men in class blushed and she saw them pull away in their seats, as if they wanted to leave the room.

She found the book so distasteful that she didn't want to waste time on it, until she came to page 284, on which began the case of a woman who was labeled by yet another new word: "*urlind* (homosexual woman). This unfortunate woman, born illegitimate with a drunken father. Her first sexual experience was forced upon her and gave her a sexual disease. Turning to prostitution, she had spent most of her life in prison." The book then quoted her as saying, "most girls handled one another at night and from that time on no man could interest me. I have intercourse only with girls who are pretty."

So these were "homosexual women." But she was not illegitimate, her father drank only on Purim, she would never be a prostitute or go to prison, and she had always heard that only men could get a sexual disease. This wretched woman's life had nothing to do with her own.

In their last year of classes before field work, Sack won a prized internship with Stewart Culin, the curator at the Brooklyn Museum. When he told her, she'd snapped back "so maybe not just the boarding school princes of the department are getting the plum jobs?"

"Jealous," he said in a low growling voice.

"No, you just won't admit you were wrong."

"Oh come on. I know you wanted this. Working with a friend of your precious Frank? The Director of the Brooklyn Museum? The guy who designed the Southwest Hall with Frank Hamilton Cushing?"

Henrietta turned away.

"I'm sorry. Don't be angry. I got it because I'm a guy, and guys get the best jobs. And you're right, I got it even though I'm not rich. I guess just being a man is enough. It's not fair. But I'll tell you about it. And maybe sneak you in sometime? Your special tour?"

"Thanks. Anyway, I didn't even interview."

"What! You were so excited."

"I was sure he'd remember me from that day I wore the suit, and he'd tell the department how crazy I am."

"I'll sneak you in and we'll find Frank's suit in a drawer somewhere and you can try on the real one."

Henrietta smiled. "I'll bet the pants are way too long. And the sleeves. Don't think I'd fit those thin hips either."

"Doesn't matter. You'll be stepping into Frank's real shoes someday, out in the field, with the Indians. This is just school. It won't be forever."

Henrietta didn't seen much of Sack once Stewart Culin took him on as an intern. They did no more than wave as they ran past each other. But one day near the end of term they met in the lunch room.

"At least I have all that time on the trolley from Columbia to Brooklyn to study. I'm working the night shift on the docks to make up for extra time during the day. All I'm missing is time to sleep."

Henrietta looked at him before answering. "You look like it, too. Maybe it's too much."

"It is too much. And it's making me angrier."

"Why?"

"Because I'm killing myself trying to do it all, meanwhile, they're just a bunch of thieves."

"Stewart Culin? The Brooklyn Museum? Come on!"

"It's true. Even your precious Frank Hamilton Cushing. Do you know what a Twin War God statue is?"

"Of course, it's the most precious object to the Zuni people. They believe the statues bring rain and protect them. They believe the original was carved by their Sun Father, and they carve new ones every year."

"Well, Frank Hamilton Cushing kept one on his mantel. Culin's trying to get it from the widow."

Henrietta started to speak, but her mouth fell closed.

"Don't try to tell me the Zuni people gave it to Cushing as a gift. They didn't even like him. And maybe because he stole their idol."

When Henrietta didn't say anything, Sack continued. "Yeah, and that's just one stolen object. Culin isn't going to give it back to the Indians. He wants it for the Museum. They're just thieves. And grave robbers. But mostly they just find some pathetic member of the tribe who is desperate enough for the fash cash to sell. And given how poor all the Indians are these days, there are plenty of those, enough to fill up that beautiful hall in Brooklyn."

"At least it's being kept safe, especially now."

"Pooh! When will she give it back? You think Culin has that day on his busy schedule? Nobody will come to an empty museum. In fact, he's always looking for better stuff to steal. And you know what?"

"You're going to steal it for him?"

"No, I'm going to deal it for me. Because that's where the real money is. Get the artifacts and sell them to the rich old ladies from Boston. They have tons more money than the museums. They need to decorate their haciendas in Santa Fe, and their mansions on Fifth Avenue and Beacon Hill. Lucky for me, Culin is teaching me the whole racket. I feel like that kid in "Oliver Twist."

"For God's sake, Sack, look at yourself. If you don't like what Culin's doing, why would you do it?"

"Somebody's going to do it, and if I worked for Culin, he'd pay me nothing. I'm going to work for myself. Maybe I'll give the Indians a bigger cut. Would that make you feel better? Because it's still nothing compared to what rich people are drooling to pay. Face it, the stuff is going to get taken one way or the other. I'm just going to grab my share of the action."

Sack picked up his books and headed off. Henrietta called after him, "I don't believe Frank would do that. He wasn't like that."

Sack turned and said something she couldn't hear, but he his cynical expression said it all.

A few days later, Sack ran up to Henrietta in the hall.

"I figured something out. It's the end of the term. I don't have to stay more boring years for a degree I don't have to graduate! Out West I'll just say I'm a student. When people ask where I work, I'll imply I'm one of those rich boy perpetual graduate students. People will think I'm really smart. Wouldn't you trust a student more than a guy without a job?" Not waiting for Henrietta to swallow her food and answer, he went on. "I'm leaving for New Mexico now, and I'll come back to New York City a rich man. The boarding school princes will be a memory. Except when I drop their names, of course."

Without waiting for Henrietta's answer, he ran off. "I've got a train to catch," he yelled back. "The Santa Fe Chief, here I come."

Henrietta stared at the letter, reading it over and over. Holding it at arms length, she tore it in half and was about to rip it again when she pieced it together as if the words would change. But it still said that despite all her recognizably outstanding work, she would not be receiving a placement or funding for a fieldwork position in the Southwest, or anywhere.

Not enough funds! Last week, she had been relieved when she heard that Margaret Mead was going to Zuni, since she had assumed that meant that she would recieve a less studied place in the Southwest. Only yesterday, she had heard the hearty congratulations for Edward and Sam as they boasted of their field assignments. Other students had consoled her that her letter was late because she must be getting the bulk of the money. But no, her letter was late so that her fellow students would be busy packing for their trips while she stood alone, with no one to see her failure or join her anger. Sack was right, the cream always went to the rich and connected, and the poor and Jews were last in line.

It was all carefully engineered, and she knew just who had let her down, although it was painful to think: Ruth had not stood up enough for her. She had favored Margaret Mead, her pet student. Henrietta imagined stabbing them both with the spears that hung over the archway into the department. There was a buzz around her, an aura of unreality, as if all the hairs on her arms and legs were not standing up so much as cringing. In any uncertain situation with huge consequences, you had to have hope, but then you were never ready when it didn't go your way. It hadn't gone her way. All she could see down the road ahead were her worst fears realized. There was a knot in her chest and butterflies in her stomach.

How could this have happened? She couldn't have worked harder. Like Sack had said, she should have paid more attention to the people than to the books. But her goal hadn't been to advance a career, but to study the Indians. Maybe doing things the Frank Hamilton Cushing way wasn't in vogue at Columbia or any other school, but it was for the Indians and it was the only thing she could do.

Her father was at work and the people they boarded with weren't home to complain about the hot water she used, so she turned on the taps full blast and filled the bathtub. She wasn't going to school. She didn't want to see the happy faces of those who had received support and those who assumed she also had. What could she say to them when for the last three years the one thing anyone knew of her was that she was going to do her fieldwork in the Southwest They would all know that anything else was nothing less than a total smack in the face from the department, especially Professor Benedict.

Why hadn't Ruth fought for her? Maybe not as much as she would fight for Margaret, but Ruth's intellectual honesty was almost as appealing as her sad mysterious eyes. Ruth knew how well-prepared and dedicated Henrietta was. How could she deny the Indian people this opportunity? That's what it came down to. It was the Indians who would suffer. And the department, which would not have the honors that her work would bring to them. It was their loss.

But it was her loss. Her bent knees ached and her neck crimped in the short tub. Someday she would bathe in the Rio Grande. She would stretch out in the cool clean river, the hot sun heating her face.

That had been her fantasy during every bath she had taken for years. Up until minutes ago, the reality had been only a few months from her grasp. Now it would be nothing but lukewarm baths in city water, or the screaming crowds of Coney Island beach. Her dream was over like the last gray water swirling and disappearing down the drain.

Instead of the Rio Grande, her dissertation research would send her trudging up and down flights of New York City tenement stairs, interviewing immigrants, like other graduate students who didn't make the cut for the field. Like herself, many came from those very same tenements, but the department pretended that the observer could be fresh and impartial to the situation.

Bells clanging, a fire engine ran by floors below. Somewhere, someone's life was changing. Their home was burning, or they were struck by a streetcar. The day had started as usual for them, but it would end as never before, as something they had never expected, like herself today. She had never thought that she wasn't going to the field. It had only been a question of exactly where in the Southwest. Her elbow smacked against the faucet and hurt at the funny bone. Little problems, no house on fire, no gruesome collision. But it wasn't little to her. It was the end of her dreams. Everything had changed, but it would all be the same. She would stay in New York, she would live here with her father, she would slog off to work and a parody of fieldwork, if not classes. Her life wouldn't change, but her life was changed.

She couldn't stay here. She had put up with it just to reach her goal. It wasn't simply a matter of moving out of her father's apartment. She must leave New York. There was only one place she could go and that was the place she was supposed to be going. So they hadn't given her money. They didn't give everyone money. Many students had rich parents, or inheritances of their own. Others just went, like Sack had. People went west all the time and found ways to survive. She would find a way. She would go to Santa Fe. There must be work there for someone with all the skills she had from the jobs she had held since she was fourteen years old, and before that, sewing piecework at home with her mother. She could do just about anything. She would rather work hard there than here, and she would save until she had enough to support her own fieldwork. The department would be relieved that she wouldn't be a burden. All she had to do was make her way west.

Ruth and Margaret would be so surprised to see her. They would be awed. They would be impressed. Ruth would see what a spoiled child Margaret was and what a worker Henrietta was. She knew what she was going to do. She was practically on her way already. She climbed out of the tub. She had no time to waste.

She shivered in the cold bathroom, discovering there was no towel because normally she did the laundry on Wednesdays and it was in the basket. How would she get the money to get to Santa Fe? Her father was barely holding onto his job at the cigar factory, and he was saving for his own trip to Palestine. All her wages from her current job were paying the last tuition bill of the semester. There was nothing for a train ticket.

Could she stowaway on a train? She had heard of women doing that, disguised as men. But that wasn't the way she saw herself heading West. So many times, she had pictured getting on the train at Grand Central Station, sitting on the velvet seat to watch the beautiful country open up before her, not hiding on a boxcar floor, terrified she would be raped or worse.

She would get the money somehow. Maybe she could she get a job on the train, just long enough to get off at Santa Fe. Would anyone lend it to her? The students often talked of those who ingratiated themselves with rich patrons. Names like Rockefeller, Cabot, and Lowell were mentioned, with gossip about how one met them and how to act if one did. Some students had internships in museums and met the patrons. But no one had offered her those jobs.

Or maybe she did have something for her train ticket. There was her mother's silver candelabra for Sabbath, very ornate and crafted, like something you would see in a museum. Her mother had inherited it from her mother, and she in turn had given it to Henrietta . It wasn't her father's, it was her own legacy, and the only wealth she had. The candelabra was treated like nothing else they owned. It was wrapped in a soft chamois cloth inside a velvet bag, hidden from the people they boarded with inside a more modest box behind her father's phylacteries and tallit. On Friday night, they lit candles in their own room so that the others wouldn't know they had it. If she took it to another neighborhood, the pawnbroker would not tell her father. Her father wouldn't know it was gone until a Friday night came. By then she would be on the train crossing the prairies.

Part 3

Waiting at Grand Central Station for her train, Henrietta watched the Twentieth Century Limited arrive with passengers from California, thrilled that she would be taking this same train to the country of her dreams. Businessmen carried important looking satchels and anxious parents herded their excited children. Loud screams rang out as everyone scanned the crowd for whoever was meeting them, and there were many hugs of reunion. Henrietta laughed at those torn between making sure they had all their bags while trying to keep up with their greeter pulling them along through the crowd. She envied the warm hugs, the smiles, the screams of recognition and pleasure, as the passengers left in little flocks.

Only one woman stepped off alone. Her long dress was a bright checked calico and she wore a bonnet like a schoolmarm in a cowboy movie. Was that how women still dressed out west? Would Henrietta look as strange getting off the train in Santa Fe in her dark, solid, eastern dress? Where could she buy a western dress? Maybe she should trade with this poor girl, who looked terrified by the crowds and whose eyes flickered from sign to sign and up to the high ceiling of the station, where pigeons swooped.

The girl hoisted her one small suitcase, so much like the one Henrietta had bought for her own trip. She straightened her bonnet, shook her head, and headed off toward the sign that said "Downtown and Brooklyn."

Henrietta started after her, for a moment imagining helping her, as the girl disappeared down the stairs to the subway.

That was how it would be to arrive in New Mexico with no one to meet her. But when had anyone ever met her? Her father had sent her off to the first day of school alone, and she remembered enviously watching the other children met by their mothers at the end of the day. She had returned from school to their empty kitchen.

Sack had sent her a postcard with a photograph of a Navajo woman weaving near a beautiful cliff. It had no address, but was postmarked Santa Fe. She would find Sack. She wouldn't be completely alone in New Mexico.

She studied the train schedule and map. She would have only enough money to go to Chicago and then take the train called the *Navajo* to Santa Fe. The other students laughed about Santa Fe because it was the biggest city in New Mexico, but compared to New York it was just a sleepy Spanish village. She knew that, yet she pictured herself stepping off the train into a station as grand as Grand Central, but in Santa Fe, New Mexico.

As her train came out of the dark tunnel under Manhattan and headed into the sunny west, Henrietta was confident that no matter how hard some moments or days might be, she would be sustained by her love for Ruth. She had decided that Ruth had fought for her and lost. It was the only way she could bear to think about losing the field placement.

Henrietta was so excited she barely slept until Chicago, although it was also the discomfort of having to sleep sitting up, because she could not afford the cars that turned into cribs with up and down beds and curtains drawn across them. After changing trains to the *Navajo*, she had finally fallen asleep and missed the long-awaited crossing into New Mexico and the first few stops there, so it was at a barren railroad stop that she first saw her Promised Land.

To her surprise, the train didn't go into Santa Fe, but let passengers off at a tiny railroad station called Lamy, seventeen miles away. The conductor explained that a car would take them to Santa Fe. She hesitantly followed the other passengers crowding the aisles, thinking of the girl she had watched in Grand Central Station.

She took the huge step down from the train, the conductor holding her arm. There was only a second when she felt as alone as the girl she had seen get off the train in New York. Immediately a young woman in a dark dress, her face almost hidden by a kind of veil, held out a clay pot to her with one hand and put a warm hand on her shoulder with the other. Henrietta felt such pleasure from the touch she closed her eyes.

"San Ildefonso" said the woman. "Maria pot," and drew her away from the huffing, ground-shaking departing train. The sun was so bright Henrietta wanted to cover her eyes. Everything was glaring and dusty pink. There was a clean scent like newly bleached sheets that had dried in the sun. She recognized the simple, low buildings but was amazed at how beige, almost yellow they were. She had thought of this world as only black and white as in the photographs and drawings she had been looking at for all these years.

Dropping her hand from Henrietta's neck, the woman pulled a shiny piece from a pocket deep in her dress. She held the silver bracelet before Henrietta's face. The sun flashed off it into her eyes and Henrietta gasped with pain. The woman's hands went soothingly to press against her face, and Henrietta felt the heated metal of the woman's rings against her cheek.

"Five dollars," she said. "Zuni."

Henrietta forgot her eyes and her head bobbed with the thrill. "Zuni!" she said. "You're from Zuni pueblo? Do you know Frank Hamilton Cushing—" It all came out of her before she realized how ridiculous the question was. Frank had died before this young woman was born. But maybe her grandmother knew him?

The girl only held the bracelet up again. "Zuni? Zuni?" she said eagerly, "Five dollars!" She pressed the bracelet into Henrietta's hand.

Henrietta knew she couldn't buy it, but she turned it over in her hand, looking at the silver band of tiny blue beads. She had seen many like it in the Brooklyn Museum and in books, and on the wrists of some of the students who returned from field work, but she had never held one in her hand. She felt she was holding all of her dream, all of Frank, and Zuni pueblo and the treeless plains she had crossed, and the mountains she now saw —it was all in her hand now, and she closed her fist tightly on it like an infant, her hand reddening from the pressure.

"Five dollars" said the Indian girl again. All around them Henrietta's fellow passengers passed handfuls of greenbacks to girls like this. She was the only one not buying, and they both noticed it. "Five dollars" the girl said more sharply.

Slowly, the metal sticking to her palm, Henrietta opened her hand toward the girl. She shook her head and gave a sad smile. She wanted to hear "you must keep it—you need it for your journey" like a character in a folktale. Instead the girl plucked it from her hand and moved on toward a man whose black velvet hat was probably burning his scalp, but who showed more promise than Henrietta did of a sale.

It didn't matter. She would soon have all of this, not just a souvenir for a tourist passing through. She was here to stay, to belong, to be taken into the warm fire, the delicious food, the loving faces of the family that would become hers. A bracelet was nothing but a trinket. She was not a tourist, but here to stay. With the other passengers, she climbed into a long bus-like car for the last leg of the journey.

As they approached Santa Fe, thrills and fears overwhelmed her. The dry, hilly land had few signs of people, just occasional fenced fields where horses ran. Finally, they reached the cluster of mostly beige adobe buildings that was Santa Fe. In New York City, this would have been a child's town of one-story tiny houses. As they approached the center, she saw more wood and brick buildings like those in the East, but none more than two stories. The car parked in front of a sprawling adobe hotel called "La Fonda," where a small crowd was waiting to greet most of her fellow passengers. Faces that had become familiar on the train disappeared into the hotel or turned the street corner, the car itself drove away, and Henrietta stood on the sidewalk, alone with her suitcase, with no idea where to go next.

In her first few hours in New Mexico, Henrietta barely blinked from staring at everyone and everything she saw. She was shocked to see Jewish names like *Ilfeld's* and *Gold's Curios* on some of the two-story buildings that lined the square main plaza. The big Catholic church that blocked her view of the mountains had a window in the shape of a Jewish star over its door. Another tourist explained that the Jewish merchants who had been in Santa Fe for decades had helped pay for the construction of the cathedral. Henrietta thought they should have given their money to the Indians.

She could easily tell who lived here, because these people were creatures of another species, the species of not-New Yorkers. They were tall and blond and moved gracefully in their powerful bodies, or they had short and barrel-like stocky bodies and long slick black hair. One man had the longest handlebar mustache she had ever seen. Just like in the illustrations and photos she had seen, many Indian women wore bright-colored woven shawls, and Indian men had huge silver disks on their belts.

Henrietta wanted to look into an adobe building, so she walked until she found a quiet narrow alley. A burro cart was parked there, and she towered over the little animal. An adobe archway behind her opened into a little courtyard café with brightly colored painted chairs and tables. She heard a piano and laughter. She walked into the courtyard just as three men came through the swinging doors of the building behind the tables.

The men came right towards her. One reached out for her suitcase, which she gripped tightly.

"Look at this! It's time some fresh fruit showed up in this town." Another of the men touched her cheek.

"She's dark for a white woman, but she'll do. I like a curly-headed one myself."

Henrietta tried to back up but now there was a man behind her.

"Leave me alone. Get your hands off me!"

"Oh, a virgin act," said the first man. "She's mine. How much, honey?"

Trying to get away, she butted right into the man behind her. His arms circled her as she pushed against him. Hold on to the suitcase, she told herself as she tried to swing it to batter the first man. Should she scream for help?

"Let me go, you ____." She had never said the word aloud before, only under her breath.

"Wow, you're some virgin!" said the first man. She whacked him in the knee with the suitcase and he let go, cursing. She dashed through the archway, past the little burro, and back into the larger street, crowded with pedestrians.

In New York she knew to be on her guard, but she had never thought about it for here, dreaming only of the good times she would have. Maybe she should look for Sack right away. Maybe she couldn't be on her own here.

Standing outside a restaurant called "Tia Sofia's," looking through the window to read the menu board inside, she puckered her lips at the strange words. What was carne? Sopapilla? Pollo con huevos? "Caliente?" Why hadn't she taken Spanish in all those years of school? With so little money left, she couldn't afford to buy food that she wouldn't like.

She didn't see any women inside eating alone. If she could find Sack, they could have lunch together, just like old times. She could tell him how she'd managed to come west, and he could tell her what he had been doing. Maybe he even knew a job she could get. She imagined the conversation more than the food, until her empty stomach got to her again. She had better eat. Hungry as she was, wouldn't everything taste good?

She felt conspicuous alone, scared that the men from the alley would come in. The waitress didn't speak English, so she pointed at the cheapest thing on the menu. Her mouth burned from the first bite. She would never taste anything again ever. She grabbed for the glass of water, trying to cool the fire. That made her choke and cough. Her cheeks were blazing, her eyes tearing. She didn't want to open them and see everyone in the place laughing at her.

There was a hand on her shoulder. A woman patted her back and spoke softly in Spanish. As she calmed down, the woman placed a puffy bread coated with honey in her hand. Soon her throat felt better.

She sipped her coffee slowly, the food gone to the last peppery lick, out of money but desperate to stay. She grabbed the menu and pretended to be considering what to order next, while stealing quick glances at the other patrons.

Soon a cowboy came in. The word "stubbly" came into her head, not just for his unshaven face but also for his turned-in, shortened bowlegs. He rocked from side to side in his tight high snakeskin boots, stumbling with confidence in his puffed-out chest. He didn't remove his tall hat so she couldn't see his hair, but his beard was gray specked with bright silver spots. His skin was dry and darkened by the sun. Although he had come in as if he owned the place and everyone in it, the café was crowded, and he surreptitiously glanced around for an empty seat. He tossed his jaw at a table filled with dude tourists in unlikely bright new western clothes. Henrietta was expecting a scene as in a cowboy movie. He would walk up that table, challenge the tallest man by spitting at his boot, and wait impatiently while they, terrified and humiliated, scrambled to their feet and backed away. He started in that direction, one knee kicking high, his chaw circling in his mouth, but then he put the knee down and stepped back. No one but Henrietta had noticed him.

He turned and headed right for Henrietta. He must have spotted her when he came in. Of course, a real cowboy would notice a calf that had strayed from the herd, and that was how she felt, sitting alone in this busy place. She pushed back in her chair, ready to stand.

"No need to leave, ma'am," he said, tipping his hat. "Would you mind if I joined you? It's busy today, Sofia must be raking in her dollars."

Henrietta let the front feet of her chair drop back, and she felt her jaw drop, too. Studying anthropology had taught her to let go of her preconceptions, yet the first thing she had done was misjudged this fellow as belligerent. He stood patiently, his smile starting to weaken, until she realized she hadn't answered.

"Oh course, oh please sit down. I'm sorry, I didn't mean to make you wait. You just startled me out of my thoughts, that's all. Can I get you some coffee?"

"That's ok, I'll just wait. Sofia don't like it if you touch her coffeepot, I sure learned that."

"You've been coming here a long time?"

"Just this summer. I live on the Panhandle."

"You're a cowboy?"

"No, I work with leather. Make it into quoits and bridles and all. You cut the leather into strips, and you braid and knot it. Here, like this-" He reached into his pocket and pulled out a loop of soft, intricately braided, chocolate brown leather. The keychain was delicate more than horse-y.

"That's beautiful. Do you have a store?"

"In Texas people just know me. Here, I'm trying to get a start, hook up with the tourist shops for orders. That's why I'm here this summer. And to get a new car. My old Model T busted its last axle getting here. I've got to sell a lot of these to go home. Course, I won't buy a new car here, it will just get broken on the way back. I just want to get the money together. I shouldn't tell you that, though. You won't be watching out to rob me at the end of the summer, will you? You look like a dangerous type to me. Where's Wyatt Earp when we need him?"

"You look like a tough cowboy to me."

"Oh, stores like it better if they think a real cowboy made the leather. Truth to tell, I'm from Chicago. Busted my legs in a trolley accident, and folks kept saying I walked just like a cowboy. I learned the leather from another fellow in the hospital. I kind of modeled myself after him. It makes a difference. Would you buy a bridle from a fellow that looks like him?" He pointed towards a tourist walking by in a black business suit and vest, not unlike what professors wore back at Columbia.

By afternoon Henrietta still wandered the plaza, being careful to stay out of empty alleys. She didn't know what she would do for the night, but she was glad she was here watching a magpie flap its slow flight to land on a delicate olive tree, and not back in Brooklyn watching pigeons on a roof. Here she had seen a dust devil rise from the earth like a tiny tornado. Here the streets were hard pink dirt where no street sweeper could ever hope to make progress. In the patio of the adobe house across the road, a Hispanic family chomped happily on burritos, each bite sending the scent of chile peppers and beans her way. She told herself it wasn't quite dinner time yet, and that something would turn up. But she didn't want to be anywhere but Santa Fe, no matter how hungry she became. For all the years she had spent dreaming of being here, it was well worth it. It was only a matter of time until the rest of her dreams came true. Even the one about Ruth. Everything was possible here.

If only she could find Sack. The other students were always chatting about running into each other at the Museum of New Mexico. She expected a huge building like the Museum of Natural History in New York, and was surprised to find it in just a one-story ancient looking building called the Palace of the Governors. This was a palace? It had crumbling adobe walls and dry, splintery wooden rails on the porch. Huged carved wooden doors stood open, revealing a ticket taker.

On the covered porch Indians squatted selling pots, blankets, and jewelry to tourists. They seemed as desperate as the peddlers on the lower East side with their carts of fabrics and books and Shabbat candles. As she walked past, the Indians looked at her only as a tourist and a customer. With no money to buy, she didn't want to catch their eyes so she took furtive glances at their faces and the colorful blankets many were wrapped in. Their slight smiles at other tourists indicated both accommodation and contempt at the same time, and reminded her of how her face had felt at the garment factory when the sweatshop owner stopped by, the sharp edges of her teeth catching on her curling lips. This was their unpleasant job. Maybe they were dreaming of escape as she had at her work.

She walked towards the end of the porch pretending she was looking for someone in the Plaza. A broad-backed man crossing the street reminded her of Sack until she saw his old man's shuffling walk. Smoky cars and trucks chugged among wagons and burro carts pulled by the delicate taps of horse and burrow hooves. At the corner, an Indian man unloaded boxes. A white canvas canopy stretched high over the small wooden body of his wagon, billowing like a huge cloud over a tiny hill. Suddenly the man cried out and something small brown and furry flashed past her eyes, galloping desperately down the porch, running across the rugs and scattering the jewelry with its feet. Tourist and vendors screamed and jumped all the way down the corridor, and then a laugh followed from where she stood down to the other end. Everyone was pointing at the wagon and then running their fingers to show how the animal had jumped out of the wagon and run frantically, disappearing now into the streets past the Palace. As fast as she could push her way through the crowd, she followed in its path to the grassy lawn of a huge church. Out of breath, and still excited from the surprise of the animal rushing past her, she sank down in the grass, telling herself that she could see better at ground level.

It was quiet in the churchyard. The vendors and tourists and busy Plaza were behind her, the silent, huge church looming above her. She stared blankly at its grotesque statues, which meant nothing except to make her feel slightly guilty for even being near a church. She didn't know why she had followed the animal. Just then she saw it, camouflaged by the grass, sitting as she was stone-still, just looking. Did she look as scared? Perhaps she felt that its story was her story, that she had been trapped and transported and suddenly let loose in a strange land where shock and laughter reacted to her, where there was nothing to be done but freeze and survey the territory. She was afraid to move, not wanting to scare it again. She wished she could hold it in her lap and pet it.

"You found her" a woman said softly behind her. Slowly turning her head, she was surprised to see not a woman, but the man who had been unloading the wagon.

"Poor little prairie dog. I'd like to catch her and bring her back to her home," the high voice continued. "Please don't move, I've got an idea."

The man circled slowly and quietly so that he stood between the animal and its most likely escape route, because the wall of the church was behind it and Henrietta was sitting in its other path. They all froze in their positions. The prairie dog shivered in the glaring sun. It was trapped, and she felt its fear. She wished she could tell the creature that it would be much safer if the Indian man caught it. The man began to sing in a soft voice and slowly lowered himself to the ground. The animal leaned closer to the sound and he reached his arms out, creeping slowly on his belly. Just then the church bell, high above, rang, and all three jumped. The prairie dog almost crashed into her and then veered to the street and out of sight. Henrietta reached out helplessly, too late to grab it. "I'm so sorry," she said. "It was just too fast." They stared as a car cut off their view.

The man let out his breath, and she realized she had been holding her own. He lay back on the grass, leaning on his elbow, his chin in his hand. "It was a long shot. You're nice to go after him. Everybody else just thought it was funny."

"But the poor little animal, all alone in this strange place. I feel so bad. Do you think we should try to find it?"

"We'll never catch it now." He turned his face to the sun. It was a beautiful day, with bright blue sky over the towers of the cathedral.

She couldn't figure his high voice out. There was something just not right. He was dressed like other Indian men, but something was not the same. His stiffly pressed dungarees, velvet smock tied at the biceps with leather thongs, and wide bandanna holding the hair over his forehead and tied behind his ears were all typical of the Navajo Indians she had tried not to stare at all day. His beardless face was not as leathery as the men she had seen, but perhaps he was younger than she realized.

"I'm Henrietta."

"Ned."

She wondered what his name really was, since many Indians had at least two names, one for whites, and the others for their own people or secret only to themselves.

"I should have checked more carefully when I loaded the wagon. She got into my grandmother's lunch box, I think. She's travelled a long way from her home and family, and it's all my fault."

For a moment, Henrietta felt as lost and alone as the prairie dog. She shook the thought away and asked, "Which one is your grandmother?"

"She's wearing a red, brown, and orange blanket."

"I saw that beautiful blanket. It looked much older than the ones for sale."

"You're good to notice that. It's not for sale to tourists—oh, didn't mean to insult you."

"I'm not a tourist. I mean, I just got here but I plan to stay."

He looked at her skeptically as they leaned in together. They both still looked down the street as if the prairie dog would appear again. Henrietta realized she was doing it because she was too shy to look Ned in the eyes. She wondered if Ned felt the same way.

"You have people here to stay with?"

"No, I have to find a job really fast." Then she regretted saying that. He seemed nice but it was never good to let a man know you were alone.

"Hope you do, it's not easy here. I better get back to my wagon," Ned said, getting to his feet. "My grandmother's probably wondering what happened to me. Maybe I'll see you again. Thanks for trying to help."

As he walked away, a cloud drifted over the sun and Henrietta felt too cold to stay on the grass. She had to find a job or Sack or something, very soon.

With no sign of Sack and a very flat purse, Henrietta felt that just about every man had an eye on her. She cringed as strangers passed by, worried they would say what the man in the burro alley had said. Carrying a suitcase was telling the world she had nowhere to go. But in her suitcase was the pamphlet about the dude ranch called San Gabriel, where the rich women went. So many times she had looked at the lovely woodcuts of meadows and mountains of the ranch. If only she could afford to go there! But she was going to be broke wherever she went. So far, things hadn't felt right in Santa Fe. Her dream of going west had not been to be in a city, even of this size. Why not go see San Gabriel? Would it be any worse than staying here without money or connections? Maybe somehow there would be a job.

From the directions on the pamphlet, she located the road to San Gabriel, and soon she stood there, thumb in the air. She turned away when a car with a man driving alone came toward her, but was soon thrilled when an old truck crowded with kids and chickens slowed for her. Soon she balanced on top of a crate in back, watching the beautiful country open up behind her.

The country turned flat, with steep hills to the west and distant mountains to the east. The land was barren except for the small trees which she guessed must be the pinon and juniper she had read about. She imagined Margaret leading a trail of women on horseback through the brush, but she couldn't picture delicate Ruth.

The truck sputtered and stopped at the side of the road. The driver tapped on the window behind him and pointed at her to get out. The Spanish family had not understood what she had tried to say to them, except for nodding knowingly at the words "San Gabriel." She dropped her suitcase over the back of the truck and jumped down, her heart thumping. The tires spun and the truck pulled away. There was no one in sight and the nearest building was far down the road. There wasn't a sound, not even birds. She had never been so alone. For a moment she missed the frenzy of New York.

There was a grove of trees across the empty road. At least there would be shade. As she got close, she saw an archway with a sign made of little branches that spelled out "San Gabriel Dude Ranch." Through the arch and down a rutted road she saw a two-story adobe building more substantial than so many of the crumbling places they had passed on the road. She walked under the archway and strained to see more. The quiet was broken by a buzzing sound through the trees and then a motorcycle burst through on the road ahead of her.

"Hey you," shouted the driver as she bounced on the dried ruts, then came to a dead stop, staring at Henrietta. Her yell was high-pitched, and as the driver stiffly unwound from the barrel of the bike and stumbled to stand, Henrietta saw surprisingly wide hips, even in jodhpurs.

"Just wait right there," the motorcyclist called out, trying to make her voice low and gruff and having it end in a high creak. Henrietta was already frozen in her tracks at the strange sight. The driver walked up to her, moving from the stumble into a swagger that was a parody of a man. Henrietta was torn between wanting to laugh and feeling fascinated. New York had no women like this.

"This is private property. I'm in charge of security." The cyclist gestured proudly at her outfit, which consisted of the jodhpurs, a blue work shirt of the kind prisoners wore, and a man's tweed suit coat. Her big bosoms pushed out against the shirt and meant that the little coat would never be buttoned. But she apparently saw it as a costume of authority, and the anthropologist in Henrietta was totally delighted. She wondered if it were the pants, the shirt, or the coat that the cyclist saw as her symbol of authority. Perhaps it was the cowboy boots, for now she put one foot against her other calf and scratched, bringing Henrietta's attention to the fancy leatherwork.

"Those are beautiful."

"Well, thanks. Hey! What are you doing here? I'm in charge, like I said. This is private property. Where do you think you're going? Where's your car?"

"I heard there might be a job here."

"What job? From who?"

"Well, it wasn't a specific job. Some women I know stayed here and they mentioned women working here. I thought maybe there would be something."

"What women were they?" Henrietta wasn't sure she could drop the names. She wished the woman wouldn't be so gruff. She needed to get this conversation to a friendly level. It was like starting field work in a primitive culture, and this woman sure was primitive.

"Let me introduce myself. My name's Henrietta, but folks call me Ree." She surprised herself saying that. No one had ever called her Ree, but on the train she had been thinking about how people in other cultures often took new names at turning points in their lives, and she had decided that since she was starting a new life, she would like a new and more modern name, something short. You had to be as conceited as Margaret Mead to have a name longer than two syllables. She thought that was probably a cultural rule, and what an interesting paper she could write on it. She had played with her name Hen – ree – etta. Etta sounded old. Hen was no good. Ree sounded western. Not feminine, either. Very to the point. Ree was a confident woman traveling on her own. Henrietta—well, she was a hen, what more could you say? That must be why she had always disliked the name, and often hesitated before saying it.

"Ree? Never heard that name before."

"What's your name?"

The motorcyclist wasn't expecting the question, and didn't answer right away. Maybe she had been reading anthropology, too. Maybe she knew this was a way of undercutting her authority.

"Karen, but what's it matter? What are you doing here?"

"Karen," Ree said slowly. It was important to honor a name, to give it a lot of weight. At least that was true according to her professors in lectures about their studies in New Guinea.

"Karen, I heard this was a really great place. I go to Columbia University, and quite a few of the professors have mentioned it. I wanted to see for myself."

"Columbia in New York City?"

"Yes, maybe you know some of my friends." She tried to think of a name that would impress Karen.

"Maybe. This is a private place, discreet." She said 'discreet' slowly and reverently, as if she had been trained to do so.

Ree remembered the students giggling about San Gabriel back at the cafeteria. She was glad she had hesitated. This place had rules she would have to guess at before she broke one. It would be like field work to be here.

"Who would I see about a job?" Ree tried to act too sure to be refused. If there was one thing she knew, it was how to talk her way into a job. She had been doing it since she was fourteen years old.

"That would be Senora, the housekeeper. OK, jump on the back."

It was hard to hang onto her suitcase and Karen's large but muscular waist as the motorcycle pounded along the rutted sand road and through a few groves, passing some outbuildings. Finally Karen poked her foot out into the dirt and brought it to a choking, coughing halt in front of an L-shaped wooden stables that mirrored a big adobe house.

"We have to walk from here," Karen said. "The bike scares the horses." There were corrals in the fields beyond the stables. Ree could smell the horses, but she couldn't see any.

Karen led Ree into the house through a back door. "Only the guests use the front door, except when they go out the back." There was an insinuating snicker in her voice. "It leads to the stables," Karen continued. "That's where the workers live." The foyer they were in had wallpaper of boots and saddles. Horse stencils decorated the coat rack.

"Do you think I could wash up first?" Ree asked as Karen led her into a kitchen. The cabinets had brightly colored curtains instead of doors. A huge can of lard and a stack of pie pans lay on the well-worn wooden table in the center of the room.

"You get covered with dust real fast out here. But we'd have to go back to the stables. Senora Sanchez will be back in a minute."

Next to the sink was a long list of rules for the staff, detailing much about storing, preparing, and serving food, as well as cleaning and preparing the kitchen and dining room. At the bottom of the list, underlined with thick blue ink, the final rule was "No fraternizing with guests. Know your place!" It was signed with the same blue ink, Caroline Stanley Pfaeffle, Manager. Ree wondered if she wanted to work here after all. It was isolated and it was all about horses, which she had only seen on New York Streets pulling peddler's wagons or used by police to intimidate people. Even though she had told herself she was willing to do any kind of work to stay out West, she was suddenly very conscious that even as the lowest graduate student on the totem pole at Columbia, she was still miles above being a maid. Which was bound to be the only kind of job she could do here, because she certainly wasn't going to clean the stables.

Karen perched on a tall stool by the table, looking at some cans.

"Looks like peach pies tonight. We'll have fresh ones before too long. Lots of fruit trees on this property. Ever picked fruit?"

Ree pictured herself up a ladder and wondered if she would be desperate enough for money to test her fear of heights. Karen didn't wait for her answer.

"Ever rode a horse?"

Ree shrugged no.

"I don't like them either. That's why I like the bike. They didn't want me using it here at first because of the horses, but now they see the benefits. Don't need to be cooled off, exercised, or brushed. I also drive the truck. Can you drive?"

Ree had expected the housekeeper to wear a long black Mother Hubbard, a white smock, and a white lace head covering, like an illustration in a Dickens novel, but when Karen said, "Oh, here's Senora Sanchez," a round-faced, short, Hispanic woman with a pleasant smile entered the kitchen. She wore dungarees and a plaid wool man's shirt. Her belt had a large silver buckle. Karen had her pants pushed into her boots, but Senora Sanchez' dungarees hid all but the leather tips, which ended in a silver point.

"This is Ree," said Karen. Ree was excited to be called her by her new name. She was going to have a new life, be a new person. "She goes to Columbia University in New York City."

"So, how long will you be staying with us?" Senora Sanchez asked. "We should go to the parlor to talk. Guests always want to stay around the kitchen, but have you seen our beautiful portal? So many lovely rooms here to sit in." The housekeeper gently grasped her arm to lead her out of the room. Ree saw her shoot Karen a berating glance.

"Oh," Karen said, "she's not a guest. She was hoping we might have a job open."

Senora dropped her arm. The pleasant smile turned severe, then returned.

"This is no place for a professor."

"I wish I was one, but I'm still a student. I need to do my research here, but it's not so easy to get money. I thought if I came to New Mexico, I could get work and get to know people and be able to continue eventually. For now, I need to find a job, and I came here because it always sounded so nice. People are always talking about San Gabriel."

"Hmm," said Senora. "Well, the work here is hard and dirty. This is no school. What could you do here?"

Cleaning stables. Scrubbing bathrooms. Washing pots. Ree hadn't been thinking what work she could do when she had hitchhiked out here. Her goal had been just to get here. From the stories she had heard, she had pictured San Gabriel as a paradise for women like her. That was because it was a vacation spot for the professors she had heard talking. It was no vacation for the workers, and she had no vacation coming. Senora turned to her pie crusts.

Just then a mouse ran across the orange tiled floor, skittering on the smooth surface, which was gleaming clean.

"Damn," said Karen. "Good thing you're not a guest." She reached for a broom leaning in the corner.

The mouse saw them all and froze with fright. In a flash, Ree slammed her foot on its tail, grabbed it, calmly walked out the door, and released it several feet from the building. Senora and Karen followed her out and watched as the mouse disappeared into the brush.

"I could have killed it for you," Ree said, "but I didn't know what you wanted."

"Wow," Karen said. "I took you for a city girl."

"The places I've lived in probably had more mice than this place does. Actually, rats."

"We do need a new house boy," Senora said. "They do all sorts of things, whatever comes up, mostly cleaning. And the best thing about you is you're no boy." She smiled at Ree.

Ree spent the rest of the afternoon in a high loft of the horse barn, following Karen's instructions to sort out boxes of tangled ropes, leather straps, and other mysterious pieces of horse equipment. As she placed them into neat piles, the sun grew low and women on horseback drifted in, some in couples and some alone, each group led by a tall cowboy in a big hat.

When the horsewomen returned to the corral, a stable hand met each one and led the horse away while the rider, sometimes staggering from a day in the saddle, headed toward the main house. As Ree grew more hungry, she pictured them at a table covered with steaming peach pies. Karen hadn't said anything about meals, just put her to work and then left. Occasionally, Ree heard the motorcycle chug past the stables. The few times she went to the outhouse, she only saw the stable hands in the corrals working with the horses.

Senora hadn't told her where she would be sleeping, but on the top floor of the stable was a row of little rooms, each with one bed and a little window. Most were decorated and the beds carefully made, but there was one empty room which she hoped was for her.

Her stomach was grumbling as half the sky blazed red, the rest dark. There was no sign of Karen. Her work was done, the floor covered with neat piles of each length of rope or leather strap or metal rings by sizes. She went down the narrow, steep stairway into the stables. In each stall was a horse, covered with a brightly colored blanket and munching from a bag attached to its head as a stable hand brushed it.

"Be careful, there!" she was warned, but the kick of a horse against the stall door had already caused her to jump back. She fell over a big square block of hay and was on her back. The hay was sharp and scratched her. She sneezed immediately.

"Allergic?" asked the same woman who had called out. "Are you OK?"

"I'm fine. I'm Ree, I've just started working here, I hope."

"Trying you out, are they? I went through that, too."

"You did? How long does it last?" This had been on her mind all day. The conversation in the kitchen had ended abruptly when Senora had told Karen to put her to work for the day, and that was it. She hadn't dared to ask any questions.

"Let me think, it's been a few years. Hmmm." The woman continued to brush the horse while she talked.

"I think it just kind of happened. They just kept giving me stuff to do until all of a sudden one day they handed me a paycheck. On the other hand—" she stopped and pulled on something near the horse's mouth. The horse bucked its head angrily.

"I've seen quite a few come and go pretty fast here. I've seen a few just walk back down the road without even saying a word. I think some women were expecting there would be men to do the hard work, the stuff that takes a lot of muscle. When they find out it's gonna be them, they aren't so eager to work here. How about you? Got the muscles for it?"

"I'm used to hard work. I was ok today, I was upstairs sorting out ropes and stuff."

"You did! That's great, that's been sitting there for weeks. They bought out some other ranch that got foreclosed, and that stuff just got thrown in boxes and dumped here. They haven't bought any new ropes or straps since they got that stuff, so when we need something, everyone's pawed through it. Finally! By the way, my name is Emmy."

"I'm Ree."

"Where you from?"

"New York City."

"Uh-oh, a starry-eyed Easterner. Ever live in the West before?"

"No, but I've wanted to for a long time."

"Hope you like rock slides and mud holes." Just then a bell clanged in the distance.

"Oh finally! Chow time! Come on!" Wondering if she should wait until Karen told her to go, Ree followed.

Ree was so hungry by the time a plate of food was finally in front of her that she could do nothing but chomp away. After a minute or so she slowed down and felt embarrassed with her self-absorption, but there was no sound other than chewing mouths and clinking cutlery. Looking around the table at the faces of those who she hoped would be her friends, she saw a dozen tired, ravenous women. Some faces glowed red from sunburns on top of their deeply tanned skin. Some still had their hats on. She had never been at a table like this, although she had seen it in the movies: the cowhands chowing down, usually by the chuck wagon campfire. But these cowhands were all women, although with some it was hard to tell.

She was bursting with all the new sights and sounds, from the chug of Karen's motorcycle and the way she felt riding behind, grasping Karen's body, to the smells of the barn, the way the ropes felt against the delicate skin of her palms as she unknotted some and coiled others, the sounds of the horses kicking their stalls, the sight of the horsewomen returning at sundown, the look of these toughened women. She wanted to tell them all how new it all was to her, and how happy she was. At last, she was here.

"Karen," said Emmy, "do you know what the plan is yet for the back corral?"

Karen finished chewing and looked up. "Naw, she just keeps changing her mind."

"She's like that," said Emmy.

Ree wanted to know who 'she' was. Was it Senora Sanchez? At last there was some conversation. Karen and Emmy had been friendly to her, but now they acted as if she wasn't there.

Maybe that was it. No one knew her name. What kind of anthropologist was she, not properly introducing herself to the community? No one in any culture relaxed until a stranger was fully introduced. It was human to fear the unknown. She raised her gaze from her plate and drew in her breath. No one looked up.

"I'm Ree," she said. There were a few murmured 'hellos' from mouths full of food. Maybe she should have waited until they weren't eating so much. Should she continue?

"I'm new here," she continued. A few faces looked at her to see if she was as stupid as that indicated.

"This is a really great place. I'm from New York City. This is my first time out West."

One of the women let out a puff of air and shook her head. The rest went back to their food. Ree wished she hadn't said anything. You couldn't fault her for introducing herself, could you? Why did they have to be so unfriendly? Karen and Emmy had been nice on their own. She consoled herself that perhaps this culture had a rule not to talk at dinner. She put her attention to the food, which was better than she had ever eaten, although she was very aware that it was also the least kosher food she had ever eaten. Just as she dipped her spoon into the peach pie, all the women suddenly put down their spoons and stood up. She saw that they had eaten so quickly their dishes were empty. They all filed out the back door as the cowboys came stomping in through the front. Ree threw down her spoon and followed Karen, wanting to grab a handful of her uneaten dessert. Karen showed her to the closed room over the stable and Ree was asleep in minutes.

From that day on she did chores all over the property, walking, carrying, pushing, pulling. When an extra hand was needed, she was called. She struggled with sore muscles, splinters, and banged knees, but her body grew hard and lean.

The dungaree pants were the first trousers she had ever worn. She felt so free in them that she didn't care that her week's wages were taken to pay for them and two work shirts and a dungaree jacket. She felt herself standing taller, her clothes hanging looser, her jaw firmer. Her olive skin darkened so much she wondered if someday she might be mistaken for Hispanic or Indian. She felt like an Indian, even if no one else saw it. She let her hair grow wild and curly, instead of the daily struggle to pin it down and tie it back. With her hair free, her whole face lit up happily.

The cowboys were notoriously clean and pressed. Their shirts were always starched and gleaming, their pants ironed to a stiff crease along the middle of the back of the leg. Back home she had never had the money, time, or motivation to care about her clothes. Here she used an iron, formerly the most odious of household tasks, to create the new woman she was becoming: tightly pressed, a cowgirl of sorts, Ree! Not Henrietta.

What would they think at Columbia if she walked into the department now, dressed in her working duds? Even if it was the women's version of what the cowboys wore, it was not at all the costume of a woman graduate student at an eastern university. They would never recognize her as quiet Henrietta, who they didn't think qualified for a field placement. Now they would beg her to work on their sites! Maybe she should head back to New York right away and be reconsidered before the tan faded.

One day Ree was assigned to the housecleaning staff.

"Tonight's the fanciest party of the summer," said Senora. "The guests are all out, so we can get to everything."

At first Ree was angry when handed a polishing cloth and light feather duster that made her sneeze, but as she moved through the rooms she realized this was a great opportunity to take her time and look at everything. She had never been in the rooms restricted to guests. In the library, a sizeable parlor with big oak Morris chairs and shiny side tables covered by woven Navajo runners, she dusted a collection of various-sized Indian drums. The bookshelves included one area exclusively for the works of Willa Cather, including Cather's latest book. There was no one around so she flipped it open just to get a taste. She forgot where she was until the door pushed open. She slapped the book closed, dropping the feather duster. She scrambled to pick it up without even looking at who came in.

"What are you reading?" She looked up and saw Ned, the Indian from the Plaza who had chased the prairie dog, smiling at her. She smiled back and for a moment they just looked at each other.

"It's the new Willa Cather," she said. "I'm supposed to be dusting." She frantically pushed the feather duster over the tops of books, looking back at him all the time.

"You're going to miss a lot of dust that way," he laughed. "I'm supposed to be looking for a closet in which a very heavy wagon wheel is stored that has to go out to decorate the portal. There it is." Ned headed for a small door covered with paintings. The door opened with a rusty shriek that made them both laugh.

"I didn't know you worked here," Ree said.

"I haven't for a long time, but they just called me back. They hire me then they fire me, depending on how many cowboys they need. They don't need Indian cowboys so much."

"I didn't know any of the cowboys were Indians."

"They keep us around to excite their romantic fantasies. Sometimes they let me show how I make jewelry. I'm not supposed to be in the house, I'm just here to get this wheel, since the guests aren't here."

He rolled it out of the closet. "These things have cast iron in them. Really heavy! But they don't want the floors damaged." He struggled to move the wheel along gently. "I might see you later, but I'm just hired for the day. If something big is happening, I might be around."

After that, Ree flew through the dusting so fast that the housekeeper congratulated her and said she would think of her for it in the future. Ree regretted her fastidiousness.

As she moved through her various chores at San Gabriel, Ree wondered what Ruth did when she stayed at the dude ranch. Did Ruth ever sit in that chair? Did Ruth ride that horse? What would it be like to sit here with Ruth and watch the sunset? The more time that had passed since she had left New York, the more she was thinking lovingly of Ruth again. Ruth must have fought for her, but against all those men in the department with their loyalty to other men and rich women, what could Ruth have done? Ruth was struggling to keep her own career.

Lately Ned invaded her thoughts. She expected to see him around every corner. It confused her feelings and she wanted to push Ned back and enjoy the pure happiness of her fantasies of Ruth. But she liked thinking about Ned. She pictured him showing her his hogan, taking her riding out on the wide open Indian land, letting her sit by him as they watched a healing ceremony. She tried to drive the thoughts of Ned out with her dream of sitting beside Ruth working on their scholarly writings. Life with Ned was a more exciting picture. But delicate Ruth needed her, while Ned was strong and confident. She was sure there was a place for her in Ruth's life, once Ruth saw the truth about Margaret. But with self-assured Ned, she would be the weak one.

She didn't understand her thoughts about Ned, because no man had ever made her feel this way before. Her fantasies of Frank Hamilton Cushing had been about wanting to live like him, not wanting to live with him. Sack's insinuations about wanting to get close to her had made her skin crawl. But how she felt about Ned made sense. Indians had fascinated her since she first read about Frank. Ned was the first Indian who had spoken to her as a friend, not a tourist or co-worker. Just having a friend here was a relief. She wanted to tell Ned about Frank Hamilton Cushing, about Columbia, maybe even about Ruth.

On Thursdays, merchants showed their wares to the guests at San Gabriel. The portal was set up like the portal at the Palace of the Governors, except that the guests stayed comfortably seated while the merchants moved from person to person. Most of the sellers were Indian women, carrying small trays. Watching from the distance of the garden where she had been assigned to squeeze dead buds off the bushes, Ree couldn't see what was on the trays, but she knew it must be jewelry, small pots, and small beaded objects.

Some Anglo traders were also allowed to sell. Ree finished the gardening and was headed to the kitchen for her next assignment when a man said "wait a—uh, pardon me," and tapped her shoulder. "Ma'am," he said, and then stood back staring.

"I knew it was you!" he slapped his knee. "Henrietta?"

It was Sack, staring at her denim trousers and work shirt and straw cowboy hat.

"Oh my God," she gasped. "I've been looking for you. I can't believe you're here."

"So you finally smartened up and left school, Henrietta," Sack's voice boomed out.

"Shhhh," she said, looking around to see who had heard. "Everyone calls me Ree here. I'm not supposed to be talking to guests."

"I'm not a guest, I'm here to sell." He held up a tray of old coins and silver buttons.

"I can't talk to you. I'll lose my job," she said and turned toward the house.

"What are you doing here, Henrietta?" he said as she went into the house.

"Ree," she called back.

In the kitchen, waiting for instructions, she couldn't believe what she had seen. Was Sack likely to say anything that would threaten her job? What did he know about San Gabriel? But she was also glad to see a familiar face. How could they get a chance to talk?

Her next assignment sent her behind the stables. She heard angry voices as she approached. Two men were arguing.

"You can't do that. That's ours to sell, not yours to steal."

"Don't tell me what to do."

They were faced off, near to blows. One was Sack, facing her, the other a Navajo man from his clothes.

"Sack!" she said.

"Henrietta," he looked her way and smiled. "Good. Now we'll have a chance to talk, maybe?"

The Navajo man turned toward her.

"You know this man?" Ned said.

"Just a little," she said. "In New York we—"

"This man steals from my people," said Ned. "You can't sell that, it belongs to my people," he said, turning back to Sack.

"You keep your hands off it," said Sack. "I bought it fair and square. If you don't want it sold, keep a better eye on your women. And I'll bet you can do that well," he said with an insinuating sneer.

"Sack, why are you doing this?" Ree asked. "You know better than this. You should give it to him."

"Hey, I paid good money for this, are you some kind of a Red? Hey that's pretty funny—a Red and a Red man!"

Ned glared at both of them.

"I don't think it's funny. Come on Sack, I can't believe you're doing this. I thought you cared about the Indians."

"You never understood me, Henrietta."

"That's Ree!"

"Ree? All right. Hiding from the law? Anyway, you never understood why I was in school. I learned what I needed to learn and now I'm here to use what I learned. You think I wanted to stand on a stage and excite all the little girls from Manhattan, like your precious Professor Benedict? Hell no, what kind of money do you think she makes? And spends her time squatting in the dirt asking Indians what they cook for dinner? That's not my life. Haven't you ever heard of the Gold Rush? There's been money to be made in the West since Coronado marched through, and I'm here for my share. And if you don't like it—" he glared right back at Ned, "then you stay poor and watch the government take the diddley-shit little that's left for you. And march you off to a cave and shoot you. If you were smart, you'd do what I do, make the money and then you know what? You'll have power then. Not the power of some old magic arrows or whatever you believe. The power of this!" He pulled a wad of greenbacks out of his pocket, in a silver money clip with a turquoise bead on it.

"That too!" said Ned. "I hate that. We never used to make money clips. It's all for the tourists and the grifters like you."

"Sure, call me names," said Sack. "But you know something? I like your people a hell of a lot more than most of the anthropologists coming here to stare at you. I've been to school." He laughed heartily. "With Henrietta—no Ree—here. At least I know something about the Navajos."

"That's Navajo people, not Navajos," snapped Ned. "Don't talk about us like you would about horses. And you just said you learned so you could steal from us. You expect me to thank you for that? I'll do my best to keep you out of here. At least out of my country. Not this white people's place. They can have you, I don't care." He backed away, not looking at Ree.

"He's right," Ree said to Sack. "I didn't come here to steal. Not everyone thinks like you, Sack." She wanted Ned to hear her, but he was walking away fast and she felt that he would forever link her with Sack.

"Tell me," said Sack, "how are you going to live out here? Little Miss Garment Worker? What are you going to do for money?"

"I've got a good job here," Ree said. "I'm doing fine."

"When the summer ends, you'll be out on your ass," Sack said. "Come find me, I'll help you."

She was glad Ned had disappeared around the corner of the stables before Sack said that. Nonetheless, she spoke loudly, hoping he could hear.

"I would never! I don't need your help. I would never do what you do."

"What do you think I'm doing?" Sack said with a grin.

"Whatever Ned didn't like."

"Oh, so you know the young, uh, fellow," Sack said. "I'm not surprised. "

"What are you doing here?—no, I guess I know already," Ree said.

"That saves us a lot of conversation," Sack shrugged.

"I need to get back to work," Ree said.

"You'll be seeing me," Sack said. She started to walk off when he continued in a low voice. "So you finally blew off those pompous asses at Columbia." She turned, startled, at this comment.

"I'm glad to see you," he said. "I always liked you. I'm glad to see you here. This is where you wanted to be."

She softened toward him. "You're the only one who really understood," she said.

"I'm not kidding," he said. "I've got a feeling you'll need me. Don't be afraid to ask."

"How do you know I'll be the one needing you? I'm doing fine so far. Got a great job here."

"Oh, I haven't got your ideals, so I figure I'll go further, even if doesn't look like it now."

"Jeez," said Ree. "You're impossible. It's always been like this. Just when I think you're a decent person, you always turn on me."

"You, more than anyone around here, or at Columbia, should understand. We're both from where we're from. We're not them. How many times do I need to tell you? What do you think you're doing here, in this rich girl's diamond playpen? You think they'll let you play along? This is just Columbia gone West."

"That's not true. It doesn't feel that way at all. Aren't you the one who talked about all the opportunity here? Everyone has an equal chance here. Not like New York."

He thought for a moment. "That's true. I used to think that. But I've been here a while now and I'm not so sure. It's not as easy as I thought. But you know, you're probably doing better than I am, you're right."

"See! Thanks."

"Yeah. Listen, once you get cozied up to one of these rich gals here, how about letting me know? I can sell her the little love presents she'll give you."

"What are you talking about? Sometimes you seem to speak another language."

He laughed loudly. "You're still the world's stupidest virgin, aren't you?"

"I have to get to work."

"Sure, go on, plow those filthy rich fields and see what comes up."

"I don't know what you're talking about."

With that, she was finally able to walk away from the conversation, wishing that just once she could feel as confident as Sack did, knowing more than him, able to leave him embarrassed for once. Well, he wasn't the one working here at San Gabriel, learning all about how these "rich people" lived. She was watching and studying and she would know more. He was looking through the window while she was inside, like in that fairy tale.

Before she could stop him, he ran up and kissed her cheek with a resounding smack. "Don't die a virgin, honey," he said and walked off, calling back over his shoulder "Anyway, I can get all the rich old money bags I want!"

Ree had offered to Senora that she would like to work in the attic, which she had seen on a "to do" list.

"It's so hot up there. I was leaving that until fall."

"I don't mind. I love attics. What do you need done?"

"There's a lot in this old house over so many years. Who knows what was dragged up there and forgotten? Make sure nothing's rotting up there, with dead mice or squirrels or leaks. Are you sure you want to do that? We can send one of the Indian girls."

Ree winced at this attitude, which she heard almost every day. Sometimes it seemed to her she heard them say "Jew girls," not "Indian girls."

"I'd really like to do it. While I separate out anything that's too ruined, what if I took an inventory? I'll make a detailed list of everything up there." Going through the attic would be a treasure hunt worthy of an archaeologist. What if she found Indian artifacts, collected long ago by a hobbyist?

"That's just what's needed. I don't see an Indian girl doing that."

Ree turned away, holding back what she wanted to say to that. "I'll take the back stairs that start at the kitchen," she said.

"My, you notice everything. I'll bet most of the staff that's been here for years have no idea how to get up there."

"Well, like I said, I love attics. I've been wanting to see what's there."

"Mind you, just take an inventory," said Senora, a bit sharply, looking at Ree more closely.

"We do something very much like this in my archaeology classes," said Ree. "So I know just how I'll do it." She started for the little door behind the pantry.

From up in the attic, unsteadily perched on a pile of old trunks to look out a high window, Ree watched some of the guests ride off toward the distant hills. Cobwebs were in her hair, and she kept a wary eye on a hornet's nest between the rafters nearby. The window was so thickly covered with dust and grime that two women on horseback, framed by the pane, looked like an illustration in a storybook. "That could be Ruth and me," Ree whispered to herself just before the bottom trunk collapsed, and she and the top trunk tumbled to the dusty hard floor.

Stunned for a moment, she sat listening to the buzz of the awakened hornets. She struggled to breathe from the heat, the dust, and the tumble. She looked through the dim light at the unpromising piles and tangles of junk in the attic, while somewhere out there, in the freshest, cleanest air, in the most beautiful vistas, her beloved and her unworthy rival were as free and as happy as could be. She was Cinderella and the Prince had run off with her awful stepsister.

Everything she touched was so grimy that the skin on her hands dried. She kept dropping things and she had to try over and over to separate the layers of fabric and piles of newspapers that were everywhere. She sneezed so loudly she was afraid Senora would make her stop so she wouldn't disturb the guests. She choked and coughed to clear her throat of dust. But she barely cared, for the thrill of opening each box or trunk or plowing through each pile had her so exhilarated she went faster and faster. The newspaper from the day the Spanish-American War ended! A wedding dress with a wine splatters on the front. Had someone thrown their glass at the bride? A wooden tortilla press, the handle carved with intricate birds and flowers, the wood shiny and soft with the oil of the cook's fingers. How many thousands of meals had begun in those hands, and then passed from daughter to daughter?

As she worked her way through the trunks, the piles grew. Much of what she touched crumpled to dust and splinters in her hands, often with the toothmarks of mice or squirrels. If only it had all been left in a cave to survive like the baskets and rabbit fur blankets of the Anasazi. Indians from a thousand years ago had left better records of their lives than white people of a few generations back. Just then she saw the tip of a large brown feather sticking out from under a bonnet in a crunched-in wicker ladies trunk. She reached for the feather, but it stuck.

Remembering her archaeology training, she patiently removed the hat. There were two large feathers, mostly brown on top and white below. They were tied to a a flat, crumbling stick of wood. As she reached for the branch, she heard a clacking sound as some objects tied to it by leather strings clicked together. Pulling it all up carefully, she saw that the rattles were delicate deer hooves. Little leather bags gouged by the nibbles of mice fell away from it, the last of their leather strings breaking. A piece of red cloth was under it all. It might have been wrapped around to hold it all together.

This had to be a sacred object for an Indian ceremony. What tribe did it belong to? How had it ended up here? It was far too sacred to be sold. Perhaps an Indian had lost it. Or someone like Sack had managed to buy and sell it, and the new owner had left it here with other forgotten souvenirs.

Maybe it wasn't really Indian. Maybe a visitor to San Gabriel had made it, just for fun. Feathers, wood, leather—anyone could get these. She had no idea if was authentic. She wanted to rush to the library to see if other anthropologists had written about such objects. But there was no library like Columbia University's here. Maybe in Santa Fe? She could ask Ned! If she saved it, she could give it to Ned to return to his people or another tribe. She looked around the room for something to wrap it in. She would hide it in the trash she was accumulating, then sneak it back to her room.

"So has your precious one turned up yet?" Sack asked. "I heard she's in the area. Any day now, she'll be here."

"What are you talking about? And stop sneaking up on me." She hadn't known he was around when he came up to her as if in mid-conversation. She was sitting on a railing, polishing a harness. Many of the guests were about to leave for a three-day trip to the mountain camp of San Gabriel called Canjilon Camp.

"Why your darling Professor Benedict, and her very own darling Miss Mead."

"What about them?" She said too loudly from the sudden excitement of hearing Ruth's name here.

"Hey, don't knock me over, I'll tell. I ran into Ruth Bunzel at the trading post at Crystal. She mentioned Mead was here. My guess is it's a little love tryst. So of course they're going to head this way."

Ree couldn't hide her interest.

"I thought you'd like to know. What are you going to say when they see you here?" he asked.

"What about when they see you?" she said.

"I don't think they care."

"Do you think they'll care that I'm here?" she asked eagerly.

"Of course," he said.

"Why?"

He moved his head back on his neck and studied her like a cat about to decide whether to pounce.

"Maybe they've noticed you watching them."

She turned away so he couldn't see her blush.

"Sack, how come you watch me so much?"

"You might be hearing that same question yourself soon." With that he walked away.

When Ruth saw this new Amazon Ree, perhaps she would forget the infatuated sycophant that Ree now saw she must have appeared to Ruth. It was no longer a mystery why Ruth never fell for her, and why Ruth preferred Margaret. Margaret had a vigor that could not be denied. Even in her femininity, she had strength and liveliness. Ree had tried to impress Ruth with her studiousness and devotion, but she was embarrassed now to picture her lifeless self back in the city. The only fervor and vitality would have been her unconcealable desire for Ruth, so naked, so exposed. She had been pale and shrunken, with the pasty skin of a man who has stayed too long at yeshiva. She had thought she was impressing Ruth with her devotion, but all she had shown was her inadequacy.

Here, she felt red-blooded and healthy. The air, the physical activity, being outdoors, not bent over a book or a sewing machine-- she felt her breath and blood moving and filling her body, as if she was fully opened for the first time. She found herself reciting the "Nishmat" morning prayer, understanding it, because now all her ducts were open, and they had been all but closed before, and she thanked God for the vitality she felt. It made her want Ruth not just as an ideal and an idol. She wanted the two of them together, vigorous, bursting with life, pumped with blood and joy.

"Hello, we're back," announced a happy voice. Those three words were said by so many of the guests when they arrived, but Ree recognized this voice. She never greeted guests and rarely was sent to work near the entrance, but she had been on her way to the front hall closet to pick up a kerosene lantern to be refilled.

Through the screen door she could see Margaret. Ree flattened against the wall.

"Oh, no, they've taken away that Dasburg painting," said Margaret as she stepped inside the hall, holding the door open for Ruth. "They've put up something more conventional. Looks like a Remington. Oh dear, cowboys." She leaned over to examine the signature.

"Let's see," said Ruth. She glanced toward the painting, but Margaret was blocking her way, so she looked around.

"Here at last," Ruth said. "Everything else looks the same. Oh!" As she turned, she came face to face with Ree, who cringed backward looking for a way to run out. She readied herself to greet them, realizing her posture had reflexively slipped back to the wormlike drudge they knew her to be in New York.

"Hello, we're back," said Ruth. "Don't mind Margaret, I'm sure it's a lovely painting. She just has to comment on everything."

Ruth looked relaxed, not the imperious pose of the professor. Ruth didn't recognize Ree, and Ree didn't know this Ruth, either.

"I can't believe it!" Margaret said as soon as they closed the door to their room behind them.

Ruth circled the room. "Look, they've painted the wall. The one where there had been a leak. They've taken out that awful flowered wallpaper."

"That's nice. But didn't you see that was Henrietta? Pretending not to know us?"

"Are you sure? That little cowboy with short hair?"

"With a nose like that? It isn't like she looks like a lot of other people. I'd know those eyes anywhere, she's always glaring jealously at me."

"Well, she'd like to be first in class, too."

"I told you she stares at you. She should be embarrassed to be so naked in public."

"Funny to hear that from you. Shame is just a cultural constraint."

"Most cultures want the eyes to be down and away, not revealing desire like that."

"Most, hmm."

"I'll bet there's a publishable paper in that. Desire is universal, but showing it so baldly, it's just universally repulsive."

"Margaret! Be kind. I swear, you're so arrogant sometimes."

"Anyway, what's she doing here?"

"If she didn't want us to recognize her, maybe she'll disappear now. Maybe we won't see her again. I'm going to enjoy my vacation."

"So you do think it was Henrietta?" said Margaret.

"Perhaps."

"If it wasn't her, she wouldn't have stared like that. It was a dead giveaway. That woman does not know how to hide anything. She's the last person to disguise herself. And besides, what's she doing hiding here? She must have heard we come here. Do you think she came to San Gabriel because she knew we'd be coming?"

Ruth sat daintily on the bed. "I just want to relax. We're together, my darling."

"Don't you think that's kind of creepy? She followed us here."

"It looks like she got here first."

"You know what I mean. What are we going to do?"

Ruth stretched out on the bed, patting the space beside her. "Come on, forget about her. We can't let anything ruin our time together. We've waited all year for this."

Margaret stood over the bed. "You can relax? Even when not much is happening, you're always working, working, working, and now when something really strange is going on, you relax?"

Ruth held out her arms. "Please, darling, there's nothing we can do right now. We're here at San Gabriel. We're free here from everyone back home. We're going to have a few days of fun before I head for Zuni pueblo and you go home. It's our place to be ourselves, to be free."

Margaret sat on the bed without touching Ruth, so Ruth reached out to rest her hand on Margaret's back, rubbing lightly. In a moment, Margaret jumped up again.

"Why is she spying on us?"

"Maybe we're her fieldwork. Maybe she's here to study our women's culture, here at San Gabriel."

"That's not funny. It's none of her business."

"Well, now you know how the Indians feel. Do you think they want us spying on them? They don't even know us. We know Henrietta."

"What do we know about her? Tell me everything you know about her."

"Ok, but only if you lie down. Then maybe you'll calm down."

Ruth settled back on the bed, and Margaret pulled off her shoes and lay stiff beside her.

"OK, I think she's from Queens or Brooklyn, one of those subway students."

"Must be Brooklyn, she's Jewish, but not a rich one from the Bronx."

"Right. Where do you think she went to school?"

"She hasn't got the polish of a private school. She sticks out. Who let her into the program anyway?"

"Oh, well, you know Boas. Always finding those diamonds in the rough."

"She's no diamond."

"Margaret, you're too harsh. She worked really hard. Not a great mind, but a very hard worker. Her papers were twice the length of most others. "

"You're so naïve, Ruth. She doesn't care about anthropology. Just another one of your admirers. She's just wants you to fall in love with her, like in a fairy tale. She thinks you'll fall in love with her because she wrote a long homework assignment."

"Margaret! You're jealous!"

"Of what? I work hard, too, but that isn't why you're with me."

"Are you so sure?"

Margaret poked Ruth in the ribs and they sparred until they fell back on the bed, breathless. Margaret reached her arms around Ruth and kissed her. They relaxed into the kisses.

The dinner bell woke them up.

"Oh, dear," said Ruth, trying to shake the wrinkles out of the blouse Margaret had thrown to the floor. "We've got to be careful with our clothes. I've only brought so much."

"What are we going to say to her?"

"Again? Let it go."

"I'm worried for you. I'm worried for me. It's no coincidence that she's here. What about that actress who shot her husband for seeing another woman?"

"Margaret, you're being ridiculous. If you want to know so much, go ask her why she's here."

"I will. I won't let her hide like that. Wait a minute, maybe she's still angry about not getting that field placement out here. Do you think she might want revenge?"

"It wasn't me who made that choice. It was a whole committee," said Ruth. "Maybe she's angry that you got the placement and she didn't. Oh, dear, this probably doesn't look fair to her, you here with me, sharing a room."

"That's where we have an advantage over couples like Gladys Reichard and Pliny Goddard. Everyone knows about their affair, even his wife. They can't be seen together any more. There are rules for married couples, but not for two women. She can't see into our bedroom. We're teacher and assistant, sharing a room to save money. She's got nothing to complain about."

"Perhaps. If it's easier for you to think so."

The next morning, seeing Margaret and Ruth walking toward the stable, Ree headed away. She made it to the far end of the L-shaped building when Karen called her name.

"Ree, can you run to the kitchen and ask cook for some apples? Bring back a bushel if you can."

Karen was holding two horses for Margaret and Ruth. She was sure they were watching her as she ran towards the kitchen as fast as she could. Maybe they wouldn't think that "Ree" was the same person as "Henrietta." Maybe cats could fly.

As she walked back carrying the heavy bushel as slowly as she could, Margaret and Ruth were patting a horse and talking with Karen. It looked like they were asking questions, which she hoped weren't about her. She couldn't think of any way to bring the apples to Karen without getting so close to them that she would have to acknowledge them. Why had she ever thought coming here was a good idea? Her cheeks must be as red as the apples, and she wished a horse would chomp her down and swallow her fast. She would like to die as quickly as possible at this moment.

"Why Henrietta," said Margaret, "what in the world are you doing here?"

"What! You know each other?" said Karen.

"Henrietta is a student at Columbia University," said Ruth, filling in the silence. Why couldn't she have said, 'Henrietta is my student at Columbia?' Ruth was such a cold fish, why, why, why did she do this to herself over her?

"What are you doing here?" Margaret asked again. Damn Margaret! She knew damn well what Ree was doing here, the same as she herself was, only for some unknown reason the gods and Ruth Benedict had blessed Margaret with good fortune.

There wasn't any point in pretending it was coincidence.

"I heard so many people at Columbia speak highly of San Gabriel," said Ree, "that I wanted to see for myself. I was lucky enough to get a job here. It's as wonderful as they said. It's a great place to work."

"But what are you doing in New Mexico? Didn't you get turned down?"

"Margaret, no need to be rude!" snapped Ruth.

"I did, but I saved my money and came out on my own. I'm saving more working here and I'm hoping to go into the field."

"Don't you think there's a reason they didn't send you here?" said Margaret.

"Margaret, really!"

"Lots of anthropologists pay their own way," said Ree. "Many aren't even students anywhere. I'm not rich, but I'm going to do it, too."

"That's something about the field we're trying to put an end to. Amateurs!"

"Margaret, that's going too far."

"I have the benefit of Professor Benedict's training, among many others." Ree stood taller as she spoke. "I've done all but my dissertation. You can hardly call me an amateur. If I were a man, I think I would have received a grant."

"I think it's admirable of you to be so dedicated," broke in Ruth, which of course put Ree in love with her again, regardless of the company she kept.

"If that's the case, why do I get grants?" Margaret asked. Ree wished she had the nerve to point at Ruth, but no matter how angry she was at Margaret, she couldn't do it.

"And what about your friend, Mr. Sackmann?"
Margaret continued. "I saw you with him often back at
school, and I saw him out here selling to the other guests.
You didn't see him getting any grants. The professors know
who can be trusted in the field, and from what I've seen him
doing out here, they were right."

"Margaret, stop," said Ruth.

"Anyway, the horses are getting restless," said
Margaret, "I want to ride." With that she turned away from
Ree, then turned back to snatch an apple for the horse, as if
Ree's function was to hold the basket for her pleasure.

Sack was right, Ree thought as she watched them ride
off. We don't fit into their club. What was it he had said one
day at Columbia? That the poor like them had only two
choices in a rich man's world: to be a whore or a con man. If
you were poor, you whored yourself to get what they had. Or
you could be a con man and patronize the rich while stealing
from them. Sack had chosen to be a con man. He was just
waiting for her to make her choice.

What was it she wanted from Ruth? In her wildest
fantasies, she wanted everything that she imagined Margaret
had, and maybe more, because Ruth hadn't left her husband
for Margaret. At more sober moments, she just wanted to
explain herself to Ruth. She wanted Ruth to understand her.
At best, she wanted Ruth to soothe her for all she had gone
through.

One day it struck her that if all she wanted was to talk
to Ruth, why couldn't she do that? But she would never have
the nerve. Whenever she saw Ruth, all words vanished. She
stumbled, she stuttered, her mind went blank. Or, it was
clouded with too many dreams and hopes and fantasies,
leaving no room for the real woman actually there before her.

"She's right," Ruth said as their horses trotted off
toward the mountains and the woods, and away from the flat
pink plain on which was the road and San Gabriel. "Rich

women pay their own way out here. Why shouldn't poor women do it, too?"

"But they fit in."

"Margaret, don't be a snob. You sound like Mabel Dodge and her stuffy salon."

"Before she went native."

"Well, there's a good example. She's rich enough to do what she wants. She's studying the Pueblo Indians, in her own chosen way. Why can't Henrietta do the same?"

The soft thuds of the horses was all that could be heard. They were far enough from the road to Santa Fe that not even the chug of a Model T sounded.

"But those other women were never students, so no one told them they couldn't go. Don't you think it degrades the department if a student ignores the faculty's wishes?"

"She's right, though. Women were among the first anthropologists here. Now the men get almost everything, except for a few stars like you. Most of the women now have rich patrons, and Henrietta didn't attract anyone's attention. It is about the money, not her qualifications."

"Come on Ruth, do you think she should be doing field work here? She's just not right for the job. Something off about her."

"Not properly socialized to the culture of Columbia University?"

"Maybe that's it. She just doesn't fit in. Nobody wanted to be around her much at school, and certainly not out in the field where you're really thrown together sometimes."

"I'm not the most sociable person myself."

"For obvious reasons, everyone loves you anyway, even if you don't try very hard for it. Henrietta's the opposite. She's too intense. Wow, there's grass here!"

They had come to a grassy patch, and the horses were balking, wanting to stop for a snack.

"Maybe you're right. She could do some damage," Ruth said. "Working unsupervised. She might stumble on something new, and not handle it right."

"That's what I mean. She should be stopped."

"I don't think we can do that. Maybe she should get supervision. Maybe the department should give her an assignment where she's satisfied, but out of the way."

"Stop thinking about work," said Margaret. "This was supposed to be our vacation. These are supposed to be the forget-everything few days. I hate that you're having to think about this. That's the thing about Henrietta, she's always pushing herself in where she's not wanted."

"What is it about her? You have no heart when it comes to her."

"All my heart is for you, my dear."

"Is it something about the Jews?"

"Of course not. You know I love Franz Boas. But she's just never in synch."

"But she's not the only Jewish student. There's Goldfrank, that woman from Queens."

"She doesn't seem so Jewish, you know what I mean? Henrietta is closer to the ghetto. Not like the German Jews, like Franz. She's Fresh Off the Boat."

"I don't think that's true. I'm sure she was born here."

"It's culture. Who would understand that more than us? She's just not melted into the melting pot enough."

"Margaret, you're awful."

"I am. Try this!" Margaret clicked the reins and took off on the trail, with Ruth, after an awkward few seconds of steadying herself, following behind.

Ree was relieved when she saw Ruth and Margaret ride off to Canjillon, the rustic campground that San Gabriel ranch had up in the mountains. Relaxing as she did her tedious tasks, Ree amused herself by studying the confident, women at San Gabriel—how they talked, held their bodies, rode the horses. She always knew when Karen was around, with her strong footfalls and her gasping breaths, because she was somewhat fat and always in a rush. Karen had a loud, deep voice and sometimes slipped out a curse word that only men used. As western as Karen was in her dungarees and plaid wool shirts, her strong presence reminded Ree of the balabustas back on Fulton Street, the tough yiddishe mamas who would fight over the best cut of brisket, who would argue about the superiority of their children, who would complain the loudest about the inadequacy of their husbands.

There was Kate, one of the cowgirls. Ree had been told that it was rare for women to lead horse trips from dude ranches, because most tourists preferred the romance of hearty, handsome, cowboys. But things were different at San Gabriel because the single women guests weren't all looking for cowboys. Kate was tall with powerful shoulders and unusually lean hips. Near or on a horse, she was confident and sure, her green eyes flashing. But in the dining room, Ree had never been able to catch her downcast eyes. She spoke so rarely that Ree watched her through an entire meal eyeing the salt shaker across the way but unwilling to ask for it. Ree finally offered it to her, but instead of smiling back gratefully, she took it and stared down at her plate.

Ree wondered if this was how she herself appeared to her colleagues at Columbia. At the few parties or formal occasions, she found herself tongue-tied. Why then was she perceived as too pushy, too Jewish? Maybe she spoke up too much in class, challenging the teachers. She often caught them in trivial errors about the Indians, especially when it concerned Frank Hamilton Cushing's work.

One morning the usually grumpy staff chattered with excitement at breakfast. Before Ree could ask what was going on, Senora Sanchez came into the staff dining room. Ree had never seen her do so before. There was a hierarchy among the workers and Senora was served at the kitchen table by the cooks, the queen of a low-ranking land.

"For the barrel contest and the worker hunt, we'll need all of you to do work you don't usually do. I'll give out the assignments now."

Ree was assigned to the cowboy hunt, but she had no idea what that meant. She asked Karen.

"We dress up in cowboy clothes and as the sun starts to go down, we—oh, you'll see."

Meanwhile, Ree's day was busy. For the pig roast barbecue, she peeled and chopped potatoes, carried wood, and cut vegetables. She had never been this close to a dead pig. She wondered if the workers would be given any to eat.

As she worked, Ree watched the cowboys Curly and Shorty roll a wooden barrel to the middle of the corral. They tied a long rope to each end, so that it looked like a giant's necklace with one big cylindrical bead in the center.

"OK, let's try it," Shorty said. They each held one end of the rope and walked away from the barrel. As they moved further apart, each pulling tightly on his end, the rope grew taut and the barrel began to rise into the air.

"Tighter, you wimp, pull tighter," jeered Shorty.

"Yeah, let's see who's wimpy," said Curly. Each set his feet firmly in the ground, spat, gritted his teeth, and the tug of war was on. Soon the barrel rode waist-high and parallel to the ground, and Ree heard each man mutter a curse as he pulled. Just then Jack Lambert, the head cowboy, walked into the corral. Shorty pulled so hard that Curly tumbled forward and the barrel fell. Jack shook his head and threw up his hands.

Ree's next job was to chop ice for drinks from a huge block set on an anvil. She had an ice pick and had already been firmly told to chop smaller pieces. She was concentrating on this when Ned came over with a wheelbarrow of huge blocks of ice, which he smashed with a sledge hammer, then handed her the chunks. They worked side by side, silently. He hadn't even said hello, and the moment had passed for Ree to greet him. She was miserable, wanting to explain herself and Sack to him. Soon his task would be done and she might never get another chance.

"You don't understand," she blurted out. "Sack's not my friend. I hate him. You left before I told him off."

"It's not important," Ned said. "I don't care."

"But it is. I don't want you to think I would do anything like that. That's not why I'm here."

She was hoping Ned would ask why she was here, but he turned back to chopping ice. If she told him her hopes of living with the Indians, would he think any better of her? He might think she wanted to steal more of his culture than Sack did. But she couldn't let it drop now. He was the only friend she'd made here. She hardly knew him, but she felt he was a friend.

"I'm here because I want to learn how your people live."

Ned let out an annoyed sigh. Oh God, she sounded like every anthropologist who had ever pushed through a teepee door.

"I don't mean like an anthropologist. I don't mean so I can publish your secrets." Well, that wasn't exactly true. She had fantasized the articles she would write about her life with the Indians, just like Frank Hamilton Cushing had done.

"I mean, I just think your way of life is wonderful. It's the way I want to live. I come from New York City, but that's not the way I want to live. I hated college and people like Sack, who just want to exploit and steal. That's not what I want. I'm—."

Ned held the hammer tightly and impatiently. She didn't even know what she wanted to say next. What was she? How was she different from Sack, or Margaret, or Ruth?

"I'm different," she said. If he didn't say something soon, what was she going to babble out next?

"You're too late," said Ned. "If I could live that way, would I be here, chopping ice for rich women's drinks?"

"Don't say that," said Ree. "You should see New York. Then you'd see how much better it is here. Not here at San Gabriel, but well, where your people are."

"It's not the way it used to be."

"Is that what you want? Are you making money here so you can move off the reservation?"

"Is that what you think I want? Is that what I look like I want?" He stood up and his biceps flexed under the tight leather thongs tied around his arms. It made her think of her father in his phylacteries, but he had never looked so muscular.

"No, not at all. That's why I want to talk to you. You're what I'm looking for here. Your argument with Sack, it was wonderful. I just wish you'd heard what I said to him after you left. Then you'd believe me."

Ned looked at her doubtfully.

"Well, I hope you would, anyway."

He began to chop again.

"I don't have the money to just go where I want, and I wouldn't want anyone to just take me in. That's why I'm working here," Ree said. "Not every white person from New York is rich. I'm not a guest here. I'm saving all my wages and then I'm going to--. Well, I don't know exactly where I'm going. I was hoping you could help me."

"Oh great! Why me?"

"I haven't met anyone else. I mean, Indians. You're the only one who has been friendly. I know I'm an outsider, I know no one really wants me here, but I'm going to try. Because this is the only thing I've wanted to do my whole life. They didn't understand me at Columbia, and maybe you don't either, but I just have this one life and this is what I want to do." She looked out at a guest, swinging in a tire from a tree, and two others who sat on the portal in rockers, heads back and eyes closed soaking up the sun.

Ned didn't say anything. What could he think but that she was a spoiled child having a temper tantrum, which maybe was true? She certainly had it better than the Spanish maid who walked past them with a bucket and mop.

"I can't get what I want either," said Ned quietly. "I can't turn the clock back. I can't make my people stop selling off our culture. And I can't get to do what I want, either."

"What's that?" she whispered, afraid to break the spell that he was finally talking to her. He didn't say anything. In the corner of her eye, she saw Karen heading their way, no doubt to hurry them up.

"I want to be a healer, a medicine man. I want to learn all the chants and herbs. White people have libraries like the big one in Santa Fe, where all their memories and knowledge are stored, but my people save it in the minds of the healers. I want to be that. There are hardly any left, and when they die, what they know will die, too, like the buffalo that are gone now."

"Don't they want you to learn? I'd think they'd be so glad to teach you."

"Yeah," Ned said bitterly. "Yeah, you would think that. I would think that."

Just then Karen walked up to them.

"Why are you two working so slowly? Let's go, let's go." She clapped her hands as she looked at the pile of ice chunks.

"OK, you're done here," she said to Ned, "you go ask Jack what he wants next."

Ned and Ree looked at each other. She wondered if his heart leapt too, wanting to keep talking.

"Go," said Karen, "I thought you were a fast worker, well, now I don't know."

Ned started off toward the barn.

"Hey! Take the wheelbarrow and hammer," Karen snapped at him.

"Thanks for breaking up the ice," Ree said weakly. Ned grabbed the tools and walked away without looking at her. Karen glared at her.

"Don't get too friendly," Karen said. "No talking on the job, and not to one of them. Everybody has to know their place here, you know."

Ree knew she shouldn't look at her so sullenly.

"Hey, I'm just trying to help you. If Senora had seen you guys chatting away, he would have been fired for sure, and you'd be on the chopping block. If you want to stay here, don't let it happen again." She looked towards the house as if watching for Senora. "Finish up that ice and clean up, you're going to help serve food."

While the pig roasted, sending woody smells over the property, the cowboys gathered all the guests outside the corral. The barrel hung at waist height, the rope ends tied to sturdy posts at each end of the corral. Curly and Shorty each stood by a post, wearing heavy leather gloves.

Jack Lambert strode into the corral carrying a saddle. Everyone watched Lambert whenever he went anywhere, with his handsome looks and proud walk. His boots were the most elaborately colored and stitched Ree had seen, and he had the biggest, widest white hat at San Gabriel. He placed the saddle on the barrel, tightening and tying off the straps and buckles with a dramatic flourish, well aware of his audience but never acknowledging it. Finally he stood back, raising his arms so that his biceps swelled through the tight black sleeves of his shirt, which had a green yoke, silver buttons and turquoise embroidery. He pushed his hat back on his head and his curly brown locks, heavy with sweat, showed on his forehead. Each woman unconsciously bent toward him, causing a surge in the crowd in his direction.

"Who's the best rider here?" he boomed out to the crowd. "Who's going first?" All the women bent backward and away. The barrel bobbed on the springy rope.

"Let me show you how it's done," he said. "I know we've got lots of great riders here." He grabbed the barrel to stop its bobbing and jumped on the saddle. His weight brought the barrel so low he steadied himself with his feet on the ground. Curly and Shorty pulled on the ropes and the barrel rose a little.

"See, it's easy," he said, bouncing lightly on his toes. "Anyone can do it. Come on, who's the best rider here?"

No one answered so he scanned the crowd of guests.

"I think it's Miss Blackstone," he said, picking out the tallest, most muscular woman in the crowd. Miss Blackstone had her fans among the other guests, some of whom called out, "Oh Marty , you can do it!"

"Come on, Miss Blackstone," said Lambert, "Come on out here and try. You have a reputation to uphold."

Miss Blackstone swaggered up to the barrel as Lambert climbed off. He reached out for her arm to help her mount, but she shrugged him off and confidently mounted the barrel.

"Nothing to it," she said. "What's the point? The oldest horse at San Gabriel is wilder than this."

"Let's find out," said Lambert. "Curly and Shorty, let's go."

Each pulled so tightly their muscles bulged. The barrel jerked, twisting as it rose. Miss Blackstone shrieked and gripped desperately with her knees.

Blackstone's fans pressed forward to watch.

"Yahoo, Marty, you can show that cowboy how it's really done!" called a short woman with tight blonde curls. A woman behind pushed her aside and called out "Who's the best cowboy, Marty, Marty!" and then stepped back embarrassed as Miss Blackstone shot her a terrified look.

"Hold on tight," Lambert said to Miss Blackstone. "You haven't ridden any horse like this. This is no old nag." He waved his hand and Curly and Shorty pulled hard and shook the ropes. The barrel bucked like a rodeo horse. Miss Blakestone's legs lost their grip and flailed wide open as she squealed and screamed. She slid over to the side, grabbing at the barrel, digging her nails in for a handhold.

"Stop, stop," she said, and Lambert immediately signaled the cowboys, who loosened the rope to stop the motion. Lambert ran over and grabbed on to Miss Blackstone. She looked humiliated.

"I didn't know—you didn't warn me. That was a dirty trick!" she sputtered. Her fans were quiet, except for the one who had been loudest. She called out "dirty trick, dirty trick" and ran right up to Lambert.

"I'm sorry," Lambert said to Miss Blackstone, patting her back. "I know you're a great rider but that does take some practice." He turned to the crowd. "I think you gals all got the idea now. Who wants to go next?"

"No," said Miss Blackstone, straightening up. "Now I know what to expect. I'm staying on." She pushed Lambert away and wriggled on the saddle to get a steady seat.

"Good sport," said Lambert, "and that was a bit mean. Now you've got the idea." He pulled a round silver watch from his pocket. "We've got the same goal as the rodeo riders," he said. "Try to stay on for eight seconds. We'll all count for you, right ladies? Let's rehearse: One, two, three," the crowd, including Ree, joined in.

With a signal to Curly and Shorty, the bucking began and the crowd counted. Miss Blackstone slid off by three, but Lambert caught her and broke her fall.

"Four," Lambert repeated with the crowd as he helped her off the barrel.

"I can do better the next time," said Miss Blackstone.

"That was great," said Lambert, "That's the record for San Gabriel Ranch."

The crowd applauded.

"Who's next?" Lambert asked the crowd.

Ree wished she could try. She knew she would be terrible at it, but she wished she were a guest and could do more than chop at a block of ice. As the afternoon went by, more of the guests tried the bucking barrel, some eagerly and others urged to it by their admirers. Ree watched as much as she could. A cowboy always stood by to make sure no one fell off, although there were many near misses. As the game went on, Ree saw that some of the guests had a new plan.

Sarah Ross, who even the staff knew followed Curly at every opportunity, had barely sat on the barrel before she screamed 'Help me" and slid in his direction. In a second he had caught her, and she threw her arms around his neck and clasped her legs around his torso.

"Hey," said Curly, "you're holding me tighter than that barrel!" Sarah hugged him tighter. "Don't let me fall!" she called out. Curly politely but firmly put her back on the ground. She immediately lined up to go again. After that, Ree saw many of the guests who had crushes on the cowboys join the line.

"Marty, since you're so good at it, maybe they'll let you be one of the catchers," Ree heard a tiny, slightly graying woman say to Miss Blackstone. Blackstone shrugged her off, embarrassed because she saw Ree was listening.

Finally the guests tired of the game and drifted back to the verandah, where cold drinks were served. "Let's rest up for the cowboy hunt," she heard Sarah Ross say to one of her buddies. "Watch out, Curly!" said her friend.

Dinner was the roasted pig. Ree dished out gravy, standing at the next station from the blackened, shrunken, yet very recognizable pig. The first time Ree had been served bacon and sausage at San Gabriel, she hadn't known what it was and had eaten it tentatively, then eagerly. When she finally realized it was pork, she started to gag. Then she reminded herself of all the chicken pot pie and biscuits with gravy she had already eaten in this new land, and decided that if she wanted to eat, she could not set any rules for staying kosher. But she could barely look at the pig, with its floppy ears and stiff black tail, let alone eat it. She focused on doling out the gravy and overhearing the guest's conversations.

"The trick is," Sarah Ross told her friend, "you pretend you don't know who he is. And he pretends he doesn't know who you are. Then there's a lot less to be embarrassed about in the morning." Ree wanted to know what they were talking about.

As they cleaned up from dinner, Senora Sanchez gave out assignments for the evening. Ree wasn't surprised when she was told to finish cleaning and then come back at 11 pm to help serve something called "midnight snack." Ree headed back to the stables, glad to have some free time. But the stables, normally quiet at night, were busy with all the cowboys and hands. Some cowboys were wearing their finest cowboy clothes, but others were dressed as Indians, in buckskin pants and shirts, moccasins, and bandannas around their heads. She didn't see any outfits as fine as her own Frank Hamilton Cushing outfit.

"What's going on?" she asked Shorty.

"You've never been to a cowboy hunt?" he said, so loudly the others stopped talking. "Why if you were a guest, Miss Ree, you would have a golden opportunity to jump my bones in the hay, in the dark, in the romantic moonlight. And I'd pretend it was too dark to see who you were."

"And if he likes you, he'll stay a while. And if he doesn't, he's going to run out of there like you're coming after him with a horsewhip," said Curly.

"Just hold on to your pants," shouted one of the burliest cowboys, Cal. "Last year those sex-crazed women pulled them right off me." There was a lot of shouting in response to that, but Ree was embarrassed and headed for the stairs to her room.

"Don't tell me you're going to miss this, Ree," said Shorty. "This is your big chance. We all know you've been craving Cal all summer." Ree liked the cowboys, who were friendly and open and treated her like she belonged, unlike most of the guests.

Just then a truck pulled up and more cowboys and a few Indians jumped off and ran into the barn.

"We're here to help," yelled one. "We hear you guys can't handle all those horny women."

Ree thought she saw Ned, in the sparkling white shirt and headband he had worn the day she had met him in Santa Fe. Perhaps it was her imagination, but it gave her an idea. Up in her room, she pulled out her Frank Hamilton Cushing outfit, which was packed deep in the suitcase she hadn't opened since arriving at San Gabriel. By the time she put the outfit on, it had grown so dark that only the moon and the stars were visible, other than the lighted glow of the main house. The men were loud and excited, some bellowing a cowboy song about a girl and the moonlight and a handsome stranger on a horse.

Ree struggled with the dry leather of her outfit. The weeks of hard work made it tight against her muscles. It felt so good to wear it again. She felt more like an Indian, not a Jewish girl from Brooklyn in a costume. She hadn't worn the outfit since that time at the Brooklyn Museum, but now she felt the joy of wearing it that she had before that awful day.

She kept the light out in her room while she dressed, and now she leaned out the window, watching the cowboys file out, quieting each other with punches and insults. They huddled outside the door while Jack Lambert addressed them, and she could hear his loud whisper.

"Now you guys scatter to anywhere you can find to hide. In fifteen minutes, you'll hear the dinner bell ring, and then it's fair game for everyone. Except for you Indians! You braves are here to make those ladies all excited, but you don't so much as shake their hand—or you'll be hanging in the town square!" He didn't say that in a joking way at all. "You Indians run like I hear you do and head for the post office—there's a truck parked there to take you back home, cherry as these ladies."

" Cowboys, remember, don't anyone take this game too seriously and do anything that will hurt or scare any of the women." A loud contemptuous laugh from one man brought Lambert right up to him immediately, grabbing his shoulder.

"What's your name, son?" Lambert said.

He answered so quietly Ree couldn't hear.

"Well, Jeff, you're from the Lazy Bar, aren't you?" said Lambert. "You guys were invited because we were told we could trust you, but this has me worried. Jeff, this is no laughing matter. This is all in fun and if any of the ladies wakes up tomorrow filled with regret—or more—there's going to be hell to pay. Jeff, you're staying by my side tonight, I don't trust you. Anybody else think they might be a problem for us?

"Aw, these ladies don't want us anyway," said Shorty.

"OK, Shorty," said Lambert, "you never want to do this, do you? You can stay with me and Jeff.

"I got a gal of my own in Espanola that won't like it," Shorty explained to the others, but Ree didn't believe him.

"Anybody else?" Lambert said. "Speak up now, you won't get fired. This has to be all in fun, innocent kisses. If you can't handle it, speak up now. I can't take that chance."

Ree heard Lambert loudly whisper "Gentlemen, remember that these are ladies." She heard the pounding march of the men as they followed Lambert to the corral where the barrel contest had been held. At the main house, she could see a procession, barely lit by a kerosene lantern heading toward the corral, and she could make out a line of women. In the expectant quiet, a horse snorted and an owl called out.

As the two lines grew closer, there was an explosive pop and a burst of flame. Immediately the scene was lit by a bonfire higher than a horse's head, and the cowboys and Indians stood together, facing the cluster of women.

"Get ready everyone," Lambert called out. "Get ready for the 1925 San Gabriel Dude Ranch Cowboy Hunt. Everybody on your marks, get set—" one of the women shot a few steps out of the crowd, and everyone laughed.

"It's when this gun goes off," said Lambert, and he held up a long-barreled pistol which gleamed in the firelight. "And when the dinner bell rings, it's time to come in and see what other surprises the night holds." With that he waved his gun in the air, teasing, and both crowds swayed back and forth with his movements, as if he were conducting an orchestra. Suddenly the gun went off and the men dashed out of the gate running. Ree could barely see them as they left the fire's glow, but there were shrieks and yells from every direction as the women ran after them. In seconds the corral was empty except for Lambert, Curly, Jeff, and the women hands who were tending the fire.

She snuck out of the stables, ran across the corner of the field and into the woods. Her plan was to take a wide circle around the area where most people had run, and then turn back to end up at its periphery. There was an orchard on the north end of the property that bordered a hay field. The mowers had been working the last few days, rolling the hay into huge mounds with rounded tops. Now she realized that had all been part of preparation for this event. Stumbling and losing her breath, she headed for the hay field. Thinking she heard someone nearby, she ran faster.

She landed with a thud against the wall of a haystack she hadn't seen in the dark. Sharp twigs of hay stabbed her, and she couldn't hold back a roaring sneeze that blasted in the night air. She stiffened against the haystack. As she sat there, she realized she didn't know why she was doing this. If she was trying so hard to hide, why had she put on the clothes and come out here? Just then, she heard breathing and footsteps and a hand grabbed for her, landing near her breast. She pulled back, but the hand closed on her tunic and held tight.

"Aw shit," said a man's voice. "Another damn Indian." But then he felt her breast against the shirt and squeezed, sending a startled thrill of pain and pleasure through her.

"Wait a damn minute," he said, and now she was sure it was Sack. He put his face up to hers. "Henrietta?" he said. She shoved his hand off her clothes and ran as fast as she could, ducking behind another haystack.

For the next few minutes, Ree crouched back and let her eyes adjust to the light. She saw shadowy figures moving around the field, sometimes coming together with a scream, then disappearing into the new grass at their feet, which had grown in the days since the hay was cut. A fruity scent from the fruit trees in the orchard mixed with the pinon smell of the bonfire. She sat back on the soft ground next to the haymow and watched the stars.

There was a soft, high, not quite smothered sneeze from around the corner of the haymow. She didn't think it was a man, but froze anyway. A mosquito buzzed her ear and she slapped it away. The person on the other side of the mow giggled. There wasn't any movement, but she could feel that they both sat stiffly, each waiting for the other to make a break.

Ree bolted for the next darker blotch she could see, which she hoped was another haymow. But the moment she jumped, the other person did too, and they collided in the dark, tripping each other and both falling to the ground, Ree on the bottom and someone not much bigger trying to break the fall and catch Ree at the same time.

"I'm so sorry," said a soft familiar voice. "Are you all right?" They were on the soft grass, their arms around each other. Ree almost spoke his name, but suddenly she knew why she had wanted to do this. Her lips went to his and she hugged tighter. He drew back but then relaxed into it. She was embarassed about the Indian outfit. The kiss continued as his hands explored her. She knew he could feel her breasts and relaxed about her clothes. She let him touch her, but she kept her arms around him. She was surprised at how soft a man was, how sweet his breath on hers. His cheeks were smooth against her face. Why did men have so many variations, from Sack's whiskery, blustery graspingness to this tender being in her arms? All women looked equally soft to her. It made sense that the man she was attracted to was more like a woman. There was nothing attractive to her about Sack. But Ned felt just right in her arms.

They kissed for a while, then lay back together, sometimes squeezing each other slightly, as if to make sure the other was there. She prayed she wouldn't sneeze and break the spell.

Finally a woman tripped over them, calling out "I've got your boot, Shorty, don't you want it back?" With a final kiss, Ned drew away and disappeared into the night. Ree crawled through the field, not wanting to encounter anyone else. She went back to her room, changed her clothes, and headed for the main house well in time for the midnight snack, which turned out to be a picnic of candy and cake served only to guests who had put on their pajamas and bathrobes.

"It gets them to bed after all the excitement," said Senora. "And we can check if anyone's missing and make sure everyone is all right. Jack's back at the barn counting the men." Some of the guests looked sparkly-eyed and pink-cheeked, and they all looked to be hiding a secret. Ree had never seen them so quiet. Even the woman couples among them looked happy, although the women known to like men had more grass and hay stuck in their hair.

Heading back to her room, a group of men passed by. Sack broke away from it and came up to her.

"So, how'd it go for you?" he said in a low voice. "Had a good time? You don't have to wait for the fancy ranch to arrange it, just let me know." He moved in closer and patted her still hot cheeks. "I see you got what you wanted, and it wasn't me, huh? But if not—"

She broke away, leaving Sack laughing at her.

All the next day, Ree felt spasms of excitement run through her body whenever she thought of Ned and the haymow. She was surprised at herself and she was surprised at Ned. Maybe he was as curious as she was. Maybe he had never touched a woman before any more than she had touched a man.

If she and Ned were together, he could take her to his home. She could live with the Indians even more closely than Frank Hamilton Cushing had. She had never seriously thought of doing this as an Indian's wife, but she had never thought that an Indian man would be like Ned. She had always thought of them as she had thought of any man. But Ned wasn't big, hairy, smelly, and bossy like Sack, or cold and pasty like her father.

If it had been Ruth in the hay mow, would she have feelings for Ruth like these new feelings she had for Ned? Had she ever wanted Ruth that way? She had always imagined herself sitting with Ruth by their fireplace, reading together. Lately, watching Ruth go off with Margaret, she had wished to go riding and hiking with her. But the way she felt touching Ned? She had never felt that before, not even in her imagination, and she hadn't pictured it, either.

It wasn't that she knew nothing about sex. Many nights she had cringed with embarrassment, hearing sounds from other rooms in the apartments she and her father had shared, knowing that her father was hearing, too. More than once men had rubbed against her on the street, on the subway, even in the synagogue. It had annoyed her, and she had wondered what it meant. But it had never given her the feelings that being with Ned did. Sometimes she had thought that other women were kidding themselves, just to please men. Other times, she decided that she lacked the capacity, just as she had never felt any pleasure from physical exercise in school. She thought that her lack of physical sensuality was balanced by the passion of her emotions for Ruth. But last night, and even how she was feeling this morning, were like discovering hidden treasure in her own body.

A few days later, as the sun was just rising and the pleasant scents of breakfast muffins and cocoa blew across the paddock grass, Karen sent Ree out to woods past the far corral to look for a missing saddle blanket. Through the trees, Ree saw Ruth walking the trail alone, lost in thought. Ruth saw her before she could draw back. Ruth would think she was spying, even though she was innocent at this moment.

"Henrietta," Ruth called out. "Would you come here a moment?"

It was strange to be called Henrietta here. It was the name of that other person she had left back in New York City. Ruth must know they called her Ree. Ree was someone she hoped Ruth could fall in love with. Henrietta was not. She tripped over some roots just as she reached Ruth.

"Are you all right?" Ruth said, grabbing onto her forearm as she straightened up. Ruth had never touched her before. The touch was gone before she could get her breath back.

"I'm fine," Ree gasped out. "I didn't mean to disturb you. They sent me out here to get a lost blanket."

"Oh," Ruth said, but it sounded like she thought it was a lie. "I thought you'd come out to see me."

"I'm glad to see you. I just wouldn't want you to think I'd followed you."

A crow screamed at a hawk and they both watched it for a moment.

"Henrietta, why are here?"

Ree was tempted to say, "I'm not here, you're just imagining me," but the reverse was more true. She had imagined Ruth here. She hung her head. She was beyond her usual tongue-tiedness around Ruth. Even if she could have spoken, she had no idea what to say.

"So you're planning to go into the field?" asked Ruth.

"That's always been my hope."

"You were turned down."

"I know, but it's just the money. I didn't want it to stop my career. I figured once I got out here it would work out. And it is going well. I'm saving what I earn here. It's great because I get room and board."

Ruth was silent. They stood awkwardly until a crow squawked nearby.

"It wasn't just the money," Ruth finally said.

"What do you mean?"

"They don't think you're ready for a field placement."

"I completed all the course work. I did the practicum at the settlement house, interviewing the immigrants. My grades were high."

"It's not a matter of grades."

"What is it then?"

Ruth scanned the sky, perhaps wishing more birds would come to distract them. Ree was hoping a mountain lion would jump down on them both—no, just on her. She didn't want Ruth, so ethereal, to be hurt. She would fight the lion off, save them both and the conversation would never continue. She would be a hero to anthropology and Columbia University.

"It's not easy to pin down. Some people just aren't suited for the field."

"Who's to judge that? It's like predicting the future." Ree startled herself with the edge in her voice. But she had heard that phrase, "some people," too many times, referring to the Jews. Boas was famous for his progressive views on tolerance, but in her gut she knew she hadn't fit in. There was a difference between German Jews who had been in New York a long time, and 'greenies' from Belarus like her father. Ruth was simply becoming the first person to validate what she knew in her gut.

"Which people are those?" Ree continued when Ruth hadn't answered. Ree felt herself starting to blaze with anger. She was in a dream, but not the one in which she talked to Ruth her idol, but an impossible one in which she was angry, confronting, attacking. This could not be real. She could never be talking to Ruth in this way.

"The department—not just those of us there now—but going back to the first field work, has seen quite a few people try the field. Some just aren't right. They get too close. They aren't scientific. It's not a bad thing to be passionate, Henrietta."

"Passionate?" Was Ruth now talking about more personal matters?

"Everyone can see how dedicated you are to anthropology. But you can go too far, and that hurts everyone in the field. You have to keep a distance. Like Gladys, for example."

Gladys Reichard had spent the last summer living with a Navajo family, studiously learning to weave, and returning proudly with a hideous, misshapen little blanket and a publishable article that described every minute twist or pound on the wool, and frustratingly little about the weavers' inner lives, as far as Ree was concerned. The family was presented strictly through their "material culture" activities, as anthropologists called it. Ree had been dying to know what the weavers thought of tight-assed Gladys and her no doubt annoying questions. Everyone at Columbia, even Ree, knew that Gladys was having an affair with Pliny Goddard, a married male professor in Chicago, and that she could only stand their long separations by maintaining the most scrupulous and tedious of observations in the field.

"What about Frank Hamilton Cushing?" asked Ree. It was thrilling to say his name to her beloved Ruth.

"Frank Hamilton Cushing," repeated Ruth, shaking her head and twisting her mouth. "He's the past. Gladys Reichard is the future."

"But don't you think Frank's work is valuable?" Ree immediately regretted her familiar use of his first name.

"All scholarly fields have to start somewhere," Ruth said. "But then they have to refine."

Ree couldn't help but think that Ruth was also commenting on immigrant groups like her own. It was as if she had said, 'they come here the tattered refuge of your teeming shores, but then they must melt in' and so on.

"I don't know what you want me to do," Ree said. "Are you saying I can't go any further with my degree?"

"You don't have to do field work. You write such thorough papers. You could work with someone back from the field, transcribing and analyzing their notes."

If Ruth had offered her own at that point, Ree might have headed back to New York. But Ruth said nothing more.

"I love being here. I don't want to be stuck in some building in New York. That's not what I worked all these years for."

"I'm just telling you the truth, which Dr. Boas, who is sometimes too nice for his own good, was unwilling to do."

"What if you're wrong about me?"

"We can't take that chance. We can't let you represent Columbia University and our department in the field." Ruth stared up at a bird as she said this.

"And what do you think? Not just the "we" of Columbia?" The words came out before Ree realized that she would have to live with the answer for the rest of her life.

"I think you have to accept the limitations of life. I think we –I – can't always get what I want. And the same for you." Ree thought she saw Ruth glance at her wedding ring, the one Stanley Benedict had given her.

"No," Ree said. "This is my dream, and I'm here to make it happen."

Ruth shrugged, turned, and stepped briskly toward the house.

"And you know what else?" Ree said very loudly, as Ruth moved further away.

"You're the reason for my dream. You're the reason I'm here. You're my inspiration." The words grew softer as Ree spoke them, as Ruth moved away, as tears and mucus filled her mouth. But Ruth didn't look back, and she couldn't tell if Ruth had heard. Ree grabbed onto a sapling just to keep standing. In those few minutes of conversation, the fine house she had spent years building had collapsed on her, and she was left alone, the now bright risen sun glaring down. But it was a different sun, not the one that had warmed her all these years. That sun had vanished into the main house.

Ree wanted to find out how much longer Margaret and Ruth would be staying at San Gabriel. Since Ruth had confronted her in the woods, she dreaded any contact with them. Until their awful conversation, she had held the hope that although others in the department had not wanted to give her the field assignment, Ruth had championed her but been outvoted. That hope was gone.

If she was ever going to get to live her Frank Hamilton Cushing dream, she needed money. Her room and board was extracted from her pay, and so very little money was piling up in the First National Bank of Santa Fe. At this rate, she would have to work a year here, saving almost everything, to pay for six months in the field. Staying would be the easiest way to save, with so little opportunity to leave the property and spend it. Besides, she liked it here in this little world where women dominated and the men were decorative, dressed in the most romantic of cowboy garb and kept away from the filth of the horse barns to protect their clothes and fragrance. It was as close to a matriarchy as an anthropologist was likely to see, a topic which she had often heard discussed by the guests.

As she rounded the barn, Margaret and Ruth reached the stalls, so Ree pulled back. Just then Karen called out, "Ree, have you got that bridle?" She didn't answer. "Ree," Karen called again, walking around the corner so that they almost crashed into each other. Ree pretended she had been walking, not cringing.

"Come on, we've got guests waiting. Got the bridle?"

"Sure, here it is." Ree tried to hand it to Karen.

"You bring it. I've got enough to do without looking for you."

"I'm sorry." There was no choice but to follow her. Ruth averted her eyes, but Margaret stared at her. Ree wanted to throw the bridle down and run away.

"Where do you want it?" she had to ask.

"Put it on the horse." She had no idea how to do it, but she couldn't say that in front of the two of them. She went up to the horse—a dappled one who had stayed restless while she brushed him—and held the bridle up. She wasn't tall enough to reach the top of his head.

"Oh for God's sakes," said Margaret. "You don't know what you're doing. Give me that." She grabbed the bridle from Ree while the horse whinnied.

"That's ok," said Karen, "I'll take care of it." She gave Ree a dirty look as she came forward.

"I'll do it," Margaret said in a fierce tone that made Karen stop. Ree was thinking that Margaret must never have held a job where a customer could embarrass a worker in front of her boss. It made her furious, especially when Karen shot her an even more disapproving look. Ree wanted to explain that she was only filling in with the horses, but decided it was more important that Ruth not see her whining. Maybe that was one of the characteristics the department didn't like.

"This is how you do it," Margaret said as she proceeded.

Ree started to walk away, towards the main house.

"Don't you want to learn how?" Margaret said. Ree stared up at the attic windows of the main house. No matter how hot and stuffy it was going to be, she wanted to be up there with all the old, crumbling things, where no one would follow her. She kept walking.

"If you only want things done your way, I don't want to learn at all," Ree called back.

"Huh?" said Karen.

"Margaret— "said Ruth.

"Oh shut up," said Ree, whirling around to face Margaret. "You're so damn perfect, aren't you! Have everything handed to you. Everything you ever want you get. Like her." She couldn't look at Ruth.

"Ree!" Karen said, "you can't talk to a guest that way. Mrs. Pfaeffle will have a conniption."

"Stay out of it," Ree surprised herself by saying. "This isn't about this place."

"This place," Margaret said, "Where you have no business being."

"I can be anywhere I want," Ree snapped back. They were both getting louder, but she couldn't help herself. "You don't own the Indians. You don't own New Mexico, you don't own Arizona. You don't own—" she was shrieking at this point, and couldn't think of what to say next, while Ruth and Margaret stared at her, jaws dropped, waiting for her next word. "Scholarship! You don't own scholarship!" Where had that come from? It wasn't wrong, just so pretentious from her hysterical lips.

Karen moved between them, as if she were afraid Ree would strike Margaret. "Now Ree, that's enough. Let's take a walk." She grabbed Ree's forearm and tried to lead her away, but Ree pulled out of her hold. The horses whinnied and stomped. Karen took Ruth's hand and led her and Margaret away from the horses.

"This is upsetting the horses. I'm sorry," Karen said to Ruth. "I'm very sorry. You know we don't treat our guests in this manner. Mrs. Pfaeffle will take care of this. Let's calm the horses down for a few minutes, then you can ride."

Ruth and Margaret obediently followed Karen. Ree backed away, watching them pat and caress the horses. Watching Ruth whisper soothingly to the horse turned her anger to envy and sadness and grief. She had just lost everything, and she knew it. She could never face Ruth again. Margaret had defended her mate, driving away Ree, the intruder. They were birds in their cozy nest, and Ree was the lonely male, not colorful, aggressive, or enticing enough to win the female away. She had no nest, she had no flock, and she was more alone than she had ever been, because she had no hope now. She ran through the open doorway of the barn, up to her little room, knowing that this was her last day at San Gabriel.

Beneath the wooden floorboards of her room, Ree heard a horse kicking the stall, then the tap of a stable hand's boots as she crossed the barn. She grabbed her suitcase from under the bed, threw it open, swiped all her clothes from the little bureau drawers and pitched them on top, and ran to the bathroom for her toothbrush and soap. The toothbrush was covered with a layer of old toothpaste that she scraped at with her fingernail, but it wouldn't come off. She turned the tap, waiting for the hot water, which always rose very slowly, with a little shriek from the pipes. She kept plunging her fingers in to check it. The sound changed when the hot water finally started. She scalded her cold hands jabbing at the toothbrush, and had to run cold water on them. Tears were pouring down her face. She heard footsteps and jammed the toothbrush into her pocket and went back to her room, as the footsteps faded and a door shut. She pushed the suitcase and clothes to the floor and sat on the bed.

She was breathing so hard it filled the room. Was this how a boxer felt when the round ended? But that hadn't been the round, that had been the whole fight, and she wished she were knocked out so she wouldn't have to feel what she felt. It was all over for Ruth, for Columbia, for her career in anthropology. No other school was going to have her, even if she had the money.

It was also all over for her at San Gabriel. She needed to pack and leave before Mrs. Pfaeffle let her have it and then fired her anyway. The customer was always right. And as comfortable as women "friends" were here, no one ever talked about it out loud. There was plenty of feeling here, thicker than the air in the stables. She hadn't missed how Karen blushed when Emmy, the pastry chef, urged a jelly roll on her, even though Emmy was married to Joe, the blacksmith. Everyone had seen Katherine's dramatic exit last week, leaving a weeping Julia behind, after they disagreed over whether to go on a five day pack trip into the mountains, or that's what Ree thought it was about, anyway.

All these dramas were going on, everyone knowing, like a radio soap opera.

Now the scene of she, Margaret, and Ruth by the stables would be another episode. She hadn't wanted to be one of the players. She was happy to stand back, holding up the scenery, enjoying her fantasies. Now it was all smashed, and there was nowhere to hide.

She picked up the mess on the floor. Was there anything else of hers here? There was the Indian feathered stick she had found in the attic. She hadn't told anyone about it. Why not take it? She wasn't going to be able to collect her last paycheck. To them it would be one more souvenir, sacred to the Indians, but just a decoration to white people. There were so many displayed in the house already that one had been forgotten in the attic. She would honor it and it would comfort her as it had the Indian who had made it out of feathers, wood, and bone.

Ree dragged her suitcase behind her along the road, hoping for a ride but also reveling in her misery. She was still wearing her ranch clothes, not a dress. Maybe she could spend some time disguised as a male tramp. She could take notes as an alien in a strange culture. Maybe that would be her ticket to fame in anthropology—her study of hobos. That would show them!

Might as well think of the benefits of her situation rather than the realities, which at the moment were that she had no water or food, and the sun blazed down on her lonely retreat. In Santa Fe she had that little bank account with which to start the next phase of her life. She wouldn't have to be a hobo right off. But if only she could stay away from her little nest egg, if only she could continue to add to it, because it was the way to her dream and she didn't want to chip at it. How soon could she find more work? Would word get around about her? Would the staff from San Gabriel talk to people in Santa Fe? Could she get a job before the gossip arrived? One thing they couldn't fault her for at San Gabriel was her hard work. They would find the attic clean and organized, her clipboard of inventory placed prominently on an upturned barrel in the center of the room.

She knew for sure she wasn't going back to New York. That train could leave without her, day after day. And she wasn't heading out for the territories, either. She was already where she had wanted to go for so long. Frank Hamilton Cushing would always stay tucked in her dreams and in her suitcase as she followed his path. Ruth Benedict would always be somewhere in her heart, even though when she thought about her professor its pounding felt like Ruth hammering to break out. Ree pictured herself old, looking back on these two passions of her youth with pride, forgiving herself for her failures. But she was making her dream come true, as much as real life would allow. Being in New Mexico was hard today, but she was here and not back in a steamy tenement. Here dustdevils rose from the earth like tiny tornadoes, but there was so little rain that she could imagine what a New York downpour would do to the dry cracked land, turning it to a raging flood in minutes. She didn't want to pretend she was anywhere but where she was, no matter how hungry she became. For all the years she had spent dreaming of being in New Mexico, it was well worth it. It was only a matter of time until the rest of her dreams came true. Except for the one about Ruth. That was over forever now.

Part 4

A rattling truck stopped and the Spanish driver indicated that she could ride in the back with his hay. She hadn't even stuck her thumb out. Maybe some luck would come her way.

The truck left her on the plaza in Santa Fe. Maybe she could find Ned or his grandmother among the Indians selling on the portal of the Palace of the Governmors. As she walked past each spread blanket, the Indian proprietor would say hello, sometimes eagerly, sometimes coolly. Now that she wasn't seeing it for the first time, she recognized that it was just sales technique, as she had done herself when she sold clothes from a pushcart at one of her many jobs back in New York.

At Columbia, she had heard that the museum at the Palace of the Governors was the place for anthropologists to find out what jobs were available. She had only to walk through door, but she hesitated at the entrance. Anyone she knew from Columbia could be inside or might walk out at any moment. How long would it be until they heard about her shame? The heavy wooden doors were covered with deeply gouged carvings that she imagined were telling her story to everyone who entered. She stepped off the portal and down a side street.

After a few hours wandering on the hot sunny streets trying not to spend money, Ree's head and eyes ached. She cursed at a child who walked across her path. She couldn't stand still or walk in a straight line, because where that line would go she didn't know. She paced in circles near the Plaza, hoping it would calm her down.

A short man with a brightly-colored shawl sold firewood from a burro cart. When winter arrived, where would she be to stay warm? How could she have messed it all up for herself at San Gabriel? She couldn't blame it all on Margaret. Sack was right; her feelings for Ruth had been too obvious and she had probably disturbed their vacation. But she had been at San Gabriel first, and she hadn't known they were coming.

Tired of circling, she veered off onto a side street called Burro Alley. Honky-tonk music was being played, even though it was early in the day. Three cowboys staggered out a big open gate and stopped in front of her. One rolled his tongue at her, then stuck it out, then they walked off. Through the entrance, she saw a circle of cowboys and some men in business suits surrounding something she could not see, but she could hear a woman's giggles and then a screech. Just then a man in workman's clothes walked past her, went through the gate, then turned back and stared at her. "Wanna job?" he said, "there's always work here for a woman, you don't have to be pretty" then laughed and went in.

Ree's face stung and she headed for the row of stores facing her on San Francisco Street. A plate of tortillas and tamales in the window of Tia Sofia's Restaurant made her stop and wet her lips, but she turned abruptly and headed for the Palace. She went through the heavy doors trying to feel some hope.

As she had heard, there was a bulletin board in the anteroom of the Palace. "I'm at La Fonda, please stop by. Edward." "Has anyone taken my sunhat, last seen at the Aztec dig? Contact Earl Morris c/o University of Colorado." "Seeking partner for horseback trip to Rainbow Arch." Finally, "Anthropologist sought for interview transcriptions. Contact Mary Cabot Wheelwright, Los Luceros, Alcalde."

There were no other job ads. At San Gabriel, she had heard gossip about Wheelwright. She had once been a regular guest there, but then had bought the old hacienda a few miles down the road. They said she was too much of a spoiled rich old lady to share the space at the dude ranch, and that she wanted cowboys of her own, although she probably wouldn't know what to do with them.

Going to Alcalde, so close to San Gabriel, was out of the question. But there were no other job ads. Hearing voices down the hall, Ree left the Palace quickly, heading up Washington Street, hoping she was moving away from anywhere she might run into any anthropologists who might know her. Suddenly someone was in front of her, reaching a hand to her shoulder.

"Why if it isn't Henrietta! Taking a day off from the hens? Too much carousing in the haymows?" Sack, in a cheap New York business suit, but with a cowboy hat and pointy-toed boots, was laughing at her.

She didn't know what to say. They stared at each other.

"Never mind," he said. "Do you have the afternoon

off?"

"I quit," she said. "I'm ready for something new."

"Me, too," he said. "Want to get a burrito?"

"I don't have much money."

"Me neither. Oh well." At that he gave her a huge smile, and they both laughed. "I've got some deals just about to come in."

"Me too," Ree said. "And I'm Ree now, remember?"

"Sack and Ree," he said. "Sounds like some kind of western tune. 'Sack and Ree and flat-busted.' It must be harder for you though, a woman alone out here. Or are you alone?"

She probably shouldn't answer that honestly, but she had no one else to trust, so she might as well.

"Sort of. I guess so."

"So what's next?" he said. "Did you see that Wheelwright job on the bulletin board?"

"Yes, but—." Before she finished her sentence, he continued.

"I bet we could hitch there. What do you think, thirty miles? We could walk it if we had to."

Ree didn't want to explain why she didn't want to try for it.

"If it doesn't work out, maybe we'll find something else on the way. That's my attitude. Think positive. Let's get going."

Sack headed down the street, not giving her time to back out. Ree was glad to see a familiar face. If she ever got up the nerve to tell him, he would understand about the fight with Margaret.

The first ride was easy to catch, a Model T truck driven by an Hispanic farmer who didn't speak English, but let them squeeze onto the seat beside him. He took them about halfway, then had to turn off to his own farm. For the next few miles they walked in the blazing sun, hot, slow and thirsty. The road was not much more than a wide dirt path, surrounded by the flat country of pinon and juniper, and the ring of mountains in the distance. She had spent the summer in the sun and was tan and fit, but if he hadn't had the cowboy hat, Sack would probably be bright red and flat on the ground by now.

"So you struck out with those rich gals at San Gabriel?" he said, in a consoling way.

"We weren't allowed to talk to the guests."

"They didn't try to talk to you?" She shrugged. She had never thought about this as a failure.

"Their mistake," he said. "Anyway, you must have seen something going on. Didn't some of those rich dames go for those cute little cowgirls?"

"I guess so. I wasn't paying much attention."

"Yeah, you only have eyes for your one true love. Did she leave? Is that why you quit?"

"Sack— "

"OK, I'll drop it. Anyway, I want to get to know some rich women. This Mary Cabot Wheelwright, she's got to be one of the richest, buying that hacienda and all. And she's a Cabot, do you know what that means in Boston?"

Ree wondered if Sack was going to embarrass her by coming on to Wheelwright. She looked back toward Santa Fe, but she saw only the hot, dry, lonely road she had traveled away from San Gabriel only a few hours earlier.

"Maybe we should have sent a letter. Do you think it will be all right to just show up?" she asked.

"Good point. But too late now. Anyway, I have a theory about that. Ever been in sales? You got to get your face in their face. Let me do the talking. Let's see, I'll vouch for you and you'll vouch for me. We both were anthropology students at Columbia. That's one hundred percent true."

"How will we explain why we're looking for work? Or traveling together?"

"I always think something up on the spot. I need to see the mark--that's the customer--and then I know just what to say."

"Wish I could do that. I always think too much."

"Let me do the talking, Ree. You got to have a goal. Here's our goal: jobs for the both of us. She was looking for one but she's going to get two. Right off the bat she'll think, is there enough work for two? We're the ones who went to Columbia. She didn't. We're the experts. We'll convince her two can do a much better job. We can check each other's work."

Ree was feeling lighter, either because she the sun was heating her brain too much, or because it felt good to let someone else be in charge of her fate for a while. If this didn't work out, all she wanted to do was sleep in the shade somewhere. If she just had some water, that was all it would take to make her happy.

"Hey, there's a car coming. I just know this one will stop." Ree was terrified it might be a car from San Gabriel. It wasn't, and they got a hitch to Alcalde. The driver let them off at the lane for Los Luceros.

"I don't know what happens from this point," Ree said. "We can just walk down that private road and hope we don't get shot."

"Think positive!

Vegetable gardens and newly planted orchards lined both sides of the lane. The workers in the fields ignored them. Not far past a little adobe chapel was a tree-lined boulevard leading toward a large two-story house with an impressive pillared verandah on the second floor.

"Doesn't look Mexican, does it?" Sack said. It was adobe, but didn't look like most of the squat brown houses. "Looks like something European."

"I've heard people call this a hacienda, now I see why," Ree said.

The gate was substantial between thick adobe walls, and carved deeply with intricate designs. The front door was equally forbidding. A man in formal butler's clothes answered their knock.

"May I be of service?" he said, and Ree was afraid Sack would laugh in his face.

"We're here to see Miss Wheelwright," said Sack.

"Have you an appointment?"

"We're the anthropologists she's advertised for."

"Please wait, I'll return."

"Going pretty well, don't you think?" Sack said. He toyed with her hair, and Ree shook him off and moved back. Still, she was glad she had come. The butler led them up a narrow stairway into a living room so large that the grand piano at one end looked small.

"This way," said the butler, leading them toward the piano. Navajo rugs covered parts of the painted green floor. An Indian drum the size of a tractor tire was next to a wrought iron standing lamp with a flowery shade. It was as if a room from Boston and a room from Santa Fe had been forced to live together. At San Gabriel, the decor had been uniformly cowboy and western. Ree wondered if Wheelwright had moved out of San Gabriel so she could express her own taste in furniture. Near the piano a woman sat on a velvet-covered sofa.

"I'm Miss Wheelwright," said the woman on the sofa. "So you are anthropologists."

"Yes, ma'am, I'm Pelagius Sackmann and this is Ree--." He hesitated and Ree realized he didn't remember her last name. Why hadn't he let them plan?

Before she could say her name, Sack continued.

"We're from Columbia University," Sack said. "Dr. Boas' department."

"A fine man," said Wheelwright. "Have you letters from him?"

"To tell you the truth," Sack said, "we weren't expecting to be looking for jobs. We were out here to see some of the field schools and digs, to decide where we might do our dissertation research. But we love it so much here we began to think of staying for a while, and then when we saw your advertisement, we just had to come right over."

"I wasn't planning to hire a couple," said Wheelwright.

"Tell us about the job," Sack said. He was a master at changing the subject. "You're doing anthropological work yourself! You must be very devoted. It's so important to find out as much as we can about this wonderful place."

Wheelwright turned more toward them with an audible crack of her bones.

"You can see for yourself," she said. When she stood, her unusually long bones and outstretched neck unfolded from the sofa and reassembled themselves into a tall woman who held her head high and neck stiff. She didn't motion for them to come along, just assumed it as she headed out of the room. Ree and Sack looked at each other and followed.

Wheelwright led them down the narrow staircase. Ree felt clumsy behind the stately woman. She glanced back to see Sack mimicking Wheelwright's walk, but she couldn't take it that lightly. She had seen many rich eastern women at San Gabriel, but none as patrician as Wheelwright. The others had picked up the casualness of the West in their clothing and bearing. Wheelwright didn't act superior, yet she hadn't gone native.

Wheelwright led them into a more comfortably sized room that would normally have been a parlor, but it was empty of furniture except for a huge Navajo weaving loom. Pegs in the wall held a hat and water pots. It reminded Ree of photos she had seen of the inside of hogans. But this was a rectangular room with windows looking out on the orchard.

A small man sat cross-legged on a small rug on the floor, dwarfed by the loom which was almost as wide as the room and almost as high as the ceiling. The half-finished rug on it was larger than any rug Ree had seen at San Gabriel. The weaver's back was to them, moving yarns and sticks too fast for Ree to follow, the rhythm of clicks and thumps enlivening the room. Instead of the usual stripes and diamonds, the rug was an intricate tapestry on a beige background. The design was like a clock, with stick people at the three, six, and nine o'clock points. Their long thin bodies wore little skirts. On their heads were headdresses of long horizontal sticks with feathers jutting out of them. Ree thought of the candles of the Hanukah menorah, because the center of the design was a row of tall thin cornstalks. Above and below that were triangular mountain designs crossing at their peaks.

"I've never seen a design like that," Ree said. Wheelwright turned to look at her, beaming.

"Of course you haven't. This is a sand painting design. It's called a Yei rug."

Ree gasped and Sack let out a word for which he then began apologizing.

"I don't care for your language," said Wheelwright, "but I'm pleased you understand the significance."

"How'd you get him to do it?" Sack asked. Before Wheelwright answered, the weaver looked up, as if awakened suddenly. His face was a deeply lined mirror of bronze, and his eyes looked somewhere beyond Ree, not at her as most men would. A loose white blouse draped his small body. He wore the clothes of a Navajo man, but there was something about him that made her think of her first impression of Ned. She had seen many other Navajo men but none looked like these two.

"I'm sorry, Mr. Klah," said Wheelwright. "So sorry to disturb you." She bowed slightly and hustled Ree and Sack into the doorway. The weaver turned back to his work.

"He works in a kind of trance," whispered Wheelwright. "You're the first people to come about the job. I have to think this out better. His religion says he shouldn't be revealing their secret designs, and I don't want him to change his mind."

"But don't they believe they'll die if they do this?" asked Sack.

"He's upset because the young Navajo boys forced into American boarding schools for Indian children aren't learning the old ways. He's afraid it will all be forgotten, because nothing is written down. They must have the sand painting designs in order to hold their healing and religious ceremonies. Without those rituals, there will be no Navajo people. Until now, all we have had to preserve the sand paintings are the watercolors on brown paper that Franc Newcomb has been doing. She's a trader's wife, and she introduced me to Hosteen Klah. He offered to weave the designs. We haven't decided yet where the tapestries will go. For now, he feels safe here in the workroom I've made for him.

"But Navajo men don't weave," said Ree, hoping she sounded as informed as Sack had.

"Some do," said Wheelwright. There was a tone in her voice that made Ree realize she'd better not speak up so fast if she wanted this job.

The old man nodded without turning to face them. He looked quite comfortable in Wheelwright's parlor. Ree had the feeling that Mr. Klah was as glad to work for Mary Cabot Wheelwright as she herself would be if she got this job. "I was surprised by that, too," Wheelwright said in a kinder tone, and for the first time Ree began to like her. She remembered a discussion back at Columbia, when several students discussed the meaning of the word "well-bred," and said it wasn't just about being born with a silver spoon, but being taught a set of rules for graciousness and making others feel comfortable.

"Weaving is women's work, but Mr. Klah is very open. He's willing to try new things and break the rules. He's my model." Wheelwright laughed self-consciously, looking at Klah proudly. Ree realized that for Wheelwright, formal as she seemed to Ree, being in New Mexico was a rebellion not so different from her own. Wheelwright was so different, and yet so like herself. They were both Easterners who had come West to live differently than their parents.

Ree wanted to be Wheelwright's friend, talking and sharing their experiences. She was surprised at how strongly she felt this, because she had had so few women friends, and no men friends before Sack.

"Do you know Frank Hamilton Cushing?" Ree gushed out, then blushed, because of course he had been dead since 1903.

"Why, I did hear him once," Wheelwright said. "A lecture he gave in Boston. Mother didn't want me to go, but I just had this feeling I should. Everyone was so excited. I think maybe that was the beginning of my own wish to come here."

"Oh," said Ree, "you actually saw him." The two women looked into each other's faces with delight. Sack shot Ree a congratulatory look.

"Have you seen the piece he did on the Zuni fetishes?" asked Wheelwright.

Ree had read it many times, but she said no.

"Let me show it to you. It has the most wonderful illustrations. I'll just have the butler--no, he won't be able to find it. I'll just get it from the library." She left the room with a light step. How many times had Ree wanted to share a favorite book, but there was no one to do it with?

"We should leave him alone to his work," Wheelwright called back. Ree had never seen a weaver this close and wanted to watch. Could there be a dissertation here? Gladys Reichard had lived with Navajo weavers and recorded their every move, so that topic was done. But what Klah was weaving, Gladys was never going to see. To most Americans who read the funny pages in the Sunday newspapers, the Yei figures would look like nothing more than little cartoon men, boring because they were so repetitious. But to those who knew about the Navajo culture, showing these designs to white people was the most defiant rebellion against immense power, against all the beliefs that Klah had been taught from his first smile during his baby smiling ritual. For a Jew, it would be like carelessly unrolling a torah scroll and ripping off pieces. The thought horrified Ree.

Did Klah have no fears as he sat before her, expressionless but somehow also satisfied, a silent man whose fingers moved like a flock of birds, this way and then that way, flashing in the sun as the figures grew on the field of wool? She needed a teacher who would help her learn to defy and rebel more. And he did it not out of revenge or bitterness or envy, but with the purest of motives, to save his culture and history even when others had lost their commitment. Klah was a hero and a model and Ree was a woman who searched for those. Compared to Klah, even Frank Hamilton Cushing might pale.

All she had to do was stay beside him and learn. She knew he wouldn't teach her anything directly. That was not the Navajo way, and even a rebel probably wouldn't do it.

Soon they were back in the huge living room. "He doesn't talk much," said Wheelwright, "not in our ways of small talk or conversation. He feels his time is too precious. He just shows us what he knows, whether it is telling one of their stories or singing one of the chants, or weaving or making sand paintings."

"Don't you wonder what he thinks of you and your way of life?" asked Sack.

"It doesn't matter," Wheelwright snapped. Ree suspected Wheelwright would love to know. "He's like a water bottle. He's preserving his culture, pouring it out or holding it up for us to see. He doesn't think he matters. That's why he's willing to take the risks involved."

"So he believes that he'll get sick and die from telling these secrets?" asked Sack.

"He must," said Wheelwright, "but he's been very clear that he wants to do it, anyway. All he asks is that we help him."

"I understand," Ree said, "all I want to do is help. What is it he needs? Transcription? And I'd like to record how the weaving is done, too. I could be his camera and voice recording machine. I want to learn to to be like him, putting my own doubts and fears aside so I can go forward toward my goal."

"Well said," Wheelwright responded.

"I'd like to see you try it," Sack said almost simultaneously. Then he blushed, realizing his sarcastic tone. "I mean, I'd like to also."

"You can stay," said Wheelwright, smiling at Ree. "You understand my mission. So few do. It was very nice meeting you, young man, but I only need one helper and I feel Mr. Klah will be more comfortable with the young lady. I wish you well. My man will show you out." She pulled a bell cord on the wall.

Wheelwright rose in her chair to offer her hand graciously. Ree lifted up from her seat, also, realizing there were a lot of fancy manners she was going to have to learn to stay on Wheelwright's good side. Wheelwright's hand was spiny but not as cold as Ree would have imagined. She wondered what Wheelwright thought of her own clammy hand.

"Wait," said Sack, "we're together. We're a team. Two heads are better than one. You haven't seen how we work together yet."

"Oh," said Wheelwright. "I'm very sorry to hear that because I just don't see it, and Mr. Klah didn't see it either. My decision is based largely on his response."

"He didn't say a word," said Sack.

"We've spent a lot of time together." said Wheelwright. "So, Miss Ree, my offer is to you alone."

Ree wondered what she would do if she cared more about Sack, but she couldn't even picture it.

"He's misrepresenting—uh, he's mistaken—uh..." all the words choked in Ree's mouth.

"You're right," Sack cut her off. "You're right, Miss Wheelwright. This isn't the job for me, but Ree has a real affinity for it. But there are other tasks I could probably do for you." He looked around the room, stopping his gaze on the various rugs, baskets, and pots on display. "These artifacts are lovely and unique. Your taste is not only aesthetic, but conspicuously knowledgeable." He paused to let Wheelwright beam. Ree was amazed she could be flattered so easily. But hadn't she done it herself when she spoke of her excitement about Klah?

"I can be of service to you in other ways," Sack continued. "Artifacts often come into my possession, though rarely of such quality. It is one of the many talents and connections that I have. May I bring some by for your appraisal? I value your opinion, and it has been such a pleasure to meet you." He stood as if he held an artifact in his hands.

"That is of some interest to me," said Wheelwright, and Ree had the impression they were agreeing to something else entirely. Sack had endless tricks up his sleeve. Somehow he had made her trust him again today. He could charm women, and apparently even charmed Wheelwright, whose aging body and graying hair didn't seem capable of any juicy thoughts. Would something happen between Wheelwright and Sack, or as Sack was more likely thinking, would something happen between Wheelwright and herself? Just then the butler came up with a tray of little white sugar cakes, the kind she had enviously watched the guests eating at San Gabriel.

"Albert," Wheelwright told the butler, "Please show Mr. Sackmann out and show Miss Ree to the guest bedroom and arrange for her things. She'll be staying with us."

Ree walked out of the big living room feeling as excited as when she first stepped off the train in Lamy. She followed the butler step for step, afraid she would fall. When they reached the ground floor, the butler stopped and turned. Sack stopped also, trying to catch her eye.

"I'll bring up your suitcase," said the butler. "Sir," he said, indicating for Sack to follow.

"Just a moment," said Sack. "Why don't you get it and I'll go in a minute." He turned to Ree as the butler left. She couldn't look him in the eyes.

"You're great," he whispered. "Played the rich bitch just right. You had me fooled with that little girl lost act, but you've got a real talent for this."

"Talent? For what?"

"There you go again. Well, I always thought you were smarter than most of those girls back at Columbia. Always sitting in the front seat, taking all those notes, ass-kissing Benedict, while the rest of them were showing off their pretty dresses."

"That's what you saw? I never--"

"I see everything. In my line of work, you never know what pays off. Like you, right now."

"What is your line of work? And what do you mean I'm paying off for you?" Ree realized her voice was rising. They leaned their faces so close she felt the heat of his body and smelled his breath. It almost felt like they were about to kiss. He drew back and laughed.

"There's nothing I can tell you about my line of work," he guffawed.

"Shhhh," she said.

"Hey, I just want to say goodbye, and wish you well," he said in a normal voice, as if he knew that Wheelwright was listening. "This will be a great opportunity to advance the study of man." He was mimicking the speeches they often heard at Columbia. He leaned in close and whispered, "of course, with that boss, I don't think it's man you're going to be studying."

He grabbed his own bag and pushed the door open before the butler could get to it, calling back "Do your best," and was gone.

The butler led her into her new bedroom and delicately laid her suitcase on a window seat created by the thick adobe wall. As he snapped it open, she yelped "No, I'll do that," and almost knocked him over.

"Let me know if you need anything," the butler said as he bowed and backed out.

The pleasant room was in the corner of the building with windows on two walls and a kiva fireplace in the corner. On the brass bed lay a hand sewn quilt, mostly white with a pattern of blue and gold rings. There was a small built-in bookcase and an oak bureau. The view out the window by the bed was of a long adobe building with roofs at several levels, clearly built up over time. Out the other window she saw corrals and wooden stables. Ree leaned over the window seat. Through the open window was the verandah which ringed the whole house. It had a wide floor and a low, simple railing that barely blocked the view. She almost climbed out the window to get onto the verandah, then realized this couldn't be dignified, so she left the room and went through the French doors. The railing was covered with dense vines and tree branches hung over it. Delicate red flowers shaped like ice cream cones draped from the trees and curled around the posts. Sweet smells drifted up from the garden below. A tiny hummingbird swooped in and fed from a red flower, its long beak stuck deep inside the horn like a straw. Only a few hours earlier, she had expected to sleep in an alley. For this, she did feel grateful to Sack.

Walking back into the hall, she looked through the open door which faced her new bedroom. Glancing to see if anyone was watching her, she leaned in the doorway. Wheelwright's narrow, cradle-like bed had a striped crimson and jet black Indian blanket tucked into its tall sides of polished walnut. A painting of a bright yellow flower hung over the headboard and dominated the room. A nondescript wooden desk was next to a plain bureau with a row of books on top, and over that hung a straw Jesus on the Cross. The room had two color schemes—the innocuous furnishings at one end, and at the other the bright blanket and flower painting.

Wheelwright, as little as she had seen of her so far, was a combination of rigid gentility and deeper needs that had brought her far from genteel Boston to this remote place. In her dainty parlor, a man in a trance state, challenging his gods. The leather medicine pouch hanging from his belt probably contained bones, teeth, and animal skulls representing all that European-inspired Boston was not. Wheelwright must have both a tamed and a wild side, and

Ree recognized these in herself. Was she a nice Jewish girl who could lie and steal and do whatever Sack accused her of doing to convince Wheelwright to trust her? Yet she knew she was sincere. She wanted to learn from Hosteen Klah and she wanted to understand Wheelwright. More than anything else, she wanted to continue her adventure so far from home.

But what Sack had said when he left felt as if he had put a curse upon her, like an angry troll in a fairy tale. At Columbia, some of her success as an anthropology student had come from her ability to analyze folk tales. Wasn't she in a fairy tale now, with Sack an angry troll, Wheelwright a fairy godmother who if pleased could bestow all riches and privileges upon her, and Klah a mysterious trickster for her to figure out?

Back in her room, she unpacked her clothes into the bureau, as the butler had tried to do. She hadn't wanted him to see the soiled clothes she had thrown in it when she was expelled from the ranch so suddenly. So much had happened in just a day: from San Gabriel to Santa Fe and back to Alcalde again. This beautiful valley must want her here. She laid her clothes on the bed, straightening out the wrinkles so she could wear them until she found out how the laundry was managed here. Then she laughed at herself, realizing the servants would take care of it and say nothing to Wheelwright.

This room, in the corner and by the doors to the verandah, was not a servant's room. She wasn't here as a servant, but as a respected anthropologist. She had the feeling Wheelwright was looking for something more from her. Was Wheelwright looking for what she herself wanted, someone who shared her interests and her excitement about them? Was Wheelwright looking for a friend?

In a bookshelf cut into the adobe wall was a neat row of books, held in by heavy bronze bookends shaped like books. A few were George Wharton James' accounts of his travels in the Southwest and California, studying how Indians made baskets and blankets. Charles Lummis' *In A Strange*

Corner of the Country had a green cover, with the title in bright golden embossed letters. She had always meant to read it. Now it would be there when she went to sleep, brass reading lamp by her bed.

What would Wheelwright have her do, besides transcribing and observing Klah? Back at San Gabriel, she had heard that Wheelwright had talked of opening a store in Boston to sell Navajo rugs. She couldn't imagine an Easterner buying one, so much plainer than the Oriental carpets fashionable among the wealthy, but perhaps there were more people like Wheelwright and herself, fascinated by the West and the Indians. She would buy a rug if she could ever afford it. Maybe Wheelwright would have her help choose rugs for the store. She had a vision of Wheelwright sending her to Boston to work in the store, but that made her shudder. What if Wheelwright wanted her to leave the Southwest and go back East? Even for a good job, she didn't want to do it. She wondered how long it would be until she had to say no to Wheelwright. Her position felt both idyllic and precarious. She felt herself already beginning to suck from Wheelwright as desperately as the hummingbird sucked from the flowers. Was that what Sack implied? Did he have to throw a blot upon her good luck?

Dinner was so formal that she kept feeling she was breathing too loudly. The heavy oak table almost filled the small dining room. She was afraid of breaking the dainty China, while the heavy silverware was hard to use. The centerpiece candelabra surprised her the most—not for its elaborate silverwork, but for the thick candles. She would have expected elegant white tapers.

"You've never seen such bright orange candles, have you?" asked Wheelwright with a squeal of delight. "They are my whim. I feel they cheer things up so. But it agitates my Boston relatives. 'Mary, must you be so unconventional?' they say. I've only had a few visitors here, so if they only knew!" Ree giggled along with Wheelwright, wishing she felt more sincere.

She had once heard a fellow anthropology student saying that the food of the rich white New England Protestants should be studied for its amazing contrast to the wealth available, and now she saw it for herself. The food was so sparse she forced herself not to gobble too fast. A few slices of cold roast, a small pile of peas, a wrinkled baked potato, a glass of apple cider, a sliced pear, and the meal was over. Too bad Wheelwright hadn't developed a taste for the thick steaks and mounds of steaming mashed potatoes bathed in sweet gravy that were the standard "cowboy food for dudes" at San Gabriel. But maybe that was why she had moved to her own place.

After the meal Wheelwright headed for the living room, and Ree knew to follow without being asked. Wheelwright took her place on the sofa in the corner again. The butler stood at attention by the gramophone, which was in a large oak cabinet in the center of the room. When Wheelwright was settled, nodding at Ree to sit, the butler ceremoniously placed the needle on the record and a hissing sound was heard, followed by a trumpet call. "One of my favorites," said Wheelwright.

The music began, a muted faraway sound because the gramophone was so far from where they sat. Wheelwright sank back into her seat, her eyelids dropped shut, and she leaned back with a contented smile. Ree was thrilled to get a good look at her, although she was worried those eyes might suddenly spring open and she would be caught staring. Wheelwright was unusually tall. Her body was flabby but not fat, limp and rounded where she might have been muscular. Her face, even while relaxed, had a forbidding strain that Ree couldn't help but contrast with the round, open faces of the Hispanic and Indian people she had been seeing so much of in New Mexico. She tried to remember what she had learned in anthropology classes about phrenology, the study of the bumps on the heads of various ethnic groups. She couldn't see bumps on Wheelwright's skull because it was covered by her simply styled, slightly gray hair. Wheelwright's looks were average, but even if she hadn't known Wheelwright to be a rich heiress, Ree would have noticed her self-important and dignified bearing. The butler, even at his stiffest, looked more approachable.

While her own unsociability may have been a factor in not getting a field placement, she felt normal compared to Wheelwright. She tried to picture her new employer as a little girl, but could only imagine a lonely adult in a little girl's body, a shorter version of the aging woman in repose before her. Meanwhile, Wheelwright's head bobbed slightly with the loudest swells of the music, and her hand twitched as if she wished to swing it like a conductor.

While Wheelwright was lost in the music, Ree wondered what she should call her. She hoped it wouldn't be "ma'am" like the butler said, which would make her feel like she was speaking to a Duchess. Even with their almost adjoining bedrooms, she doubted it would be 'Mary." She wondered if Wheelwright had a preferred secret name for herself, as Ree had chosen instead of Henrietta. What name would Wheelwright pick? All Ree could think of was the cowboy names at San Gabriel: "Lad," "Wrangler," and "Curly."

Just then Wheelwright's eyes fluttered and she must have seen Ree's face.

"You don't like the music?"

"I'm sorry, it's wonderful. It just affects me so emotionally," Ree said, hoping this was the right thing to say. Wheelwright's eyes sank down again. Her eyelids had the blue sheen of an older woman. The summer night was too hot for a fire, but Ree thought how much cozier this room would be with blazing logs. She wanted to shut off the rest of the large space, in which the sparsely placed objects—the large red, white, and black Navajo rug; the wood and animal skin tom-tom drum the size of a garbage can; and the Indian pots—were an unblinking audience facing them as they sat as if on a proscenium stage at the narrow end of the room.

"We heard this often at symphony," Wheelwright said, sitting up so suddenly her bones cracked. Ree threw her eyes down to the floor, hoping she hadn't been caught looking unappreciative. Wheelwright said nothing more, and soon looked as if she had fallen asleep. Deciding she had better show proper appreciation for the music, Ree closed her eyes as if carried away. Meanwhile her mind ticked madly, reviewing the surprising events of the day, wondering how Sack was, and telling herself he was mean and it was not her worry.

The next thing she knew, Wheelwright coughed, startling Ree. Wheelwright must have thought she had fallen asleep.

"Lovely, lovely, isn't it? So peaceful." Wheelwright's polite discretion was going to be Ree's best hope for staying on. She hoped that Wheelwright liked her enough to ignore her shortcomings.

They went to their bedrooms early, Wheelwright asking if Ree enjoyed reading in bed as she herself did. Ree, whose days had always been so full that she usually went to bed late and slept immediately, nodded enthusiastically. She fell asleep wondering if Wheelwright had ever been so cold in an unheated tenement that she had to burrow deep in her blanket to read by a streetlight. Don't be resentful of the rich woman, Ree told herself. She's being perfectly generous to you.

The next morning, breakfast was on the verandah under the flowering vines, as hummingbirds buzzed in and swooped away. Then Wheelwright led her into the parlor where Hosteen Klah was already weaving.

"I've offered him breakfast," Wheelwright said, "but he insists on getting up before sunrise and eats outside over a little campfire. Cook gives him the food. I believe he has a ritual for the sunrise. I'm hoping he'll show us sometime."

Ree liked the "us" implying a sense of permanence for her stay. Or was it more of a royal "we?"

"Now we just sit quietly, and when Mr. Klah is ready, he will begin to tell us stories or sing chants, or he may say nothing. I've learned he follows rules about the weather. He can't say anything sacred if a storm is coming." They both looked out the window anxiously, but the sky was clear blue.

Klah sat cross-legged on a folded blanket of intricate and colorful weaving. Under it was a simple rug of brown and white crosshatch. Scattered around him were woven baskets holding balls of wool and various sticks used to prod and pick at the weaving. The loom was made of logs about five inches in diameter, forming a large, box-shaped frame about ten feet wide and five feet high. The countless vertical strings formed a shimmering waterfall of light on the frame. Ree could see how this warp doubled back, allowing the finished portion to be rolled so that the final rug would be longer than the height of the loom.

Klah didn't look up when they entered, but continued weaving. Compared to other Navajo people she had seen, whose clothes were always so immaculately cleaned and pressed as to always appear new, Klah's clothes were shockingly ragged. Most Navajo men dressed as Ned did, in shining white blouses with leather thongs tied tightly around the biceps, but Klah wore a brown smock. The cloth had the thin polished sheen of age, the threadbare parts showing at the elbows and a hole near the wrist. The shirt had a long slit up the middle, then buttoned right under his chin. On his head was a winged, crown like hat, something like the bishop's hat in a chess set. Ree had never seen anything like it. He wore more jewelry than most Navajo men did, including heavy turquoise and silver bracelets on both wrists. The cuffs were rolled high on his denim trousers. There was something feminine about him.

Klah must have thought they were suitably quiet, because he let out a sudden deep roar, like a growling cat. Ree worried how long she could listen to that, but he immediately began to speak in a soft sing-song that she could barely hear, and she realized he must have first cleared his throat. His voice was distant as on an Edison wax cylinder record.

"Take notes, take notes," Wheelwright said, pushing a pen and notebook into her hand. At first Ree couldn't understand what Klah was saying, which didn't sound like English, but she wanted to look busy, so she wrote whatever she saw: "uses right hand to pluck strings of loom. Pushes so hard down with cross-stick that a thump is heard. Constant banging of cross-stick." She should know the names of the cross-stick and the strings. Before Gladys Reichard had left to spend a summer studying Navajo weavers, she had bragged about preparing by learning all that was known about it, even studying the Navajo language. Here Ree was at last with an Indian to study, but completely unready. What was she doing in this parlor with lace embroidered curtains at the windows? She should be sitting in the dirt on a mesa, with a woman weaver, not an androgynous man. Stop worrying and take notes, she told herself. Here's your big chance and you're not even paying attention.

Klah settled into a repetitive, quiet chant, sunk deep into himself, his hands still, his eyes staring at his groin, so self-absorbed that Ree felt intrusive and embarrassed, not only for herself but for him. But Wheelwright, perched on the window seat, looked at Klah possessively, as if she were showing him off to Ree. The secret here must be to butter up Wheelwright for her amazing ability to get Klah's cooperation. It was impressive, because Navajo people did not want their sacred stories told, their secret chants sung, or their mysterious sand paintings reproduced by outsiders. Klah was doing all of these, despite the ancient belief of his people that this would cause sickness and death to him and those around him.

Was she herself in danger? If she fell into thinking that way, she would be more scared than if she had ended up wandering Santa Fe or spending the night with Sack.

Ree transcribed his sounds. After writing the same simple syllables several times, she wanted to stop. But then she remembered something Benedict had said about her field work at Zuni pueblo, and realized she should count the number of repetitions. She wished she could tick them off on a bead necklace like Catholics with their rosary. Instead, she made a tally mark for each one.

"What I really want to know," Wheelwright said when Klah went back to working the loom, silent except for the thump of his stick, "is about their religion. He has folktales that he'll share easily, but the actual ritual and beliefs are a different story. Do you think you can discern which is which?"

Ree had no idea, but she wasn't going to admit it. "Maybe it's in his tone of voice." She shouldn't have said 'maybe.' She must be more authoritative to pull this off. How would Sack answer? Ree started again. "I've been trained to be aware of his voice tone and other body give-aways," she said as confidently as she could. She was aware she was suddenly holding her body like Sack, her shoulders spread like his broad ones. Wheelwright, whose posture was always rigid, somehow sat up even straighter, and watched her like an admiring pupil. For the first time Ree had a sense of being respected for her training.

Mary—in her head she must call her Mary, instead of Wheelwright. That was the way to think if she were to maintain this superior attitude, instead of feeling like a lucky bum who had been given a warm bed for a night. Thanks Sack, she thought, for your lesson in arrogance. "For example, in the writing of Professor Reichard," Ree continued, and Wheelwright leaned forward, eager to suck at her well of knowledge. Ree had never felt so powerful in her life. If only Ruth could see Mary listening to her with such respect. "Don't be afraid to tell me what Reichard has discovered," Wheelwright pleaded, "even if it is immodest," and Ree realized Wheelwright must have seen her blush at the thought of Ruth.

Ree had spent so much time alone that it was hard to turn off her endless thoughts and pay attention to another person. She was going to learn a lot from this experience, even if Wheelwright wasn't a Navajo. She was going to learn about herself, not about Indians. But that wasn't her goal. She would use this and move on. She would save her money and soon she would be in a hogan, not a parlor.

Wheelwright hadn't actually mentioned money. But it had been advertised as a job. What if it were strictly for room and board? How would she find the nerve to ask for the details? How would Sack ask? He would spring up right now, practically knocking over Klah, with his hand out, saying "so we've agreed to ten dollars a week" before Wheelwright even knew what was happening. Ree couldn't do that. Maybe she could ask the other servants what to do. But she wasn't one of the servants. She was doing anthropological work while they mopped the hallway outside.

Klah unfolded his legs and stood up. He began a slow dance around the room, shaking his hand as if holding a rattle, grunting rhythmically. Wheelwright looked pointedly at Ree's still hand until Ree started writing again. Klah stopped for a moment and looked intently at Ree. She dropped her eyes, not staring back, which apparently was the right move because he went back to his dance.

The butler came in and whispered something to Wheelwright. While they talked, Klah stopped moving and stood almost over Ree. She smelled onions from his breath and sage on his clothes. It was her first good look at his face. His nose was wide, with a deep crease between his eyes, from which two strong lines ran into his forehead. His eyes were narrow and long, with barely any lashes or brows. His cheeks were bulging and hard. His skin was dark brown and shiny, like the hot chestnut treats she sometimes bought from street vendors in New York. His face was as far from a Jewish face as could be.

Klah was examining her. He murmured something and shook his head, then smiled. She wished she knew what he had said. She must have looked puzzled. He said again, very softly, in English, "you are a woman, you are a man. You are changing" She was embarrassed, looking around to see if anyone else had heard, and began to rise from her chair defensively, but then he pointed at himself and said the same Navajo words. Did he mean that he was both a woman and a man, also? He wasn't exactly smiling at her, but his face was not challenging or hostile either. It was as if he recognized something in her that he saw in himself. She wondered if he had ever said this to Wheelwright. It wasn't something she could ask.

Later, as she followed Wheelwright out to the stables for what was apparently going to be a daily horseback ride, she thought about Klah's remark. She had been mortified. The thoughts she sometimes had about Ruth – did it mean she was not as much a woman as others? At Columbia, there had been much talk about the writings of Doctor Freud, the Viennese doctor who claimed to understand the deepest secrets of humans. Ree tried not to see herself in Freud's perspective of the consequences of sexual abstinence and lack of healthy desire for the opposite sex. Was Klah, in the mystical ways of his own culture, intuiting what Freud wrote in long, scholarly papers? Was she not as much a woman as others, but instead a pseudo-man who desired other women? It was a thought she was ashamed to think, but Klah had said it right to her face. But the way he said it and the composed way he pointed to himself suggested he understood something that she didn't.

At lunch, she dared to ask Wheelwright a direct question for the first time.

"What is it about Klah that most interests you? Is it just the weaving?"

"I'm so glad you asked," Wheelwright responded, and Ree realized she had been as eager to talk and as shy as Ree to start a conversation. "It all started when I was on a pack trip from San Gabriel. We stopped at Arthur and Franc Newcomb's trading post up near Toadlena. Have you been there?"

Ree didn't want Wheelwright to know how little of New Mexico she had seen so far. She knew Sack wouldn't hesitate to answer, so she said "a fascinating place."

"And the Newcombs, aren't they wonderful?" Wheelwright gushed. Fortunately, before Ree answered, she continued. "The whole idea started with Franc and her friendship with him, but she's busy with the trading post so I've taken over the chants and stories. Franc is doing watercolors of the sand paintings, while I'm giving Klah what he needs to get them woven.

"But as to your question, the night we arrived the Newcombs took us off to a night ceremony, deep in the hills. It was a black but starry night, lit only by crackling fires. There was smoke everywhere, chanting, people coming in and out of the haze. It went on all night but I was so transfixed I didn't dare blink for fear of missing something.

"By morning my eyes were swollen shut, but I didn't care. I felt changed—not felt, I was changed. No Sunday services at Kings Chapel, not even Christmas Eve, had ever moved me like that. I hadn't known what I was looking for. It wasn't religion, and maybe not the God I'd been brought up on, which all seem so small compared to what I saw that night. It felt like an opening into the mysteries of life. I suppose I should think about it scientifically, as our times demands, but I can't. Perhaps that's why it affected me, because it felt beyond science and rational thought. But it was nothing like the incense-swinging ceremonies of the Irish Catholics, who are everywhere in Boston now with their over-decorated churches. I don't think it could happen in a church, or it never had to me. It must happen in the secret kivas of the Indians, and I know now, because he has taken me there for ceremonies, that such things can happen in the log hogans of Klah's people. That night, something broke open in me and I've never felt the same."

She took a deep breath and stared off before continuing. "In small ways, I find this again from working with Klah and having him show me the chants and stories and ceremonies that make up their grand ceremonies like I saw that night."

Ree was astonished by Wheelwright's sudden brightening. While she talked, the formal and self-conscious aging woman disappeared, replaced by a youthful, curious eagerness that Ree wanted to reach out to in the same way that she had been drawn to Ruth during all those classes. She had sat in her seat, her pen tight in her hand, furiously taking notes while what she wanted was to touch the marvelous woman speaking. She hadn't felt this way for any woman but Ruth. Was Klah was right about her, that she was part man? Did she want women like men did? But was that what she wanted from Ruth and Wheelwright?

"I'll take you along when there's a night ceremony," said Wheelwright. "Perhaps you'll feel the same."

"I would hope to," gushed Ree, "but that's so unusual, so unique. You're such a lucky person. It sounds like what I've studied, how a primitive might feel at the end of a vision quest."

"A vision quest?" asked Wheelwright.

"It's an ordeal of starving and suffering in order to have a mystical experience."

"Of course," said Wheelwright. "But I didn't suffer to have mine. We drove all day, had lamb stew at Newcomb's, and then the loveliest ride in the dark up to the ceremony. From a distance, we could see the fires burning, so beautiful." She was quiet for a moment then continued. "Do you think I could feel it again if I suffered? What a wonderful idea! I shall ask Mr. Klah how to do that."

Ree suffered trying not to laugh. Wheelwright was so sincere but so innocent. Should she suggest that Wheelwright be dropped off on the streets of Santa Fe as she had been, hungry, with no money, a heavy suitcase, and knowing no one? That would be as jarring to Wheelwright as when the Indian youths were sent out into the wilderness alone on their vision quests. She would certainly have experienced suffering.

On the other hand, perhaps Ree herself would have been better off if Sack hadn't shown up. If she herself suffered more, perhaps she would have experienced a revelation like Wheelwright's. But what was she thinking, that she would see the Burning Bush? Jews hadn't had magical revelations since the days of the Prophets. Why not? Had the people who could teach them to see visions died with their secrets, as Klah probably would if Newcomb and Wheelwright hadn't convinced him to create a permanent record in watercolors and wool?

"So ever since that night," Wheelwright continued, "my purpose in life became clear. Mr. Klah is old. His parents were in the Long March, when the U.S. Army forced the Navajo people to walk hundreds of miles, cold and hungry, only to be corralled. So many died they finally had to let them go. His relatives told him many stories which are among those I want you to transcribe. His people have a place to live and raise sheep now, but the children are forced to go to boarding school and learn Christian ways. The boys don't have time to learn the old ways. He's afraid all the knowledge will be lost. He knows more than almost anyone. He is like a living library. None of it is written down. Can you imagine, your mind being the Library of Congress for all that America has learned and thought? That huge building in Washington—and all of that would be in your head? And in your body, too, because what he knows is more than words and memories. It's in every cell of his body, as Professor Agassiz might say at Harvard College."

Ree thought of the Torah, the library of the Jews. There were also the books of the Talmud and so much more, but all that could be lost if only the Torah was left. What would Wheelwright think of her if she knew she were Jewish? She shouldn't, but she couldn't help but ask.

"Have you ever seen a Torah?" she asked.

Wheelwright pursed her lips anxiously, as if afraid to be caught without having done her homework. Not knowing whether to prompt her, Ree decided to wait.

"The sacred scrolls of the Jewish people?" wheelwright spoke hesitantly.

"Yes, that's it. They've managed to save them for thousands of years. It's what's kept them together through all their wanderings." As she said this, Ree thought that it made no sense, since they had dispersed through all their wanderings. But Wheelwright didn't catch the contradiction.

"So admirable," said Wheelwright, "and of course the Gospels are more than nineteen hundred years old themselves. But if all those writings had to be remembered by people from generation to generation, what would be left? And taught from one man to the next? Think how lucky we are, to help to preserve this legacy! Back in Boston, my family has silver cups made by Paul Revere that are passed from generation to generation. They're beautiful, and I respect the effort that has been made, but it's nothing compared to what the Navajo people have done. The Nightway Ceremony alone has twelve nights of chants, and Mr. Klah knows them all. We're in the process of transcribing that right now. I'm so glad you understand how much this means, not to me, but to the—no, not just to the Navajo people, either. I believe it is important for the whole world. Did you know that the Pueblo people believe that if they don't do a certain ceremony every year, the world will come to an end? Mr. Klah hasn't said anything like that to me yet, but I suspect he will. There are many secrets he hasn't revealed. But I don't want the secrets to die with him! Just the thought of him dying..." She rose excitedly from her chair, an Amazon warrior, then fell back, a pale lady from Boston. Ree thought of Klah's words "your are changing" and what she had seen at this lunch table embodied that. Like a character in a folktale, Wheelwright had changed from one magical being into another before Ree's startled eyes.

What was happening? Was Ree herself changing? Even without fires and smoke and chanting medicine men, she felt that at last her trip had begun. The months at San Gabriel were a distant and unsatisfying dream. Her dream of going West had been a dream of having a life as different as the one that Frank Cushing had lived among the Zuni people, one that changed him. She was finally on her own journey of change, having passed through some kind of gate, with Sack a knight errant to help her move on, to enter this world of wonders. She didn't believe it was magic, although she suspected Wheelwright thought Klah had magical powers.

Ree looked at Wheelwright, now picking at crystal cup of stewed prunes, and wanted to fling her own cup, so discreetly placed before her by the butler, across the room at the porcelain samovar with its etchings of Greek maidens draped in winding sheets. She wanted Wheelwright to wake up and be that Amazon again who she had felt desire for as she had felt for Ruth for so long. Wheelwright looked up, saw Ree had stopped eating, and fluttered her eyelids, keeping her eyes blank, embarrassed by their momentary intimacy. Ree bent down to her prunes, glad Wheelwright hadn't asked her why she had mentioned the Torah and not the more obvious Gospels. She should have mentioned that instead.

Ree was glad she had done enough riding and spent some time watching the cowboys at San Gabriel to keep up with Wheelwright on the daily horseback ride. Being a companion to Wheelwright was as much the job as working with Klah, and it was clear now that Sack never had a chance to be hired, because Wheelwright could not have dominated him the way she dominated Ree. She never asked, but always assumed Ree would join her for all meals, the daily rides, and evenings spent listening to music. Sometimes Wheelwright would ask her to read aloud, or even worse, Wheelwright would read to Ree, which meant a struggle to stay awake. Wheelwright loved George Eliot novels, but the European settings bored Ree.

Breakfast was a treat, served on the verandah outside the bedrooms. The table was always set with the finest linen tablecloth and napkins, and the napkin rings were silver stamped MCW, as was the China and silverware. Had Wheelwright been given these as a trousseau? She had learned by now that Wheelwright had never married because she had cared for her dear mother. Wheelwright had been forty when her mother died, and soon took the trip to the Southwest that had given her an unexpected obsession with the place. She also traveled to Europe and was planning to go to India and the Holy Land.

"Now that I've seen a different way among the American Indians, I want to see all the ways that people feel this feeling that some call God," Wheelwright told her one morning at breakfast. In the formal garden below, two Indian men were planting a bush, seemingly unaware of their employer watching. Wheelwright must have pushed her silent food button, for the butler appeared suddenly. She sent him downstairs to tell the gardeners that they had placed the bush too close to the fence.

They had settled into a routine of sessions with Klah. Ree was surprised a man of his age could be so vigorous, for he was up before sunrise, busy all day at the loom, and telling all he could remember of what were proving to be very repetitive stories and chants. Sometimes she could follow the stories of twins and changing women and bees, finding in them some guidance for her own life, but other times the words were so symbolic and surreal that she wished he would stop talking and let her sit there with her thoughts as his batten thumped against the wool. It was pleasant to think along with this rhythm. She knew she would hate weaving, with its tiny exacting finger movements, need for perfectly balanced tension across the strings, and endlessly repetitive motions, so she was relieved to merely watch.

Wheelwright often took her along to teas, lunches, and dinners with her friends in Santa Fe, so Ree had been meeting a strata of society she had only stared at from a distance at San Gabriel, and never encountered in New York. They were rich women endlessly discussing horses, architects, second homes, and yachts. Some, like Wheelwright, were funding archaeological or anthropological expeditions, many of which Ree would have loved to go on. But because they met her as Wheelwright's dining companion, no one was ever going to offer her a job or even a chance to do anything not by Wheelwright's side. She felt decorative, a pretty object, a fancy button on Wheelwright's dowdy dresses, despite being pretty dowdy herself.

One day while Klah was focusing on a problem with the weaving and Wheelwright was perched on the window seat, she asked Wheelwright about her Beacon Hill home. "Does the kitchen there have all the latest electric appliances? I read there is one that toasts bread so you don't have to turn on the oven?"

"I wouldn't know what is in the kitchen there. I've never had reason to look. The servants..." As her voice trailed off, Wheelwright looked thoughtful, then added, "Should I?" The remark delighted Ree, and she thought she saw Klah suppress a giggle.

At that moment, Klah turned to her with a smile, and from then on, she didn't find him so otherworldly. For one thing, she realized he understood English better than she had thought, and for another, she saw him as another one of Wheelwright's servants, entertaining Wheelwright's whims, as covered over in mysticism as they might be.

At Columbia, she had heard much about the rich women anthropologists like Elsie Clewes Parsons and Mathilda Coxe Stevenson. They came to the Southwest with money and attitude at the end of the Indian wars, when most of the Indians were in terrible poverty and powerlessness. These women saw themselves as helping the Indians by preserving the culture and encouraging an economy based on weaving, pottery, silversmithing, basketry and other crafts. Most ethnologists paid their informants, if not with money then with cigarettes or food. Did the Indians see it as a business of selling information to strange rich white people from the East? Did Klah see it this way? His rugs would be worth a fortune. There would be a parade of millionaires eager to put them on their walls. Maybe he was afraid of the bad fortune he might bring on himself with all the secrets he told and wove, but maybe he was more afraid of hunger. Didn't his simple old clothes show he didn't care about material things? Didn't they prove his sincerity? Wheelwright said that when she gave him new clothes, he never wore them, apparently giving them to his many relatives. She had stopped doing it, because he would leave Los Luceros to deliver the clothes.

Every few days, Wheelwright went to Santa Fe to meet with bankers and dressmakers. Ree sat in the waiting rooms, wishing she could explore the city. Wheelwright never offered any time off, and Ree was afraid to ask. Finally, as Wheelwright was heading into a meeting with an architect for some outbuildings she wanted to add, she told Ree to meet her at La Fonda in an hour. Ree rushed off to enjoy every minute. She had just stepped onto the portal of the Palace of the Governors when she spotted Ned talking to an old woman. She walked up to them and tried to look casually at the jewelry and rugs. When Ned saw her, they each jumped back as if from static electricity. She hadn't seen him since the night in the haymow, and she had no plan of what to say. They looked at each other awkwardly while the old Indian woman smiled and ducked her chin curiously.

"Hi," Ree finally said, as Ned stood frozen.

"Um, hi," Ned gulped out. "This is my grandmother, Frances Yazzie.

Just then a tourist interrupted to ask Frances about a rug.

"I can't believe I found you. I hardly ever get to Santa Fe," Ree exclaimed.

"I haven't seen you at San Gabriel in a while," Ned said. So he had been looking for her. Ree felt more confident.

"I'm working at Los Luceros now. Do you know it?"

"Sure, I've ridden through there when I've come in on horseback. So you left the dude ranch?"

"I wanted to see more. Now I'm helping this woman," Ree hesitated, unsure how much she wanted to say. What Klah was doing was very controversial among the Navajo people. Maybe Ned would not want to talk to her. "I'm helping this rich woman from Boston. She's got a big estate. I help her with stuff."

"Are you talking about Hosteen Klah?"

"You know about it?"

"Everyone knows about it. Most are angry."

"What about you?"

"I've always wanted to meet him. I've seen him a few times at chants, but never to speak to him," Ned answered.

"Do you want to come to the house?"

"The rich woman's house? No, I can't meet him there. But I want to meet him."

Ree felt stuck. She wanted to see Ned again. "Let me help you," burst out of her.

"Would you tell him Ned Leeds wants to meet him? From Lost Wash? Ask him where he would be willing to meet me."

"How can I reach you?"

"Oh, I'm working here for a—" Ned looked embarrassed—"for a rich man from Boston, with a big house off Old Santa Fe Trail. His name is Witter Bynner."

"I wonder if he knows Mary Cabot Wheelwright. That's who I'm working for."

"He has a lot of parties. It looks to me like they all know each other, at least the ones who live in Santa Fe. Artists and writers and archaeologists. They all drink a lot."

"Not Wheelwright. She has people to dinner, but no wild parties."

"I'll give you my address."

"What work are you doing now?" Ree asked.

"Right now I'm helping to put in a kitchen. It's very Mexican, all bright colors. I'm an apprentice to the carpenter. I'm learning to lay that pretty Mexican tile."

"That sounds wonderful. Want to hear something funny?" Ned nodded and she continued. "Wheelwright—my boss—never goes into the kitchen of her own house. She won't go where the servants go. That's what they told me, and I've never seen her go in there."

"Never?"

"Maybe when she first bought it, but not since then. The servants all laugh about it."

"So, you're not a servant?"

"No, but I feel closer to them then to her."

"What's your job?" Ned asked.

Too late, Ree realized he might not like her answer.

"I was going to Columbia in anthropology so she hired me to transcribe what Mr. Klah tells her."

Ned looked startled, then concerned.

"So it's true then. Is he telling her the ceremonies?"

"I know a lot of Indians don't like it. I understand why, too. But he says if there isn't a more permanent record, so much will be forgotten, because the young people aren't learning it."

"Because we're forced to go away to boarding school," Ned said.

"Were you? Did they treat you badly?" Ree asked.

"I ran away," he said, shaking his head. "The things they wanted me to do! The clothes they made we wear! They couldn't keep me long. The trouble is, then you can't go back to your family or they'll find you. I've been hiding from them since I was eleven years old."

"How old are you now?" She had thought he was much younger than herself, because of his high voice and smooth cheeks.

"Nearly twenty-four. I've spent most of my life on my own," he said proudly. Ree was more shocked at his age.

"We're about the same age," said Ree.

"We've lived very different lives," said Ned. "I wanted to go to school, but not the one they wanted me to go to. Where I work now, at Mr. Bynner's, I've met a lot of anthropologists. They always want to talk to me. Sometimes I make stuff up, just for fun. They take me so seriously!"

Ree had heard sad tales from field workers whose work was discredited and ethics questioned. One weeped in the cafeteria after a devastating rejection of a dissertation, crying "but that's what the subject told me. How could I make that up?" She hadn't known what to believe, her confident professors or the fellow student. Should she trust Ned? Had Wheelwright ever considered that Klah might be misleading her?

"I have to get back to work," said Ned. "I was at the Plaza to help my grandmother unpack her wares, and then I'll come back tonight to pack her up again. In between, I work on Bynner's kitchen."

"Oh my gosh," said Ree, looking at her watch. "I was supposed to meet Wheelwright at La Fonda." They both stood up. "I'll ask Mr. Klah about you. And I'll ask Wheelwright if she ever goes to Bynner's house. I'd love to see what you've done in the kitchen."

"Once it's done, he'll be showing it off, that's for sure." They walked across the Plaza towards La Fonda.

"Will you still be working there?"

"After the kitchen, he's building a library. I'll be there for a while. If not, his friends will hire me. Mary Austin, William Henderson, they all have adobe houses that need work."

"Don't you miss being home? I mean, did you ever go back to your family once you were too old to be sent to school? I guess you see your grandmother."

"I used to sneak back, but my mother died and my father got a new family. He doesn't think much of me, he has a lot of children from his other wife. But my grandmother, she's my family. I see her as much as I can. I make better money here, and send some back. I see her when she's here to sell her rugs. Everyone is so poor back home, there's nothing to do but raise sheep. I don't like sheep, do you?"

They both laughed. "I guess I'd rather live in a rich man's house for now, but not forever."

"What do you want to do?" Ree asked. She hoped Ned wasn't going to say he wanted to go to the city.

"I want to live like my ancestors did, before the Long Walk, before they were prisoners on their own land. Now the government tells them what to do, where to live, how many sheep to have. I think they had a better life, but it's not there any more."

"Me too," Ree said eagerly.

"You want to live like a Navajo?" laughed Ned.

"Sort of. I feel the way you do. The old ways were a better way to live. I come from New York City, I know how I don't want to live."

"I shouldn't have laughed. It's great you feel that way."

"But what can you do if you think those days are over?" Ree hated to put the thought into words.

"I want to be a healer like Hosteen Klah. He's one of the last who knows the old ways. Even as things have changed, my people still go to healers if they're sick and want to hold the ceremonies and the chants. What's left of the old days is because of Hosteen Klah and others like him. But he's right, young people have to learn it, or it will be forgotten."

"You've got to study with him!" Ree said. They were almost at the entrance of La Fonda. Frantic tourists pushed past them going in and out of the carved wooden doors. A few scowled at Ned, while others stared at him.

"It's not that easy," said Ned. "You have to be accepted as an apprentice. I've tried, but so far nobody wanted me."

"How can they do that?" said Ree. "You'd be perfect."

"Maybe not exactly," said Ned as if he could say more on this. "But if I could meet Hosteen Klah, that might help. He might understand me better than some others."   Ree wondered what he meant by that. If Ned hadn't met him, why would he think so?

"Anyway, I have to go. Here's my address —" he pulled an envelope from deep in his pocket and ripped off the address. "Let me know if you can set anything up. Tell him I'd meet him anywhere he wants. I don't think he'll want to meet me at Wheelwright's house, anyway I hope not."

"Why not?"

"It would be better. It's not about her. The white people want to watch everything and write it all down. Oh, sorry," he caught her eye sheepishly. "Really, it's a good thing she's doing with Mr. Klah, but mostly it's just," he hesitated. "It would mean a lot to me to talk to Hosteen Klah. He's very, very special. I just don't want anyone watching, do you understand?"

"Sure." Ree pictured the old man and the young one meeting, the young man's face so excited, the old man's face so questioning, yet so pleased—and she didn't want to see Wheelwright hovering over the moment, pleased to have engineered it.

"I won't tell Wheelwright anything about this. I sometimes get time alone with Mr. Klah. I'll ask him. Is it all right if I ask Wheelwright if she knows Mr. Bynner?"

"Sure, maybe she goes to his parties. I'll ask him if he knows her. Maybe we'll see each other again." Just as they smiled at each other, the doors opened and Wheelwright burst through.

"Ree, there you are," Wheelwright said as Ned briskly walked off without a shrug of goodbye. Wheelwright glanced at Ned slipping away, then turned back to Ree. "Do you realize what time it is?" she asked. Ree hoped Ned hadn't heard that.

"I can't sit here alone, you know, I've had to wander through the shops waiting for you." She was angry, and Ree was pretty sure it was because of her glimpse of Ned. "Well, it's too late now for treats at the restaurant, I have to be at the dressmakers now." She headed down the street, with Ree expected to follow. Ree didn't even want to see if Ned was watching, she was so humiliated.

Wheelwright was huffy through all their errands and on the ride home. Ree couldn't think what to say. Finally, as the car was pulled up to the house, Wheelwright asked "Who was the Indian boy you were talking to? Why were you late?"

"I'm sorry, I didn't mean to be. He was telling me how much he admires Mr. Klah. He's glad for the work you're doing."

Wheelwright preened. "Well, why didn't you say so? Maybe he could come to the house and we could interview him. Did you get his name and address?"

"No, it was just a quick conversation." Here she was, lying again, but she felt more loyal to Ned than to Wheelwright.

"If you make a contact like that again, find out. Any Navajo who supports our work could be very useful to us."

Ree nodded, understanding Ned's attitude even more. She wasn't sure how to disqualify herself from being lumped in with Wheelwright, but maybe it would help if she told Ned she had been kicked out without finishing anthropology school. He might admire that. There was so much she wanted to say to him.

"I think I'll go see if Mr. Klah feels like talking," she said to Wheelwright. Maybe she could get some time alone with him.

It took a few days to get time alone with Hosteen Klah, and when she did, she felt it was almost as if he sensed that she had something to ask him, because it seemed he never took a break from chanting or being so deeply in thought that she couldn't interrupt. The right moment never came. She wasn't sincere in the question she wanted to ask. Klah was very open to her honest, ethnological questions about the knowledge he had. Although she was skeptical of his powers as being magical for healing or affecting the weather or even human behavior, she had no doubt that he had an unusually strong intuitive sense of the people around him. He would be sure to notice if someone was exploiting him.

But would it be exploitation to ask Klah to meet Ned? Wouldn't the old man be delighted to find a young man who wanted to carry on the traditions? She decided to launch right in. The next time Wheelwright left the room to discuss an upcoming dinner party with the cook, she made her move. At that moment, Klah was in the midst of starting a new piece of wool, which he did by breaking it from the ball of yarn with a sharp pull on either side. The new string was then cleverly laid over the old one, and only a few whiskers stuck out in the final product, not noticeable.

"Mr. Klah," she began, "I met a young Navajo man who would like to meet you." Klah did not look up. She couldn't tell if he was listening or deep in thought. "He likes the old ways. He has heard of you, but not met you. When I told him I knew you, he asked me to find out if you would meet with him."

Still, no response.

"He lives near Lost Wash. His name, he told me to tell you—" she said this so he would know it was a name for the white people, not his real name—"is Ned Leeds."

At this, Klah twitched slightly, but he said nothing. Ree decided she had done all she could, so she stopped talking and he kept up with his work, soon starting to tell her a story which she dutifully transcribed. It was a story about a boy who flung dirt at people, and then set bees upon them. But when the people gave the boy a prayer stick, he sucked the bees back into his mouth. She had heard a lot of these stories, and was always so busy transcribing that she had no time to think about their meaning. When she did think about it, she found she had no idea what it meant.

Her last paper before she had left Columbia had been about a story told by many tribes. The Navajos told it to explain the origin of their enemies, the Utes. The story was of a man who wanted to have sex with his daughter so much that he faked his own death, came back in another body, and seduced the daughter. She hadn't chosen the story, it had been assigned by a male professor who had a way of looking at her that made her squirm. She hated the story, which made her feel self-conscious around her father. In all the years growing up without a mother around, it had never crossed her mind to think that her father had sex. She had been glad to finish the assignment, and felt more uncomfortable than proud when the professor had said he would submit it to a journal. She hadn't heard anything back about its fate. If her career ended now, she hated to think that would be her one published work, the only concrete evidence that she had been an anthropologist. People would think of her as having a perverse interest in incest. It was so unfair and so unlike her. But she shouldn't think that she would never publish again. She would write accounts like Frank Hamilton Cushing had, of her life among the Indians, the friendships that would develop, the adventures she would have which no white person had ever been allowed.

Maybe someday Klah would look at her with admiration instead of his usual attitude, which was that she was somewhere between an audience and an interrogator, but always, without doubt, an employee of Wheelwright. Ree had seen that he had a genuine affection for Wheelwright that didn't seem to be based on her riches. The intuitive man saw in his patron a depth other white people didn't have, and Ree wished he could see it in herself.

Did she want Klah to see something special in her? Wouldn't that be creepy? Her father had taught her to not take seriously Jewish folktales or superstitions. But the more time she spent with Klah, the more Ree realized that her own heritage had its own strange tales and probably even healing processes. She had seen old ladies cover their eyes and wave their hands and talk about keeping away "Kinehora," the evil eye. After a funeral, everyone had to wash their hands. After a death, all the mirrors were covered for a week. From an anthropologist's point of view, it was no different from many of Klah's stories. Her father never told them to her, but she had seen the old ladies in their tenement building who followed these rules.

One old grandmother of the family in whose apartment they boarded for many years sometimes told these stories. Her pale blue eyes were covered with a teary veil of blindness, but she could still darn immaculately. Everyone brought their worn out stockings to her, and she somehow wove the tiny damaged threads into a strong patch. Ree was wearing a pair of those now. While she darned, the old lady told stories of the old days, but Ree barely listened, impatient to get back to her Frank Hamilton Cushing books. Perhaps she should have transcribed the heritage of her own culture as she was doing for Navajo myths now, but she couldn't have done it even to publish papers and earn academic prestige. Some Navajo was going to have to go to Brooklyn and record those stories from those old people. It was not going to be Ree. Didn't every culture have some version of the proverb "the grass is always greener?" She certainly wasn't the only Brooklyn Jew who didn't want to examine the stories of the bubbemeises, the grandmothers. In this she was like everyone else.

One day Ree sat up, her joints cracking. Klah turned suddenly and stared at her. She had been lost in thought and not writing down what he said. Both their heads swung up to see if Wheelwright was watching, but her chair was empty. Klah's face widened into a somewhat guilty smile and they grinned at each other. For the first time in weeks, he felt like a real person she was connecting to.

"Who are your people?" he said. "Where do you come from?"

"Brooklyn." He looked blank. "New York City." He nodded slightly.

"What are their stories?" he asked.

"Stories?"

"What do they tell their children? How do they explain how the world came to be? How do the children know what to do to be good? How do they know what is bad?"

"Oh, well," she bought time, thinking about the grandmothers and their stories about Kinehora. Could she remember enough to tell him?

"About Jesus and how he made the blind man see? That was good medicine," he said.

"Jesus?" she said weakly.

"You don't know about Jesus?" he said. "Do you have other people? Do they have other stories? I thought all the white people had the same story about Jesus."

"Not me," she said. She was listening for Wheelwright's footsteps. She had never said outright to Wheelwright that she was Jewish. With Wheelwright's interest in other religions, her employer had never gone to church or questioned or offered that Ree do so. Ree had worried that she would be expected to attend Christian services at the old adobe chapel on the estate, but it was boarded up, although the Spanish staff carefully tended the graves. Apparently Wheelwright no longer practiced Christianity.

She didn't want her religion to be an issue, the way she sometimes suspected it was at Columbia, no matter what was said outwardly about tolerance. Boas was a Jew but she had heard some students use the words "Jew down" more than once, even in referring to him. The space between stated ideals and actual practice was no less in the academic world than it had been anywhere else. In her Brooklyn neighborhood, there were Yiddish words for the Negroes and the Italians and the Irish and all the other groups of strangers that life had marooned together in America. The tone of voice for the words in Yiddish was one of superiority. In her anthropology classes she learned that every group had these words for other groups, and that feeling superior to other groups was a way of feeling more a part of your own group. That was why most groups named themselves "the people." The Navajo word for themselves was "Dine," which means, "the people." If you name your own group as "the people," then members of all other groups are less than people. She wasn't sure what Jew or Jewish meant, but suspected it meant "the people who have a covenant with God," or "The people who God promised he would never send a catastrophic flood to again."

Meanwhile, how should she answer Klah? She was pleased to finally have him see her as a real person and didn't want to lie to him.

"My people don't believe in Jesus," she said. He looked puzzled.

"I didn't know that could be. Miss Wheelwright has told me about the people of Japan who have their own gods, and she showed me the pictures of the gods of the people of India, but they are yellow people and brown people. What other gods are there for white people?"

"I'm a Jew. Jews don't believe in Jesus. In the Bible we're called the Israelites. We were the people before the Christians, who believe in Jesus." She felt strange speaking in this tone of voice, which was like Klah's when he told his stories.

"Tell me what your people believe," said Klah. "Who is the first of your people to emerge from the world below?"

Ree tried to think what to say. She had never known the Bible stories well. In recent years her father had become more religious, but when she was younger her father took her to Workmen's Circle, a non-religious organization that provided cemeteries and social gatherings for the many like himself who did not believe enough to go to synagogue. There had been some classes she had been forced to sit through, with an emphasis on the history of the Jews. They had sung Yiddish songs. She could read the Hebrew alphabet, which was used for writing Yiddish. But she didn't know much about Judaism. She was intimidated by the religious Jews in Brooklyn, the men with their dark clothes, huge fur hats, and long, unruly full beards. A tall gangly one who lived on their street always smelled of onions, as if he had just crawled from a muddy forest floor, like a spring onion pushing through the soil, green roots first, and then the dirt-covered bulb. She pictured him shaking the dirt off his huge fur hat, blinking behind his thick spectacles, crying out in Yiddish, "here I am, Ruler of the Universe, tell me what to do to obey your Laws." She giggled to herself.

"Please, your story," said Klah.

A voice broke in, saying "and God said 'let there be light,' and he created the earth and the sky, and all the animals, and then finally he created a man, Adam, and out of his rib he creates a woman, Eve." Wheelwright stood in the doorway, hands on hips, looking proudly at Klah and not at all at Ree.

"I was hoping you would ask about our beliefs," Wheelwright continued. "Have you never studied the Bible?"

"Oh that story," he said, "I've heard that story. But she told me her people have a different story. They don't have the story of Jesus," he said, looking at Ree.

With Wheelwright staring at her, and clearly jealous of the conversation she had been having with Klah, Ree wasn't sure what to say.

"We just have the really old stories," said Ree. "Jesus is a new one to us."

"What are you talking about?" asked Wheelwright.

"He asked me what my people believe. I was trying to tell him."

"You don't believe in Jesus? Oh, of course, you're Jewish. I knew that, but I never thought of it exactly that way. What Jesus means to you."

So Wheelwright knew Ree was Jewish. Since when? But apparently it hadn't mattered. She had been hired anyway, and was taken to meet people who might not want Jews around. But now that it had been spoken of openly, how would it affect their relationship? She was always on pins and needles around Wheelwright, as much as she tried to relax. Would she feel even more self-conscious now? What had happened to that free life she had come West for?

"That's right," she said, hoping the conversation would end quickly. "Mr. Klah was telling me a story of his people, and then he asked me this question. But I'm eager to hear the rest of your story, Mr. Klah," she said, "what happened after the man sucked the bees back into his mouth?" He gave her a sharp look, not fooled by her change of subject, and probably angry that she hadn't been paying attention earlier. Fortunately, Wheelwright fell for it.

"Oh, the one about the bees. Now I've heard a little of it. What have I missed?" Klah turned back to his loom, leaving them both looking at his back. Ree didn't want to look up and face Wheelwright.

At least Klah had talked to her like a normal person. Ree felt lighter than she had in a long time. It bothered her to spend so much time with Hosteen Klah and feel that he was something other than human, the way Wheelwright seemed to worship him. Hadn't she romanticized Indians for so long, seeing them through Frank Hamilton Cushing's eyes? Maybe the other anthropologists were right that the field needed to change. Still, why would she do any of this if it was all about emotionless science with no room for her fantasies and wishes?

It was a relief to see Klah as a human being and hopefully she would see others that way. Like Ned? But smiling at what had happened that night in the hay mow, her feelings for Ned didn't feel the same as she felt for any other Navajo man.

"Anthropologists are wrong to dismiss the role of money in saving these objects," said Wheelwright. "There isn't a culture where money doesn't matter." It was easy enough for Wheelwright to say that. To Wheelwright, if an Indian was willing to sell, then she was willing to buy. Some Indians were willing to sell their heritage and protection, even though they believed sacred objects would keep them and their families safe.

As Wheelwright spoke, the sun blazed on the silver teapot and flashed in Ree's eyes. She thought of her mother's Sabbath candelabra. Selling it had provided enough money for her trip west, so she had done it without a second thought. But when she packed for the trip, about to close her suitcase, she saw a space that would have been just right for the candelabra. It was then she realized that it was truly gone. Her mother had carried it across Poland from the shtetl of David Gorodok, deep in the Pale of Jewish Settlement near Minsk. Her mother, who had traveled across the ocean for her dreams, had never been desperate enough to sell it, but Ree had turned it in for a ticket on the *Santa Fe Chief.* Where was the candelabra now? Did it light the Sabbath for a family more loving than her own? Had it been melted into an incense burner for a Mass?

This was what it meant to take objects from the Indians. She thought of the feather-covered stick from the attic, hidden now in her suitcase. What family had sold it to survive?

One night, after a long day spent riding way out over the sage-covered hills almost as far as Espanola, Wheelwright wearily announced that they would go to bed early. Ree was full of energy and wished she could at least shut the door of her room so she wouldn't have to worry about Wheelwright across the hall, hearing every creak in the floor. After tossing and turning in bed, she considered sneaking across the wide adobe windowsill, out the window, across the verandah, down the outside stairs, and into the kitchen. Could she do all that without waking Wheelwright? What would Wheelwright do if she heard her? Ree had been too scared to test her situation before. There was a lot to lose if her employer got angry. But if she got caught just this one time, she could say that she had gone down for warm milk. She could try it just this once. She slipped over the sill and padded down the verandah. In the distance she saw the small home of the estate's stable manager, brightly lit. She heard a fiddle and people laughing and talking. There was a sweet scent in the air from the trumpet vines that the hummingbirds so loved. The grass tickled her bare feet as she pushed through the screen door of the kitchen.The butler, the cook, and two stable hands looked up from their seats around the table. But they didn't look surprised, even though she was barefoot and in her bathrobe, and she wondered if past companions of Wheelwright had used the same escape route.

"Saturday night, I thought you would all be out having fun," she said, trying to sound as if she always did this.

"We are," said the cook. "We're trying something Mr. Klah taught us." In the center of the table was a piece of oilcloth, and on that was a layer of dirt. A tic-tac-toe board had been drawn in it, and they were in the middle of a game.

"Mr. Klah plays tic-tac-toe?" asked Ree. It felt so good to have a conversation without Wheelwright hanging on her every word.

"Have you seen him do the pictures with the sand?" asked the butler.

"That's not a game."

"It is the religious symbolism of his spirit world," said the butler, mimicking Wheelwright's tone of voice. They all giggled into their hands, trying to stay quiet.

"The artifacts of a culture and so on," said the cook in a falsetto, causing another round of laughter.

Ree was surprised that the butler, who was always so formal and respectful, was such an instigator behind Wheelwright's back.

"What do you think of Hosteen Klah?" Ree asked.

They were all silent for a moment.

"He's all right," said one of the stable hands. "Most Indians, I don't have much to say about. They just get poorer and drunker all the time. They won't let their kids go to school and make something of themselves. But he's different."

"What's school ever made of you, Charlie?" said the other stable hand, still jovial, but no one paid attention.

"He's interesting," Charlie continued. "I know his sand paintings aren't really like these." He waved his hand at their efforts. "But that's why we tried this. We wanted to see if we could do it too, so I got some sand."

"Brought it back in his hat. Now his head is full of grit."

"Shut up, Tom, this is serious. You understand, don't you Miss Ree? Haven't you ever wanted to try it, see if it's magical for you like it is for him? He says if you do the pictures exactly right, you can heal the sick."

"And have good luck," said the cook. "I could use some of that."

"Oh come on," said Tom, "you believe that? Hey, it's just Indian superstition. White men should know better. Besides, he's a strange Indian, you can't tell me you haven't noticed. Navajo men don't weave. They don't spend all their time sitting in the parlor with women. You know what I think?"

"Don't think I want to," said Charlie. "I like the man. I learn a lot from him."

Tom ignored him. "I think he's some kind of pansy Indian. Just what Wheelwright would like. She don't like real men."

They had all but forgotten Ree was there. She thought of how Frank Hamilton Cushing had written of slipping quietly to the edge of the crowd around the fire so the Indians would forget him and show their real selves. She felt like a real anthropologist, and right here in Wheelwright's kitchen.

"That's not true," said Charlie. "You've been out riding with him, Tom, you know he left us behind in the hills. He goes up god knows where and in all kinds of weather. Like to see you last that long with nothing but a pony, a blanket and a hat."

"But he's up there picking flowers, Charlie, that's my point. He's different, the Indians know that. They treat him different, too. Kind of scared of him."

"They think he's a witch," said the butler. "They believe in that."

"Those flowers are good medicine," said the cook. "He gave me some once, when I had that terrible cough. Tasted awful but it helped. He's just a medicine man. They're a dime a dozen among the Navajos."

"No, he's different," Tom continued. "I've known medicine men—remember Begay? I used to cut wood with him in the mountains. Tough as nails, I couldn't keep up. But it's not that Klah isn't good with a horse or tough for weather. No, it's something else about him. The only word I have for it is pansy. But he's not like the pretty boy artists in Santa Fe, either."

Tom had stopped joking and Ree could hear some anxiety in his voice. He wanted to understand Klah. She thought that was the thing about Klah, you couldn't make fun of him. He was different, but like the cowboy, she didn't have a word for it.

"I know what it is," said the cook. "I'm part Indian myself."

"Sorry," said Tom, "I didn't know that."

"I don't like people to know. Wheelwright doesn't. It's too hard to get a job. Anyway, most of the time I almost agree with you. My dad was a terrible man when he was drunk. But about Klah, he's what Navajo Indians call a nadle."

"A what?" murmured Charlie.

"It's someone who isn't all man or all woman. Some of the other Indians call them a berdache."

"I saw that at the traveling Wild West show," said Tom. "In the side show. It was a bearded lady, with a big thick beard. If you paid more money, you could see her bosom. And if you paid even more money, well, I can't tell you what they said you'd see."

"Did you see?" asked the butler.

"Didn't have the money," mumbled Tom. "Guy I knew did, and told me, though."

"Oh yeah," said Charlie, "I saw that once at a carnival. A hermitdyke, or something like that. Half his head was short hair and half a mustache, and the other half was long hair. Half his clothes were a man's suit, and the other half was a dress."

"How'd he go to the bathroom?" Tom asked.

The cook stood up. "It's different for the Indians. It's not a joke like that. It's a good thing. The Indians think so, anyway. They have the best parts of each. What's best about men and what's best about women."

They waited for the cook to say more when Wheelwright's voice burst in:

"Ree, are you there?" She was near the kitchen, but she hadn't come in.

Everyone jumped, and Ree thought they all looked at her pityingly.

The butler went to the doorway.

"Can I help you, Miss Wheelwright?"

"Miss Ree left her room some time ago and hasn't come back. I can't imagine where she's gone."

"Oh, dear," said the butler. "Let me help you back upstairs, and cook will bring you some warm milk while I look for her. I'm sure she's fine. Maybe she sleepwalks."

"Sleepwalks? I never thought of that," Wheelwright's voice faded as the butler walked her away from the kitchen.

"Quick," said the cook, spinning in her chair towards Ree. "Get going—" Ree headed for the door she'd come in, but the cook grabbed her arm. "This way," she whispered. She opened the door of a large cabinet, and pushed Ree into it. She snapped a light switch, which did nothing. "Damn, it's out," she muttered. "It's steep, tiny little stairs. When you get to the top, just push and you'll see where you are."

The steps were so shallow that Ree's heels hung over the back. Suddenly she crashed into a wall, but when she pushed it opened with a loud creak she found herself in the hallway near her bedroom. Down the hall, the butler was saying good night and reassuring Wheelwright that Ree was fine.

From then on, Ree often snuck down to the kitchen. It amazed her that she had lived in the house for weeks without knowing about the passage, which she now saw that the butler used often. It let out into a panel in the hall at the other end from Wheelwright's bedroom. She had only to pretend she had been to the bathroom and Wheelwright wouldn't know that she had been in the kitchen, or wouldn't let on if she did.

Sitting with the teapot brewing on the stove behind them, she felt she had made friends at last. The butler, the cook, and the stablehands Charlie and Tom were the first people she had met in New Mexico that she felt comfortable with, except for Ned, who she still thought about a lot but had no idea how to see again. Wheelwright probably knew what was going on, but chose to pretend she didn't. The old lady had some heart in her after all. No one knew why she never came into the kitchen, although that was one of the topics they discussed repeatedly. It just felt good to be with them and not just with Wheelwright or alone all the time.

Ree was disappointed that they never talked about Klah again in the same way. She wanted to hear more, especially from the cook, about Klah being a "nadle." There was a word for what he was, and that exhilarated her. To the Indians he wasn't a freak in a carnival. She had heard in anthropology classes that sometimes other cultures had a word with no equivalent in your own culture. She could tell that "pansy" was a bad word for how people saw Klah. So "nadle" was a positive word for this.

But why should it surprise her that the Indians had a positive word, because hadn't she always thought they had a better way of life? She had so many questions: could a woman be a nadle? Did her professors know about this? Did Ruth and Margaret? How come she had never heard of it before, in all the lectures, books and articles? Had her time at Columbia been for so little that she had to come this far to hear this important thing from a humble cook in a remote ranch?

Could she ask Klah if he knew the word? Could she ask Wheelwright? What an awkward conversation that might be, because Wheelwright had that quality, if a woman could have it. Something about her was too independent for a woman, but not masculine. Maybe that was why Wheelwright was so obsessed with Klah. Maybe Wheelwright was looking for the same answers that Ree herself was. Ree had spent her whole life with words, and here was a new one, but she was frustrated that she couldn't learn more about it. She wished she could use the library at Columbia and research this. Maybe the library in Santa Fe would have something. She had to get Wheelwright to let her spend time there.

One day Ree and Wheelwright were in the living room going over the transcriptions, when the butler came in without being called.

"Just checking if you might want some tea, ma'am," he said. "It's getting a bit nippy."

As he turned and walked away with his order, Ree felt he had signaled her to meet him. A few minutes later, she made an excuse and left. He was standing at the bottom of the stairs and waved to her to come down.

Ned was in the kitchen, drinking coffee with the cook.

"I came to see you," he said, "and to meet Hosteen Klah." He looked even handsomer than she remembered him. His high voice seemed to her to be who he was, rather than some freak of nature. The cook and the butler looked very curious.

"I can't stay," said Ree. "I have to get back upstairs. Wheelwright…"

She caught her breath and tried again. "I'm sorry, what a terrible way to say hello. Especially when you've come so far to see me. I'm so glad to see you. But I don't know what to do, because Miss Wheelwright is waiting for me. I've never had a visitor before."

"I think you should take Ned upstairs and introduce him," said the butler. "She's always interested to meet Indians who support her work with Klah."

"As long as she can listen in on you two, she'll be pleased," said the cook. "She likes to watch us Indians," he said to Ned.

"I understand," Ned said. "I've seen that before." He and the cook laughed. Ree and the butler stood by knowing they couldn't join in.

Ned avoided looking Ree in the eye, but she looked at him questioningly, remembering that he had said he didn't want Wheelwright watching.

Ned shrugged. "I really want to meet Klah, and nothing else has worked."

"You have to do it," Ree said. Ned smiled and finally met her eyes. A thrill ran through her, remembering the haymow. "How do we do this?" she asked the butler.

"Go back up," said the butler, "and I'll announce we have a visitor to see Mr. Klah. She doesn't need to know he came to see Ree. That's how I'd do it."

"Fine with me," said Ned.

Ree hurried back upstairs, trying to put a sober face back on, hoping Wheelwright wouldn't notice the color that had to be in her cheeks. Would Wheelwright remember seeing Ned with her in Santa Fe?

Wheelwright was puzzling over the latest transcript of Klah's chanting.

"Do you think this is eight repetitions here? It just shows seven, but it's usually eight." Not waiting for Ree to answer, she continued. "I'll make a note to ask him. He'll probably want to go through the whole chant again."

Minutes passed but there was no sign of the butler or Ned. Ree wondered ifNed had backed out. Finally, she heard footsteps on the stairs, and the butler entered.

"Miss Wheelwright, you have an unexpected visitor, Mr. Ned Leeds."

"Ned Leeds? I don't know the name."

"He's from Lost Wash. He has heard of your work with Mr. Klah."

Wheelwright smiled with self-satisfaction.

Ned was dressed as he had been the day Ree met him, in crisp dungarees, a sparkling white shirt, leather thongs tied around his biceps, and a leather medicine pouch hanging from his belt. He stumbled on the rug as he walked through the huge room, so bug-eyed was he at what he was seeing. Ree remembered how overwhelming she had found it on her first visit.

"Miss Wheelwright, I've heard so much about you and your work," he said, offering his hand. "I wanted to see. I hope it's all right. I'm Ned Leeds from Lost Wash."

Wheelwright looked at Ned with no sign of having seen him before.

"I'm pleased to meet you. This is my assistant, Ree," said Wheelwright. "Please have a seat." Ned winked at Ree as he sat down.

"So you've heard of my work with Mr. Klah."

"Yes, and I've heard of him for so long. I've always wanted to meet him."

"You're not offended or scared that he's preserving your heritage?"

"I know a lot of people are, and I have to admit you just never know what might happen, but I know that if it isn't done, a lot of this knowledge will die with him and the few others that know the old ways."

"I'm so glad you feel that way. Mr. Klah isn't here now, but we expect him back soon. Do you know anything you would like to share?"

Ned started to shake his head no, but Ree flicked her eyes at him.

"It might be something he told you already," he said.

"Maybe you have a variation," said Wheelwright. "That's always valuable. Lost Wash, hmm. Isn't that close to where Mr. Klah is from? Ree, take notes. Would you like coffee or tea?"

Soon, his head bent low and body swaying with the slow beat, Ned sang. His songs had something of the rhythm and sound of Klah's chants, but the words were few and uncertain. Ned repeated himself more than Klah did. But Wheelwright beamed happily. Ree saw a desperate look on Ned's face as he struggled with the words. Was he trying to tell her something? She shook her head slightly, not understanding.

"So have you heard this already from Hosteen Klah?" Ned asked. "Does his song sound like mine?"

"Somewhat," said Wheelwright.

"How so?" asked Ned.

Ree realized that he was faking the whole thing. He didn't know the secret chants at all. He was making it up. Was he doing all this for her? To be near her? She had to help him.

"I wonder," Ree asked in as natural a voice as she could. "Mr. Klah has a song something like that which goes" and she hummed it.

"I know that one!" Ned said, and proceeded to repeat it exactly, over and over. Wheelwright didn't catch on. Ned and Ree grinned at each other, even as her hand cramped from writing.

They went on like that for some time. When Ree suspected Wheelwright might catch on to the repetitions, she dug another song out of her brain from the hours spent with Klah and asked Ned if he knew it or a variation. Ned nodded knowingly and sang exuberantly.

Was Ned catching on to the nature of her role in Wheelwright's life? What was that role anyway? Did Ned think she was more intimate with Wheelwright than a transcriptionist? She wasn't, and she didn't want Ned to think this. She couldn't wait to get alone with Ned. How would that ever happen? Wheelwright was already treating him like a new exhibit in her growing museum of living Indians.

Ree had wished to see Ned again, so she couldn't complain that her wish was granted. But this was almost more frustrating. There was so much she wanted to say to Ned, and so much she hoped to hear. Yet as they sat with Wheelwright between them, Ree felt more than ever that she was Wheelwright's bird in a gilded cage.

Finally Wheelwright left to talk with the butler.

"Wow," Ned whispered. "Wow. Anyway, we pulled it off."

They both suppressed their giggles.

"When Klah's here," said Ree. "she just sits and beams at him. She was doing that at you."

"I can't believe she didn't catch on," Ned said.

"She worships Indians," Ree said. "She hangs on every word and movement."

"That's a lot better than whites beating us up," said Ned. "But it gets tiresome. How does Klah stand it?"

"He doesn't have to make stuff up. Wait a minute—."

They both broke up into smiles together.

"Or maybe he does," they said together. Ned reached over to put a hand over her mouth, because Ree began to laugh uncontrollably. His palm was calloused but small. She remembered how it felt that night in the hay at San Gabriel, and wondered what he was thinking. They both drew back, the laughter ending.

The butler came in to announce lunch. Since Wheelwright wasn't there, he whispered "How's it going?" and Ree and Ned both gave him a thumbs up. Ree felt the best she had since arriving at Wheelwright's. She had friends—the butler, the cook, the cowboys and Ned. They were all together. She felt a little bad for Wheelwright who could never be part of this and who probably desperately wanted to be. It made her think of those days in the cafeteria at Columbia, feeling so alone as she watched the rings of other girls chatter away. But Wheelwright had her own rich friends whose circles she fit into. Ree was so happy to not be so alone. She felt so close to Ned, even with the awkward memory of the haymow. Her future was falling into place! She was sure she would soon be living her Frank Hamilton

Cushing dream. As they went into lunch, she had to hold herself back from touching Ned. She wanted to run her hand along his bicep, which bulged in the leather thong.

When the butler announced that Klah was at his loom, Wheelwright beamed at Ned.

"Let's see what Mr. Klah thinks of you." She led them to the parlor with an expectant air of showing off a prize bull to a judge. Ree couldn't catch Ned's eye.

Klah looked up from his weaving to greet them, then turned back to his work. He had to have seen Ned but he didn't react. This left Wheelwright standing awkwardly, her hand upraised, her mouth open, ready to make an introduction. Ree was always interested in how Wheelwright handled awkward etiquette situations. She had made a game of outguessing her employer. In this case, she thought that Wheelwright would continue to make the introduction, after this slight pause of silence. But instead, she waved Ree to her usual place and pointed Ned to the window seat. She settled into her own chair. They all sat silently and watched Klah, who said nothing and continued his weaving. Time passed. Ree tried to look busy, taking notes on his hand movements as he wove, but she had seen this all before and noted it all down. Maybe his silence was in itself significant.

She expected Ned to get restless as any young man might from sitting still. But he looked content, watching Klah's hands move. He caught Ree watching him and smiled appreciatively.

The room was hot, the air still, and Ree was almost asleep when Ned spoke. He stood and walked close to Klah. Klah looked up, ran his eyes up and down Ned's body, and said nothing. What did he think of the small, hairless hands?

Klah said something to Ned in Navajo.

Ned nodded and they continued speaking in their own language, while Ree and Wheelwright sat by awkwardly. Ree sensed that it started out friendly, but Ned asked something that made Klah stiffen up. Ned got more demanding, almost pleading or promising, but Klah grew more adamant. Their talk died and Klah sulkily went back to weaving. Ned stood staring, his mouth working as if to find the right words. Then he said humbly what must have been 'thank you,' bowed slightly to Klah, turned to Wheelwright and said "thank you very much," and left the room.

Ree wanted to run after him. She looked at Wheelwright, who looked back at her as shocked as she herself felt. Wheelwright couldn't follow Ned, it would have been rude to Klah. If Wheelwright couldn't leave, then Ree couldn't leave. A low rumbling noise came from Klah and he beat at the weaving like a drum. It was the way he started his chants. As she turned to her notebook, Ree stretched her neck to see out the window and maybe catch a glance of Ned as he left, but the garden stayed empty, the gate closed.

As she wrote out Klah's words, Ree was desperate to talk to Ned. Why had the older man refused to teach him?

Hours went by. Wheelwright wasn't watching Klah as intently as she usually did, and after a while she walked out. Klah's chanting wound down after Wheelwright left, and he looked more thoughtful than transfixed as he wove. How could Ree find out what she wanted without asking what she so much wanted to ask?

"Mr. Klah, that design is so beautiful," she said, hoping to start a conversation.

"Not everyone can have what they want," Klah said and began to chant loudly again. This felt like his final word, reminding her of how her father would end conversations, especially when she wanted something he didn't want to give.

When they finally broke for dinner, the butler whispered to her that Ned had asked him to tell Ree goodbye and that he hoped to see her again. "Do you have any idea what happened?" Wheelwright asked Ree that evening, not even specifying what she was talking about.

"I guess whatever he wanted, Klah didn't want to give him."

"What do you suppose he wanted?"

"I think he wanted to study with him."

"Maybe they're rivals."

"Maybe he wanted herbs or flowers. The secret ones."

They shrugged at each other.

Ree had her own unanswered question. Why had Ned avoided what had happened that night in the hay? Wouldn't most men have indicated they wanted to pick up where they had left off? Was it something about Ned, or something about her that Ned didn't want? She pictured herself in Ned's arms, their bodies tight together. She let out a breath, shocked at herself.

Ree was becoming restless with the predictable daily routine when Wheelwright announced that the next day they would go to San Gabriel for lunch. Ree stumbled right into the grandfather clock in the hall, too filled with sudden terror to care about a stubbed toe. Her worst fear was that the women at San Gabriel would tell Wheelwright the truth about her, and she would be thrown back on the streets of Santa Fe again. That night she barely slept. She told herself she had lost everything before and yet things had worked out. She had lived through the disappointment of losing the fieldwork assignment and leaving San Gabriel, so if she lost her safe haven at Wheelwright's she would find something. But although her fascination for Wheelwright was nothing like her passion for Ruth, it had its own driving force. Whether happily working or sometimes exasperated by Wheelwright's attitude of entitlement and power, she would miss it.

What would happen when the women at San Gabriel saw her with Wheelwright? What would be said? How would she be disgraced?

When morning came, she forced herself to put on an agreeable face for breakfast on the verandah. If she could talk Wheelwright out of going to San Gabriel, she could buy some more time. She looked out over the distant hills.

"Have you ever ridden out that way? she pointed.

"Oh yes, would you like to do that sometime? It's wonderful, plenty of arroyos and rocks." Wheelwright was excited by difficult trails that terrified Ree.

"How about today?" Ree said, her voice cracking with doubt.

"We're going to San Gabriel today. I thought I'd told you last night. You'll love it, it's a wonderful place. It's the reason I bought this property and built Los Luceros." Just then the butler entered and Wheelwright gave him instructions for the gardeners.

This was her chance to tell Wheelwright that she had worked there. But how could she explain why she hadn't mentioned it in the job interview? Wouldn't it be easier to tell now, alone with Wheelwright at ease at her breakfast table, than at the dining table at San Gabriel, with others listening in and shaking their heads at her shame? She pictured Wheelwright pointing at her, gesturing for her to leave immediately. But Wheelwright was far too discreet for that. She would smile politely until they got out of site of San Gabriel, and then have the chauffeur leave her off on the road with her bags to be sent ahead to Santa Fe.

"San Gabriel is the most wonderful dude ranch," Wheelwright said, having dismissed the butler but keeping an eye on the gardeners. "The guests there are almost all women, and most are anthropologists. Why, haven't you heard about it from your Professor Benedict? She stays there often." Ree had hoped Wheelwright had forgotten that Ruth Benedict's name had come up during her job interview. Did Wheelwright know Ruth from San Gabriel? What if Ruth were there now? What would Ruth say to Wheelwright?

With Wheelwright going on about her good times there, it was too late to confess. It would be too humiliating to say she knew San Gabriel far better than Wheelwright did.

Breakfast ended with a bowl of fresh strawberries dusted with white sugar, a treat that Ree had learned was the only sweet Wheelwright served. She ate it with the glum feeling that it might be her last meal at Los Luceros. Each sweet bite felt like a train retreating in the distance, carrying the hopes and dreams she had brought to the Southwest.

Although they often rode horses near San Gabriel, Wheelwright ordered the chauffeured car for the formal visit, ending Ree's desperate hope that she would be sent off to deal with the horses while Wheelwright had lunch in the main house. To look as little as she did at San Gabriel as possible, she wore her frilliest clothes and pulled her curly hair back in a tight knot, which Wheelwright complimented.

Driving to San Gabriel, Wheelwright chattered about her good times there and her wonderful friend Mrs. Pfaeffle, whose husband had won the ranch in a card game.

"She married a cowboy, can you imagine? A woman of good breeding and education from the East! It's been a scandal. But she's the reason San Gabriel does so well. He can't do a thing but look good on a horse."

Ree knew the story, and the Pfaeffles, well, if from a distance. Since she had always reported to Senora Sanchez, the housekeeper, she had never directly spoken with either Pfaeffle, and hoped they wouldn't recognize her. As the car turned off the road to San Gabriel, she hoped that Senora Sanchez might somehow be gone. She was pretty sure Ruth and Margaret were far off in Zuni pueblo, because their stay at San Gabriel was to have been a brief one before a summer of field work.

As the car turned off the road and headed toward the dude ranch, Wheelwright chattered away about how much she enjoyed the informality and friendliness of San Gabriel. Too soon they were at the main entrance. The chauffeur held the door open while Mrs. Pfaeffle greeted them.

In her time working at San Gabriel, Ree had never entered through the front door, but had scurried in back doors and back stairs with the rest of the staff. Now she followed Mrs. Pfaeffle and Wheelwright through the grand hallway, glancing at the decorations. Cowboy designs were cut into the woodwork and banisters. Paintings of cowboys hung on the walls, with beautifully crafted cowboy hats,

lariats, boots, and spurs. Lamps and bookends had cowboy
motifs. Ree's eyes darted everywhere, looking for the person
who would betray her.

"I've got to come over and see how your garden is
coming along," Mrs. Pfaeffle was saying. "I'd never think to
plant an English garden in this climate. You're so bold to
try."

Wheelwright beamed as they sat down in the parlor.
Apparently they would be chatting for a while and then have
lunch with the guests, who were out for the morning ride.

Wheelwright introduced Ree as "this is Ree, an
anthropology student who is transcribing Mr. Klah's stories
for me. I thought she would enjoy meeting our neighbors."

Just as Mrs. Pfaeffle turned her attention to Ree,
Senora Sanchez stood in the doorway.

"A moment please, Mrs. Pfaeffle," she said. "There's
a question about the delivery."

"I'm sorry, Mary," Mrs. Pfaeffle said, "running a
business certainly takes a toll on the amenities." As Mrs.
Pfaeffle left, Ree saw Senora's face react to her. First she
looked angry, and Ree was sure she would tell her employer
about Ree as soon as they were alone. But then she had an
insinuating smile on her face, looking from Ree to
Wheelwright and back again. Ree realized that she probably
couldn't tell Mrs. Pfaeffle anything without implying
something about Mrs. Wheelwright that simply wasn't said
aloud. It was the way nothing was ever said aloud about the
many inseparable pairs of women among the guests. Even the
romances with cowboys were not spoken of, and
Wheelwright would never have mentioned Mrs. and Mr.
Pfaeffle if they hadn't been married. All the embarrassment
about sexual taboos might just work in her favor. Perhaps she
would write a paper on it for the *Journal of American
Anthropology*. Americans could be ruled by what some called
"primitive" beliefs just as much as any fellow romping
through a jungle eating grubs for food and wearing nothing

but a shell codpiece, because there were also those "taboo" things which could not be said aloud in American culture.

Mrs. Pfaeffle returned and settled back down again.

"I'm so sorry for the interruption," she said, turning to Ree. "Where were we? Oh yes, so you're an anthropology student. You must know some of the ladies who stay with us," said Mrs. Pfaeffle. "Many are anthropologists. What school do you go to?"

"Columbia University," Wheelwright said proudly, relieving Ree of speaking one more lie, since she no longer went there, although in the interview Sack had told Wheelwright they were both working on their dissertations. Outside, Ree could hear the guests returning from the morning ride.

"You must know Professor Benedict," said Mrs. Pfaeffle, "Isn't she wonderful?"

Ree nodded, knowing she could answer this without lying.

"You'll be delighted to hear that Professor Benedict will be joining us for lunch. She's working at Zuni Pueblo this summer, but she's back for a few days break from the sun..."

Ree didn't hear any more, because her last bits of hope and optimism drained out so fast that her toes and fingers turned to ice. Through the windows she studied the wide flat pinon-covered plain leading to the ring of crisp, jagged mountains beyond. She could excuse herself and before they knew she was gone she could run through the brush, hide for a few days, and then hitch back to Santa Fe. No, she couldn't go back there, she would have to go further, to somewhere no one knew her. Perhaps she could go to a pueblo to hide out. If she presented herself as a fugitive, maybe the Indians would take her in. Would they have more sympathy for white people who defied the laws? She didn't actually have to do something terrible, like rob a bank, she just had to imply that she had done so and hope they were sympathetic. It was a new way to make her Frank Hamilton Cushing dream work, and it conveniently meshed well with her immediate and desperate need to escape the humiliation that was about to fall on her at any moment. All she had to do was excuse herself and walk out that door and never see Wheelwright or Benedict again. Her future was in her hands. This moment was as decisive as when she had stepped on the train to go West.

Just then the dinner gong rang. Mrs. Pfaeffle stood up. "You'll love the meal today, Mary, it's your favorite lamb, cooked the way the Navajo people make it." Ree knew this wasn't at all true. As the cook had explained to her, no Navajo would eat lamb with mint jam, as the guests did. For the staff, the leftovers were made into a real Navajo stew, with potatoes and carrots and puffy fresh-baked bread, not dinner rolls. It had made Ree glad she was a worker, not a guest. But no matter how it was prepared, how much of the meal would she get to eat before Benedict exposed her? She had no appetite, but she had better eat all she could quickly, for she would soon be running for the hills. These clothes were not going to serve her well for that. Maybe she should just head for the highway right now while Wheelwright was admiring a new painting.

Mrs. Pfaeffle returned and led them into the dining room. Ree kept her eyes to the floor, which caused her to stumble into the woman next to her. They grabbed for each other so as not to fall. She looked up to apologize, and Ruth's big liquid eyes looked back at her. Ree had a momentary thrill, because she had never actually touched Ruth before, and just now her hands had been on Ruth's waist and elbow as she helped her up. Ruth gasped as Ree whispered "I'm sorry." Ruth started to say something just as Wheelwright asked "Ree, are you all right?" and Mrs. Pfaeffle said, "Mary, do you know Professor Benedict?" and introduced them. Ruth sat down next to Wheelwright, and Wheelwright motioned for Ree to sit on her other side. Ree was relieved not to face Ruth.

An aperitif of halved grapefruits was served. The maid serving Ree shook her tray, the crystal bowls clinked, and Ree looked up. The server met Ree's eyes. It was Johanna, who had slept in the room next to hers and who she had often talked to while waiting for the bathroom. Johanna had come West from a Pennsylvania coal town, filled with dreams of marrying a rich rancher, and had been disappointed to realize that most of the guests at San Gabriel were women. In their last conversation she had told Ree that she was asking the cowboys which dude ranch had rich men. Ree hadn't wanted to point out that rich ranchers were unlikely to stay at dude ranches. Now, she gave Ree a puzzled look. As she leaned over Ree's shoulder to put her dish down, she whispered "caught a fish, have you?" and rubbed her arm against Ree's shoulder affirmingly.

Caught a fish? What did she mean? But of course. Although Johanna hadn't wanted a woman, she had wanted a rich male patron. In her eyes, Ree had done it. And it was true. Ree had only had to bear up to Wheelwright's whims and tastes and endless desire to sit on her sofa listening to music and reading aloud, and she now had a life so much easier than poor Johanna, who had just been ordered to take a guest's grapefruit back to the kitchen to be sliced again. Ree sat at the table, enjoying fresh fruit that Johanna was not going to be eating after she had served, cleared, and washed up from this meal. In Johanna's eyes, Ree had attained her dream. Her fear that the servants would expose her was turning out to be quite the opposite.

But what about Ruth, still chatting with Wheelwright? Ree strained to hear, blocking out the other conversations, but caught only the word "Zuni." As long as the word wasn't "Henrietta" she was all right for the moment. What would Ruth be willing to say at the dinner table anyway? Wouldn't she want to take Wheelwright aside discreetly and warn her? If Ree stayed by Wheelwright's side, she could prevent that opportunity.

Other conversations lulled as everyone took interest in the animation with which Ruth and Wheelwright were talking. Ruth was explaining her current fieldwork.

Wheelwright asked questions, which gradually came around to Wheelwright telling Ruth about her work with Hosteen Klah.

"He's living in your house and you're transcribing the chants and stories?" said Ruth.

"Yes, I've hired transcribers to help me. Ree is my current helper. I'm surprised you don't recognize her. She is a student at your university." Ree's heart went to her stomach, which suddenly burned. This was the moment. She felt heavy, beginning her emotional walk to the death chamber. This was it, the moment had come, the game was up, it would all end now.

There was a long pause. The last thing Ree wanted to do was look up, but she felt all eyes on her, especially Wheelwright's, who she knew was beaming proudly, showing her off. She could sense Ruth struggling with how to handle the awkward situation.

"Oh, I'm sorry," said Ruth. "Of course, Henrietta. I'm sorry, I didn't expect to see you here. I hadn't heard that you had taken this position. It's quite an honor for you to work with so dedicated a supporter of our work as Miss Wheelwright. I'm so pleased you have hired one of our students, Miss Wheelwright."

"Please call me Mary," said Wheelwright. "I only want the best to work for me."

At that, Ree and Ruth's eyes caught. Instead of the suspicion she expected, Ree had her best chance ever to look deeply into Ruth's large pale dreamy blue eyes, and she saw something like the admiration Johanna had expressed with an affirming touch of her shoulder.

"What you learn from Mr. Klah is so important," said Ruth to Wheelwright, "So significant to our understanding of his people. I'm in awe that you have gotten him to open up to you. I know the difficulty of that."

"You're so lucky to work in the field and know so many of the Zuni people," said Wheelwright.

"Yes, but I feel I have so much more to say from the theoretical aspect. I have a book about comparative cultures that I'm working on between teaching and fieldwork, in the little time I have. It's such exciting work and I'm always so eager to get to it."

"Please tell me about it," squealed Wheelwright.

It was a side of Ruth that Ree had never seen, and not just because it was a private conversation rather than a lecture to a hall filled with attentive students. Like the bowing and scraping of the housekeeper and the serving maid, Ruth too was obsequious to Wheelwright, squeezing what she could out of the attention of this rich woman who could do so much to change her fortune. Even for a professor at Columbia, Ruth lived modestly. If she ever left her husband, Ruth would have to support herself and as the women students at Columbia knew well, the women faculty were not paid as much as the men. Had Margaret paid for the holiday at San Gabriel for Ruth and herself? Margaret never seemed concerned about money and had bragged of her family's home in a wealthy suburb of Philadelphia. Ree had heard that Ruth had grown up somewhat poor near Buffalo and had managed through a series of jobs and scholarships to become a professor.

She didn't want to see Ruth like this. She wanted Ruth to be ideal, to tower over all other petty humans, which was why Ruth's interest in Margaret was so grating to her. If Ruth was to love anyone but Ree, it should not be grasping Margaret. But grasping Margaret was Ruth's choice. Margaret wanted what Ruth could give her in field placements and job references and connections for a stellar career-to-be in anthropology. Ruth wanted Wheelwright to give her money so she wouldn't have to do the fieldwork she disliked. Ree was seeing Ruth from the other side of the table now. This was Ruth trying to get something from someone else instead of the Ruth who pushed away those who wanted something from her. Why did she have this need for Ruth, who took for granted the opportunity to do the work Ree dreamed of doing, who was not at all above human desires as she tried to manipulate Wheelwright to give her what she wanted?

Wheelwright seemed oblivious to Ruth's motives, happily bragging about her work with Klah. Without her money, would anyone even notice this awkward, unattractive aging woman with a high, unpleasant voice?

Ree sat back in her chair and sighed so loud that Wheelwright glanced back at her. Ruth wasn't going to embarrass Wheelwright by exposing her. Wheelwright had become Ree's protector. It was a phenomenon her professors described from field work in the Pacific. The Big Man, because of his wealth, fortunate marriage, and physical strength made everyone around him an extension of his invulnerability. Wheelwright's money was just the American form of an excess of yams and blankets. These genteel women with their delicate porcelain teacups were no different than the non-Bibled, non-schooled, and often non-dressed people in the jungles.

Ree wondered what would happen if she were to break these taboos and speak up: "Benedict and her student Margaret Mead are lovers!" and "Professor Benedict isn't telling the awful things I've done because she thinks Wheelwright will protect me and hurt her!" Because she didn't have the nerve to say these aloud, she felt compromised, small, and diminished, just another member of her own culture, fearing the anger of the gods as much as anyone on an island or jungle or tundra or plain. The cowboy decorations of the dining room might as well have been huge stone statues or piles of skulls or trees carved with grotesque faces, because she was as scared as anyone of the reprisals of the gods if she were to speak up against the local customs. She saw herself cowering in the grass as lightening bolts struck all around her, volcanoes rumbled in the distance, and great waves broke over her bobbing body. She wanted to be like Jonah, oblivious enough to sleep calmly in the hold of the ship while others cringed and screamed and cried out.

If she could only get to her dream of an Indian community, like Frank Hamilton Cushing had, she would be safe. She was even thinking of it as "her Indian community" now. Whatever gods the people there believed in, they weren't her gods and they wouldn't scare her. She was too comfortable living with Wheelwright, and it was slowing her progress. She had to move on. Wheelwright's house wasn't where she was supposed to be, and what whim of her employer would it take until the good fortune turned against her, and without even breaking the taboos, the protection would be taken away? Wheelwright was a protective god as false as the plaster casts of South American graven images she had seen in the Brooklyn Museum.

As the conversation turned to other topics and dessert served, Ree stopped thinking of running off into hills and thought instead of getting back to Los Luceros, this lunch behind her. She stuck by her employer's side as the meal ended and the guests scattered, many heading off for an afternoon ride. She lost sight of Ruth when Wheelwright turned back to speak to Pfaeffle. Ree waited on the verandah for the car to be brought up, when someone stepped close to her and whispered.

"Whatever you think you're doing here, working with Klah makes it harder for all of us!" Ruth's forceful tone shocked Ree as much as that Ruth was speaking to her.

"What Klah is doing makes the other Indians not trust us. If you keep this up, your career is over. The faculty will never allow this."

Wheelwright was watching them curiously. She had only a moment. Softly, but firmly, Ree whispered back.

"The faculty! They want it all, and they don't want anyone else to have anything."

Ruth's startled eyes stared back.

"Coming here, learning the Indian ways, that was my dream all those years, and since Columbia won't let me, I'm doing it without them."

"Go back to New York, and I won't tell anyone," Ruth said. "But you've got to stop this!"

"Would you let anyone stop your dreams?" Ree whispered back just as Wheelwright's car pulled up, and Wheelwright and Pfaeffle stiffly hugged goodbye. Wheelwright, never letting on that she had been trying to eavesdrop, headed for the car and Ree followed. As she sank into the deep leather seat, she caught a last glimpse of Ruth through the little triangular window. Ruth looked thoughtful, as if the words had touched her. At least Ree wanted to believe that.

She couldn't deny what Ruth said. She could be angry that Ruth wanted her to give up her dream, but it was true that working with Klah infuriated many Indians. If it got around that she was doing it, some would cut her off worse than the anthropology department at Columbia had.

Wheelwright was silent until the car wound along the private road to Los Luceros.

Probably Ruth had counted on Ree to not tell Wheelwright what she had said, as much as she had counted on Ruth to keep her own secrets. But she didn't have to cover up for Ruth.

"Professor Benedict doesn't approve of our work with Mr. Klah," Ree said, emphasizing the word "our" to show her own position.

Wheelwright ran her tongue around in her mouth, her forehead tightened, and her self-assured mask dropped further than Ree had ever seen it. Thinking of how two-faced Benedict had been, she felt sorry for Wheelwright.

"They just want to keep it all to themselves," Ree said. "They make all the rules so they can take credit for themselves."

"That's right," said Wheelwright. "I'm so glad you said that." The car stopped and the chauffeur opened the door, but Wheelwright made no move to get out. "Have you ever been to Boston Public Library?" she asked, then continued. "Oh, of course not, you haven't been to Boston.

But, I'm sure you've been to places like it in New York. It's a cold place with marble floors, big stairways, high ceilings, and huge portraits on the walls. The house I grew up in is like that. From my first trip West, seeing how different life could be, I knew that was everything I wanted to leave behind."

Ree nodded, picturing poor little rich girl Mary dwarfed by her monumental surroundings.

"The hot sun here made me feel so free of all that. But I'm always worrying that the East will stick out its cold skeletal hand and pluck me back, always telling me what I have to be."

"Not letting me be who I am!" broke in Ree. "Telling me how things have to be done!"

"Yes," said Wheelwright. "And Mr. Klah, old and respected as he is, has his own skeletons. I guess we three have something in common, different as we are. It gives me hope." She said the last without looking at Ree, while climbing out of the car, but Ree felt as close to her as she had ever been.

Ree had expected to hear from Ned after he left so suddenly, but no letters arrived. Every time a visitor was announced, her heart jumped, hoping he would show up unexpectedly again. Finally Wheelwright announced that they would go to Santa Fe for an afternoon.

While Wheelwright was having her hair styled, Ree got permission to go to the library and immediately set off for the Palace of the Governors next door. Which old woman on the portal was Ned's grandmother? She worked her way down the line, admiring the jewelry, trying to start a conversation, and finally asking each vendor if they knew Ned Leeds. After the first few vendors shook their heads, a woman walked up from behind and tapped her shoulder.

"What do you want Ned for?" she asked. She was one of the oldest women on the portal and had many strings of silver and turquoise necklaces.

"I just wanted to talk to him. You're his grandmother Frances, right? We met when I was here before.

"I might see Ned sometime. What's your name?"

"It's Ree. So Ned's not in Santa Fe?"

"I have to get back to work, but you can come," Frances said as she headed down the portal, stopping at a spot where the display of jewelry was covered with a blanket.

As she pulled off the blanket she said "You stand there and look like you've found something wonderful, and another tourist will come along and want whatever you found." She pushed a necklace into Ree's hand.

"I'm not exactly a tourist," Ree said. "I'm—"

"I hope you're not another of those anthropologists."

"I'm sorry," said Ree.

"Sorry! Don't you think it's interesting that the word 'apologist' is inside the word 'anthropologist?' You folks are always apologizing. Or you should be, except the ones that wouldn't think to."

"I'm sorry," said Ree.

"There you go again. Well, don't you folks ever talk to each other? How many of you can study one person?"

"What?"

"You should talk to all those others that want to study Ned. Are you one of the ones who pay? You don't look it. I know a few good stories myself, by the way."

Ree didn't know whether to get furious or laugh. Frances said everything with a twinkle in her eye.

"Ned's so lucky to have such a funny grandmother."

"You think I'm not serious? And who said I was his grandma?"

"Sorry, I just thought—"

"Did you say your name was Miss Sorry?"

Just as Ree started to answer, a real tourist pushed her nose almost into Ree's palm to look closely at the necklace she was dangling from her hand, having forgotten she was supposed to pretend it was wonderful.

"Can I see that? Are you buying it?" The tourist all but snatched it out of her hand. She was a tall white woman with a squash blossom necklace on, the kind that Ree felt should only be worn by Navajo women.

"Well, wait, I'm probably buying it. We were just talking about the price."

"Hold off a minute, will you? I know this jewelry well, I can help you out."

"Well, I guess you can see it," Ree said reluctantly.

The tourist turned it over, twisted it, and even bit it. She rubbed her finger on the turquoise. "How much does she want?" she asked Ree.

Ree turned to Frances, who named a price.

"Are you taking it?"

"I think—"

"Hold on. Let me take this into the sunlight," the tourist told Frances, moving without waiting for an answer. "Come on, I'll show you," she said to Ree. She walked to the railing and bent over the necklace so Ree had to bring her head close.

"Look, if you want it and we end up in a bidding war, one of us will pay far too much. I'll give you two dollars to let me have it."

Ree weighed the sure two dollars against helping Frances make some good money.

"I'd really like it. I'm going to offer her more."

"All right, three dollars to you to let it go."

"There's no point in this," Ree said. "They don't always sell to the highest bidder, either. Sometimes they sell it because they like you."

Without answering, the woman spun around and went back to Frances. Still holding the necklace, she pulled bills out of her purse.

"Here's the money."

"Wait a minute," said Ree. "I'll pay three dollars more." Frances looked at them both with an equal blankness.

"I'll pay that," said the woman. "It's such fine work. Did your husband do it?"

"Make that four dollars more," said Ree, trying to catch a sign from Frances. She didn't know when it would be safe to stop. If she went too high, the sale would be lost. And did Frances understand she couldn't buy it? What if she didn't? Frances would never help her find Ned.

Just then Frances said to the tourist, "You seem like the right person for this necklace. You really understand this silverwork. My grandson made it."

If she meant Ned, Ree wanted the necklace.

"I want you to have it," Frances said to the tourist. "I want you to have it for your last offer."

"Deal!" said the woman, gloating at Ree.

"You're so lucky," said Ree. "You're right. You sure know what you're doing. Maybe I should follow you around and learn how to trade like this." Frances shot her a look to be quiet.

The money was exchanged, and the tourist moved on.

"Thank you," said Frances.

"I'm glad I could help," said Ree.

"I am Ned's grandmother."

"Does he do the silverwork?"

"Oh no, that's my grandson. But Ned's learning."

"Don't you have to start really young?"

"Well, Ned had other things to learn then. Ned can weave beautifully."

"You're proud that he can weave?" Few Navajo men wove. Klah was an exception. Ree didn't think a family would brag about an aberration like this.

"I taught Ned myself."

So that was part of why he was so close to his grandmother.

"Want something to eat? I've got plenty." Frances offered her a puffy flat bread. "That's Navajo bread."

"It's so fresh."

"Baked this morning. Rises up with the sunrise."

"I bet you live in a beautiful place."

"Maybe. But why do you want to see Ned?"

"He came out to where I live. Where I work, actually, it's not my home. I work for Mrs. Wheelwright."

Frances drew back.

"Did Ned meet with Hosteen Klah?"

Ree didn't know what to say. She had already said too much. Ned would be angry at her.

"They met for a moment."

"Oh," said Frances. Ree was relieved she didn't ask any more. Just then a tourist wearing an obviously just-acquired woven poncho asked Frances about a ring, and then another tourist had a question about where the turquoise came from, and Ree had to decide whether to stay longer and risk saying more than Ned would want, or leave and let the trail run cold. Who were those other anthropologists studying Ned, and why?

She had to get back to Wheelwright and think up something to say about the library research she hadn't done. Frances was patiently answering the tourist's questions. Wheelwright had no monopoly on graciousness.

"I have to go," Ree broke in. "I'm so glad I met you. If you see Ned, will you tell him that Ree would really like to talk to him again? He can write me at Los Luceros."

"I will," said Frances. She smiled at Ree. "I'm glad I met you, too. I never know where Ned's going to be, but I'll tell him."

As the summer days grew shorter, the staff complained to Ree that when Wheelwright left for the winter, she wouldn't leave money to heat the house. There would be no leftovers from her meals. Someone that rich just didn't understand what it meant not to have a bottomless bank account to draw on. Picturing herself huddling with the staff by the kitchen fireplace together, counting the days until Wheelwright returned, she realized she couldn't spend the winter here. Although they were friendly in the summer, the staff would resent her as one more mouth to feed.

The only place she could think to go was Lost Wash. Her one beam of light in all this was meeting Ned. The more she thought and fantasized about Ned, the more she was convinced that he could solve all her problems. He could get her entrée to his community and get people to trust her and talk to her. He could bring her into Lost Wash like Frank Hamilton Cushing had been brought into Zuni by the chief. But what would it be like to be with Ned? How would they be together, if they were alone, without Wheelwright's gaze? Why did she feel so strongly about him, a feeling she didn't understand? Meanwhile, why was there no word from Ned?

As they watched the sun set far too soon after finishing dinner, Wheelwright talked about going back to Manhattan, where she lived in a women's hotel.

"Ree, have you ever worked in a store?"

Ree had occasionally worked at the front of the garment factory, where buyers would look at samples and put in wholesale orders. She had also been a salesgirl at Macy's department store during the Christmas season. But she didn't want Wheelwright to know that much about her. She wanted to keep up the appearance of having come from a middle-class background, not anything like Wheelwright's wealth, but from a comfortable home where young women did not work before marriage.

"No, I haven't."

"Do you think you could?"

"Why do you ask?"

"I've decided to open a store in Boston to sell Navajo rugs. Whenever people from the East see my rugs, they always ask how I got them. I think they would love to own them, and it would provide money for the Navajos. They get so little right now. Did you know the traders used to pay them by the pound? Even now, they don't get much for all their work and skill. I could make some money, too. I'm always worried I'll have to sell my island in Maine to keep Los Luceros."

Wheelwright had whined about this before, but it was hard for Ree to feel or act sympathetic.

"The store must be in a place where there's lots of money, but it wouldn't look right for me to be seen as a shopkeeper, so it can't be where I live in Manhattan. I want it on Charles Street on Beacon Hill, near where I grew up. You will be the manager in charge of the store."

Go back East! Ree didn't want to go to Boston, or anywhere backwards. The wages Wheelwright finally grudgingly gave her were saved in the bank. She had been thinking that when Wheelwright left, she would find a cheap place to live in Santa Fe, probably a boardinghouse for women, and try to get by until she found Ned and convinced him to take her to his home.

"I thought you wanted me to stay here for whenever Mr. Klah shows up."

"He's told me he won't be back this winter. He's promised to help his sister. Her husband has been sick. Anyway, you'll love Boston," Wheelwright said. "I think I'll call it the 'Carry-On Shop.' And I've purchased your ticket to Boston."

Ree was startled. She hadn't expected events to move this fast, but wasn't that what the servants had been saying? Wheelwright always acted as if her employees had no needs of their own.

"But I don't want to go to Boston. You should have asked me first," she blurted out.

Wheelwright stared at her.

"I don't want to go back East. All I've ever wanted is be in the West. It's a very generous offer." She said this even though there had never been an offer, just an assumption. "But I don't want to go. I want to continue with my dream that brought me here, which is to live with the Indians."

"I didn't know that was your dream."

"It's hard to talk about a dream. Sometimes it has seemed so impossible. Working here with Mr. Klah has brought me closer to it than I would have thought. I even know some of the language now. This has been a terrific opportunity. I want to continue this work. Your store in Boston will help the Navajo people make some money, but I want to be with them."

Wheelwright pinched her lips tight together.

"Who will run the store then? You could do it so well, and I can trust you. I know what! You can do it for just this winter and get the store going."

"It would feel like going backwards. It took me years to get here and I want to stay and continue studying the Indians."

Wheelwright looked out the window.

"All right," she finally said. "When are you leaving?"

This was not going the way Ree wanted it to. She didn't want Wheelwright bitter at her. She needed the reference, if nothing else. There was a lot she admired about Wheelwright, and she didn't want it to end with her running away, as she had from her father and San Gabriel. She wanted to think better of herself.

"I'm glad to work with Mr. Klah. But once you leave for Manhattan, I just assumed I'd leave also. I'm sorry, we've misunderstood each other. I should have spoken up earlier, but I didn't know what to say."

"I don't know why this keeps happening to me," said Wheelwright, turning away without looking at her. "There's a new recording that came in the mail today. Would you please put it on."

The discussion was over.

In the next few days, she reminded Wheelwright of her plans, hoping she might become a patron, but Wheelwright became more formal than ever. She hadn't found anyone to run the store. Whenever Wheelwright called in the butler and the housekeeper for many discussions about closing the house for winter, Ree was pointedly excluded. It was clear that on the day Wheelwright left, she should be leaving. She wondered how they would part.

Maybe Klah would help her. She waited to find him alone.

"Mr. Klah, when Miss Wheelwright leaves for the winter, I'm going to head for Lost Wash." She waited, but he continued to weave without acknowledging her.

Finally, Wheelwright's last evening at Los Luceros arrived. They sat in their familiar chairs in the corner of the living room, the fire crackling and comfortingly warm. Ree knew that the butler resented every log on the fire, since he would have less to heat the kitchen and the servant's living quarters all winter.

Wheelwright said nothing about the future, just sat in her usual daze, listening to a recording. She asked Ree to continue reading to her from *Vanity Fair*. It was the section where the Thatchers are shunned by their friends after they lose their money. Ree knew that Wheelwright would never see the connection between the class differences in the books they read aloud and her own treatment of people around her.

Ree put the book down. Wheelwright was awake, but said nothing.

"I wish it wasn't ending like this," Ree said, shocked at her own boldness, but what was there to lose at this point? "I've enjoyed working for you and especially working with Mr. Klah. I need to go on with my work. Don't you think I can do more for the Navajo people here?"

After a long silence, Wheelwright spoke. "It's just I have such plans for the store, which will do so much for Mr. Klah's people. I thought I was also helping you to have employment. I feel you are ungrateful."

"No, I'm very grateful. I just don't want to go back."

"I see. And what are you going to do for the Navajo people?"

This was her big chance.

"I'll live with them and be more than an anthropologist studying them." Saying it, she saw how unlikely it was. Why would they want her there? Just then a log fell to pieces in the fire, sending up a blast of sparks. Her fantasy world of Ned and Frances crumpled just like that. Even Wheelwright would know this wasn't going to work. She saw herself running through her nest egg all too quickly in Santa Fe and then back on the streets again, with nothing.

"That's very brave of you," Wheelwright said. "It sounds like Frank Hamilton Cushing. I hope you have the luck he did when they took him in."

"He's my model, "Ree said. "That's the dream that's driven me this far."

"But he had a whole expedition behind him," Wheelwright said, "and a museum and a magazine. He wasn't on his own." Ree knew that she meant well, but each word hammered her.

"I know, but this is all I have. But all I have is how much I want to do this. That has to count for something."

"I admire that," said Wheelwright. "It's something I've dreamed of doing myself. Please write and let me know how it's going."

"Of course I will. I hope we'll stay friends."

Wheelwright smiled so happily that Ree was glad money was not involved. She had always thought that Wheelwright was desperate for a true friend, but she had to admit that she was, too. Things could have gone differently, but she didn't know how.

Part 5

Ree stood far enough away that she hoped no one would notice her. It was hard to approach this little shack of rough boards with bark showing, hammered into a frame and chinked like a log cabin. There were no windows on the side she faced, but still she felt watched. The sign said "Food" and she should have felt welcome, but she didn't. What she did feel was hungry.

Wheelwright had left Los Luceros first, leaving Ree without a ride to Santa Fe. The staff had shrugged knowingly. The butler flagged down a mail driver to take her. He protested that he was heading toward Ship Rock, but Ree gleefully took this as a sign that she should head directly for Navajo country.

The mail driver hadn't stopped for all the hours of the long bumpy ride. He had begrudged picking her up, and he hadn't shared from the food he occasionally nibbled out of a tin lunch box. She had been so glad for the last minute ride that she hadn't had time to pack a meal from whatever the kitchen staff might not notice missing. She couldn't stop thinking about which she wanted more, water or food. She tried instead to picture the mail truck leaving her at a trading post, where a generous meal would be served up by a lonely trader's wife eager for a woman to talk with.

As she looked at the unpromising shack, she knew that was just her fantasies running wild again. She was in the real Wild West now, where it was every man for himself, and bullets and life were cheap. She laughed at her joke, squared her hat, and decided to stride into the food shack with all the confidence she could pretend to have. She took long, strong steps, her suitcase firmly gripped, holding her head high and straight with pride because she was in Indian country at last. No longer on her way, she was walking into the adventure she had chosen back so long ago in Brooklyn.

Instead of a door to the shack, a moth-eaten, scraggly Navajo rug hung like a curtain. It was one of the heavy old rugs made when the traders paid by the pound. The weight caused it to hang straight and not flap in the wind, and she had to put her bag down to push it aside. Having lost some of her confident posture, she went through the curtain and immediately collided with a waitress who stumbled, then straightened up, her stack of used coffee cups wobbling, but not falling. Ree, the waitress, the cook who was leaning over the counter, and two Indian men frozen with their tortillas held in midair all let out a sigh of relief and then laughed. The waitress, wearing what Ree recognized as a Harvey girl apron, but cinched up several times for her short round Navajo body, laughed loudest.

"Din't ya see the sign that sez knock first?" wheezed out one of the men.

Ree felt her face redden even more than her latest layer of sunburn.

"I'm sorry, I didn't, I'm so sorry, are you ok?" This caused everyone to laugh even harder. The waitress put the stack of cups down on the counter, where they tottered and one finally fell off, crashed and bounced, setting off a new round of laughter.

"I'm so sorry," said Ree.

"It's ok," gasped out the waitress. "Not much happens here. This is pretty much our excitement for the day, wouldn't you say, Joe?" The cook nodded.

"You must be one of those anthropologists," said the waitress. "I thought they had all left us in peace for a while." She drew back the rug and looked out.

"How'd you get here anyway?" she asked. "I don't see a car or a horse."

Ree wished they hadn't pegged her for an anthropologist so soon. When Frank Hamilton Cushing arrived at Zuni pueblo, they thought he was a fur trapper or a soldier, because they had never seen an anthropologist. It was only after he had lived with them that they learned to watch out for more.

"I got a ride with the mail truck," said Ree. "I'm not an anthropologist. "I'm an ---." But she didn't want to start off lying to them. She had done way too much of that this summer.

"I'm an —," she stuttered again. They all stared at her skeptically. "Well, I sort of am. I've studied it. But I'm here because I want to learn about your ways."

"They all say that," said the waitress.

"Are you or aren't you?" asked one of the customers. He had rolled his tortilla into a cigar-like tube and was delicately nibbling little bites from it. The other man had already finished his and was licking the last of the beans from his fork.

"I'm here on my own," said Ree, "I'm not with any school." She hoped this would impress them, but instead the man eating beans ran his eyes up and down her body. She was vulnerable here, a woman without the protection of a man or a school, which was a surrogate for a man. But Navajo men weren't known for aggressive behavior toward white women, or white men. It was one reason why she had wanted to be here instead of in Apache or Ute country.

"Jenny—" said the man who had been eating beans, holding up his coffee cup as if saluting the waitress.

"Drinks a lot," muttered the cook. "Yes, Drinks a Lot" said the other customer and held his tortilla tube as if pouring coffee from it. "That should be his name." Ree was relieved their attention had moved off her.

"And what would you like?" the waitress asked Ree.

"French toast or eggs Benedict?" asked Drinks a Lot.

Ree looked for a menu or a sign with prices.

"He's a troublemaker,' said the waitress. "We've got eggs on Navajo taco, take it or leave it."

Ree hesitated.

"Ten cents," said the waitress, and Ree nodded gratefully.

"So, what do you want to learn about my people?" smirked Drinks a Lot. Ree thought back to an article she had read that said hat Navajo people never asked direct questions. Maybe she could debunk that for her next publication.

"It's none of your business," snapped the waitress.

"Sure it is. She came in here, it's our business."

"No, it's my business," said the cook. "Built it up from my first tortilla sold out of a bucket. If you want to keep coming in here, Joe, you'll remember that."

"Sure, I know that," Joe hung his head just the littlest bit. "But you know I didn't mean it that way. What are you doing here? What's it mean to be 'sort of an anthropologist?' Got kicked out of school, did you?"

Was he seeing right through to all her failure and shame?

"Maybe she didn't like school any more than you did. Maybe she didn't want to be one of them," said the waitress. Someone was sticking up for her! Ree wanted to sink into the arms of the soft, round woman, wanted to bury herself in the mountainous breasts under the white apron, wanted to be held while she cried out all the loneliness and fear. Having someone defend her made her feel it all. She shook her head to drive the thoughts away. The waitress turned back to slicing into a peach pie.

"That's right," said Ree. "I didn't want to be one of them. I just want to learn—" she had to be careful. How could she phrase it? It was the condescension of her colleagues that she hated. "They—." Everyone in the diner waited for her next word, ready to judge her. She wasn't one of them and she wasn't one of the anthropologists. It was as if she had to invent herself as something totally new. Had Frank Hamilton Cushing felt this way when he first arrived at Zuni pueblo? He had come with some others on the exploratory Hemenway Expedition, but he had stayed on. How had he explained himself?

All the dark-haired, dark-eyed, round faces stared at her. They were a tribe, looking at a woman alone, trying to fit her into their ways of categorizing the world. Ree had studied the myths of many Indian tribes, compared them and found the commonalities. There was a story for every human possibility, so there must be a story these people had that would explain her. What story would that be? Had Klah told it? Back at school, it had all been sorted out, labeled, charted neatly in her notebooks. But at this moment, her mind went blank. Or rather, it was filled with coyotes, ravens, turtles, and bears all scurrying across her brain, but none stopping to help as they so often did in the stories.

"I just want to learn." She almost said, "to listen to your stories," then realized that nothing would label her more as an anthropologist than that. "I just want to learn how you live. The way I live hasn't worked well for me. I don't like the city and the people there. I heard that you know better ways. I just want to try."

"We don't run schools for white people," said Joe. "They send us to school. Haven't you heard?"

"Joe, be quiet," said the waitress. "Give her a chance."

"I've heard, "said Ree. "I've heard about those schools and I think it's terrible. I think white people should be sent here to learn how to live by your ways. That's what I want to do." It had never been so clear to her before. Already she was learning, from the kindliness of the waitress to the brutal honesty of the customer. It was no wonder she didn't want any more of the hypocrisy back at Columbia. People who wouldn't tell her to her face that they wouldn't give her a field assignment, or even tell her why. Ruth and Margaret and the farce they put on every day, pretending to be like all the other women when they were no more that than she was as they hid their love away.

"We don't have any school like that," said Joe. "You want to start one?"

"No, I just want to learn. I don't have any grand plans. Just want to find a place for myself here."

"We'll just clear out a room for you," said Joe, and she looked at him with hope, until he finished, "there's an empty hogan right down the road." Ree knew that meant someone had died there and that no Navajo person would enter it. She didn't know how to answer politely.

"I wish I could think of something," said the waitress.

Joe shot the waitress a glance that in any language didn't look pleased. He slammed his cup on the table and walked out, throwing a dime on the counter.

"Too much coffee," said the waitress. "Don't mind him. But this probably isn't the place for you. Too many think like he does."

Thankfully, a mining company truck pulled in and she caught a ride to a trading post in the Crystal Mountains, north and west of Los Luceros. She was surprised by the mountains and woody greenery, expecting more flat, desolate land dotted with rocky towers. Seeing this forlorn trading post lost in Navajoland, she realized that what was called a trading post in Santa Fe might as well have been Macy's. The Santa Fe store had been a large emporium where she had to walk carefully to avoid knocking over piles of food, cooking supplies, tools, clothing, rugs, pots, and toys. This dark adobe had almost bare shelves, holding only a few boxes of crackers, canned tomatoes and peaches. A few dusty white-speckled blue enamel pots and ladles hung from hooks behind the cash register.

At the counter, a Navajo woman talked to the clerk. He was a tall white man with a distinguished face, the kind of man she had often seen striding the Manhattan streets in their sharply-pressed business suits. But this man wore a grimy white apron over blue dungaree overalls with no shirt. His sunburned skin was peeling in the way of people who could not tan. He towered over the tiny and cringing woman, holding a rug up, showing her how the light coming through the dirty window showed through holes in the weaving.

"No one's going to buy this when there's so much better out there. Work slower, be more careful, Attencia. Isn't that what your name means, 'attention?'"

She answered softly in Navajo. A Navajo man stood at the other end of the store looking at some tools, listening intently while trying to appear disinterested.

"No, I won't try to sell it. My customers expect quality, and this isn't it." Ree wondered if the woman understood anything he said beyond 'No.'

"And I can't give you any more wool, it's a waste. Take this one apart," he said, handing it back to her. Just then he saw Ree. "Can I help you?" he called out, turning away from the weaver.

"Just browsing," said Ree, as if they were in a well-stocked grocery in New York. She pulled a can off the shelf and read the label. Her last hitch had left her here and she had no idea what to do next. The weaver stepped back from the counter and slowly walked toward the man who had been listening.

"Golney," called the storekeeper to the man, "I can use rabbit skins if you can hit them in the right place for a change. I can't sell them full of buckshot."

There was a Navajo wagon and mule tied out front. Ree could offer to pay them for a ride further into their country. Clearly they needed the money. She walked up to the man.

"I was wondering if I might get a ride with you."

He stared at her without answering.

"I have some money—I mean, I can pay a little. How much would it be to go to your town? Where you live. I mean." The storekeeper had an amused smile on his face as she struggled, but didn't offer to help. Maybe the man didn't speak English. But the storekeeper had spoken to him in English. The Navajo man looked at his wife and jerked his head, indicating she should go out the door. The woman walked slowly, looking at the big jar of peppermint candies on the counter. Ree decided he wasn't going to answer, so she shrugged and turned away from his increasingly angry glare.

Suddenly turning toward her, the man asked "What would you want in 'my town'?"

The woman stopped in front of Ree and held the rug up by two corners, her eyes asking if Ree would like to buy. For a moment the man held his anger. It was a lovely rug, brown and white striped with diamonds of red, but the weaving was tight in some sections and loose in others. After a summer of watching Klah weave, Ree knew what an artist could do. This was the work of a normal woman, but they were all expected to weave, regardless of talent or interest. It reminded her of the garment factory, where she could sew well enough to keep her job, but she could never have been one of the fine needle workers who added embroidery or made custom-fitted clothing. Just being born Navajo didn't mean being born a fine weaver. She wondered if this woman wanted to escape her life's destiny as much as Ree wanted to leave Brooklyn. Perhaps the woman dreamt of going to New York.

The two waited for her answer.

"It's very beautiful," Ree said to the woman. "I wish I had the money for it."

"What do you want in 'my town'?" the man asked again.

"I just want to live there," said Ree, before she thought.

"You're rich enough to live where you want, but you can't afford a rug to stand on," said the man. "Go home to your own town. And take that moneygrubber with you—"he indicated the storekeeper with his chin.

"Get the hell out, Golney," said the storekeeper. "And don't come back. You don't talk to white women that way." Golney glared at him, pushed his wife, and walked out.

"You can't let them get uppity," said the storekeeper to Ree. "And you shouldn't be out here alone. What are you doing here anyway?"

Through the open door, Ree watched Golney grab the rug from Attencia and shake it in her face, an angry parody of the storekeeper's actions. Attencia looked at the ground, stepping back from him, afraid of a blow. Just then they saw Ree watching. Golney pushed Attencia's shoulder and stomped off, jumping onto the seat of the wagon, while Attencia scrambled to join him.

Ree was shocked. Didn't the Navajo women own the possessions and bring in the money with their weaving? Shouldn't she have been the one in power? This looked no different from so many couples she and her father had boarded with over the years, ignoring the occasional sounds of arguing and then wails of pain. She wanted the Navajos to be different, to be serene and gentle, like Klah. But Klah didn't have a woman, as far as anyone knew. She couldn't picture Ned hurting anyone. She thought of the day they had sat on the grass together and talked. He was everything she had imagined about Indians, and nothing like what she saw now as Golney snapped the reins and the wagon drove away, Attencia sitting so far from him on the bench seat that she could have fallen out. She was glad she had seen this before getting a ride with them, but now she had nowhere to go again.

"If you're looking for those anthropologists, they went through about two hours ago. Heading to Mummy Cave. But where's your car?" said the storekeeper.

"Oh, I just missed them this morning and I'm hitching to catch up. Do you think another ride will come along?"

"You better hope so. You better hope it's not another fellow like Golney. He'd as soon kill you. There's no place to stay around here. Did you want to buy anything?"

"Usually the Navajo people are so friendly."

"If you're buying their rugs and skins they are. It's all about money with them. Some of them just can't make it, like those two. Probably starve again this winter and expect us hardworking taxpayers to take care of them."

Ree had read about the hospitality of traders back in the early days of Southwest exploration, when a visitor would be invited to join at the table and given a warm bed for the night. Clearly those days were over, even in this remote site. The trader didn't offer her a cracker from the barrel. She bought a few and waited by the cold woodstove, as far as she could stand from where he sat behind the counter, polishing silver jewelry, bent over protectively as if he feared she would pull a gun on him. Many of the books she had read were memoirs by traders, filled with stories of their adventures. This fellow had no stories, no crackers, and no patience with her. She knew he wanted her to leave so he could go back to his solitude. Perfect job for him! Through the open doorway, she looked far into the empty miles, wondering if he would ignore her until she starved.

When a small wagon pulled in and a little old Navajo woman stepped out, Ree ran right out to talk to her. With hand motions and the few words they had between them, the driver understood that Ree was alone and wanted a ride to Lost Wash. The woman, whose name was Augustina, asked why she wanted to go there. How could Ree explain it with almost no words? What was the name of Ned's grandmother? "Frances Yazzie" popped out of her mouth and Augustina nodded with recognition. I can throw Navajo names around! Ree told herself, and she felt proud, part of the new land where she had chosen to live.

Instead of having a white canvas top, like all the other Navajo wagons, this wagon had a barrel-shaped roof covered with cedar shakes. Ree sat on the buckboard next to Augustina, who dozed as the mules kept up their slow rhythmic pace. At one point the reins slipped from her hands, but the mules didn't seem to notice. Ree was unable to resist taking the reins. The mules perked up their ears knowing something was different, but plodded on, following a barely perceptible trail through the desert. At one point a mule staggered against a rock and the wagon shook. Augustina woke up, reached out for the reins, saw Ree holding them, smiled and went back to sleep.

Riding along, Ree felt excited to be away from Wheelwright. She could make her own decisions, set her own schedule, and go where she wanted. She had pointed a course north toward Ship Rock and Lost Wash, choosing not to go to Santa Fe and cling to the familiar. Now no one knew where she was. It was scary and exciting. It was more than Margaret or Ruth would risk. Her mind was on the future, on finding Ned and Frances and Lost Wash. She was far from the students and faculty at Columbia, far from her father's home in Brooklyn, far from that other life she had lived.

Every minute she was farther from the strange, restricted life she had lived at Wheelwright's. She was sure she could handle hardship, even after having had the brief easy life of a rich woman's companion. The freedom filled her with energy.

She loved Augustina's wagon. It was a wooden cabin on wheels, with a woodstove and a stovepipe. The inside of the wagon was much like a hogan, with hooks on the walls to hold Augustina's hat, cooking pots, weaving tools, and some clothes. Most of the floor was soft with piled up rugs and blankets, creating one big bed. There was a small loom affixed to the floor and a rug in progress. The ceiling was painted blue like the sky.

As the sun went down there was nothing but empty trail ahead. Augustina guided the mules across some bumpy terrain, ending up at a lone tree with a waterhole, much to Ree's amazement. She let the mules loose to drink, anchored by a simple tether. They slurped happily. Augustina took some firewood from a shelf underneath the wagon and made a fire. Soon she was patting flour and water into tortillas. She pulled a cast iron pot from what appeared to be countless niches and hiding places and drawers and shelves to the wagon. The pot was filled with beans swollen from soaking, and soon they were eating hot bean tortillas with melted cheese and chiles. What Ree suddenly wanted to do more than anything else in the world, even more than finding Ned, was to stay with Augustina, be her apprentice, and learn all these skills. She would live in her own cozy wagon, knowing all the trails and tricks of the road, free as a bird, free as a lizard, freer even than most Indians.

The sunset was the most beautiful Ree had ever seen, or maybe it felt that way being here. Augustina pulled out a thick blanket and handed it to Ree. Then she climbed into the wagon, apparently turned in for the night. Ree wished she could sleep in the wagon, but she settled on the ground, her suitcase for a pillow, the stars coming out, feeling that all her western dreams were coming true at last.

At what seemed like the middle of the night, Augustina woke her as she lit the fire. There wasn't a crack of sunrise, but Ree saw she should get moving, for Augustina had made coffee. Soon they were on the road again.

As they rode on, a Navajo horseman appeared and rode alongside, keeping time with the wagon, chatting with Augustina. Her hostess pointed her chin at Ree with a puzzled look. The horseman startled Ree when he spoke in English.

"Why do you want to go to Lost Wash?"

Ree wasn't sure what to say. It had been the simplest answer to Augustina to say the names of Frances and Ned, but now she was afraid that would presume on their hospitality. Plus, the horseman would surely get there before the wagon, and she hoped to surprise them.

"I heard it was a beautiful place," she said. "I heard there are nice people there. I wanted to see for myself."

"Oh, an anthropologist?" said the Indian.

"I used to be. I don't feel like one much anymore. To tell you the truth, I got kicked out of school."

"That's great," he said. "Glad to meet you. My name's Tom Billy."

"I'm Ree. I love this wagon. I've been wishing to learn more about it, but Augustina and I don't have enough words between us. Can you tell me what it is?"

"That's a sheepherder's wagon. You can go out for months in that with the sheep. Grandmother Augustina has just delivered her sheep in Two Gray Hills, and now she's heading back home."

"Does she live near Lost Wash?"

"Not too far."

"Can you tell her that I thank her so much for her hospitality? She's been wonderful."

Tom Billy and Augustina talked for a few minutes.

"She said she's worried about you. A woman alone out here!"

"She's alone here, also."

"But she knows all there is to know. She can survive out here even better than I can."

"I would love to learn from her. Do you think she would take me as a student?"

Tom Billy laughed and said something to Augustina. They both laughed.

"I'm serious. I'd like to live the way she does, in a little wagon."

"You ever herd sheep? They're dumb and dirty and stubborn."

"I could learn. I want to learn." He was probably right, but she wanted to live in the little wagon so much.

"How do you get a wagon like this? I'd love to live in one. Even if I didn't get to have sheep." She tried to sound regretful.

"Are you thinking of spending the winter in Lost Wash?"

"I'm hoping."

Tom and Augustina talked.

"She'll rent it to you. She doesn't use it in the winter. You know how to use the woodstove?"

"I could rent it! That's wonderful! I can learn about the stove. I'd like to learn from her. How much to rent it?" Her heart was in her throat, she wanted this so much. While the two talked, she pictured her little wagon pastured for the cold weather not far from Frances' hogan, with easy walking to wherever Ned stayed. Would Ned be there in the winter?

"She'll rent if for five dollars."

"For a month?" How many months could she afford?

"No, that's until spring. She'll need it back as soon as the ground thaws."

"Five dollars for the whole time!"

"I'll tell her to ask for more."

"No, please, don't!"

He laughed. "OK, I won't tell her. She thinks it's a pretty good deal. Usually it just sits outside her hogan. She wants you to come home with her, so she can teach you all about it. When you're ready, she'll drive you to Lost Wash and then she'll take the mules back. You'll need to arrange for a place to keep it in Lost Wash, but between you and me, there's a lot of empty land there. If the people there don't mind you being there, they'll rent you a place to stay. Just as long as you tell them you got kicked out of anthropologist school."

She loved the way he smiled at her. Maybe the Navajo people were her lost tribe that she had been searching for all her life. She reached a hand to shake with Augustina, who instead smiled at her. From her wallet she pulled out five dollars and held it up. Augustina took it and it disappeared into her clothing immediately. That was a big chunk of her nest egg, but Ree could not have felt happier, and in a strange way, she could not have felt more secure. She had a house, she had a teacher, and she had a likely plan to live in Lost Wash.

She was so exhilarated she almost asked if they knew Hosteen Klah. She wanted to break more common ground, but what if they reacted as Frances had? It wasn't going to make her any friends to let it be known that she had been getting their secrets from him.

"Well, I've got to get going," Tom Billy said. "I come to Lost Wash once in a while. I'll watch for your wagon. Good luck to you."

After he left, she wondered how Augustina would teach her with so few words between them, but the lessons started right away with learning to drive the mules, to the extent that they were actually driven. When they stopped for the night, Augustina showed her how to make a fire and store the firewood. Ree felt she was living her Frank Hamilton Cushing fantasy at last.

The next day as they pulled off the little road that there was, Augustina beamed and Ree understood that she was heading home. She felt sad that she had no place to feel that way about, but she could think of the little wagon as her home for now. She hoped Augustina would leave the soft blankets and rugs for her to use. She wished she had asked Tom to find out. She would just have to see, and if not, she would somehow have to get what she needed. If only she could find a way to make money. There was a trading post at Lost Wash. Maybe the trader could use some help.

Before she saw it, camouflaged by dirt walls that blended in with the land around it, they stopped beside a hogan. As the wagon pulled up, children ran out, followed by a young woman with a baby at her breast. They hugged Augustina, then stopped in their tracks seeing a strange white woman on the wagon. Augustina jumped down and Ree followed, stumbling a little.

Ree spent the next few days with Augustina. Without words, she showed Ree all the tricks of living in the little house on wheels. She rubbed the mules' ears and held out corn for them to nibble, then gave Ree some corn to do the same. She showed her how to build a fire, and how to warm or cool the house.

Augustina was training her granddaughters to be shepherds, and Ree eagerly joined them, although the girls thought it was hilarious and Augustina didn't seem to think it was proper etiquette for a guest. They walked the sheep far from the hogan, Augustina showing her where to find water. Walking in the sun. Ree was glad it was autumn. Finally they reached a slightly grassy area where Augustina left the younger girl with some sheep and walked on with the older one.

"Can I stay?" Ree asked. Augustina would think she was tired of walking, but Ree wanted to see what it was like to stay with the sheep. Augustina walked away, leaving Ree with the little shepherdess, Lilly, who giggled and hid her face when Ree looked directly at her. They huddled in a spot of shade under a butte. The sheep clustered along a tiny spring where more grass was visible than there had been on the whole walk so far.

The sun was high and Ree groggily watched the cloudless sky. The sheep didn't need any attention.

Everything was slowed down and peaceful. Had she ever spent so much time so calmly, with no work to do? Even if sheep were dirty and stubborn and dumb, she wanted to be a shepherd and live in the sheepherder's wagon and roam this beautiful land.

And beautiful it was. She had a momentary image of herself, leaning on a rock with Lilly and the sheep nearby, but in the middle of Central Park watching the new skyscrapers grow. But she had never sat quietly in Central Park. Back home, she was always too busy, always working, studying, planning, or worrying.

Was she thinking the Indians had carefree, lazy lives? She knew that wasn't true. In the time she had spent with Augustina, the woman had showed her many conveniences of living in the wagon, but each one took work. Augustina chopped firewood, cleaned the stove, repaired the wagon, prepared each meal from basics of flour, salt, sugar, lard, and beans, and fixed the wagon wheels which apparently broke often against the rocks of the road. That was all in addition to caring for the sheep and weaving. At home she took care of the grandchildren.

Augustina also cleaned, spun, dyed, and wove the wool from her own sheep. Ree knew how painstaking this was from watching Klah. She wondered if Augustina lived off the sheep income alone, or if it all depended on weaving. For the little girls who were growing up out in the sun, learning their responsibility for a major part of the family income, it could not be carefree.

A shadow covered her and she opened her eyes, which she hadn't realized she had closed with relaxation. The sun glared in a corona over Lilly's shoulder, for the girl was leaning over her. It was so cool she wished she could ask Lilly to just stand there. The little girl looked curious. There were so many questions she would love to ask Lilly about her life, and Ree realized that the girl probably felt the same about her. Ree sat up and smiled. It was all she could think to do.

Lilly pointed past the sun and looked at Ree questioningly, then pointed in the opposite direction, and then the two others. At first Ree thought she was referring to the Navajo rituals concerning the four directions, but then she realized it was a question: from where did Ree come? She discerned which way was east and pointed to it, saying "New York City." Lilly didn't react to the words, but nodded her head at the direction, then pointed toward herself and east again, indicating she wanted to go there.

Ree's inclination was to say, "oh no, you don't want to go there when you have this beautiful home, the most beautiful in the world," but she stopped herself, understanding that this child's wanderlust was like her own. A girl could feel as restricted watching sheep in this wide open space as Ree had at Lilly's age, carrying a heavy basket of laundry from the tub where she had scraped it against the washboard, through the living room full of the crying, fighting babies of their landlords, dragging it across the kitchen windowsill and onto the fire escape, where she clipped the clothes to a clothesline to flap five stories above the courtyard below.

That had been her childhood, but from the moment she had first read the article by Frank Hamilton Cushing, she had dreamed of a place like this. She understood how Lilly felt, especially when one of the sheep pooped right in front of them. She and Lilly laughed and moved on, looking for another slightly shady place to sit. She wanted so much to tell Lilly that she understood her. She tried to do it with a smile.

The days with Augustina went by fast, but Ree was in no hurry to leave. The best part was at night, when she crept into the wagon and curled up in the blankets. The windows of the wagon were like barn doors, opening to the entire star-filled sky. The blanket-covered floor was a soft crib, surrounded securely by the walls of the bed of the wagon. The wagon truly felt like her home.

Augustina taught her to cook stew and make the Navajo bread at the same time as she taught the littlest girls.

They found Ree's participation cause for endless shy giggles. They all struggled to pat perfect flat breads that would rise fluffy on the inside and crisp on the outside as it cooked over the fire. The strength of the fire and how to get it just right for cooking was another lesson. Ree had hated cooking for her father and learned as little as necessary. Her challah breads had always been too dry. But now she wanted perfection.

She wanted to learn to build a wagon like this. When she had enough money, she would find a man to teach her carpentry. Maybe Ned would. He wasn't like other men. She didn't think he would keep the men's skills secret.

One morning Augustina packed the wagon with food and other supplies, and taught Ree to hitch the mules to it. After lunch, Augustina's whole family gathered and hugged Ree. Ree couldn't stop crying. Her friends were puzzled as she sucked back her tears.

As Augustina flicked the reins and they headed away, she felt sadder than ever, a pit in her stomach. She had been joyous to leave Brooklyn, frantic to leave San Gabriel, and exhilarated to leave Wheelwright, but this was a new way to feel, with love for the people and the place, wanting to stay longer. In her plans for the future, this bittersweet feeling hadn't been a factor she anticipated, but she hoped to have it again.

Part 6

The ride to Lost Wash took most of the day. The landscape was more familiar than on the trip up, and Ree amused herself by spotting hogans in the distance. Finally, the road began to look better traveled and they rode into a cluster of stone and adobe buildings, passing a crumbling stable and a church with half-built walls and the hand-painted sign "Lost Wash Mission." On the trading post a faded sign read "Lo

W h Trad r Rug old." Augustina pulled up the wagon and hitched the mules. Ree followed her into the store.

This was the most neglected trading post Ree had seen. At Crystal the shelves held cans and a glass display case of pawn jewelry, but in this one only a few sacks of food stood in a pile of spilled cornmeal. There were some cans of peaches, their water stained labels peeling. The display case had broken glass in it instead of jewelry. There was no sign of the trader. Augustina pantomimed holding a bottle to her lips and drinking, then smacking her lips.

Sawdust on the floor barely covered dried shoe prints. Just then a door opened in back, and they heard men's voices. A man came through a curtain that separated off a back room. He was a white man, emaciated, unshaven, with eyes that popped from dehydration. His skin was burnt bright red right through a leathery tan. Ree wondered if he had passed out drunk in the desert. But all thoughts of him left her mind when she saw the man who walked in behind him.

"Well, if isn't Henrietta? By God, it is!" Sack was dressed in dungarees and a plaid shirt instead of his elegant suit. He slapped a western straw hat on the counter. He looked more like a dude than a cowboy, and she knew he would rather be wearing the suit.

Ree was too startled to speak, but Sack kept going. "What are you doing here? What happened with old Wheelwright? I heard she was treating you like a lap dog."

Ree's face fell to hear that she had been the subject of gossip.

"Who said that?"

"Dunno, some dumb anthro student. I spent some time with Earl Morris' group, excavating at Aztec. They got nothing better to talk about all day down in their dusty holes. That archaeology's not for me."

"Who the hell's this?" spat out the emaciated man.

"This is Henrietta."

"Ree," said Ree.

"Sure, Ree. I know her from New York. We used to go to the same college. But what she's doing here, I don't know."

"College!" said the man. "You all go to college than you end up here looking for handouts from me!"

"You know that's not true," said Sack.

"I say you chea—"

"Don't say it!" said Sack. "A card game's a card game, and we weren't the only ones there. I'm being as nice to you as I can. You take your time packing up. What do you think?" he swung his head back at Ree. "I'm a trader!"

At first she thought he meant he was a traitor, and she knew she looked confused.

"This place is all mine," he said. "Won it fair and square."

The former owner said something angry to Augustina in Navajo. But she smiled at Sack, pointing at him and then at the decrepit store.

"I think she's glad about it," said Sack. "No one likes to see an empty store."

"Oh you shut up about it," said the trader. "Like to see how well you do. In fact, I'll come back next year to see this place boarded up and you dead by the road, because you think you're so smart. We'll see about that." His voice dribbled off at the end.

"Just pack up your stuff," Sack said. "I'll even give you a ride out of town if you want. I'm trying to be fair," he said, turning to Ree. "Anyway, what are you doing here? I thought you were living in a mansion, eating off silver platters, ordering the servants around."

"There were some nice things about it, but I was glad to leave. All I've ever wanted is to get out here and live in a place like this."

"Whew, that's sad. That's the last thing I want to do."

"But what about this trading post?"

"For now, it's a lucky break. I'll get it going, then I'll live off the profits."

"Oh for God's sake!" said the old trader, who had grabbed the last box of crackers off the shelf, defiantly ripped it open practically under Sack's nose, and dropped a few on the floor as he stuffed others into his mouth. Sack didn't take the bait and Ree was relieved. She suspected they were both wearing guns, probably in their boots. Or that was the way it went in cowboy movies, anyway. She didn't want to find out.

She wasn't sure what to think of Sack right now. This was a twist of fate she hadn't anticipated. She had expected to be alone and new in Lost Wash, except for Frances and Ned. She had envisioned gradually gaining the trust of the people so they would take her in like the Zuni people had with Frank Hamilton Cushing. But if she became associated with Sack, Lost Wash might be ruined for her. What would they think of him? Even if they were glad he had driven this failure of a white trader away, Sack was loud and aggressive and everything Navajo men tried not to be, and everything they thought of as the worst of white people.

"So how'd you end up here?" Sack asked.

"After I left Wheelwright's, I was hitching this way and caught a ride with Augustina here. She's renting me her wagon. Want to see it?" They walked outside while the old trader continued to chew defiantly on a mouthful of crackers.

"Very nice. I hear they get these from the Basque sheepherders that are up in Montana. You planning to do an article on it?"

"I hadn't thought about it. Anyway, my anthropology days are behind me."

"I'll bet," he said. "Mine sure are. All I want now are the valuables. Rugs, jewelry, and—"He stopped abruptly. "This sure is a cute little place to get cozy in the night," he said, peering into the bed of the wagon.

She was sure he had stopped before saying "artifacts," and she knew that if she stayed in Lost Wash, Sack would tempt her with this possibility. They both knew that the real money would be in selling rare and ritual objects to a collector. Even Wheelwright was likely to buy. Ree sensed

Sack's brain calculating, wondering on what terms she had left Wheelwright, and if she could set up a deal for him.

On the way to Lost Wash, Augustina had stopped at a dry river bed and dug clay for pots. There was a foot-high tower of rocks, which Ree suspected was a marker for ritual objects hidden there. It had to be a secret spot, and she had been flattered that Augustina had trusted her, although she doubted she could ever find it again in the miles of repetitious shrub-covered hard land they went through to get there. Her whole future with the Navajo people relied on their trusting her as Augustina did, and Sack would never behave in a way that would make the people trust him.

Augustina touched Ree's arm to get her attention, pointed at herself and then back in the direction of her home. Ree hadn't thought out this part yet. She had to find a place to park the wagon.

"Who else owns land around here?" she asked Sack.

"Just a crazy preacher," he said. "He's been trying to get that church built for years. The Navajos don't want much to do with him."

She was not surprised that he had only answered about white people.

"I need to rent a space to keep my wagon," Ree said. "Maybe I could ask this preacher. Do you know where he is?"

"What for?" said Sack. You can park it back there, behind MY trading post," and he laughed so heartily she thought he would pound on his chest like an ape in the Bronx Zoo.

Worried about how it would look to others to be living on Sack's land, but looking at the deserted church, which had a wooden lean-to against it which she suspected was the preacher's house, she decided she had no other choice.

"What's your price?"

"For what?"

"To rent the space."

"I'd do it for a friend."

"That's all right, I like to keep things business-like."

"You can help out around the trading post. Want to trade for working for me? It could use a woman's touch, that's for sure. While you're cleaning it, I can head for Santa Fe to get food and goods to sell. How's that for a trade? You pick your spot, anything within one hundred feet is mine, except where the church is. Or where the church wants to be. I'd like to buy him out. I don't want any preachers stepping on my toes."

"Okay, but just at first. I'm going to be part of the Navajo community here, not the white one."

"Sure," said Sack. "Who am I to interfere with your dream?"

With her few words of Navajo and hand signals, Ree pointed to the few trees behind the trading post, as far as she thought one hundred feet might be. Augustina nodded approvingly, and Ree walked the mules, pulling the wagon behind them. Soon it was parked and the wheels blocked with stones. Sack looked on possessively.

"This will be great," he said. "They like it better if there's a couple. Then they aren't afraid their women will go after me."

"Don't tell them we're married!" Ree said.

"You're right. I want their women going after me." Sack grinned.

She gave him a look and he hung his head, pretending to be ashamed. As Augustina hugged her, mounted one of the mules and headed out, she wished her mind was on this moment of parting and not on how suspicious she was of Sack. She almost wanted to tell Augustina to hitch the mules up again and help her move on to another place.

"You have nothing to be scared of," he said.

"I'm not scared."

"Hey, I don't win trading posts in poker games by being a bad judge of faces. You've got nothing to worry about. This is purely a business deal. I've got plenty of women in Santa Fe, just so you know."

Ree looked away at the flat horizon and distant hills beyond. She didn't know what to say.

"Why don't you get settled in?" Sack suggested and walked back into the trading post. Augustina and the mules had disappeared from sight. This was it. If Sack hadn't been here, just the drunken old trader, things would no doubt be worse or not even possible. Funny how Sack turned up at certain moments. Maybe he was good for her. There were Indian tales with characters like him. But too often the savior turned out to be coyote, the trickster.

In the dark of that first night, Ree was lonely. The time she had spent with Augustina and her daughters had given her a need that she had never had. She wanted to be in a home where all around her women worked on the wool, carding and spinning until the fire ran low, and men polished silver bracelets, and stories were told by the fire. It had been more like what she had read of Frank Hamilton Cushing at Zuni than she had ever experienced herself, and now that she had known it, she missed it. But instead she was alone in the sheep wagon. It was cold and she could light a fire, but she would be too lonely beside it. She pulled the heavy woven blankets more tightly around her, tucked in her toes and wrapped a shirt around her head. Still, she was cold. She reached out to close the window flap. All she could see was blackness, not even a fire in sight.

Was this her dream come true at last, the dream she had carried since childhood, the dream she had spent years studying for, the dream she had come west for, and the dream that her adventures had carried her to? Had it led only to this: shivering in an old wooden wagon in a desolate, dark place?

Hearing footsteps approach, her cold body tightened. There was a knock on the wood frame of the wagon. She was so scared she didn't answer.

"Hey, if you're not in there, you're lost on the desert. Come on, open up or whatever you do with one of these."

Glad to hear Sack's voice, Ree opened the flap.

"I'm here, I'm ok," she said.

"You must be freezing. Why haven't you got a fire going?"

"Oh, I was just tired from the trip, thought I'd just go right to sleep."

"Can I come in?"

"It's really small in here, I don't know how you'd fit."

"Let me try it. Where's the darn door?"

Not sure she should do it, Ree struggled to pull back the doors and make a space. Sack handed her his kerosene lantern to hang. When Sack jumped up, his weight made the whole wagon shift with a loud creak. He tumbled in, falling on her legs.

"Ouch!"

"Sorry." With a lot of shifting around, Sack somehow settled down, his knees almost in her face.

"I fit in here just right with Augustina, but you're a lot taller," Ree said.

"So you got really comfortable with her?" said Sack.

"What do you want anyway?"

"I just came to be friendly with my old friend. Boy, I sure haven't seen much of you since you hooked up with the old rich bag."

"Don't call her that."

"Oh, I just figured you'd seen through her the way I did."

"She was very nice to me."

"Well, what are you doing here then? Why'd she throw you out?"

"I left. I chose to leave."

"Are you crazy? You could have ended up owning that whole place. She doesn't even have an heir."

"And how would you know that?"

"I learned to research at Columbia University," said Sack. "You sure you don't want to light your fire? It's getting cold at night."

"No, I've got to get to sleep soon." That would get rid of him, she hoped. She felt peculiar with a man sitting on the bed. For a moment she had the strangest flash go through her mind, that instead of Sack awkwardly perched with his big feet poking into her thigh, Ned would be here, and it wouldn't be uncomfortable or awkward. It would be graceful, like everything with Ned was. And it would be warm. Sack's breathing reminded her of the horses at San Gabriel, the air filling with his frosty breaths, the tiny space heating like a horse stall. She imagined Ned here, the wagon toasty and Ned's soft breath curling on her bare neck or ear.

"Anyway, are you crazy? How could you leave Wheelwright? Come on, you can tell me. You've got to tell me."

"She wanted me to live in Boston for the winter, and sell Navajo rugs at this store she has there."

"Let you live at her mansion on Beacon Hill, I bet."

"I didn't come all the way here to live in Boston, even just for the winter."

"Do you have a job when she comes back?"

"She was kind of mad at me for not wanting to go to Boston. She just assumed I would, and didn't even mention it until the last moment. She even bought my ticket without asking me. So she was shocked when I said I wouldn't go."

"So it's all over."

"I guess. But I never meant to stay so long. I only ever wanted to live near the Indians. This is the field assignment I didn't get. I'm assigning myself to this, and I'm going to learn all I can. What's it like here?"

"I just got here a few days ago myself. Practically had to put a gun in the guy's back all the way from Santa Fe to make him pay off the bet. But watch out about asking questions. I've been around Navajos enough to know they don't like it."

"Oh, I know that. I'll be more subtle. I learned a few things at Columbia."

"Thanks to me you did. Have you ever thought to thank me for helping you get out of Brooklyn and into college?"

"Oh, sorry. All right, thanks, Sack. But I got there myself."

"Wouldn't have known about it without me. And the same goes for working for Wheelwright."

"What are you trying to say? If you want something from me, this is all I've got. And this wagon sure isn't mine. I'm renting it and everything in it. What I've got is my one little suitcase still."

"What about what Wheelwright paid you?"

Ree's laugh was more of a snort.

"It's pretty much gone getting to here and paying the rent in advance. She was really tight! You think I had it made with a rich woman, but they don't get rich by giving it away—or even paying the help decently."

"Oh for God's sake, you didn't know how to get it out of her. I could have told you. I know how to play those old ladies. You acted like a goddamn servant, I bet. Well the trick is to act like a prince. Or in your case a goddam princess. Or maybe in your case a goddam prince."

"I don't know what you're talking about."

"Never mind about the prince. I mean if you act like their servant, that's how they see you. If you act like a prince, they think you're their long lost child and want to give you everything."

"OK, she'll be back in the spring, and you can go call her Queen Mother. But I've got what I wanted. I'm here."

Sack was silent, twisting his mouth like he was forming words.

"What do you think Benedict will say?" he finally asked.

"What about her?"

"When she hears you're out here on your own doing field work? Papa Franz Boas will split a gasket and take her down too. They're going to be really angry at you."

"Why? I've got good training and I'm going to use it."

"I thought you were too stupid in how you blew it with Wheelwright, but this is even better. Wish there was someone around from school I could laugh about this with. You never get it, do you? You think the same people who didn't want you to go out to the field officially are going to be pleased to hear you did it anyway? I'll make you a bet right now—Benedict's going to show up here to tell you to call it off and go back to Brooklyn."

The image of Ruth, also sitting here on the blankets, and somehow in her imagination squeezed in between Ned and Sack, made Ree shake her head and unfocus her eyes for an instant.

"Benedict here? She doesn't have time for me, she's made that clear."

"She'll be here, because you're making her look bad to the boss. They pay attention to that."

"I don't believe you. Why do you want to make me feel bad about this? I didn't tell Wheelwright who to pick. Stop blaming me!"

"I could get ten Wheelwrights if I wanted. I'm just telling you the truth, so you're not in total shock when Benedict or one of her lackeys shows up here."

"Well, she can't complain that I followed her here. I could complain if she followed me here." As she said that, Ree thought how amazing it would be if Ruth did come looking for her. She was sure Margaret had left for Samoa. Maybe Ruth would like the coziness of the wagon. Maybe she should keep the fire lit every night, just in case.

"But you did follow her to New Mexico. This is their territory. They told you they didn't want you here, and here you are."

"They don't own the Southwest."

"They think they do."

"I don't care. I'm here, and they can say what they want. It's a free country. What can they do to get me to leave? Nothing. And what about you? They want you out, too."

"They sure do," he chuckled.

"I'm not doing any field work! Look, I need help at the trading post. I'm no storekeeper. I couldn't stand to be here much. You work for me, run the place. If old Benedict shows up, that's what you're doing here."

"What'll you pay?"

"I'll pay a commission on all the crackers and canned tomatoes you sell."

"How much?"

"Going rate. Anyway, there's a cut for you if any Indians bring in anything—interesting, shall we say?"

"I'm not helping you deal in stolen artifacts."

"Nobody said 'stolen.' I said if they bring any in."

"It's as good as stolen if they sell it, and you know it."

"And what about your comfortable surroundings at Wheelwright's house? Lovely pots and drums. And the rugs!"

"I didn't buy them, she did."

"Well, she had to start somewhere. That's why I want a store in this godawful place. Winter comes, food runs low, and I'm figuring there will be some discreet visits and quiet offers. You be there to take them and you get three percent."

"Three percent of what?"

"Whatever I get for it, from the Wheelwrights or the museums or maybe the Harvey Company. They buy a lot for their tourist stores."

"I don't want any part of it."

"Okay," he paused, then said in a calmer voice, "Would you work in the store until I get somebody else? I can't hire Indians, because they can't say no to their own family and so they give it all away. And they'll starve if there isn't a store here." Ree thought about her thin wallet, but she had a bad feeling about this.

"Hey," he went on, "This is the best place to meet Indians. They all have to go to the trading post. And there you are, Miss Anthropologist Without Portfolio—or diploma—ready to take their family history and make mysterious diagrams. White people's sandpaintings."

It was appealing. But whatever she did here, the Indians were going to associate her with Sack.

"What were you planning to live on, anyway?" Sack asked.

"Live like the Indians," she said in a tiny voice.

"Are you kidding? You can't live like them. They've been doing it for a few thousand years and they're all related and help each other out, and they're starving anyway. Sick, too. No one's going to help you, white girl. Did you not learn anything at Columbia?"

"Like Cushing," she squeaked out. Her throat was dry. His body and heavy breath had heated up the wagon. His smell wasn't soft and sweet like Augustina, but a leathery scent that scraped her throat.

He roared with laughter. "Like Cushing! Maybe if they'd never seen a stupid white woman before."

"Don't call me stupid."

"I'm beginning to think Benedict and the gang were right about you. The Navajo people aren't going to take you in, anymore than the Zuni people took Cushing in. He forced his way in. You're not going to get that far, unless you can find a scalp to take." He roared at his own joke. "They don't have a chief's house like the Zuni, anyway."

"I got to live with Augustina and share this wagon."

"Where's she now?"

"Heading back home, I guess."

"So why aren't you with her?"

"She rented me the wagon."

"As long as you had money, sure. You think I'm not the world's nicest guy, but I don't want you to starve. Work for me! If anyone brings something that would interest me, you just get their name and tell them to come back and see me. That's all I'm asking."

"Why? Why would you want me?"

"I trust you."

"Should I be flattered?."

"Not too much, I don't have a lot of options. I can't have a Navajo run the trading post. And the white guys around here will rob me so bad, I'll lose more than I won in that card game. Did I tell you how it went down?" While he told the story of every play of the cards, Ree thought through her options. It might take some time until a family took her in. Meanwhile, if she wanted food, she was going to have to buy it from Sack. Which meant she would soon be in debt to him. That would be the worst thing she could do. What would Sack suggest as payment? But what other choice did she have? Sack was right.

"OK, I'll do it. Like you said, just working in the store, selling food. And I can judge what any new rugs and pots they want to trade are worth."

"Don't be too generous! And you'll let me know—

"If there's anything that looks old, I'll tell them I don't have anything to do with it, to talk to you. That's it, that's all I'm doing. Some of us plan a future in anthropology." But that wasn't all she was going to do. She hadn't promised him that she wouldn't tell anyone attempting to sell sacred objects or other artifacts why it was a bad idea for their people, their children, and their own safety. This would be an opportunity to protect the people from Sack. Maybe working for him could be a good thing.

"OK, but I plan to be rich." Sack looked her right in the eye when he spoke. "Not in human knowledge, just money."

"You've been out here a while. You don't look too rich."

"What I'm looking for is not an everyday occurrence. Not anymore, anyway. Your beloved Cushing and his buddies cleaned up for a while, so now the competition is fierce. If we're one step ahead of the Harvey Company man, it's going to happen."

"Don't say 'we.'"

"You sure don't miss a thing. You'd make a good anthropologist, anyone ever told you that?" He grinned with such sincerity that for a moment she believed him.

"I wish someone would say that. I still don't believe it, after all those papers and classes, everything. How can they not believe in me?"

"You still think it's about you. It's not about you, it's about them and who they think is like them and you're not."

"Boas is Jewish."

"One's allowed."

"Esther Goldfrank?"

"One man and one woman. That's the quota. Anyway, it's not only about being Jewish. You just don't fit in. You're just not one of the Columbia tribe. You didn't assimilate the cultural values."

"I did everything they asked for. Even went to those horrible departmental tea parties. Feh!"

"It's more than that. You're too obvious."

"Too obvious at what?"

"You don't want me to spell it out for you. But you know what I mean. I've got to go now." He uncurled and started climbing out. "Open the store at the first glimpse of sunrise. That's when these folks show up expecting an open store! I'm leaving for Santa Fe as early as I can."

"What if I run out of stuff to sell? What do I do?"

"Hell, your guess is as good as mine. I just got the store myself." He thought a moment. "I'll be shipping more to you as soon as I can raise the cash. I'm lucky at cards."

"Sack, thanks," she said.

"I don't believe it," he said. "Appreciation, at last."

"Don't make me regret it."

"That sounds more like the little girl I once knew," Sack said as he backed out of the wagon.

She thought he was gone but he called out as he walked away. "Do you believe it? This is not Brooklyn. Or Morningside Heights. And we're here. We made it."

"You do have a sentimental side," Ree shouted back.

If he replied, she didn't hear it.

Working in Sack's store turned out to be her only chance to talk with her new Navajo neighbors, because otherwise they weren't friendly. Ree wanted so badly to be invited into a home or just have a friendly chat, but they viewed her as they did all traders, as the judge of their economic situation, deciding from a few rugs or skins if the winter would be cold and hungry or warm and satisfied. She had never had this much power over anyone and she didn't want it. It did help her to understand how the faculty committee at Columbia had felt, deciding whether to give Ree her dream of the Southwest or keep her chained to a Brooklyn tenement.

Still, she was so glad to be here. In the dark night, alone in her wagon, her eyes learned to spot the glow of hogans in the distance, and she pictured the families together in their warm hogans. There were many people who came to the trading post who were everything she wanted to believe about the Navajo people: the men calm and gentle, the wives warm and loving, the children smiling and shy. These were the families she pictured out there in the darkness.

She wanted to forget about Golney and Attencia, the unhappy couple she had met on her way here, but she sound found that she was living in Golney's 'my town' after all. The two had come into the trading post one day, complete with several small children clinging to their mother's skirt. There had been a glare of recognition that left as soon as it sparked. Neither she nor Golney could afford to argue further, especially when Attencia asked to buy their food on credit. Golney slipped out the door, hiding his shame from her. It had to be anger, too. From then on, there were times when she thought she saw him, but he always slipped around a corner and avoided a face to face meeting.

Attencia was too desperate for shame. She had children to feed. Ree gave them candies, hoping it wouldn't add up to an amount Sack would notice as unaccounted for.

Attencia had no beauty or grace. She would never be photographed looking noble or spiritual for folks back East to admire. She was a dumpy woman with a pasty round face and slightly bulging eyes. Her face said that she wanted out, she wanted to be anywhere but here. It endeared her to Ree. Ree was learning more Navajo and looking forward to someday speaking with her, asking her where she dreamed of going.

Ree was so lonely that she was glad when Sack returned days later with a wagonload of supplies. That evening, they sat by the fire toasting bread, while he bragged about his luck betting on cockfights. When a woman on a horse rode up in the dimming light. Ree was thrilled to see that it was Frances, Ned's grandmother.

"Frances, do you remember me?"

"I heard you were here. Augustina stopped by to tell me."

"You're kidding! That's great. I didn't know how well she knew you, because we couldn't really talk. Did she tell you what I've done? Renting her wagon and all?"

"Why Mr. Sack," said Frances, making out Sack in the dim light. "I heard you own the trading post now."

"Sure do," he said.

"It's got to be better than that drunken fellow. He didn't know enough to stay out of the sun. But what are you doing to do with it?"

"I want to get it going again. Ree here is going to help me."

Ree squirmed.

"You're married to him?" asked Frances, pointing her chin at Sack. "Well, guess I was wrong about you and Ned."

"So that's why you're here," Sack muttered to Ree.

"We're not married," said Ree. "We just know each other a little from back in New York. I need a place to park my wagon for a while, and Sack said I could put it here. But I'm looking for other possibilities, if you know any."

"You want to live on Navajo land? Not that this isn't--" she said, raising her chin at him and throwing her shoulders back, although Sack just continued chewing his food.

Ree didn't know what to say. Frances' tone made her feel she had to justify herself. She thought about how Frank Hamilton Cushing had forced himself upon the Zuni people, walking right into the chief's house and claiming an area for his bed. She didn't feel much like Frank Hamilton Cushing now. How had he done that, claimed his right to be there? But that was how Sack was, wasn't it? Sack didn't question that he should own the only building with a solid roof in the community. What would Ned think of all this? Would Ned hate her for associating with Sack?

"I'd like to," was all she could think to say. "I really love living in the little wagon, and Augustina has shown me how everything works. It's just something I want to try. I'm hoping to move further out," she smiled hopefully at Frances.

"You sure you're not looking for Ned?"

"How does she know him?" scowled Sack.

"He's her grandson," said Ree. "He wanted to meet Klah and came out to Los Luceros, but Klah didn't want to talk to him."

"So that's what happened," said Frances. "He never said. But just as well, no one should be around Klah." She shot a look at Ree that made her want to kick herself and her big mouth. Hopefully, Frances wouldn't tell Augustina she'd worked with Klah, or tell Ned that Ree had spilled the beans. Was there no way to avoid betraying the people who were being so nice to her? The wagon was so simple, the land so beautiful, the life so free. Why did it have to get complicated so quickly? Was there no way of starting out fresh? But on the other hand, didn't this mean she had made relationships here, that she knew people, that they knew her, that she wasn't alone and unknown? There was something to be said for that.

Ree almost said "Working for Wheelwright was just a job," but that wouldn't have been honest. She said nothing. But Frances wasn't waiting for an excuse.

"So you're planning to stay here?" she asked coldly.

"I was hoping to see you," Ree braved. "I'd like to see Ned, but I also wanted to see you."

"Why?"

"I was hoping you would show me what you do. How you live this way."

Frances shook her head. "You said you weren't an anthropologist."

Sack snorted.

"I used to be, but I'm not. I won't tell anyone your secrets."

"What about Hosteen Klah?"

This was going terribly. Was she going to have to leave the wagon behind, taking the next ride that came through Lost Wash back to anywhere else?

"I'm sorry, Frances. It was just a job." She almost whispered it, she was so ashamed.

"I'll tell Ned you're here."

"So that's why you're here," Sack whispered to Ree.

"Sooner or later, Ned comes back. I've got to get going. Why don't you come by and we'll talk?"

"I thought you were mad at me because of Hosteen Klah."

"I have a feeling about you. But you--," she glared at Sack, but he just smiled back. "We can't keep the white people away, we know that. But at least we can try to keep the good ones here. No one's going to miss that old drunk, but Mr. Sack, you better do a better job for us. And whatever it is you think you'll get here, you won't. If you do, you better move on fast."

Sack sucked on his tongue, looking mildly chastised.

"Sure grandmother," he said, "you just bring your rugs and silver by and see if I don't do right by you. In fact, if you've got anything now I can take to Santa Fe, I can come back with food for you and for the store."

"I might have something, or not." With that, Frances disappeared into the night. The clean air was so cool and fresh. Even if the people were complicated, Ree could at least enjoy the place.

"Wow," said Sack. "Don't mess with her."

"I wouldn't. She's really nice."

"I just want to make some money. I don't know why everyone has to think the worst of me. I won this place fair and square, and they're all glad to see that hopeless drunk gone. The preacher is ecstatic. They hated each other for years. I feel like I've cleared the air around here, and instead of appreciation, I get suspicion. Is there something about me?"

"I don't know. You just seem like you're out to make a fast dollar. They don't respect that."

"Why not? That's what makes our country grow. That's one thing the Indians don't understand, and it's the reason they're all poor. Do you think they have any choice any more? It's grow with the country or be left behind, with nothing but a dirty store, some dented cans of peaches, and a half-built church. Is that how you want to live? Don't answer, I guess you do." He reached out and patted her head, which Ree backed away from.

"Oh don't worry, I'm really not interested. I know Wheelwright's more your type. Well, good night." He walked off, leaving Ree squirming.

One slow morning Ree was lost in thought, mindlessly sweeping the floor, when there was the sound of a crash and horses whinnying in fright. Ree ran to the door to see a wagon backing away from the trading post and heading down the road. With so few places to stop, why had they not come in? The wagon had knocked down the post of her clothesline. She went out to fix it when she heard a moan from someone on the ground.

A Navajo woman lay curled up and groaning. She stiffened upon seeing Ree, like the prairie dog sentries sighting a hawk. Ree put a comforting hand on her and brushed her hair away. It was Attencia, the pathetic wife. Her face was bruised.

"It's ok, don't be scared, I'll help you. I'll get some water." She rushed to the well. She had to hold the cup to Attencia's lips.

"Do you want to come inside? Can you walk?" Attencia struggled to her feet. Ree led her into the trading post and helped her lay down on the canvas cot in the back room. It stank of mildew and the vomit of the drunken trader and she gagged to get near it. She felt Attencia recoil. Ree led her out to her own little wagon home and helped her climb into the blankets.

"I'll get you some food. You stay here." Attencia pulled the blankets to her chin, her eyes grateful, still silent. A tear ran down her face.

Ree fed her soup and crackers and wished they could speak. She was relieved when she heard the bell ring on the trading post door.

The new customer was Mrs. Manyskirts. She had come by a week earlier and Ree had given her store credit for one of her rugs, which was so beautiful she was sure Sack could easily sell it. But what if she was wrong? She wondered if he would dock her wages for mistakes, as they had done at the garment factory. But what wages were those? He was letting her park on his land and eat from the store. He hadn't said anything about money.

"Do you know Attencia?" she asked Mrs. Manyskirts. "She's hurt. Can you come look at her?" Mrs. Manyskirts did not look surprised. At the wagon, Attencia tried to hide her bruised face, but Mrs. Manyskirts spoke quietly and signaled for Ree to leave. Some time later, she came back into the trading post, Attencia walking slowly behind her.

"She's coming to my house," said Mrs. Manyskirts. "She thanks you for your help."

"What happened?" said Ree, but the women left without answering.

Winter was coming, but Ree wasn't feeling any more welcome at Lost Wash. Sack had been gone since the day after seeing Frances. A shipment of goods arrived by mail truck, but not a letter. She couldn't believe she even missed Sack. The first few days had been busy, then it had slowed down and she realized that in her first few days the locals must have stopped by to check out the new woman trader. Frances hadn't come back after that first visit. This wasn't the way her dream went. This was the reality. She felt that the Indians resented her. When there wasn't a customer, she was alone. She began to understand why so many of the traders were drunks.

Whether she stood by the door or sat outside on a log, it wasn't possible to miss the rare event of any customers arriving. For amusement, she watched the prairie dogs in the field nearby. The prairie dogs had the kind of community she wanted to join. She pictured them snug and warm in their web of underground tunnels. She felt an affinity with the sentries who stood frozen at guard, protecting their village. When hawks came, she chased them away with rocks and screams, wanting to believe that the prairie dogs appreciated her efforts and considered her one of their own, although too large to scuttle down their holes.

One particularly bleak day she spotted a hawk's shadow passing over the field. She grabbed a broom and ran outside. "Get out of here, get out of here, you" she screamed out with the worst Yiddish curses she knew. It was satisfying to say it loud, letting out all the anger she was feeling toward everything that was keeping her from finding the life she had come here for. She ran into the field shaking the broom.

"Hey, I thought you liked the prairie dogs," a voice startled her, and she spun around to see Ned, dressed exactly as he had been the last time she had seen him, that day at Los

Luceros when he had spoken with Klah and then disappeared.

Ree pointed to the sky but the hawk had sped away. Mortified, she pretended to be sweeping the hilly field as she walked back to where he stood. Navajo men always rode horses or came on their wagons. They never walked, but Ned must have or she would have heard him.

"There was a hawk. I've been chasing them away. I wouldn't hurt a prairie dog."

"They're not getting into the stored flour sacks? Most traders amuse themselves by shooting at them."

Sack hadn't told Ree to check. She wondered what she would find.

"I like prairie dogs. I like how they live together and protect each other. I would never hurt them."

"Well, you know I feel about them." They smiled at each other, remembering how they had met on Santa Fe plaza.

"Do you think he made his way back home?" asked Ree.

Ned looked out at the field, where the prairie dog sentries had stayed at their posts through all the human chattering and movement. "I think I see him right now. Yeah, that's definitely him."

Approaching Ned, Ree wanted to hug him, but she lost her nerve when he stepped back as if anticipating this.

"My grandmother told me you were here," said Ned.

"How is she? I was hoping to see more of her."

"She keeps to herself. You never know when she'll show up."

"You're like her."

"I guess so."

"What happened to you? I wanted to say goodbye. Why'd you leave Los Luceros so suddenly?"

Ned turned away for a moment. "I think I see another hawk coming. Do you want to curse at it?"

"You know Yiddish?"

"No, I just figured from the tone. So I'm right? And what's Yiddish?"

"Those are the worst words I know. I told the hawk to shrivel up like an onion in the field."

"That will scare it."

"It sounds better in Yiddish. Yiddish is the language of the Jews."

"Jews? Dry goods salesmen have their own language?"

"What are you talking about?"

"The Jews. The Seligman store in Santa Fe. I didn't know you had family here."

"I don't. I don't understand."

"Everybody says the Seligman's are stingy Jews."

"Don't say that, that's a terrible thing to say. I wouldn't say bad things about your people."

"Jews are your people? Not your family?"

"There aren't a lot of Jews around here, but some of the merchants in Santa Fe are Jews. Didn't you ever read the Bible? Abraham and Isaac, crossing the Red Sea, that's all about the Jews."

Ned squatted on the ground, the way the Navajo men relaxed to talk. Ree sat on a log nearby.

"Oh, but maybe you've never read a Bible. Sorry, I wasn't thinking."

"No, I have," said Ned. "They made us read it over and over at the Indian boarding school. We practically had to memorize it. But I don't remember Jews. There were the Egyptians, the Israelites, the Canaanites —."

"That's it, the Israelites. Those are the Jews. It's all about the Israelites, being the slaves of the Egyptians and all."

"But didn't they all become Christians? Didn't Jesus come to save them all?"

"Not me. Not my family. We don't believe in Jesus. We're still Israelites, I guess. My father wants to go back there, to Palestine, to the Holy Land of the Bible, because our people were driven out of our land a long time ago. He says it's still our land and we need to take it back."

"I understand that," said Ned. "The U.S. Army made my people walk a terrible distance, in frozen weather or scorching sun, away from our lands to a place we didn't know.

"I'm so sorry," said Ree.

"Frances was there, just a little girl. She saw her mother die. And the soldiers killed her father for trying to help her mother."

So that was what was so deep in Frances' eyes. She marveled that Frances could be so kind to her when she must be seeing the whiteness in Ree's face.

"My father came to America for reasons like that," said Ree. "He came from a little village near Minsk, in Russia. The Christians hated the Jews. The meanest men would come to the village and kill everyone they saw. My father's grandmother was kicked by their horses, they rode right over her. I think he saw her die, but he would never tell me for sure."

"Wow," said Ned. "I didn't know things like that happened to white people. Here, it's the white people who are always hurting us. But there's something different about you, isn't there?"

"What do you mean?"

"It must be that Jew thing, like you said. I thought all white people had Jesus. You don't?"

"No. The Christians say we killed Jesus."

"That's right, in the Bible, now I remember. That other Bible, the little one. The Gospels."

"That's not our Bible, that's the Christian's Bible. We only have the other one, the one about the Egyptians and the Red Sea."

"So that's why the Christians kill the Jews. But why do they kill my people? We were here the whole time. Nowhere near Jerusalem. It's a desert, but not that one."

"I don't know," said Ree. "I don't understand why so many white people think they're better than Indians. I think Indians are the best. I want to live like you do." Maybe she would only get what she wanted if she said it right out.

"How do you think I live?" asked Ned.

"With your family, in a hogan. Everyone eats together and then they sit by the fire and tell stories."

"The women weave and the men make silver jewelry," Ned continued. "Every few weeks there's a feast day and all the families come together. Everyone is happy and does all the dances and rituals."

"That's it," said Ree. "I want to be part of that. Do you think it could happen?"

"You know what, Ree?" Ned said, leaning so close to her that his soft cheeks almost touched hers. "You know what? I'd like to live there, too. But I don't. Nobody lives there." The bitterness in his voice made them both jump back like magnets that repelled each other. "Look around! What do you see here, in my community? Do you see families like that? When they come into the trading post, what do you see?"

Ree pictured Attencia's bruised face.

"Well, not everyone's happy, but I figure I'm not getting to see how they really are. Because I haven't been in anyone's home yet. But they have to be happier than people in the city. I come from the city, and people aren't happy there. I think people would be happier if they never went to the city. Like your people."

"Like your father's people? Back in his little village? The Christians sound like the Apaches who used to raid our villages. And like the U.S. Army."

"I never thought of it that way. I never think of my father's village to be anything like this. I just wanted to come somewhere that was." Suddenly, she was fighting back tears. "Somewhere different. Somewhere where people are nice to each other."

"Oh gosh," said Ned. "Don't cry." He put his arms around her. It was awkward, she had never been held like this and it felt like he had never held anyone before. He held her face to his shoulder as she cried.

"That's not a bad thing to want," Ned said, patting her back. "I'm sorry, I was being mean to you. That's what I dream of, too. I want to believe my people were like that before the Long March. Before the white people changed things."

Ree was unable to stop herself from sobbing loudly.

"I don't mean you. You would never do that. Anyway, that's what I dream of, too. I don't like seeing my people so unhappy, drinking, men beating their wives. My people used to live together like you said. They had a way of life that was good for everyone. That's why I wanted to meet Hosteen Klah. He knows the old ways and I want to know them. I want to live that way, too."

"Why did you leave so suddenly?"

Ned stepped back, out of the hug. Ree wished she hadn't spoken. It had felt so good.

"You don't have to tell me. I just wanted to see you again. I didn't want you to leave." The second time she said it, she was embarrassed and her voice trailed off.

"You were very kind to me," said Ned. "Thanks for helping me get to meet Hosteen Klah. I hope I didn't get you in trouble with Miss Wheelwright."

"She never caught on," said Ree. "Those songs you were singing! I couldn't believe she fell for it."

"I wasn't trying to trick her," Ned snapped. "Well, I sort of was. You must think I'm an awful person."

"No, not at all. For all I know, Klah's doing the same thing. I know you believe that terrible things will happen if you tell your secrets to white people. And I know you didn't want to talk to her. She pushed you into it. I thought you did the right thing. She always has to be the center of everything. She just couldn't believe you wanted to see Klah and not her. That's why I left there."

"That's right, what are you doing here?"

"She just wanted to boss me around. I came West to—well, like I just told you. I want to live the Indian way. I don't want to live in a mansion with Wheelwright, even if some people think I'm crazy. I want to live in a hogan. I want to learn. Do you think anyone will teach me?"

Ned stood and paced. He pulled at his hair and looked at the sky for hawks. He smiled at the prairie dog sentries.

"We're so alike," he said. "All I wanted from Hosteen Klah was to learn from him. But he won't teach me."

"Why not? He's always saying the chants and stories will die out if he doesn't find young men to teach."

"Well, I wasn't what he wanted."

"Ned, you're perfect. How could he say that?"

"He did. I guess you've learned by now my people aren't easy. You've got to prove yourself or something. I don't know, I don't know what else I can do."

"My people believe that if you want to become a Jew, become one of us, but you're not born a Jew, then you have to ask and get turned away and come back again, three times. Then they know you really want it. You'll really stick with it."

"Huh, " Ned grunted. He squatted to face her again. "Maybe I should go back, ask him again. But I don't know, he was pretty sure. Hey, thanks, maybe it won't work but at least I feel a little hope about it. I've been feeling that I'm at the end of the trail on this. I wish I could learn on my own, but I can't. Only a medicine man can teach it, and Hosteen Klah knows stuff no one else living knows. That's why I had nothing to tell Wheelwright."

"Ask again. What's the worst that could happen?" said Ree.

"Thanks," said Ned. "Where do you think he is?"

"Wheelwright said he would be taking care of his sister for the winter."

"I've got to go," said Ned, standing up.

"But you've only just got here. Oh, don't," said Ree.

"But," said Ned. "That's a great idea you gave me. I've got to go find out."

He hadn't even walked inside the trading post, and he was gone. Ree replayed the conversation, telling it to the prairie dogs. She imagined Ned returning, happy from his travels, grateful to her.

That night in her lonely wagon, she pretended he was still holding her. She had a new strategy. Ned had said he wanted to live in the old way, like she did. Ree wondered if he had the same picture in his head. She saw the two of them living together in a cozy hogan. If she were Ned's woman, they could live that way and she would fit in here. But could she live with a man? She thought of Sack and his crude implications. She shuddered that off and thought of Ned, whose face was soft and beardless. Ned didn't step into her space and occupy it the way Sack did. When Ned came back, she was going to—to what? She had no idea how a woman got a man. She laughed, thinking of how Margaret had gotten to Ruth before her. She had no idea how a woman got a woman, either.

The next day Attencia walked into the trading post. Ree hadn't seen her since the day her husband dumped her out in the yard. She didn't see the children or Golney. It was almost shocking to see a young Navajo woman walk in alone.

Ree started to say 'how are you?" but was afraid it would imply she remembered seeing how the husband had treated the woman. What could she say that wouldn't bring up the shame of that? And she didn't know how much English Attencia could speak.

"I want that—"Attencia said, pointing to the jar of licorice candies. "I want that and I have money." She held out her hand and surprised Ree by showing a few coins.

When Ree looked surprised she said, "And I can speak English. When I want to."

Ree counted out the candy. "Traded some rugs?" she asked.

"Maybe," said Attencia. "Don't tell Mr. Sack." Trading post owners expected the local weavers to sell to them exclusively. Ree was surprised Attencia had said this much. Was it possible Attencia trusted her?

"I didn't steal it," said Attencia.

"I didn't say that," said Ree. "You work very hard, you should have some money. And some pleasure." Attencia chewed on the candy and stuffed the rest deep into a pocket hidden in her skirt.

"You think so?" Attencia smiled.

"I didn't know you could speak English," said Ree.

"I speak English when I want, not when white men yell at me. I went to Indian boarding school. I should never have come back here."

"Where would you go?"

"I married a bad man. I liked Santa Fe. Where are you from?"

"New York City."

"That's very far. I think I'll go there."

Ree pictured this tiny woman in her velvet blouse and floor-length skirt on the familiar streets back home.

"You need a lot of money to go there. But there aren't many people like you in New York City. You might feel very alone so far from home."

"Is that how you feel?"

Ree felt warm suddenly. It had been so long since anyone had asked her how she felt. All her reasons for coming West suddenly flowed back into her.

"I do feel alone, but I want to be here."

"Why?" asked Attencia.

"I don't like New York City. I read about how your people live and I wanted to live your way."

Attencia looked around the trading post and smirked. "This isn't the way I live! I don't have a store with food and candy. She shook her head. "Where are your children?"

"I don't have any children."

"Where's your husband? Did he get another wife because you don't have children?"

"I don't have a husband either."

"Mr. Sack's not your husband?"

"Sack! I'd hate that."

"But you and Mr. Sack—"

"Not at all!" said Ree more loudly than she meant to. If there was one thing they'd been taught about field work at Columbia, it was to stop gossip about extramarital sex.

"I just work for him. We used to go to school together in New York. But it's nothing more than that."

"Don't you want a husband?" asked Attencia.

"Not me," said Ree, but then regretted it. What if Ned had sent Attencia to find out if she were available?

"You're smart," said Attencia. "I wish I had been smart."

"What if you married someone else?" said Ree. "Someone who would be nice to you?"

"Who's that?" Attencia asked, almost spitting.

Ree decided to be bold. "What about Ned? Do you think he'd be a nice husband?"

Attencia started to laugh and ended up choking on the candy. She had to turn away and wipe the tears off her face with some of her huge skirt.

"Ned," she finally said, turning back. "Yes, Ned would make some good husband. Good as a mule." She started laughing again.

Ree didn't get the joke and wanted to change the subject. "So I was wondering," she said, "I'd really like to live more like your people. I'd like to live more out of town, like you do." She had no idea where Attencia lived. The barely visible hogans were so hard to see that for all she knew Attencia was her next door neighbor.

"You want to live in your little wagon or in a hogan?" asked Attencia. She was wandering around the store, looking at the shelves, deciding what to spend her coins on next.

"I already paid rent for the wagon. But I've been thinking I'd like to rent a place to put it, not here at the trading post."

"Rent?" said Attencia, stopping and looking as directly at Ree as Navajo women ever did.

"I'd love to see your place," said Ree. Maybe finally she was getting somewhere.

"Maybe," Attencia said.

Ree had been so glad to see Ned again at last. He had secrets and lines he wouldn't cross with her, but she didn't care. If she thought of her fantasies of Frank Hamilton Cushing as being her last and only love affair, then who had more secrets and barriers than a fantasy man who died long before she was born?

But Ned's secrets she recognized and respected. Being an Indian was a world she could never truly share, but if only Ned would try to let her in, if only he could love her as she realized she now loved him.

How he had held her while she cried was a treasure she fondled over and over. After that he disappeared again. She would have to accept his comings and goings, as Wheelwright had done with Klah's disappearances. If Wheelwright were here, they could gossip about their Indian men. As if Wheelwright would ever discuss Klah in this manner! But she looked upon Wheelwright's relation to Klah differently now. If Wheelwright and Klah had been lovers that past summer, she would have known, sleeping in the room across the hall. Perhaps they had been so once. Perhaps Wheelwright hoped it would happen. But every time she tried to square these speculations with her former patron, it didn't seem possible.

Meanwhile life went on at the trading post, but with the layer of excitement that Ned might return. Every morning she awoke with a special feeling, convinced this would be the day, and then arguing with herself that she was only setting herself up for disappointment. But she loved the way she felt, the excitement of anticipation. Was it worth the likely disappointment? She didn't care, she loved the feeling.

One day when the store was empty, Attencia came to the counter slowly, looking forlornly at the goods. Ree had the feeling she had no coins this time. She held her skirt tight to her belly, as if her stomach ached. Unusually for a woman of her age, she wasn't wearing any silver jewelry, which was how Navajo women stored their wealth. It must have all been in pawn or sold. She leaned over to speak to Ree when the door suddenly slammed open and a chattering family came in. Attencia slunk back to the corner where the rat traps and kerosene cans were kept. Through a steady stream of customers, Ree saw that she was still there.

Finally the store cleared out and Attencia came to the counter again, still clutching her midsection. She was about to pull whatever if was out from under her blouse when Ree stopped her.

"The trader's not here," Ree said. "I can't buy anything. Is there anything you would like to buy?"

Looking confused, Attencia pulled something wrapped in calico out. Ree held up her hand like a traffic cop to say "stop" and shook her head "no!" emphatically, but the woman began to unwrap the object. Ree wanted to see, but just looking would mean crossing a line she didn't want to cross. If it had to be hidden, it wasn't meant to be shown to a non-Navajo person, let alone sold to a white trader. Sacred objects had to stay sacred. No matter what other anthropologists had done, Ree wasn't going to be the first white person to taint whatever this was. If word got around that she was even looking at artifacts, she would never be accepted here.

Before Attencia could unroll the last of the fabric, Ree turned and walked into the storeroom, hoping she would get the message and leave. She could wait Attencia out until they heard another customer coming. Attencia would wrap up her prize and leave, because if she got caught trying to sell it, the consequences would be very severe, especially if, as was most likely, the object was one that her husband Golney had been entrusted to care for. If Golney found out, Ree didn't want to think what would happen.

Just then a loud truck roared to a stop outside, and she heard Atttencia scramble back to the dark corner of the store. Ree was relieved to have handled this well. If Sack had been here, he would no doubt have done it differently, but she couldn't stop that. She just hoped word would get around that the white woman trader was not looking to buy things that shouldn't be sold.

When all the customers had left, Attencia approached her again, but did not hold out her wrapped bundle.

"Maybe my sister Juana will not mind if you put your wagon near her hogan until she returns," Attencia said.

"When will she return?"

"She went to the Los Angeles with a white man. He was building a road and he made her believe she would live in a big house with him. She went, even though he would not let her bring her sheep."

Ree wished she could be taking notes.

"How is she?"

"He made her take everything from her hogan, the night they left. His big house couldn't be so fancy when he made her take even the woodstove. We have one letter from her." From somewhere in her skirt, she pulled out a postcard. It had a picture of an orange grove with huge bulbs of fruit and white flowers. The caption said "California- fruitful land of good fortunes." On the back, under a brief printed description of California's climate, an X had been scratched in pencil.

"That's my sister, that's her letter," Attencia said.

The stamp had been cancelled two years earlier.

"That's all you've heard from her?" Ree asked.

Attencia let out a resigned sigh. "Do you want to rent the space?"

There had been no other offers. Sack might be back soon, and there was no sign of Ned. Ree was already feeling trapped within the boundaries of the trading post. This was her chance, but she was scared of Golney, and also of Attencia and her attempts at dealing. It wasn't how Frank Hamilton Cushing had lived in the chief's house, but everyone said Cushing had forced his way in, not been invited. He had compromised, but at least she had been made an offer. After all this time living at San Gabriel and Los Luceros and at a trading post, at last she could live like the Navajo people.

"How much?" Ree asked.

A few days later, as Golney's horses pulled her wagon onto Attencia's land, Ree felt so happy she ignored his sullenness. He needed the money too much to stop the arrangement. Navajo women owned the land and this time it was Attencia's choice.

Attencia brought her a stew of mutton, potatoes, carrots, and onion, all served on puffy round bread pulled hot from the outdoor oven. "Navajo stew and Navajo bread," said her hostess. The children peaked at Ree from behind their mother's skirt. They were curious but also resentful and Ree realized she was eating their dinner. She offered her bread to one of the children but Golney said something and the little girl turned away.

She slowly circled along the octagonal log wall of her new home, running her palms against the logs and chinked mud. There were a few nails on which pots and hats and clothes once hung. Two fell out as she touched them, no doubt from the shrinking of the aging logs. The tiny thud as each hit the hard dirt was the only sound but her breathing.

Within a few days, she had settled in. From her new home, her walk to work at the trading post took about twenty minutes, but it went faster because the view was so beautiful. It was up and down a few rolling hills and past a tiny stream, although Attencia said that would dry up in the winter. In one direction was a badland of big polished rocks, where it would be difficult for people or horses to travel, and no grass for the sheep. To the other side were grazing lands, Attencia's hogan hidden among them.

Ree had her wish now, but the reality was not her dream. She was in Navajo country on her own, but young unmarried women didn't have their own hogans, because there were no Navajo single women. They were all married, willingly or not. Her dream had been to share a hogan with a warm, friendly family. Maybe it was all about that. Maybe that was all she had ever wanted and had never thought she could have in New York, even in her fantasies of a cozy, domestic life with Ruth Benedict, the two of them in their reading chairs before a crackling fireplace, working on the notes from an adventurous field trip.

Maybe that was what she truly wanted, but she had been so afraid to want it that she had never realized it until the moment she ducked through the short open doorway to look inside the deserted hogan. She sat on the cold dirt floor, one bright but narrow streak of light coming through the smoke hole, as if a spotlight fell on her in this otherwise dark clammy room. When she stood up, slivers of wood fell from the seat of her skirt, and she realized she had been sitting in the remains of a fire long cold.

That night, staring at the sad hogan, Ree thought about Frank Hamilton Cushing's description of his life at Zuni. He would write notes by kerosene lamp as the Zuni chief and his family sat around the fire, the chief's wife cuddling her baby. The chief was deep in thought, occasionally speaking to the lieutenant at his side, not unlike a businessman giving notes to a secretary. The chief's two adolescent sons sharpened arrowheads. His eldest daughter polished a pot. It was cozy and domestic, and although Ree knew that the Zuni people had contempt for how Cushing had pushed his way in at first, they had assimilated him. He had his place by the fire.

Ree built a little campfire outside her wagon. It was small and smoky, too hot to sit near but too cold to warm her if she sat back. She hadn't mastered the skills that burning sheep dung required. She thought enviously of Frank Hamilton Cushing, with his adopted family, his pleasant fire, his place in that world.

Later she realized she had fallen asleep, despite all the disappointment and discomfort, but at that moment, when a white man in buckskins and Zuni jewelry walked through the smoke and sat down by her, she really thought it was Frank Hamilton Cushing.

"Now perhaps you understand," he said, as he settled his long, thin body down by the fire and crossed his arms over his knees. "You can see I had no choice. The Zuni didn't like it, but I had to take the chance of insisting they give me a room, or I'd have had no place to live. Not even this." He rubbed the smoke from his eyes, then took the fire stick from her hands and rearranged the dung coals.

"You've got a lot to learn," he said. "When I first got to Zuni, I wasn't alone. I came with a whole expedition and stayed behind after they went home. Back in Washington, they knew where I was. I had many people behind me."

This mean streak of Frank's hadn't come through in his sweet accounts of life with the Zuni people.

Soon the fire glowed brightly, with a comforting crackle and no smoke. Frank loaded his pipe from a beaded pouch and took some puffs. He settled back, the bowl of the pipe in his long delicate fingers, and studied her as a doctor might.

"I admire you," he said. "I didn't do what you're doing. People like to think I did, but they also want to believe that the West was explored and developed only by mountain men and cavalry heroes. I was brave because I wasn't alone. You are alone."

Ree began to sob. The combination of feelings: that she was such a pathetic failure and that she had outdone her hero, was too much. She wondered if Attencia and Golney could hear her wails through the night's silence. She could hear owls and coyotes at night, so surely her neighbors could hear her. Would they take pity and visit? What would they think of this strange man by her fire in his buckskin outfit and long blond hair?

When she opened her eyes, he was gone. Her fire glowed comfortingly. She must be getting better at it. She would get better at everything. She was new at this, but she was learning.

Every day she convinced herself Ned would return. One morning, as she cleaned the glass front of the pawn cabinet, her back turned to the door, someone came in. She was about to turn with a smile of greeting on her face when she saw in the mirror of the panes that it was Sack. Her shoulders fell and she threw the sponge to the floor with disappointment. She didn't want to turn around. Sack didn't say anything, but stood watching her in a way that made her feel uncomfortable.

"Hey, good worker!" he finally said. "This place looks great. I knew you'd be good at this."

Slowly she bent over to get the sponge, picked it up, and turned to face him.

"You don't look happy," he said. "What's wrong?"

"Oh, I was hoping it would be a customer. A paying customer," she improvised.

"Well, that's what the owner wants to hear," he said. "So how's it been going?"

Soon they were bent over the account books. She was proud that Sack was so pleased with how the store looked and the sales. But she wanted to see Ned coming through the door.

Sack brought fresh vegetables and fruit, which she gratefully munched. Her diet of canned peaches, canned tomatoes, and oily sardines was boring.

Throughout the day, Indian customers came and went. Sack watched her serve them, a proprietary look on his face.

"I've made you what you are today," he said, which made her cringe.

"I'm not going to do this forever."

"Do you want me to start looking for a replacement?" he countered, which sent a spasm of terror through her. Without this job, she couldn't afford to stay in Lost Wash until everything she hoped for worked out.

"No, I'll stay for now," she said, and he nodded, pleased that his bullet had found its mark. What else could she do? Maybe she could arrange to be a teacher. Word had spread that the Indian agent for the area was on his way, sending frantic Navajo customers running off to hide their children so he couldn't kidnap them to go to the boarding schools. If she could convince him to let her start a school here, she would be the hero of Lost Wash. Ned would be so pleased. Why hadn't she thought of this before?

She was in the middle of a complicated transaction involving measuring flour to the half-penny for an anxious customer with just a few coins to spend when the door must have opened without her hearing the bell, and suddenly Ned was there. Just as she saw him, he saw Sack standing to the side. Ned's eyes caught hers and her mouth dropped open, but she couldn't think what to say. Ned held a hand up in a helpless little wave, his head tipped toward Sack, then he turned the wave into pointing at the customers as if to indicate she looked to busy to interrupt, and he turned and went out. Sack had a curious, questioning look, his eyes and forehead tightened.

Sack came behind the counter and tried to help her with the next few customers, as if trying to hurry things along, but it only made it harder for her to work. She was making mistakes anyway, because she was wondering when Ned would show up again, if ever. And what was Sack going to say about this? Finally the store was empty.

"So you two did have something going on at San Gabriel," Sack said.

"What!" said Ree. "That's ridiculous."

"Yeah, but then you moved up in the world."

"What are you talking about?"

"Your Indian gal couldn't give you what rich old Mary could, so you kept her on the side for the summer."

"Gal? I don't know what you're talking about."

"Were you seeing her while you were with Wheelwright? Is that why you left? You chose love over money, didn't you? Well, I'm impressed. Impressed with your stupidity, that is. You could have had both if you played your cards right."

"Sack, did someone shoot you in the head lately, and be dumb enough not to kill you? You're not making any sense. And I did not go after Wheelwright's money, how many times do I have to tell you?"

"You and the Indian freak got some scheme going? You tell me the plan and I bet I can come up with something even better, if you cut me in."

"I don't think like you. I came here to live like Frank Hamilton Cushing, you know that. Ned happened to be here, and why do you keep talking about him like he's a wo…" Her voice trailed off at the end as she suddenly didn't know what to think.

"You don't know?" Sack said slowly, ducking his chin and looking at her almost with concern. Then he straightened up. "You've got to be! You've got to! This is too funny!" he sputtered.

"What are you saying?" Ree said. "You don't know anything."

"That's the same Indian as was at San Gabriel," said Sack. "The one I almost got into a fight with. Well, why do you think I stopped? You think I'd ever run from a fight? Is that what you've been thinking of me all this time?"

"I don't think about you all that much, if you want to know the truth."

"Of course not, you're thinking about your manly Indian girlfriend. What is she, a student of Klah? Going to the weird Indian school?"

"Didn't you learn anything at Columbia?" shouted Ree. "That's part of their culture. It's a really good part."

"I'm sure you'd think so," said Sack. "It's right up your alley. And Wheelwright's, too. And then there's those lovesick puppies, Benedict and Mead. With their little love trips to the field."

"Shut up!" Ree screamed in a way she hadn't since her adolescent days, which had only resulted in her father slamming the door on her and going off to his synagogue, leaving her more lonely than ever. "Shut up about Benedict. All you've ever done is make fun of something beautiful."

"I thought you didn't like it one bit, Benedict and Mead. Now it's something beautiful. So, I'm right, things were going on with you and Wheelwright and you and what's her name? Oh yes, Ned. Nezbah to those who knew her in skirts, I bet."

"Get out of here," Ree said. "Get out of here. You're wrong and you're mean. You don't know anything but money. And you're totally wrong about Ned. I should know." She immediately regretted saying that. To make up for it, she pushed Sack's shoulder, but it was harder and stronger than she expected. He let her pummel him, laughing.

"That's a real man's shoulder," he said. "If you really want to know anything, I'm available anytime. You've been barking up the wrong tree, honey."

"What do you know about Ned?" the words were out of her mouth before she could protect herself. In all the years she had known Sack, she had never been so unguarded, so unprotected, since that horrible day that Sylvester Baxter had spoken at the Brooklyn Museum.

"I'm sure I don't know as much as you, but I know a woman when I see one. You seem kind of surprised. How can you say "he" and "his" and not let it bother you? I find it really hard to do. You must know Ned really well. She makes you do that, right?"

"She doesn't make me do—" Ree couldn't believe she called Ned 'she.' The last thing she wanted was for Sack to know how much he was getting to her right now.

She stopped pounding on him and ran out the door. A family was just coming in, the children smiling at the prospect of candy, the mother carrying a folded rug proudly. As she ran past them, their faces fell. "Come back," the children yelled and the oldest ran after her, the younger ones following. She just wanted to find a place to be alone and hide, but there was nothing but the endless land. She sat on little hump of dirt, but the children surrounded her with hopeful faces.

"Go inside," she said. "The man will sell you candy." She waved them away. But they didn't understand what she was saying. She kept waving at them to leave, impatient to be alone with her thoughts. Finally Sack stood in the doorway looking for her. She pointed to show the children and they ran off. With the circle of children gone, Sack still stared at her, and she had never felt so naked in her life.

Hadn't she always known this about Ned on some level? She wasn't as surprised as she had acted with Sack. It explained everything, like the strange tone of voice that even Frances had talking about Ned, about why Ned didn't seem part of his--or should that be her?--own little community. She couldn't even think about Ned without stumbling on pronouns. And this must be the answer to the mystery that she had mulled over for weeks: Klah wouldn't teach Ned because Ned wasn't a man. That was why Ned hadn't explained it to her either. And Wheelwright hadn't caught on, because Wheelwright was as stupid as she was.

Stupid was how she felt. All her dreams and fantasies about how she and Ned would get married and have a hogan and she would be part of the tribe—it was never going to happen. How would the Navajo people treat a female who took a bride? Was Ned the only one? Apparently they couldn't become shamans like Klah. All she knew about this was what the cook had said that night in Wheelwright's kitchen, and the word he used, 'nadle.'

What was Ned supposed to do, put on a skirt and weave and have children? Ned was far more masculine than

Klah. She couldn't picture Ned as a Navajo mother any more than she could see herself once again in the long dresses and corsets she had worn in New York, or see herself preparing Shabbat dinner for a husband and children. She and Ned were a different breed of human. But it wasn't only about whatever Sack was insinuating. There was nothing about Benedict that was anything like Ned. There wasn't even anything about Mead like this.

There had been those tough looking horse-loving cowgirls at San Gabriel. But every woman looked more masculine dressed to go riding at a dude ranch. That was part of the fun and even Ruth had dressed that way. Ned was something else, and she was glad that the Navajo people had a word for it. But having a word wasn't all that Ned needed.

The only one who could tell her more was Ned. What would happen if she confronted her? She could hardly deny it. Or perhaps she would, and what could Ree say to that? It would be all over for their friendship. If she confronted Ned, she would have to be sure.

Maybe Ned would be relieved to have it in the open. Maybe Ned suffered with her secrets as much as Ree carried the burden of her own. Maybe Ned had never talked about it, and opening up to Ree would be the liberation she had wanted for a lifetime, and together they would share in the joy of letting go of the secrets.

Ree thought about her own secret of the Frank Hamilton Cushing outfit, which she had never shown to anyone since that terrible day at the Brooklyn Museum. Even Sack had the good sense never to mention it again. Did making the outfit mean she had wanted to do as Ned had, wearing men's clothes, dreaming of a man's life? No, her dream had been to live like Frank Hamilton Cushing, doing what women were not allowed to do, not to be him. Maybe Ned was the same, wanting to do what medicine men did, not wanting to be a man. Ned had never said that.

Ned needed her. She believed in Ned's dream. She wanted Ned to have the training from Klah, or another medicine man. She still wanted to be with Ned as much as before. Maybe this was better. Had she really thought that she could love a man? Now that she understood about Ned, she understood her feelings for him. They had never been for a man. They had been for the unique person that Ned was.

She wanted to find Ned and tell how she felt. She wanted to tell how she loved Ned even more now than she had before, wanted Ned more, had even bigger dreams for the two of them. She wanted Ned to explain it all to her, about nadles, and Klah, and what Ned's life had been like. This was much, much bigger than her passion for Ruth had ever been. She had never known who Ruth truly was. But it was as if Ned wore her inside on her outside, the men's clothes being how she really felt about herself. What was in Ned was a woman with a secret, a woman so alone in life. And that inside was what Ree wanted so much to touch, to hold, to protect. To love, in a way she had never felt love before. She had to find Ned right away, and offer all she had and was.

But first she had to face Sack again. He had left her to sit alone. She had been so deep in thought she hadn't noticed the blazing sun. Usually she avoided this time of day. She could feel the hot burnt skin on her face and arms. She had to go inside. What would Sack say? If she didn't go into the trading post, she had nowhere to go but back to her wagon, which would be unbearably hot. There was no fresh water there. Anyway, she would have to face Sack sometime.

"I don't see enough small bags of cornmeal out here," Sack said when she came in. "Can you fill ten more? And do you have a list of women with rugs to sell?" He wasn't going to say anything. Relieved, she went to the storeroom to dole out grain.

She was carrying jugs of fresh water back to her wagon at twilight when Ned appeared. She had thought the sudden appearances coincidental, but now she realized Ned was as aware of her as she was of Ned, and as uncertain of how a meeting would go as she was, as afraid to approach.

"Ree," said Ned stepping alongside her. "Want some help with those?" Ned reached for a jug.

That was very manly thought Ree—or was it just part of the act? She stopped and faced Ned. She thought Ned would see immediately in her face that she knew the truth, but Ned looked happy to see her and took the heavy jugs with a smile. What should she do? She couldn't speak. Ned smiled even more, perhaps assuming that the sight of her had left Ree speechless. Ree finally stuttered out "hi" and stood frozen on the path. Ned's face dropped too and the jug hung limply.

"Is something wrong?" Ned said, and Ree wondered how she could ever mistake this soft high sound for a man's voice. You see what you want to see, was all she could console herself with. She had thought of Ned as tall, as someone she looked up to, who looked down on her lovingly, but now she realized they were about the same height. Ned's broad shoulders, however, were real, as were her unusually narrow hips for a woman. She saw how she had been mistaken, but she also saw all that was womanly. Navajo men did not have whiskers, but Ned's face only looked mannish due to the leathery tan on her already dark skin.

"You're staring at me," Ned said, and her face darkened. The smile was replaced with a look both scared and angry. They stood silently. Ree knew she was examining Ned like a specimen, searching for male versus female. Ned drew back stiffly and stood up straighter.

"Go ahead," Ned spit out. "Go ahead and look." She spun around. Once her back was completely turned to Ree, she began to walk away.

"No," Ree said with a shriek. "No, it isn't like that. Please don't go. I—I love you. I do." She couldn't believe she had said that. Ned slowed down a little. "I didn't know about you," Ree sputtered out slowly. "I love you for who you are. I didn't know—." She was stuck for words for a moment, then continued. "about you. Please don't go."

Ree ran a few steps and threw her arms around Ned. Ned pushed her away, but they faced each other. Ned looked down and started away again.

"Please Ned, please don't go. I think you're wonderful. I've wanted to know you better since the day we met. When you left Los Luceros so suddenly, I was broken hearted. I was hoping I'd find you again, it's a lot of why I came here. I've never met anyone like you."

"I'll bet," said Ned, but he turned toward her again.

"Sack told me," Ree said. "He's mean. I wish so much he hadn't. I wasn't trying to pry, it never crossed my mind. He just wanted to hurt me by saying it."

"And did he? Hurt you?"

"At first I was upset, because I was shocked. I had to think about it." Ned shook, ready to run at any moment. Ree put a hand on Ned's forearm. "I had to think about Klah, and about nadles, and what I knew about them."

"What do you know about them?"

"Very little. I was hoping you could tell me more."

Ned pulled out of her grasp and stalked off. Ree ran after her and touched her back, but Ned pulled away.

"No, not like an anthropologist! That's not what I meant at all. You don't know much about me either, you know. You don't know my secrets. You don't know why I lost my job at San Gabriel, do you?"

Ned looked up with interest.

"You don't know why I was at San Gabriel, either," Ree said. "I was there because I was in love with my professor. I went there because it was a place I knew she liked. But she showed up and I got in a fight with her girlfriend. So I got fired."

"What's that supposed to mean to me?" Ned asked.

Ree was stumped for a moment. To her it all connected, but she didn't have the words to explain it. She was shocked at herself for putting the sad story into words to tell Ned. She had never said it aloud.

"It's supposed to mean that I loved a woman before I met you, and now I love you." When Ned just stared back, Ree went on. "That's how I am. There were a lot of women like that at San Gabriel." Suddenly Ree realized that it was no coincidence that Ned had been at the dude ranch. Her whole sense of the world out here in the Southwest was spinning.

"What were you doing at San Gabriel?" she said before she thought about her words.

"Just a job," said Ned.

"Did they know? When they hired you?"

"No, that's kind of how I got fired, too. I think your friend Sack may have told them."

"He's not my friend, he's mean. How did Sack know?"

"He makes it his business."

They stood without talking, until finally Ree set her jug down and Ned did the same.

"I don't know," said Ned. "I've never talked about this with anyone. I wasn't expecting to."

"I wasn't either," said Ree. "But don't you think I would have found out?"

"I hadn't figured it out," said Ned. "I was going to go away for a long time and hope you didn't come back."

"But didn't you come looking for me just now?"

"I guess I did. I don't understand myself sometimes. I knew I had to stay away, but I wanted to see you. I don't know anything. Sometimes I would see those ladies at San Gabriel, but I didn't really want what they had. Because it's also about being a healer like Hosteen Klah. That's what I've wanted all my life more than anything."

"So that's why Klah wouldn't teach you."

Ned hung her head, then looked up defiantly. "But that's not the end of it. Hosteen Klah is considered the best of all the medicine men, but he's not the only one. I'm going to find a teacher."

"Of course you will," said Ree. "I want the best for you. I want to help you. Since I found out, I want it even more."

"I appreciate it," said Ned. "I appreciate that you believe in me. Only Frances ever has. Everyone else just wishes I would go away. They know me but they think I'm wrong."

"It wasn't always that way," said Ree.

"That's what I've heard," said Ned. "But it's hard to believe, the way things are now. If only Hosteen Klah had been willing to talk to me."

"He has to make a lot of choices about how he spends his time. He's old and he knows what he needs to do most of all. Maybe he just felt it was too late to start teaching you."

"He could have been nicer about it," said Ned.

"I wish he had," said Ree. "I wish you could have everything you want out of life."

"You too," said Ned, and they smiled at each other.

Without saying more, they picked up the jugs. Soon the cooking fire was blazing, a pot of stew hanging over it. With nothing to do, they sat awkwardly, watching the sunset instead of each other.

"All right," Ned said suddenly, as if coming to a great decision. "I'll tell you." Ree smiled and moved closer, but Ned sat up straighter, stared into the fire, and spoke soft and uncertainly.

"I guess it began with clothes. I never wanted to wear skirts and blouses. But my parents wouldn't let me wear boys' clothes. We battled all the time. When I went out with the sheep, I would even try to get my skirt trampled and ripped and covered with dirt, but then I just had to clean and sew them. Finally I stole a pair of trousers from the wagon of a family passing through town. If I'd stolen from any of the neighbors, it would have been discovered. I hid the trousers in a small cave near where the sheep grazed, and I could wear them for a few hours. When I wore pants, I wasn't Nezbah who had to weave and cook. No, I was Ned, who could ride horses to all the old places where my people had been and where their secrets were hidden.

"I took the sheep into the most difficult to reach and isolated places so that no one would see my pants. Climbing rocky paths and carrying stubborn sheep made me hard and muscular. I found many secret, hard to reach places. Sometimes I found sacred objects--eagle feathers, clay pots, turquoise beads. The Anglo archaeologists would pay good money for those, and to be led to those places. But when I found them, I pushed rocks to make it harder to get to, or covered them more. I wanted to hide them but I didn't want to disturb them. I always pictured the quiet moment when someone like me left them as an offering. I don't even know how I knew to do all this, it was just a feeling that was so strong that I had to do it.

"Only Frances understood me. She would take me far into the land to find herbs for healing. I wanted to learn, and she taught me all she could, but she only knew what women know. One day we went two days walk from my home. I was so thrilled to be old enough to go with her.

'You're getting big,' Frances told me. 'You've got to be careful the Anglos don't see you. They'll steal you and take you away to their school. I took you out here for a few days because I heard they were coming.'

"I loved staying with Frances. At home, I felt like my mother saw me as just one more kid grabbing at her skirt. Whenever one of the older children was stolen away to go to school, there was always a new baby. I felt replaceable. But with Frances I was the only one. She picked me to save.

"Grandmother," I asked her one day as we walked hand in hand, trying to balance each other as we picked our way through a field of cactus. 'Why did you take me and not Gilda or John Billy? Aren't they going to be stolen to go to school?"

'Don't you like being with me?' asked Frances. 'You're always asking to go up into the hills.'

'I do, I love it,' I told her. "I was just wondering. So it's not just about going to school?"

'Do you want to go to school?' she asked.

'No, I want to learn about our land. About where all the herbs are. About the special songs and places.'

'That's what I thought. You're not like the others, Nezbah. You're more like me. You like the old ways.'

"Teach me more," I said, but it got me thinking something else. I didn't want to end up like my mother, surrounded by children and always kept busy by my father. But what else was there? My brothers were learning to hunt and live in the mountains and build hogans. They didn't have to sit on the ground all day learning to card and spin and weave. I hated that, I wanted to move around. My legs were always cramped and stiff. And I wanted to know other stuff that the boys were taught that they wouldn't even let girls know about. Most of all, the boys could run and climb without tripping over their big skirts."

Ned continued, "The cactus field finally gave way to an area of rounded boulders. I had to curl my toes to grip as we walked, and Frances grabbed me to keep from sliding. She hummed a chant I remembered from a ceremony. I hummed along, hoping I would remember the tune in the future."

'I wish I could remember those better,' Frances told me. 'I just don't have the knack. I don't know which tune goes with which ceremony. That's why the real chanters are so important. They remember. Now we're almost at the place where the plant for pneumonia grows. Be careful where you step and look for white flowers.'

"We both bent over to search. Frances went ahead over a rise, then she gasped so loud I jumped."

"Snake?" I yelled, but Frances turned and hushed me. She didn't wave me away as she would have for a snake. She let me creep silently up to her side. I didn't see anything but brush."

"What is it?' I whispered."

"Frances pointed toward a bush not far away. She whispered, 'look closely, there's someone there.'

Ned stopped talking and stared off into the distance, as if picturing his memory.

"The bushes shook and then I saw a man watching us. He didn't walk away, but he didn't give a friendly sign, either."

"Frances called out to him.'Please! I don't want to disturb you. I just want to know about this flower. I've picked this before but I'm not sure it's the right one for the chest sickness. Can you tell me?' She held out her collecting bag and picked one of the flowers from it, holding it up for the man to see."

"The man didn't answer at first, just looked at us. I felt I was being stared at, not Frances. He locked eyes with me."

'This is my granddaughter,' said Frances, but the man tipped his chin as if asking her to be quiet."

Ned stared off into the distance, as if picturing the memory.

"I ran right up to the man. He was dressed in the old ways, with a loose shirt. He had a bandanna tied around his forehead, and little leather medicine bags hung around his neck and from his waist sash. He was a medicine man.

'Nezbah, stay here,' said Frances. But we were already face to face, examining each other head to toe. I had never been this close to a medicine man. They come when someone is sick or dying, and the children are told to be quiet and stay out of the way. I thought he would do something magic, like I had heard. But all he did was look at me. No man had ever looked so deeply into my eyes. Men barely noticed a shy little girl like me, except to order me around or yell at me. And he didn't stand like a man, tall and angry."

'That's the right flower,' he said to Frances, but still staring at me. 'But be sure you only pick it at this time of moon.' His voice was very soft and gentle, like an old woman whose voice has gone low.

'Are you a man or a woman?' I asked. I don't even know why I said it. It came from my heart, not my head.

'Nezbah!' said Frances. 'Get back here,' but the man just stared at me.

'This is Hosteen Klah,' Frances said to me. 'He's very important to our people. He knows all the old ways. He leads the chants at the ceremonies.' She turned to him. 'I'm sorry Mr. Klah, for the rudeness of my granddaughter.'

'Perhaps she asks herself this question,' he said.

'I've wondered,' Frances mumbled so softly I've always wondered if I heard her correctly.

"Suddenly I felt really shy. I just wanted to run from both of them.

'Come Nezbah, we have to let Mr. Klah find what he needs here. We'll leave him alone now. Don't bother him.'

She pulled me back the way we had come. She didn't say anything. I waited until the man and even the hill he was on disappeared beyond the horizon.

'Grandmother,' I asked. 'I don't understand. Was that a man or a woman?'

'That was a nadle. A special person, who preserves our old ways.'

'But he looks like a man. He dresses like a man. Why do I think he's a woman?'

'That's what a nadle is. I don't know exactly myself. Only the nadles really know. They seem to be men. Some of them become wives of men, and dress and do the work of women. Some are like Hosteen Klah. He remembers our stories and songs. He heals the sick and leads the ceremonies.'

"I was very excited. I had thought being a man or being a woman was all you needed to know about someone. What your life would be was determined by this alone.

'Did he used to be a girl?' The words burst out. I already pictured myself dressed as a man, being seen as a man, or as much of a man as Hosteen Klah was.

'I don't think so,' said Frances.

'Oh,' I said. I waited a while and then I had to ask again. 'You don't think Hosteen Klah was a girl? You mean he might have been? And he grew up to be a man? I don't understand.'

'I don't either,' Frances sighed. 'It happens but we don't understand it. Hosteen Klah knows, and others like him.'

'What if I wanted to be one, too?'

'Nezbah, it's a very difficult life. The Anglos don't understand at all. They want everyone to be a man or a woman. Even many of our own people get angry about it.'

'But how do you get to be one?'

'You don't choose it. You are or you aren't.'

'How do you know?'

'I guess you just know.'

'Can Hosteen Klah tell? Is that what he meant? That I ask myself?'

'Do you, Nezbah? Do you think you're like him?'

'But that's why I want to know. Did he used to be a girl?'

'I don't think so. I have heard that a girl can be a nadle. I just never met one.'

'Grandmother, I thought you knew everything.'

'Why do you think that? You know I can't remember which song goes with which ceremony, and I didn't know about the white flowers.'

'Oh, I knew that, but I also thought you knew everything.'

'Thank you Nezbah, you have great faith in me.'

'Does Hosteen Klah know everything?'

'He knows more about our people than anyone.'

'I want to be like him. I want to be a healer.'

'He only teaches boys.'

'Why can't he teach me? He should teach people like him, the nadles.' It was exciting just to say the word. It was the most important word I had ever heard.

'I've never heard of him teaching a girl. Maybe the boys he teaches are nadles, but they are more like boys.'

'Who teaches the girl nadles?'

'I don't know,' said Frances.

'Let's go back,' I said, pulling on her arm. 'Let's go ask him. Quick, let's go.'

'We can't,' Frances said, but she let me pull her back up through the cactus and across the rounded boulders. We were both panting and sweating by the time we reached the top of the rise. But no one was in sight.

'Hosteen Klah, Hosteen Klah,' I called out. I wanted Frances to yell too, and I think she wanted to, but she didn't want to disturb him. I called and called, but no one answered."

Ned looked into Ree's eyes, then looked off into the distance.

"After that, I wanted to be a medicine man like Klah, holding all the songs, sand paintings, rituals, and other secrets of a chant ceremony in my mind so that they would not be lost and could be passed on to the next generation. Even at school when I was told that by learning to read and write what we knew we would save our history, I knew it wasn't the same. Perhaps everyone could read this knowledge, but it didn't mean they really had it. It was only what was carried inside a person that could be passed on to be held inside another person.

"I searched for a teacher but no one would have me. Hosteen Klah is very selective of his students, but even the lesser medicine men would not take me. I was friends with a boy who studied with a medicine man. He told me they learn by slow and patient listening, memorizing, and repeating at every opportunity, and especially during ceremonies. The boy told me there were techniques for memorizing he was being taught, but he thought they might be secret and wouldn't tell. Hosteen Klah studied for twenty-six years before performing his first chant ceremony. It sounded difficult, but I wasn't discouraged. I went to every ceremony I was allowed, listened carefully and tried to remember.

"Most of all, I believe that I'm like Klah. We're sometimes called the Changing Ones," Ned told Ree. Her voice was shy and defiant, as if she had never said it aloud before.

"Is that why you dress like a man?" asked Ree. "But Klah doesn't dress like a woman."

"I don't think of it that way. I dress the way I should dress. Part of it is hoping that a teacher will take me on, seeing that I'm willing to do all that a man does and don't want to do what a woman does. Although Klah does what a woman does—he weaves."

"Why is that?" asked Ree.

"When he was a boy, his legs were hurt when he was cutting wood. He couldn't walk for a long time, so his mother and aunts taught him to weave. But I think he would have learned anyway. That's the nature of Changing Ones, they don't follow the course laid out for them by tradition."

"It's funny, you know," said Ree. "To be like Klah is to be most responsible for preserving your traditions, but at the same time, to be like Klah is to most break away from them."

"I never thought of it that way."

"That's the kind of thing I studied in anthropology school. You have to step back and take a longer view."

"That's impressive," said Ned. "But my people don't like anthropologists. My grandmother Frances didn't want me to talk to Klah because he gives our secrets to them."

"Why did you try then?" asked Ree

"Because I want to study with Klah so much, and I believe in whatever he wants to do. His main apprentice, who studied with him since he was a boy, died suddenly a few years ago, and now he has no one to pass his knowledge to. I was sure he would accept me, but he wouldn't. He knew I wasn't a man."

"How did he know and I didn't?"

"I think he remembered me from when we met when I was a little girl. That's what you have to understand about him. He's not like others. He has an amazing mind to remember so much. And it's so much more than memory. He sees much more than you or I could. But I believe that I have that potential. I believe that I can learn. But I guess he's saying he doesn't see that in me."

Ree put her hand on Ned's shoulder, who didn't move away. The fire was getting lower. They sat silently and their bodies grew closer, warming each other.

"Do all the nadles become healers like Klah?" Ree asked.

"No, only a few. Most of those who are born men become wives to warriors. They can wear women's clothing and do the jobs of women.

"What about the ones who are born women?"

"It's harder. It's harder for women to live like men, like I try to do. Some never try and you would never know how they were inside. Others do it so well, you never know they are women. The people who know I'm a woman are the people who knew me as a girl, and those like Klah who can see more deeply into a person."

"How do you know Klah recognized you from your childhood? Or that he knew you are a woman? Did he say so when he said he wouldn't teach you?"

Ned smiled. "You're so nice to think that. He didn't say it, you're right. He just said he couldn't be my teacher and I should go home and learn from my grandmother."

"He didn't say you should get married and have kids?"

"You're right, it could have been worse, but well, it couldn't have been worse. I had tried for years to get to see him. And he didn't give me a chance to show what I know. But he wasn't mean."

"He was always very nice to me," Ree said. "He asked me about where I came from and my religion. He was interested to learn things."

"I don't think I can tell him anything he doesn't already know," said Ned. "But there's so much I want to learn from him!"

"But you can't give up," said Ree. "Look at me, my dream since I was a girl was to be right here."

"To be in Lost Wash?"

"Well, to live among the Indians. To be their friend, to be—" Ree wasn't sure how far she could go with this. "To be part of the community."

"I don't know," said Ned. "Sometimes I don't even feel part of it."

"You don't?"

"I feel too different. If not for Frances, I don't know if I would come to Lost Wash anymore."

"But I thought your people understood that some are Changing Ones," Ree said.

"In the old days, they would have. But these days, with so many changes, people don't believe the same. Especially with the missionaries coming in and telling them what to believe. So many people are giving up the old ways. That's a big part of why I want to study and learn and be like Hosteen Klah."

"It's funny," said Ree. "Back where I live, because things are changing, women can do more, not less. The way my people used to live, by now I would have been married and had children so young, and I wouldn't have gone to school, and I certainly wouldn't have left home and gone far away."

"So you don't want to live in the traditional ways of your people, but you want to live in the traditional ways of mine?"

They both laughed. "Life's funny," said Ned. Just then a log broke in the fire and crashed, sending out a shower of sparks that made them lean back. Ned's arm went around Ree to steady them both. As they sat back again, the arm stayed and Ree shivered with pleasure. Their cheeks touched, and soon their lips did, too.

Ree hadn't closed the curtain on the wagon, so the bright sun woke Ned suddenly. Ree was already awake, facing Ned, looking at her.

"Did you just wake up?" Ned asked.

"No, I've just been watching you. Making sure you're really there."

Ned blushed. "This is really cozy, kind of like my parents' wagon. Adults slept on the ground alongside, but little kids slept in the back while the wagon rolled along."

"I love it. You can sleep here anytime," said Ree, then turned away with embarrassment. "Oh my gosh, I have to get to the trading post. There's always someone there by sunup." She was out of bed and rushing to get dressed before she had time to think of how nice it would have been to stay longer. Ned brought the horse and Ree rode to work with her arms around Ned. Then Ned was gone.

Another day began, but it was a day like no other in Ree's life. All she could think about was Ned and the night they had spent together. It was another perfect blue sky, hot, silent, motionless day. She paced the yard of the trading post, kicking at the slightest divot in the dirt. When would Ned return to make love again? Time was going so slowly.

For so long all she had wanted had been to live like Frank Hamilton Cushing and impress Ruth. What she wanted from Ruth was vague and studious and dreamy, the two of them on a quiet evening, sitting side by side reading, perhaps with a cat at their feet. But with Ned, now she wanted a raging fire and flesh upon flesh. Was it her fantasies which had changed or she herself, switched on now to feelings she had never had in New York, released with the fury of the sudden thunderstorms she had seen in this strange land?

As the harvest season brought more money in, there were busier days at the trading post. The men gambled in the yard outside, while the women endlessly discussed the new selection of calico fabrics, and the children speculated how many pieces of peppermint were in the new jar. Friendly chatter filled the room as Ree bustled from customer to customer. They asked many questions before they spent their hard-earned money.

The bell on the door jangled so constantly she paid it no mind, but suddenly a hush fell on the room and she realized the bell had just rung. The crowd of women blocking the doorway parted the way they did when a white person entered. With a gasp, she saw Ruth Benedict in the doorway, her dark silhousette framed by the glare of the blazing sun behind her. So this was how the Indians felt during their rituals when the terrifying kachinas appeared.

Anyone coming in had to give their eyes a few seconds to adjust to the dim light inside, so Ruth stood blinking. Remembering their last encounter at San Gabriel, Ree thought first to run out the back door, but then reminded herself that she had every right to be here.

Ree's terror was replaced by a swell of pride that made her stand up straighter behind the counter. At last, Ruth had come to see her. Maybe they were hearing about her back east. They were sure to be envious of her friendship with Mary Cabot Wheelwright. Maybe they had changed their minds and would give her a field placement after all.

Ruth walked up to the counter, still struggling to see. "One of my informants told me you were here."

"Sack Sackmann won this place in a poker game, and he hired me to work here." Ree had never felt so sure of herself speaking to Ruth. Now that she was with Ned, she felt differently about Ruth. Poor Ruth and Margaret could never know the joy of what she had with Ned, she was sure. They were too intellectual, too much in their heads. She and Ned had something that came from the earth and the stars. They had found their love by a fire, in the desert, not in a college lecture hall. She felt a sort of pity for Ruth, and it amazed her. How much had changed since she had left San Gabriel in such shame!

"Henrietta," said Ruth, and then just stood there, saying nothing. She swung around and looked in every corner of the store. The Navajo customers had gone back to their own conversations.

"Ree," said Ree. "I call myself Ree now." It was exciting to use this name with Ruth. "So are you traveling through? Heading for Chaco?"

"Dr. Boas asked me to speak with you. Is there somewhere we can talk in private?"

Her tone sent Ree back to Columbia, that pathetic and desperate girl again, wishing and hoping. Just then the bell on the door clanged and she caught a glimpse of a man's hat. Was it Ned? She couldn't let Ned see her this way.

"That's all right, they aren't interested in my business. I can't leave the store, this is my job." She wondered what Ruth thought of the new assertive Ree, more like Margaret than like Henrietta. Maybe this is what Ruth liked in a woman. What if Ruth suddenly started to like her? Would she choose Ruth or Ned?

"All right, we'll talk here," said Ruth. She cleared her throat, crossed her arms, and stood up straighter. Even with all that, she was still the dainty lady who had stood at the lectern for Ree to admire so many times.

"Dr. Boas and the department are concerned that you are here. We gave you every consideration for a field assignment and didn't feel you were properly prepared. We can still offer you field work in New York City. Or perhaps Chicago? We're just starting a new project there. "

"You think I would leave after all I've been through to get here?"

"Please don't make this harder than it is. We're being very generous to offer a New York field assignment."

"But I don't want that. All my life I dreamed of living here. From when I first heard of Frank Hamilton Cushing, I wanted to be like him." Ree couldn't believe she was finally getting the chance to explain herself to Ruth. She wanted to slow down, add more details. Maybe she could also explain what happened at San Gabriel. Ruth would be so impressed to hear about Ned—no, maybe she wouldn't. Ruth had a bad marriage with Stanley, and she wouldn't think much of Ree being with a man. Ned had told Ree to talk about her only as a man. But she could tell Ruth. Ruth would be fascinated that she was so close to a nadle. It was an anthropologist's dream.

"We all have dreams," said Ruth. "Like Thoreau said, if you're building castles in the air, be sure to put a solid foundation under them. Your dream is not what the department wants. We've spent decades in this region building our reputation with the Navajo people and the anthropologists and archaeologists from other universities. We have guidelines and rules and oversight for every student we place in the field here."

"I'm following the guidelines," said Ree, although she knew that spending the night with Ned, a probable subject, was not allowed, at least for women anthropologists. Sack had told her what some men did, claiming there was a lot Frank Hamilton Cushing didn't put in his writings about his life at Zuni pueblo, but Ree had told him she didn't want to study that.

"You can't be working within the guidelines, because the guidelines include working closely with an advisor," snapped Ruth.

"I wanted to work with you," said Ree. "I worked hard all those years, wrote all those papers, you gave me A's." She heard a screechy quality in her voice and saw that the room had grown quiet. The customers were standing by, watching the Anglo women argue. Some of them knew enough English to understand and they would explain to the others. Ruth had probably been right to ask for privacy. But anywhere they would have gone it would have been talked about. Ruth didn't understand the first thing about life here.

"I'm in a perfect position," Ree continued, forcing her voice to be calmer. "I'm working in the community, making friends. I'm learning a lot. I'll be able to write some great papers about this." She immediately regretted saying that. If the customers saw her as an anthropologist here to study them, she could forget about real friendships.

What would Ned think? Ned liked that Klah worked with Wheelwright, but Ned knew that Klah controlled the information he gave. Ned wouldn't agree to be studied, it would only hurt him with his own people. Her position was impossible. What would please Benedict would hurt her with the people she wanted to join.

"No, I take that back," said Ree. "I used to want to be an anthropologist, but I don't any more. I don't want to write about my friends and I especially don't want to tell their secrets. I have what I want now, and I don't need what you offer. Why would I want to be in New York City? You never understood, I grew up in those same tenements you want me to study!" She had always wanted to say this to Ruth. "That's not even scholarly! That's not even following your own guidelines!"

Her anger was growing, and she wanted Ruth to strike back. She wanted a loud screaming fight. She wanted to give the customers plenty to talk about, as long as they didn't say that she was writing about their secrets. She wanted them to see how she was breaking with her past and with her own people, and setting her lot with them. She wanted to say those words from the Bible, to say that she had joined a new people like Ruth told Naomi. It was ironic that it was to Ruth she would be saying these words. But all that mattered was that her Navajo neighbors understood. She didn't care any more what Ruth Benedict thought.

But Ruth didn't take the bait. She was silent, although she clenched and unclenched her hands in little girl fists.

"Please don't do this to the department," Ruth finally said. "We spent years teaching you responsible ways to live in other cultures. We have a reputation to protect. Show us that you learned from us. Show me that you learned from me!"

That one made Ree stare at the floor. Then she looked up again.

"I appreciate everything I learned from you. But why couldn't I have a field assignment here? I did everything any one else did to earn it. Why?"

"I wish you wouldn't force me to say this. But just what you're doing here now shows that we were right. You just aren't," she stopped to pick the right word. "Socialized enough. The faculty could see that you were too likely to be a loose cannon. We couldn't risk that. If you'd done what we said, spent a few years being seasoned in New York—"

"But you couldn't make me any promises, right?" asked Ree. "Then don't tell me I should do more. I did all any one else did. Your pet Margaret just didn't like me, isn't that the truth?"

"I can't continue this discussion," said Ruth. "I came here in good faith to ask you to go home. It's more than just the reputation of the department. We're afraid for you. A woman can't be in the field alone, unsupervised. There's plenty of doubt even when they are properly supervised and work with others. If anything happens to you, the future of women in the field will be jeopardized."

"Then your darling Margaret won't be able to stay in Samoa?"

"That has nothing to do with it!" snapped Ruth. "Leave her out of it. You're making it harder for every woman. You could ruin it for all of us."

"What am I doing so wrong? Working in a trading post? A lot of the wives of traders are doing the work of anthropologists. Franc Newcomb has been working with Hosteen Klah for years, making watercolors of his sand paintings. I'll be able to do work like that. I'm already getting close with a local healer." After all, Ned was going to be a healer. Ned already knew some and was going to know more, especially with Ree's support.

"It's not the same," said Ruth. "If Mrs. Newcomb makes a mistake, people will say she's just a white woman who overstepped. But anything you do, they'll say Columbia University was at fault."

"Well, Columbia University is at fault. They should have given me the field assignment. They didn't, and I'm here, and it's a free country."

"For your own good, please leave," said Ruth. "Don't you understand how dangerous it is for you alone here?"

"No," said Ree. "Because I don't spend my time at fancy dude ranches with other anthropologists flattering rich people. I'm here to learn all I can and to be a part of this community. They value me here. The last trader was a drunk who cheated them. They're glad I'm here. They like me here." She pointed her chin at the customers, imagining they would clap with approval, but they were pretending not to be listen. "They do," she insisted. "They trust me, They don't have to listen to our conversation to know that what I'm doing here is all right with them." The shakiness in her voice felt as shaky as this argument.

"Listen to yourself," said Ruth. "I'm trying to help you and you're just trying to hurt me. I never tried to hurt you. I know you think that's what I did, but all I could do was be your teacher. That's all a teacher is allowed to do."

"Tell that to Margaret," said Ree. "Anyway, that doesn't matter any more to me. You don't have to worry about me. I've got a man here, he'll take care of me." She found she enjoyed this jab, this moment of superiority over Ruth, even though she knew it was completely false. But Ruth didn't know that.

"Oh my God," said Ruth, "That's just what we're worried about. Please don't do that. Please leave. Please stay away from the men. Don't you understand how dangerous that is?"

"I'm not in any danger from this man," said Ree. Would she ever learn to think before she spoke? If she hadn't had a need to impress Ruth, she wouldn't have mentioned a man. Now she had made it all so much worse.

"I'm not getting anywhere," said Ruth. "I have to leave now. But please, at least think about what you're doing and what the larger picture is for anthropology. But most of all think about what it means to be the only white woman here."

"Is that how little you think of my friends here?" spat out Ree. "That's what you don't understand. I don't want to be like you and feel so superior, and pretend to be open when really you judge everyone who doesn't look like you. Jews, Navajos. And the men anthropologists judge the women. You should understand, but you don't. You're in the club, and Margaret's in the club, and I'm not. It's just what Sack said."

"And that's another thing. We think Sack is dealing in artifacts. We want to talk to him, also. If you're working with him, you'll have the law to answer to."

"Sure, your archaeologist friends can steal all they want from the dead, but it's because they have the license to do it."

"You're stealing artifacts!"

"I didn't say that," Ree said, making her voice very low. This could destroy the trust she had built with her Navajo neighbors. "I wouldn't do anything to hurt these people. I love their culture, I want to preserve it. Sack's running a trading post here, nothing more. I think you should leave."

"Please," Ruth said. "For your own safety, please go home. I know you think you have good reason to be angry with me and Columbia, and maybe you do, but please think beyond that." She turned and walked toward the door, but her good manners got the best of her and she turned back again. "Goodbye, Henrietta. I can only hope that all will go well for you." With that she was gone. Ree and the crowd of Navajo women and children watched the door bounce to a close behind her, the bell jangling.

After all the years spent treasuring every moment and word with Ruth, Ree could not believe she had told her to go. How did life take you to these unexpected, undesired, surprising places? She wished Hosteen Klah was here, she would like to ask him. She wished Ned had the years of study to answer. How would she face herself after what she had said, but hadn't she been right? Columbia could not control her life forever. They could not take her dreams and her West away from her. If only Sack were here with his righteous indignation about what the professors did.

Ree was trying not to replay the conversation when Ned showed up, as unexpectedly as ever, to invite Ree for a ride out onto the land. "We'll both go on my horse, walking and riding. We need to leave before it begins to get dark, and we'll come back at first light so you can get to work. It won't be easy, but do you want to go?"

Ree was delighted at the thought of spending hours alone with Ned. "I came here to do things and see the land," she said. "I'll keep up."

She closed the trading post early, hoping no one would remember and mention it to Sack. What could he do anyway? He wanted her working there, and she had to have a day off sometime. She searched the trading post for a gift for Ned, then thought of just what to take.

Soon they were far out of sight of Lost Wash. There was nothing ahead but land. "People in the East call this land empty," she told Ned. "But there's so much here." Small brush dotted the pinkish earth, and rock formations of every size and shape scattered to the horizon as they rode further from the trading post.

"Do you see the elephant?" Ned asked. First Ree was puzzled, then Ned pointed until she saw how a large rock with a twisted spout made that impression. Soon they played a game of identifying each distant formation by its shape.

"Frances taught me that," Ned said. "It keeps you busy during long rides up to her mountain camp, where she takes the sheep in the summer. Since the ride was pretty much the same every year, the challenge was to find new shapes and faces in the rocks. I've got names for every one of them. But I want you to find your own."

"That one looks like a trolley car in the city," Ree said.

"Not what I would have thought of," said Ned.

"That's ok. You aren't missing anything worthwhile."

They rode on, and Ree knew that Ned smiled as much as she did. With her arms around Ned's waist, she wondered how she ever had mistaken Ned for a man.

Their trip continued at a steady pace. When the going was easy, they rode on the horse, sometimes together, sometimes one at a time. When it got rough and uphill, they both walked, with Ned leading the horse behind them.

"See that very big mesa?" Ned asked, pointing way into the distance. It was just starting to get dark. "That's where we're going."

Ree thought Ned meant they were going to the base of the mesa, but when they got there, the high walls casting a dark shadow over them, Ned jumped down from the horse and helped her down. "This is it, from this point on we're walking. I'm leaving the horse here to spend the night." Slinging a saddle bag over his shoulder, Ned searched through what looked to Ree like solid rock covered with some dangerous-looking cactus.

"Here it is," said Ned. "It's a trail that's hundreds of years old. It's sort of a staircase. Hard to climb, but well worth it."

"I can't wait to see the view," Ree said as she started up at a fast pace.

Ree was out of breath almost immediately. "Just take small steps," said Ned. "Lots of small steps and you won't feel the rise." That worked better, although Ree felt self-conscious as Ned got further ahead, looking down at her. Ned showed Ree where to step, choosing the best footholds and rocks least likely to see-saw under her weight. Sometimes the trail was covered with small stones that slid under her foot so that she started to slip. She had to be careful not to grab at a cactus in her desperation. At a few points the trail was so slick and narrow that Ned showed her how to walk sideways to move up. In other places Ned led her up ancient stairs of carved foot holds.

"Hey," said Ree, "Where's that view I thought I would see?" All she had seen so far were narrow crevices and tunnel-like arches.

"Soon," Ned said. As Ree came to the peak of a steep, rocky path, her ribs burning, it was as if the world had spun. Before her was a beautiful vista that went on forever, the flat earth far below. Hard as the climb had been, she couldn't believe they were this high, the rest of the world so far away and so endless.

"Ned, this is incredible. I've never seen anything like this."

"It's much better up there," Ned pointed higher, where the steep cliff above disappeared into brush.

"But this is perfect. Let's stay here."

"You've got to see the rest. Don't stop. You've got to keep a pace going, it's much easier to climb that way." Ned started up again and Ree followed. She wanted to keep looking at the view but she had to watch her feet carefully.

Ned hummed a tune as they continued up, and soon Ree learned it and joined in as much as she could with the little spare breath she had.

"I couldn't have done this when I first came West," she said. "I'm a lot stronger now. But not enough, I guess."

"You're almost there," Ned said. "It will be worth it."

The sun was beginning to go down and the colors became more varied.

"Look there, quickly," Ned said, pointing under a bush, and Ree saw the flash of the outline of an animal.

"A fox, I think," said Ned. Ree looked to see it again, but she almost fell and went back to concentrating on her feet.

They reached the steepest crevice of the hike.

"I'll never do it," said Ree. "How am I going to get up there?"

"I know you can," said Ned. "I'm going to get behind and guide you." With Ned's hand warm against the small of her back, and Ned's breath on her neck, Ree went up the slope slowly and firmly. The last step was a big one, throwing her leg over and pulling herself up with Ned pushing, then suddenly she was on the flat plain of the summit, twirling around, seeing in every direction the far off silhouettes of the mountains and the dim shadows of the mostly flat land far below them. There was nowhere left to climb, there was no wall on any side, and she had never felt so free in her life.

"There's nothing holding me in," she told Ned, spreading her arms wide and smiling.

"I thought you'd like it," Ned said. "You enjoy the view, I'm going to gather some firewood." There were stands of twisted little trees here and there on the mesa top. Ree found a natural seat on a rock and explored the view. It felt great to stop climbing, but even more wonderful to see all this and to feel on top of the world.

Soon Ned had a fire going and pulled food from the saddlebags. Potatoes roasted in the fire, and sharpened sticks skewered mutton above it. The scents of the food mingled with the breeze blowing over the sage. As the fire grew brighter, the sun went down and the sky darkened. In the gleam of the flames, Ree and Ned smiled at each other. Ned put an arm around her and taught her a song of the Navajo people. Ree taught Ned a tune that her rabbi hummed during prayer services.

"It's called a niggun," she explained. "The words to this one means that the world is a narrow bridge that we are all walking on, and that only God can save us."

"You should have sung that one while we were walking up here," Ned laughed.

"Let's sing it on the way down." They lay back and watched the stars appear. Ned told Ree the stories that the Navajo people saw in the stars, and Ree told Ned about the Greek mythological characters she had been taught.

"Do the Jews have their own stories in the stars?" Ned asked.

"I never thought about that. I've never heard any. I'll ask about that the next time I run into a rabbi," she giggled.

"You're far from home," Ned said. "Don't you miss it? Don't you miss your people?"

"Not at all," Ree snapped, then she realized it wasn't true. "No, you're right. Sometimes I have questions like that one, and I wish there was someone here to ask. I should write them down. Because there are Jews around. There are some in Santa Fe, and maybe I'll see them sooner or later. But for now, I just want to be here. What could be better than this? This is what I dreamed of all these years."

"Sure," Ned said a little uncertainly.

"It's not the same for you, is it?" Ree asked.

"Well, I've been up here before, but not with someone like you, so that's really nice. More than nice, it's wonderful. But my dream has been to be a healer, and right now it isn't happening."

Ree didn't know what to say. Ned smiled suddenly and stood up. "Get ready for the grand finale!" With that Ned picked up two long branches that weren't burning and used them to push the largest log out of the fire.

"Help me with this," Ned said, and handed Ree one of the branches.

"Why are we doing this?" Ree asked.

"You'll see." They pushed the heavy flaming log to the edge of the mesa top.

"Get ready!" Ned said, "and go!" They heaved the log over the edge and it bounced down, the rush of air causing it to flame and the impact breaking it into pieces, sending out a cascading stream of glowing sparks and little fires that flared all down the cliff edge. It lit up the dark night red and radiant. Ree's face was so red and hot from sitting by the fire that she felt like one of the embers herself. She hugged Ned, wanting to hold their hot faces together and also wanting to watch.

When the last red glow went dark, the moon and endless stars lit the mesa.

"There's no words for this," Ree said. "Thank you so much, this is so beautiful."

Ned gleamed proudly. "It's good to share it with you."

"I have a gift for you," Ree said. "You should have this." She took out the little package she had wrapped in a wad of uncombed wool to protect it. She carefully pulled back the wool to show Ned the stick with the two feathers she had found in the attic at San Gabriel. The deer hooves rattled. She looked up, expecting to see pleasure on Ned's face, but Ned stared at her, shocked.

"Where did you get that?"

"I found it." She didn't want to admit she had also stolen it.

"You shouldn't have that."

"I know, you take it. I want you to have it. I've been waiting for someone to give it to."

"I can't take it. No one can take it. You shouldn't have it. Don't you know what that is?"

"Not exactly. But something sacred, I'm sure."

"I can't tell you what it is, I'm not allowed. Where did you get it? We've got to put it back."

"Ned, I'm so sorry. I didn't know it was that special. I mean, I thought it was very special and I wanted to give it to you—"

"Stop blubbering. You really don't understand my people, even if you think you do. You took that from where it was and carried it around? How long have you had it?"

"Since July." Ree could barely speak, she felt so ashamed.

"We've got to get it back. Where did you find it?"

"It was in the attic at San Gabriel. They didn't even know they had it. I knew it should go back to your people. That's all I was trying to do."

"Stolen by white people, stolen by white people, my whole culture. And they taught my people to hate me, to call me a freak."

"They shouldn't do that," said Ree. "That's what I want to help with here."

"You can't help," said Ned. "It's all stealing, whether it's tourists, or archaeologists, or Wheelwright or you. To me you're all just thieves."

"I can't believe you said that. I didn't steal it, I saved it for your people."

"That's what they all say, when they take our sacred possessions and put them in museums, and then they won't let us in to see them. Did you know that? They won't even let us in to see them? Did you see a lot of Indians back in that museum in Brooklyn you were telling me about, the one where you used to love to go? Did you see a lot of Indians there? Did you ever think about the bones and the skeletons that they have? Would you want your grandmother's bones on display? Your bones?"

"Ned, I didn't do this to you. I'm not an anthropologist anymore. I'm here to learn. You aren't being fair to me."

"You should know better about this." Ned carefully placed the object back in its nest of lamb's wool and wrapped it up. "So you have no idea where this came from?"

"No, that's why I took it from the attic. It was with a bunch of junk. I thought you could find a better place for it."

Ned looked at her coldly.

"I don't understand why you're so angry at me. I'm just trying to help." Just then a log broke in the last of the fire, sending up a shower of sparks. They both looked down the cliff edge, but there was only darkness where the fire show had gleamed.

"I had a dream about this," Ned said quietly. "I dreamed that a white girl gave me a prayer stick. Which is what this is."

"That's good!" said Ree hopefully.

"No, it was a dream that meant I had lost my protection. It meant that I could die, that the powers had turned against me."

"Ned, that's--" she had almost said 'ridiculous.' She was glad she held back. "Ned, that's just a dream" was all she could come up with.

"You don't understand," said Ned. "You can never understand."

"That's not true. I'm trying. You don't always understand me."

"I'm not the one stealing your culture."

"I'm not stealing your culture."

"What do you call it then? Why are you here?" Ned moved away from her, pacing.

"I'm here to learn, because I think what you have here is wonderful."

"You don't know what we have here. You see what you want to see. Don't you see those women who come to the trading post? Don't you understand that every penny you don't give them for their rugs is a meal they can't feed their children? Don't you see how many are blind? That's a disease we get from the sand blowing in our eyes. You don't see that in New York, do you? Don't you see how sad the men are, how they try to get whiskey? Don't you see that they beat their wives? You don't want to see what's really here."

"But I thought you loved your people. Why do you stay here?"

"I want to heal them, don't you understand? I want to get them back to how it was before the white man stole it all. And the white woman."

"That was mean, Ned. I'm not like all the others, you must see that."

"I can't see that. I've been wanting to believe that, because I—" Ned's voice dropped off and in a hoarse whisper continued. "Because I liked you, because I liked being with you."

"Nothing's changed! I didn't do anything. I believe everything you believe."

"I'm just kidding myself. Being with you will just make it worse for me. They're all laughing at me enough already. I can't take any more. And I'll never get to be a healer when they see you with me. It's not worth it to me."

Ned turned away, poking at the fire to spread it into glowing coals that would burn out safely. She handed the saddle blanket to Ree, saying "Here, you can wrap up on this to sleep," and began to walk away.

"Ned, please stay with me."

"I'll be nearby. Stay by the fire and the animals will stay away."

"But, I don't want to fight. I want to be with you."

"I can't do this. I was kidding myself. I've had this plan my whole life, and this isn't part of it. I'd say I'm sorry, and I am sorry if you're hurting. But I'm not sorry to go back to my plan. You say you're living your dream, and that's what I need to do. You can't be in it."

Ree told herself things might work out better in the morning. She spread the saddle blanket on the ground and lay down, leaving half of it where she hoped Ned would join her. But when the rising sun awoke her, the fire was cold and the blanket empty. She saw Ned a few yards away, sitting against a rock, defiantly looking out at the morning's colors, lost in thoughts that were not going to include her. She wanted to cry, but the morning was too beautiful.

Ree felt hopeless about the dream she had been living out. Ned's outburst made her doubt everything she was doing. Why was she kidding herself, so far from home, trying to live a life that could never be hers? Ned was right. All she could do here was mess up and hurt feelings, as she had done by giving the feathered stick to Ned. She had only one choice now, which was to go home and spend her life back in the crowded hot apartment taking care of her aging and wretched father until he died, then suffering alone until she died, supporting them both and then herself by endless hours bent over a sewing machine in a sweatshop. She never wanted to hear the name "Frank Hamilton Cushing" again. She never wanted to think of Indians again, or western mountains, or mesas, or cascades of fire, or the soft cheeks of an Indian woman who passed as a man.

She had plenty of time to think about this on their silent ride back to Lost Wash. Ned barely nodded hello, face set angrily in a way that said there was no chance for reconciliation. Their happy walk of the day before was mirrored by the grim trip home. Yesterday's difficult walk was easy compared to this miserable climb down. Ned's hand no longer reached out comfortingly to steady her, just grudgingly gave her balance as stiffly as a staircase banister.

She had never been so miserable, even on the day of the fight with Margaret. Then, she had at least been filled with the righteous anger of being misunderstood. Ned misunderstood her too, but she could also see the rightness of Ned's position. Still, she resented that Ned could feel such affection for her but then also see her as a threat. Wasn't she the only one who truly supported Ned? Even Frances clearly had doubts, even if she didn't express them to her granddaughter.

They were walking, not side by side, but more or less alongside the horse through a flat sandy plain, punctuated here and there by small mesas and strange twists of rock, the nightmarish shapes fitting her mood.

"Ned, I have to give it one last chance. I'm with you, I believe in you, please don't cut me out of your life. I made a mistake, but it was with the best of intentions. I don't know everything about you or your people, but I'm here to learn. I thought I was doing a good thing, giving the prayer stick back so you could do the right thing with it. I didn't steal it from your people. I stole it back for your people."

Ned said nothing and they trudged on.

The day that she and Margaret had fought, she had changed that disaster into an opportunity to finally make her dream of the West come true, by moving on from San

Gabriel. But how could she transform this catastrophe? Here she was in Lost Wash, she had reached what she thought was the realization of her dream. Where else was there to go now?

Perhaps she could move to another Navajo community. But now she knew how difficult it was to ingratiate herself. Ned and Frances were her only friends here, and once Ned told Frances what had happened, they would both hate her. How could she move and start again? She had less money now because most had gone to pay the rents for the wagon and the land. Sack was paying her little more than food. This place of her liberation was now a trap.

When they sighted Lost Wash, Ned murmured "Goodbye" and rode off, leaving her to walk the rest of the way alone. She wished Ned had at least said "I'm sorry." Didn't Ned feel any loss? This couldn't be totally her own fault. How happy she had been the day before, even most of the night before. If she hadn't brought the feathered stick, if she had never found it, would all her dreams have come true? How different would her life go, even today? Would they have returned lovingly to Lost Wash, planning their next time together? But if Ned had all these doubts about their involvement, wouldn't it have come out somehow? She might have done nothing wrong, yet Ned still would have chosen other goals and dreams over her.

She tried to be too busy at work to sulk about Ned. With each customer, she considered what it would be like to be friends, but most were mothers with children, so self-contained. Ned and Frances were aberrations who traveled out of Lost Wash, with no small children or mates. No wonder they had been more open to her. Even the unmarried young women who might have been her friends spent their time at the trading post flirting discreetly with the unmarried men. It was a world for women with men, a world that she thought she could join with Ned, in an unusual way but a way after all. She wasn't likely to meet another Ned anywhere. Perhaps there were other female nadles but they wouldn't have Ned's unique charms. Besides, her heart was broken to lose Ned.

She tried to picture Ruth in the loving way that had inspired her for so many years, but all she could think of was the humiliation of her argument with Margaret at San Gabriel, and Ruth's groveling to Wheelwright, and Ruth's recent visit. There was no refuge in her old fantasies.

Sack was back before Ree expected him. He had a large box on each shoulder which he dropped onto the counter with a loud thud. "There's more in the truck," he said and ran out again without even a hello.

Later, munching on crackers which he kept poking out of his dark beard, he told Ree about his travels and asked her how much she had sold, what she had run out of, and what the customers were bringing in for trade.

"Only rugs, huh?" he said. "So how's the love affair going?" he finally asked. Ree turned away.

"Oh well, sometimes it's like that," he said with a knowing smile. "Seriously, how are you getting on with the Indians?" When she didn't answer, he was quiet, and she hoped he would say something comforting. "Well, sounds like you're going to have to do what your hero Frank Cushing did," he said.

"I am," she said, wanting to impress him. "I'm living like them now. Practically with them. I rented some land and I'm building a hogan."

"So, how much longer until you go totally native? Sure would like to see their faces back at Columbia. You're going to have to take a white man's scalp, just like Frank." He laughed at his joke, but Ree took it as a warning. Anyone could sell crackers and canned tomatoes, but he needed a clerk in the trading post to help with his other purchases and sales.

Attencia came to Ree's wagon more often lately, as if she knew how desperate Ree was for company. The Navajo woman was like a soggy old tub that washed up on Ree's castaway island with the high tide, battered against the beach, and offered the slimmest chance of an escape to Ree. But at least Attencia reached out to her, when no one else did. Today she offered some corn, her arm outstretched holding the cobs by the tassels, the ears drooping limply, as if getting closer to Ree would contaminate her. Since Ned's response to the prayer stick, Ree felt she was a contaminant of all the bad luck and bad choices in the world, although just a glimpse of the pathos of this forlorn wife and mother was enough to remind her that she had choices left that Attencia would never have. Ree straightened up as she found a slight vein of hope somewhere inside herself.

"Attencia, thank you," Ree said. "That's so kind of you. Next time you're at the store, I promise I'll give the children some candy."

Attencia stood hopefully, patiently, waiting. Not knowing what to say, Ree smiled weakly. Attencia took this as an encouraging sign, for she glanced behind and around her in all directions, squatted down, and took something from the endless folds of her skirt. It was a rolled rug in lovely pink, blue, orange, and gray pastels. Ree recognized the colors of the Wide Ruins type of rug, not often seen in these parts. It was far more beautiful a weaving than any she had seen from Attencia.

"Did you weave that? Is that yours?" Ree asked with excitement. Perhaps Attencia had a hidden talent, so that Sack could approve more credit and more money could go her way.

Attencia lay the rug on the ground and carefully began to unroll it. Ree suddenly knew what was in it. She spun around, her back to Attencia.

"Stop," Ree shouted. "You know I can't see that. Don't unroll it."

"You sell," said Attencia. "You sell, you take half. You can go away then." Ree wondered how Attencia knew, but maybe it was obvious to everyone that she needed to leave Lost Wash.

If she helped Attencia, the poor woman could feed her children, who were waiting anxiously right now. They would be hungry tomorrow. With the money from the deal, they would have food and heat this winter. Golney was not taking care of them. Who was she to stand in the way of these children eating? Attencia could explain the unexpected riches by claiming that Ree had bought some of her badly made rugs, after all. It made sense now, even if it hadn't before. She had only to say yes, and her life would move on to the next adventure, the next opportunity, perhaps her dream finally realized. How much longer could she stay stuck like this, digging a hole in land where she wasn't wanted? She had to stop kidding herself, this wasn't working out. Even Attencia only talked to her in order to exploit her. This was not her Frank Hamilton Cushing dream, this was the end of that road unless she took this chance out.

"Where did you get it?" asked Ree, turning back to see the rug still unrolled. She wanted to ask what was in the rug, but she doubted Attencia would know. It had to be a sacred object that only men would know about, and no doubt one that had been entrusted to Golney for its care.

Attencia bit her lips and didn't answer.

"Show me the place," Ree said. She had an idea in mind, but if she said it, Attencia would never agree. "Show me," Ree said in the tone that white men used to order the Indians around, a tone that threatened power and implied their powerlessness and weakness and vulnerability, a tone she had never used to an Indian before. Attencia looked as scared as when Ree had seen her with Golney, and Ree wanted so much to apologize, to beg for the mercy of this pathetic woman, but she knew that if her plan worked, it would be better for Attencia.

"Let's go," Ree said. She reached into the wagon and grabbed her jacket and hat. Attencia held the rug like a baby. Ree felt good that she had not touched it. She was also scared that Attencia would put it down and run away, leaving it with Ree. Whatever it was, the repercussions on both of them, but especially on Attencia for bringing it to her, were way beyond unthinkable.

"Let's go," Ree said again, and Attencia began to walk. Ree was afraid that she would head right back to her own house, as she was going in that direction, but just as Ree considered breaking away and running off to the trading post, leaving Attencia to her fate, the Indian woman turned off onto a dry river bed and and kept going. Ree had never walked this way. Many minutes passed. The going got harder as Attencia avoided sandy places and struggled up steep rocky ones.

Finally they were in a ravine, dry now, but the type of place that was prone to flash floods. Attencia went directly to a pile of boulders. She put her package on the ground, and with some struggle moved rocks to reveal a small cave. Ree saw petroglyphs inside, but none on the outside. It was the hiding place of a careful ancient one. Inside the hollow Ree saw the vague shapes of other objects. Attencia stood by proudly, like a merchant with a cart of wares.

"Put it in there," Ree said, pointing to the bundle and to the space. She left no room for hesitation, her voice sure and commanding. Attencia did as told. Ree pushed the rocks back as Attencia stood by disappointed, face fallen.

"Let's get out of here," Ree said. "Don't ever come back here. I will never come back here." Not waiting for Attencia's answer, Ree ran and didn't look back. She hadn't gone far when she realized she wasn't sure which way to go and no longer had her guide. But she followed the creek bed and soon was back in recognizable territory. She went right to the trading post and got to work.

She was proud of her restraint at that moment, but another part of her was saying, "That's your ticket home. Take it, hitch a ride out with the next mail truck, and whatever is in there, it will pay your way wherever you want to go." Anywhere but Navajoland. Sell it in Santa Fe, and she could go to California. She could go to the Yucatan. She could change her name. She could hope that no one recognized her. Beyond the anthropologists at Columbia, no one else in the field would know her. She could go to Bolivia or Peru, where anthropologists were reporting great discoveries. Maybe no one would ever connect her with the object. So much dealing went on, why would she get caught? The whole game was that white people didn't get caught. She could send money back to Attencia somehow. Ned already thought she was stealing artifacts, and she felt more punished by his reaction than any court of law might hurt her. Why shouldn't she at least take the reward for all this punishment?

The prospect gnawed at her like the story she had read in high school, "The Tell-tale Heart." But hadn't that man committed a murder and then been unable to escape his guilt? What had she done but the right thing to protect the Navajo culture and this desperately beaten down woman? She had nothing to feel guilty about. But the guilt was not for what she had done, but what she now felt it was in her power to do. She had never felt such power in her life, and she did not know how to let it give up its hold over her.

Her days and nights now held a misery even worse than before. There was her humiliation about Ruth, her disappointment and shame about Ned, the rejection by this tiny community, and now her horror at her own temptation to hurt the people and the culture she so admired. She had thought she had reached bottom but now she was even lower. Here were patches of quicksand she had only thought she had avoided.

Never mind her own fate. What about Attencia? Attencia would approach Sack next. Once he got all he wanted, he wouldn't care if the Indian woman was killed, beaten and then killed, or beaten and banished from her tribe, which would kill her inside and leave her vulnerable to the worst of white people.

The last time Sack had shown up, he had shown no inclination to raise Ree's salary, but only complained of how badly he was doing lately with his other businesses, which she took to mean his trade in artifacts. He had tried again to get her to help him, and she had self-righteously refused, thinking about Ned and the prayer stick. But if Attencia offered, Sack would jump, no matter how lost the object would be to the Navajo people and to the historians and anthropologists who could record and analyze and preserve and display it. Sack would sell it to a rich person to hide in their secret collection, to show only to other white collectors, to gloat at what they had taken from the Indians. If she refused Attencia, how soon would the woman be unrolling her rug for Sack instead?

The fall sheep were shorn, and the trading post was busy. Sack arrived with a wagon load of stock to trade for raw wool and rugs. Customers crowded in for flour, corn meal, tomatoes, crackers, and new pots, bowls, and blankets. Ree hoped for an invitation to the upcoming feast day and celebratory dance.

Since their visit to the cave, Attencia entered the store only when it was busy, and with so many children surrounding her that Ree suspected she borrowed a few to enlarge the barrier between the two of them.

From the talk she heard, part of the festivities was to be a dance, not of the sacred kind but of the social kind. She asked some of the customers if she would be welcome, hoping for an invitation, but they shrugged noncommittally. While Ree knew better than to her push her way into a religious rite, she thought she could go to the dance with no repercussions. How much did it matter anyway? She decided the dance would be her last attempt to stay. If she went and no one objected, she could take that as a sign that she had some acceptance, however unexpressed and grudging. If they rejected her, she would plead ignorance. It would be a test, and if it went badly, she would leave Lost Wash. She pictured herself sneaking out of town on the mail truck and letting Sack figure it all out. She wasn't going to face his sneering attitude. It would be hard enough to leave.

With nothing more to lose, she would wear her Frank Hamilton Cushing outfit to the dance. Everyone shared all the food they could at events like this, so she would bring all the food she had. Maybe showing up at the dance in that outfit and with generous food would change how they people saw her. Maybe they would see what their culture meant to her. Maybe they would see how much she wanted to be a part of their lives. Maybe Ned would be there and dance with her. Maybe they would walk out into the darkness, like that night in the hay at San Gabriel. Things would be the way they were again, the way they had started to be.

It was a dramatic move that Frank Hamilton Cushing would understand. He had forced the Zuni people to take him in by allowing no other choice. Her mistake here had been to be so timid, in the way anthropologists were trained to acclimate and assimilate. That hadn't worked and she saw the falseness of it, and knew that the Indians saw it too. She wasn't fooling anyone by insinuating her way in here. Why not be brazen and outrageous as she could be? Why not try a new tack? She had nothing to lose. Maybe Ned would hear about it and give her another chance. Maybe someone else would take an interest. All she needed was one person to welcome her, and she would have a foot in the door again.

This was the most hopeful she had felt since the night of Ned's cascading campfire. She thought of the beauty of the glowing sparks falling through the air, the delight of Ned's body, and knew she had to take the chance. Hadn't she taken a great chance coming West in the first place? She had no regrets, as badly as some parts had gone. Should she have stayed back in the garment factory, bent over the sewing machine, living a life of fantasy instead of adventure? No, it was worth everything to have left home and come here. She was only twenty-four years old and there was so much ahead of her.

Ree hadn't felt so exhilarated since stepping on the train west. She had been about to splurge and eat a can of peaches, but put it into the sack of food for the feast. She was feeding on her dreams and they had always fed her better than anything. She would eat as little as possible, which would make her lightheaded and brave to do this.

Just then she saw Attencia with her huddle of children, out in the yard of the trading post. They didn't come in, but Ree saw the Navajo woman peek through the open doorway to see who was behind the counter. Their eyes locked, and Attencia turned and left, the disappointed children following.

If Sack had been standing there, instead of counting money in the backroom—Ree's mind raced through the chain of events that would follow. Then suddenly, the words he had said rang in her brain. "You're going to have to take a white man's scalp, just like Frank Hamilton Cushing." Suddenly she knew exactly what she needed to do.

She waited until Sack had closed the trading post and was going through the day's accounts.

"All right, you're right, I'm leaving town. I need a fresh start," she told him. He was eating right out of a can of beans, his suspenders down. He gloated when she spoke, still chewing.

"But I need money," she said. "I've made you this map." She handed him a piece torn from a brown bag. "You'll find what you want. I'm leaving tomorrow. I need money for the train home."

He threw the map down on the counter and studied it.

"Don't go until the moon is up." she said. "Everyone will be at the dance by then. You know I don't like this, so you just do what you have to do."

"That's all I asked for," Sack said with a snide smile. "At last you smartened up. It's about time you learned how easy money is made."

"Just shut up and do what you have to do," Ree said.

"You always have to do it the hard way," he said as she left. Let him have the last word. She was about to take his white man's scalp and give it to the Indians.

Shamans and others taking part in rituals always dressed in special clothes. Special clothes had power, and she had given so much power to her Frank Hamilton Cushing outfit, but she had let go of that power after the debacle at the Brooklyn Museum. She was glad she had carried the clothing this far so she could have it for this special night that would change her luck at last. Why hadn't she thought of this earlier? It was so obvious now.

She opened the suitcase and unrolled the outfit from its velvet wrapping, not unlike the one in which her father kept his tallit and tefillim. She laid the clothes out on the blankets that covered the bed of the wagon. As she bound the leather straps around her biceps, she saw how they were indeed like tefillit, and she took this as a good sign, that at last she was taking the power that had even been denied her as a Jew, because she was a woman. She knew why Ned dressed in men's clothes. When Ned saw her in these, it would surely change the mind set so hard against her now. As she continued to dress, she felt more and more sure of what she was doing.

She didn't want to be stopped on her way to the dance, so she took a rarely used trail. As she walked along in the dusk, two horsemen approached. One horse reared up, the rider cursing to make it calm down.

"Who's that?" the rider called out angrily.

The other rider trotted close enough to see Ree.

"It's the white-woman-who-writes-all-night," he called to his friend. Ree was delighted. She hadn't known that she had been given a name by her Navajo neighbors. She wanted to thank him, even though he probably thought it was an insult. Many white people were given insulting names, but this name was better than any she would have thought of for herself.

"Hello," she said, but the man with the nervous horse rode up and cut her off.

"You stay away from my wife," he said, and she recognized Golney. "I don't want you around here. Go back to your home and mother. Nobody wants you here."

"Come on, Golney," said the other man. "White people will only get you in trouble." They rode off without another word, but Ree's happy mood was broken. Was that the truth, that nobody wanted her here? But all she had to do now was find Ned and tell him how to catch Sack in the act. Ned would be the hero of the town, and she would be in Ned's arms again.

The horsemen disappeared when another man stepped out from behind a rock. It was Sack, and she realized he must have followed her from her wagon.

Clouds covered the moon and Ree shivered.

"Nice evening for a walk," he said. "And such a beautiful outfit. Did you buy that at the local trading post?" he smirked.

She glared at him. "I made it myself, the goods there aren't up to the local standards," she said, but he didn't laugh.

"So I thought you might like to take a little walk with me," he said pleasantly.

This didn't feel right. It would be good for him to think someone was expecting her.

"Sorry, I'm meeting Ned at the dance."

"I'll bet you are," Sack said. He took her by the arm. "But first I need a little company. This won't take long."

If she resisted, he might suspect something. Or, she might as well admit to herself, that perhaps he already suspected something. She went along, desperately running through her options. She had drawn the map so that Ned would catch him near the cache of artifacts, but not exact enough so that Sack would have them in his hands, defiling them. They walked along silently. Clouds moved on and off the moon, changing their path from bright to dark and back again.

At the ravine, Sack excitedly compared the map to the landmarks around him.

"This damn map doesn't show where it is. You show me!"

"I don't know, I just have the map."

"Who gave it to you, anyway?"

"That's not important."

"It's Golney's wife, isn't it? Aren't you scared of Golney?"

"No, I'm not scared of anyone."

"What about me? Scared of me? Because I'm getting pretty fed up with you. You led me out here to set me up, didn't you? You were going to have your girlfriend catch me out here, weren't you?"

"No, I told you, I need to get out of town, I need a fresh start. Where else can I get money for that? That damn woman. I feel set up, too. I paid my last money for that map. Let's just go back to town, I'll find her at the dance, and I'll get the exact location."

"You're so full of crap!" Sack exploded. He pulled and scratched at the walls of the ravine, finally breaking a fingernail on a boulder and cursing loudly. He grabbed his hand in pain and glared at Ree.

"I think you know where the cache is and I'm going to find out." He looked over the damage to his hand.

"What's your fresh start going to be anyway?" Before she could answer, Sack continued. "Why do I ask? You'll go somewhere else to be an Indian, sucking the last of their life blood from them. Even Benedict and the rest don't want to do that any more."

"That's not true. I'm here to be a part of them—at least to try."

"Come on, you're a Jewish girl from Brooklyn. You couldn't be farther from an American Indian if you were the Prince of Wales."

"I can't help where I'm from. I've been trying to choose where I'm going. And I'm not going your way. That's not my way. You're stealing from them."

Sack moved toward her, his arm raised, about to slap. "Don't give me that crap. If she doesn't sell to you or me, she'll sell to the next person, it doesn't matter. It's her choice, I'm just here to help. And I have big plans for it. It will be a lot safer where it's going than buried in this ravine."

"Hitting me won't help. I don't know where it is."

"The way I see it you've got two choices—give it to me or don't. You don't have to give it to me."

Ree looked up hopefully. "I won't."

"That's your choice, but," he turned toward the town, "I'm sure the folks here will be very grateful to me for telling them what you've been up to with your best friend Attencia. And Golney will probably have to kill her to save face. Or beat her as close to dead as he can. And desert her and the kids. So go ahead, don't tell me. I can get plenty of points from those old guys in charge, and who knows, they might be grateful enough to spare something down the line. For sure, I'll be getting all the wool in these parts. So go ahead, make your choice."

Ree backed away as he talked.

"Looks like you're going to have a long walk home. Lots of time to think about what will happen to Attencia. And they won't let you stay either. And word gets around. Your time is up in Lost Wash. Hope you got the money for a ticket home, because the train is waiting for you—if you can get there in time."

A drop of rain hit Ree's cheek, and she saw drops on her buckskin sleeve.

"There's no place to hide," Sack said.

"I could kill you," Ree surprised herself by saying.

"You could try. And how would you explain it?"

"I could say you tried to rape me."

Sack laughed. "They all think we're lovers. How can I rape you if you've been sleeping with me?"

"Why would they think that!"

"Word gets around."

"Why, you piece of treyf!" Ree screamed.

"Such language for a nice Jewish girl! So what's it gonna be? Tell me where it is and you'll be fine."

"What difference would it make? You'll always have this to pin on me. I won't be able to stay here."

"You don't trust me to keep our little secret?"

"Oh," Ree said, "I think we each have a little secret."
"So tell me where it is, then you've got something on me.
"Thanks for the suggestion."

"You think I'm stupid. You think you're smarter than anyone. That was what was wrong with you at Columbia. That's why they didn't like you. Well, it's over now."
The raindrops turned to a light drizzle.

"In a minute, it's going to get pretty wet in this ravine. Hand it over! You heard the choices."

Ree froze and Sack moved toward her. "No more choices," he said. He pinned her arms painfully behind her as she struggled to bite him. As they scuffled, he kept saying "Tell me. Tell me. Tell me" louder and louder, until he was screaming in her ear.

"Stop!" she gasped out.

"You have a choice. I have no choice. Which do you want—choice or no choice?"

Ree got a fist free and swung at him. They rolled into the ravine. Cold water splashed in her face. She struggled to stand but Sack pushed her down. Her head bounced against a sharp rock.

"Aw, all that water on your nice Frank Hamilton Cushing suit," he said.

Ree was limp, her eyes closed. He shook her and her arms fell into the water.

"Are you ok? Get up! That trick won't work." But there was no response. The water rose to Sack's knees as Ree's head bobbed peacefully. He stared at her blank face.

"Stupid tourist dude bitch, drowned in a ravine. Won't those gringos ever learn about the desert? Ain't it a pity?" He let go and scrambled up the bank.

Ree awoke, so cold. She tried to move, but her waterlogged clothes held her down. It was easier to stay where she was. She remembered the fight with Sack and thought, "I didn't tell him." She pictured Attencia, safe if not happy in her hogan. She wondered if Ned would ever forgive her. She wondered if Ruth would ever think of her. Then she saw Frank coming to her, lifting her in his warm arms, sitting her beside his blazing campfire and telling her stories of his life with the Zuni people, the stories that had started her whole adventure. He said a Zuni prayer, and she answered with the Sh'ma.

Part 7

"Anybody seen anything of the white woman?" Sack asked the customers as they came in through the day. "She was supposed to be here at sunrise to open the store, and there's no sign of her. I went out to her wagon and she's not there."

Soon everyone knew that Ree was missing. The mail truck came for its weekly stop and spread the news so that the sheriff soon arrived. He organized a search party, although the Navajo people said among themselves that if the missing woman had been Navajo, nothing would have been done and the sheriff would not even have come.

Some of the customers at the trading post remembered Ree asking about the dance. A search of her wagon showed her satchel flung open and her normal clothes thrown carelessly on the bed, so it was concluded that she had put on her prettiest dress to go to the dance. But no one had seen her that night.

Sack asked to join the search party, but the sheriff told him to stay at the trading post and have food ready and take messages. "That's no job for a man," he told the sheriff. "I can't just stay here. I've known Henrietta since we were children. I've got to help find her. I think she's lost in the desert. She needs me!" The sheriff relented, although Sack struggled to keep up with far more expert horsemen. Rain and flash flooding made the search harder.

When Ned tried to join the search party, the sheriff held up his hand and pointed away with his thumb. "Go home," said the sheriff, "you don't belong with us. And if anything happened to her, we'll be looking for you." But Ned rode out alone to search, wondering if his reaction to Ree had been a fair one. If something had happened to her, maybe he had been right about her. Dealers in artifacts were in trouble if they got caught.

At the trading post, there was already plenty of talk about who had done it.

"It's the women," Frances said to Ned. "They never liked her being around their husbands, an unmarried woman. They got together and got rid of her."

"It's Sack," said Ned. "He shouldn't be in our town."

"Shhh," said Frances. "Don't let anyone hear you say anything against a white man. They'll blame you. You better be careful, everyone knows you were friends with her. And I heard that Bobby Gatewood and Golney Seymour saw her headed to the dance. They said she was dressed funny, sort of like an Indian."

Two days later, a sad procession of horses rode back into Lost Wash. A body wrapped in brightly colored woven horse blankets was tied to a horse. The town burst with questions and suspicions. As the searchers returned to their homes, the rumors spread.

Ned heard the new from Frances, who hugged him as he wept.

"She was wearing Indian clothes. That's what all the men in the search party said. Buckskin and fancy velvet and lots of silver buttons. Not something our people would wear. But it was all torn up from the fight. She was beaten really badly. They think she might have been hit with a rock, but the body is a real mess. They can't tell if she was dead first or drowned when the ravine flooded."

"I was so mean to her," Ned said. "We were her only friends and then I wouldn't talk to her."

"What happened between you?" asked Frances. She had wanted to ask since she had noticed Ned moping around with no sign of Ree.

"Well," Ned answered, "she had a prayer stick. She was stealing artifacts, probably dealing them. She said she wasn't, but why else would she have that prayer stick? She tried to give it to me and I was scared. And angry. She thought she understood us, but she didn't. But now I wonder what she was doing that night, what those clothes were, why she was at that place. I don't think the women would hurt her."

"The terrible thing," said Frances, "is that the white sheriff will be deciding who did it. Whoever they decide, that's who did it." They sat silently.

Lost Wash had never had so many white people in town at one time. There were sheriff's men, the coroner, and newspaper reporters from California and New York. They examined the sheepherder's wagon, talked to everyone, and bought all the food at Sack's store.

Sack had taken the role of the widower, and store counter was covered with condolence gifts of Navajo breads. White people scrounged the arid land to assemble bouquets of desert flowers that immediately shriveled.

"We first met when she was still in high school," Sack told a reporter. "I was the one who encouraged her to go to Columbia University and be an anthropologist. If I had only known where it would lead, I would have let her be," he sobbed. "She would probably be a teacher in New York City today and married perhaps. But she really wanted to learn about the Indians. We both did, and we both dreamed of coming here. And I thought if she went to Columbia she would be headed on her way. But she wanted more, she wanted to live like the Indians. I never really understood that. That's going too far, and I guess someone here didn't like that.

"That's what I think happened. She was going off on her own a lot. I warned her about it. Just think what they found with her body! A notebook and a pen. She was prying into their secrets. If there's one thing I've learned living here, it's to stay out of their business. I just run my trading post and trade fair and square and keep my nose out of things. Henrietta never could learn that. She was always wanting to know, asking questions, too much the anthropologist, but she wasn't one. Not able to play by the rules. That's why the folks at Columbia didn't let her have a field assignment here. I felt sorry for her, out here all alone with no job, so I gave her one. But I worried that she pried into their business. If I hadn't loved her so much, I would have had to fire her."

"You loved her?" asked the journalist.

"Yes, and I wanted to marry her. But she wasn't ready for that. She had her idols, the women anthropologists like our teachers at Columbia, and she wanted to do work like they did. I admired that about Henrietta, because I had given that up myself. She always had bigger dreams than me. I just wanted to live here and understand the people, that's why I was in school, and pretty soon I was restless to go west. But Henrietta was furious that Columbia dropped her. She came here angry and I think that's why she didn't see that she was rude to the Indian people. That's why they didn't like her. She got on the wrong side of someone. They didn't want her here. If only I had seen it in time," he wept into a bandanna.

"Is it true," asked the journalist, "The rumors that two Indian men saw her walking toward the dance?"

"That's the kind of thing she wasn't careful enough about," said Sack. "A woman wandering around alone, out where she would only run into men. The Navajo women don't do that. For one thing, they've always got their children around. Two men? Well, that makes sense to me. Probably gave them the wrong idea. It doesn't take much. In their culture, a single woman is a wrong idea in itself."

"Do you think they thought she wanted to have, you know, something to do with them?" asked the journalist.

"Henrietta was so innocent. She didn't understand how men feel around a pretty woman. And I hear she had on a very provocative Indian squaw dress."

"Thanks," said the journalist, "you've been very helpful. I'm so sorry about your loss. Have you heard from anyone at Columbia University?"

"They're very upset," said Sack. "They never wanted her out here. Did you know her professor even came here to ask her to please leave before something like this happened? Henrietta practically bragged to me about it, she was so self-righteous that they were unfair to her. But they were totally right. If only I had backed them up, she would be alive now. I thought the Indians would respect that I was her man, because even though we weren't married, they thought we were because she worked for me. But there must have been an Indian who didn't see it that way, like the ones who ran into her, wandering all alone, a single woman, the night of the dance."

Soon Golney and Gatewood were taken into custody, and Gatewood turned against Golney, who was his cousin. Frances explained it to Ned. To stay away away from local gossip, Ned had been camping alone on the mountain, morosely thinking of Ree.

"Golney's confessed," Frances said.

"That's no surprise," said Ned. "Confession, I'll bet. How long would you last taken off alone by a bunch of white men looking to prove you're the killer?"

"He says she asked him to marry her, which I don't think is exactly what she said, but she's a white woman so you can't use the real words. Then he said he was married already, which of course she knew, so she got angry and hit him, and then he felt attacked and he had to defend himself. Do you believe that? He's claiming self-defense! Bobby Gatewood said he heard her ask Golney to marry him, and he said no, he was already married, and she was so angry she hit him and ran off, and he had been to the dance and drunk some illegal hooch so he followed her. Bobby said he didn't follow, so he didn't see what happened."

"She asked him to marry her? She wouldn't do that."

"Maybe she asked him to do something else, something short of marrying her. Didn't she want the same of you?" Frances asked. "Every woman wants that at her age."

Ned was angry for a moment, trying to decide from memory if Ree had wanted Ned less after discovering Ned was a woman. Ree's excitement had certainly been from the assumption Ned was a man. Maybe that was what Ree had wanted after all. But his anger faded as he remembered how shattered Ree had been when rejected. Ree had wanted Ned, not a man. On some level, she must never have thought that Ned was a man. Ned missed her so much now.

"I don't believe it," Ned said. "She didn't want a man."

"Well then, why did Golney kill her?"

"Maybe Golney wanted her. But wait a minute, you don't know that. You don't know for sure that Golney did it. It's just what Gatewood said, and he was arrested. He had to make something up to prove his innocence."

"Maybe Golney will turn against Gatewood. He could tell the same story."

"He's not that smart," said Ned. "Everyone knows Golney is a dumb bully. He pinched and shoved me when we were little. The smaller kids learned to stay away from him."

"See, he's a mean man. He could have done it."

"It's always one of us who is blamed when a white person is hurt. They don't want to say that a white man did it. It's so much easier to put one of us in jail or the gallows."

"Do you think they'll hang Golney?" Frances said, and they both drew back in horror at the thought.

"I don't know. Nobody saw it. If they just send him to jail, nobody will look too deeply into it."

"The other thing is that Attencia's friends knew that Golney didn't like it that Ree was renting her land."

"Gatewood should have said they were arguing about that."

"This way Golney can say she attacked him first."

"Who would believe that?"

"That's what he's saying, stupid as it is."

"That's Golney for you. He's stupid enough to end up convicted for this. And he doesn't have a lot of friends in this town. I'm not the only one he bullied. But I still don't think it was him. Or at least I don't think the investigation should stop because of what Gatewood said. But I know it will. It's the white man's justice. I have an idea who it is--"

"Quiet!," said Frances. "Don't say a word, even to me. Say a word against him and you'll be the next one arrested. If you hadn't been at the dance with me, selling food, they would suspect you, too."

"That's probably why she wanted to go to the dance that night. I think she was hoping to find me there and make up. If only I had gone to her first."

"You stupid woman," Golney whispered to his wife. They were alone in the jail cell. He was to be taken to the prison in Santa Fe that night, to be held for trial. "I know what you were doing with the white woman. If you go back to that cave again, you'll find a big snake waiting for you. And nothing else. I hid it where you will never find it. Don't try to sell our family's heritage. When I get out of prison, I'll deal with you."

"Why don't you tell the truth? You didn't kill her."

"It's for you, don't you understand? If I told the truth, I'd have to tell why she was really in that ravine, near that cave. And someone else with her, too, the white man. They only want to steal what we have, and you were going to help them. Maybe I'll go to jail, but it won't be as bad as what would be done to me for letting my woman sell our sacred things."

Epilogue

"It's a telegram from Boas," Margaret Mead called to Ruth as she closed the door behind the delivery boy. She held the envelope up toward the bed where Ruth Benedict's face barely peeked out from a thick pile of blankets and quilts.

"Go ahead, you open it," Ruth said.

"Henrietta's father dropped suit. STOP. Leaving for Palestine to join Zionists. STOP."

Ruth started to answer but instead held up one hand while she blew her nose with a handkerchief held in the other.

"Columbia is off the hook!" Margaret squealed. He's admitting she brought it on herself. Where'd you put the champagne? Now there's nothing to stop me from going to Samoa. The department won't be afraid to send women into the field."

"He lost his daughter," Ruth gasped out through her stuffed nose. "He needed to blame someone."

"You can't say you didn't warn her. She broke every rule. She spit in all our faces. We were so right about her. She was never one of us. Did you hear what Sylvester Baxter just figured out about the time he spoke at the Brooklyn Museum?"

Ruth reached out for the telegram. "Here's the last line from Boas: 'Let us return to the business of anthropology and put this sad affair behind us. STOP.'"

Margaret rubbed her hands together. "What a lucky break. And the father's just as crazy as the daughter was."

"Don't be mean," Ruth said. "Idealists, maybe. Romantics. Apollonians. Not quite integrated into their culture. Every culture needs a few, to let off steam."

"And every culture has a way of cutting them off," Margaret said. They stared at the empty envelope.

"Or cultures couldn't persist," Ruth completed her sentence.

"Well, I have work to do," Margaret said. "When's he going to answer about the Samoan proposal? I thought maybe this was it."

Ruth wasn't listening. She was thinking of Henrietta. It had been flattering to be loved so passionately, even so obsessively. Margaret's love was always controlled, her heart and mind always looking beyond and to the sides. Ruth had never felt Margaret's love the way Henrietta's clung to her every blood cell. Sticky and rich and ultimately repulsive, but admirable in the way that all extreme human energies are. Henrietta had been that Apollonian spirit, a thrust, a wild dance like a warrior leaping within her, straining at her boundaries, trying to push beyond them. Ruth had cut her off, just as Margaret had said. As every culture had to in order to preserve itself. It was human, it was life, and although she could never explain it to Margaret, Henrietta had connected to the passions of the poet and adventurer within her.

She regretted that she had never given Henrietta any positive response. Her fear of suggesting more than she would ever deliver had held her back. Now that it was too late, she was able to feel the part of her that did envy and admire Henrietta. All she could do now, she promised herself, was to honor Henrietta's spirit wherever she found it.

The End

Author's Note

She's Gone Santa Fe is an historical novel in which I imagined what Henrietta Schmerler, an obscure but real person, might have thought and done in her brief life. I also imagined the interactions or passing mentions of my fictional Henrietta with many real people, including Frank Hamilton Cushing, Mary Cabot Wheelwright, Hosteen Klah, Ruth Benedict, Margaret Mead, Franz Boas, Edith Goldfrank, Gladys Reichard, Pliny Goddard, Jack Lambert, Caroline Stanley Pfaeffle, Golney Seymour, Bobby Gatewood, and others. Much is known about the lives of some of these people; little about others. I did extensive research into their lives, and although I took some liberties by inserting Henrietta, I tried to stay as true as possible to the known facts. Because this is not Henrietta Schmerler's true story, I did not use her last name in the text.

In this Author's Note, I will explain how I did the research and fictionalized the truth. I encountered much conflicting information during my research and have tried to choose the most consistent and reliable. I will leave it to the biographers and historians to provide the documented account. I apologize for any errors outside of those intentionally caused by fictionalizing.

Very little is known about Henrietta Schmerler, other than that she was Jewish, from New York City, was born in 1907, was athletic, and was a graduate student of Ruth Benedict in the anthropology program at Columbia University at the same time that Margaret Mead was there. Until her death made headlines, Schmerler was an undistinguished graduate student with one publication. There are conflicting accounts, but I believe the one that says that Schmerler, age 24, went to Arizona in 1931 without the approval of her department, hoping to live like the Indians and do field work. It is unclear why she could not get approval. She either built a wigwam-type building or lived in a shack near the Indian community and tried to ingratiate herself. Apparently she was called "the woman who writes all night." Weeks later, she was found beaten and stabbed to death in a ravine on the White River Apache reservation, dressed in Indian-style clothing. An Apache man named Golney Seymour was convicted of her murder on unreliable evidence. Her father had a civil lawsuit against Columbia for not protecting her. There was celebration at Columbia when he dropped the suit to help build what became the state of Israel (Lapsley, 206-207.)

Since so little is known about what Schmerler did during her brief time at Columbia and in the southwest, I made it up. Changing the character's name to "Ree," which was my creation, gave me more artistic license. My character, Ree Schmerler, is attracted to women, but I have seen no evidence that the real Henrietta Schmerler was. I moved the time of Ree's travels in the southwest from 1931 to 1925, so that Ree could cross paths with Benedict and Mead's 1925 visit to New Mexico. This was also when Hosteen Klah lived at Mary Cabot Wheelwright's estate, weaving rugs and having his chants recorded.

I moved the final phase of Henrietta's life to the Navajo reservation. Quite frankly, I did this because I have learned a lot about the Navajo people but know very little about the Apache people. I choose to believe that Golney Seymour did not kill Henrietta Schmerler, but was a victim of a racist justice system. I don't know who might have done it. Sack is a completely fictional character, but a composite of many who illicitly traded in culturally significant artifacts then, as still happens now worldwide.

The seed for this book was found in one sentence in *Hidden Scholars: Women Anthropologists and the Native American Southwest*, edited by Nancy J. Parezo (1993). On page 92 it says "In the early 1920s, [Florence Dibble] Bartlett was among a coterie of unmarried women who founded the San Gabriel ranch in Alcalde, New Mexico, a hospitable and stimulating respite from city life." There are conflicting accounts of the origins of San Gabriel Dude Ranch, but it apparently was geared more toward single women than most other dude ranches, which were family-oriented. It captured my imagination as a place where lesbians were likely to vacation. Photos of San Gabriel Dude Ranch can be found online in the digitized Photo Archives of the Palace of the Governors at http://econtent.unm.edu/cdm4/indexpg.php. During a visit to the Archives in Santa Fe, I viewed a photo of a woman guest on the "bucking barrel" (photo #112302 by Edward A. Kemp. An online photo shows "the oldest cowboy" on the barrel.) Vertical files at several libraries in New Mexico and online sites provided advertising brochures about San Gabriel and its annex called Canjillon Camp.

In 2004 I went looking for evidence of what had been San Gabriel Dude Ranch from 1918 to 1932. The main building was subsequently owned by Florence Dibble Bartlett, and by 2004 it was being used for offices of the New Mexico State University Sustainable Agriculture Science Center. The building was beautifully maintained and I was allowed me to walk through and take photos. It is clearly recognizable in many of the archived photos of San Gabriel Dude Ranch. I also walked on nearby streets hoping to find signs of the stables and outbuildings, but they were impossible to discern.

Mary Cabot Wheelwright (1878-1958), a never-married heiress from Boston, loved San Gabriel Dude Ranch so much that she bought a nearby hacienda which became her Los Luceros estate. For research on Wheelwright, I was very fortunate to be able to tour Los Luceros in August, 2004, during the very brief time that it was open to the public as a house museum reconstructing Wheelwright's life there in the 1920s. I was moved and inspired by the simplicity of Wheelwright's bedroom, the beauty of the verandah with its hummingbird feeders, the orchards, and the gardens. If you are driving through Alcalde, watch for the historic marker on Highway 68 heading North, and imagine as I did Wheelwright and her companion, Marie Chabot, riding their horses off into the beautiful landscape.

I had also made a very brief but very valuable visit to Los Luceros a few years earlier, when a friend who thought she had access took me onto the grounds. I was able to get a quick look at the estate before it was renovated for the house museum. This was especially valuable for seeing the stables, which did not survive the renovation. Something about the stables, a large, two-storied building, caught my imagination and it is a major setting in the book, although I moved it over in fiction to the San Gabriel Dude Ranch. We were quickly chased off by a caretaker, which was disappointing but I am glad that the property was being protected, which has not always been true in its long history. Los Luceros is currently owned by the Sundance Institute as a center for film in New Mexico.

In Boston, a tour of the Rose Nichols House Museum on Beacon Hill let me see what Wheelwright's family home would probably have looked like when Wheelwright grew up there. The Nichols House is at 55 Mount Vernon Street, and Wheelwright's family home was 73 Mt. Vernon Street. 73 Mount Vernon Street is now a private residence, apparently cut into several apartments.

From 1923-25, Wheelwright's Navajo rug store, called "the Carry-on Shop" was at 65 Charles Street on Beacon Hill, Boston. Most recently this was the Nahas Leather shoe store. The "Carry-on Shop" moved at some point to 30 Charles, across the street. Most recently this has been a gelato ice cream store. Until recently, you could still see the beautiful tin ceiling that probably was there in the 1920s.

For the time Ree spends with Wheelwright, I relied heavily on the letters of Marie Chabot (1914-2001), who was Wheelwright's companion and heir. Chabot most likely was a lesbian, or so many would conclude from reading her letters in the *Marie Chabot - Georgia O'Keeffe Correspondence, 1941 - 1949* by Lynes and Paden. There is no evidence that Wheelwright believed herself to be or acted as a lesbian and I have tried to not present her as such. A brief video interview with Chabot is on Volume 5 of the PBS documentary "American Visions: The History of American Art and Architecture."

Hosteen Klah (1867-1937) is highly revered by the Navajo people for preserving their heritage. There are conflicting accounts as to whether Klah would have been within the transgender spectrum, as we define that today. I apologize in advance for any misrepresentation of transgenderism or of Native American lives and culture, as this is well outside my personal experience. I am inspired by the tolerant attitude toward transgendered people and gay and lesbian behavior among many traditional indigenous North American cultures, and greatly appreciate the work of scholars of this topic.

The rugs that Klah was weaving in my story are no longer displayed, as they contain content sacred to the Navajo people. The museum that Wheelwright had built to display them, formerly called the Museum of Navajo Ceremonial Art and now called the Wheelwright Museum of the American Indian, provides other fascinating exhibits and is a must-see for visitors to Santa Fe. The public bus to the Wheelwright Museum on Museum Hill has to be the most beautiful city bus ride in America.

In September, 2000, I took a week long course in Navajo weaving taught by Mary Walker and Jenny Slick, based in Window Rock, Arizona. In addition to weaving lessons, we visited many trading posts and other weaving sites from Hubbell to Toadlena to Crownpoint. For a truly wonderful educational, cultural, and social experience, I recommend their course. See the website at http://weavinginbeauty.com/

For the lives of anthropologists at Columbia and elsewhere in the 1920s, there are many memoir and biographical accounts, particularly about Mead and Benedict. Nancy Parezo's *Hidden Scholars: Women Anthropologists and the Native American Southwest* is an endless source of ideas. Don D. Fowler's *A Laboratory for Anthropology* is filled with stories of the people and places that make Southwest anthropology so legendary. In Cambridge, Massachusetts, the Peabody Museum at Harvard is the home of Harvard's anthropology department. There is said to be a place in the basement where Alfred Kidder and Samuel J. Guernsey shook hands and said "Let's do the Southwest!" setting off so many adventures that I have eagerly read about. When I go past or into the Peabody, I feel that I am walking in the footsteps of all the great early anthropologists who no doubt visited that building at some point in their careers.

I may have been somewhat unfair to the 1920s anthropology department at Columbia. There were several highly successful Jewish students, although anti-Semitism in the Ivy League at the time has been documented. Franz Boas, Ruth Benedict, and Joseph Campbell are all well regarded for their work promoting tolerance of all cultures. I haven't seen the evidence of why Henrietta Schmerler was denied approval to do field work in the Southwest, if that is what happened, and I have no proof that it was related to her being Jewish, other than comments that Margaret Mead described Schmerler to Benedict as one of the "unpleasant Jewish women" who "just shouldn't be let in [to the department] at all" (Lapsley, note 39, page 331.) It was this comment, and the paragraph on page 207 of Lapsley stating that Benedict celebrated the news that Schmerler's father had dropped his lawsuit, that inspired a good deal of the plot of *She's Gone Santa Fe*.

The town of "Lost Wash" where Ree spends her last days is fictional. For my previous novel, *Land Beyond Maps*, I researched the isolated trading post community at Red Rock, Arizona, where Laura Gilpin took her highly regarded photographs of the Navajo people. "Lost Wash" is loosely based on Red Rock.

There are many contemporary newspaper accounts about Henrietta Schmerler's death. I have listed the major ones in the Selected Bibliography. These and others can easily be found on the internet. Many public libraries carry the "Historical Newspapers" database. Most give highly offensive accounts of the White River Apache people. I will leave it to the historians and biographers to tell as true an account as possible.

Selected Bibliography

Ruth Benedict and Margaret Mead

Banner, Lois W. (2003). *Intertwined lives: Margaret Mead, Ruth Benedict, and their circle.* NY: Knopf.

Caffrey, M. M. (1989). *Ruth Benedict: Stranger in this land.* Austin: University of Texas Press.

Howard, J. (1984). *Margaret Mead: A life.* NY: Fawcett Crest

Lapsley, H. (1999). *Margaret Mead and Ruth Benedict: The kinship of women.* Boston, MA: University of Massachusetts Press.

Mead, M. (1966). *An anthropologist at work: Writings of Ruth Benedict.* NY: Atherton Press.

Modell, J.S. (1983). *Ruth Benedict: Patterns of a life.* Philadelphia, PA: University of Pennsylvania Press.

Mary Cabot Wheelwright

Lynes, B.B. and Paden, A. (2003). *Maria Chabot - Georgia O'Keefe: Correspondence, 1941 - 1949.* Albuquerque, NM: University of New Mexico Press.

Rodee, Marian E. (1995). *One hundred years of Navajo rugs.* Albuquerque: University of New Mexico Press.

Wheelwright, M.C. "Journey towards Understanding" in Niederman, S. (1988). A *quilt of words: Women's diaries, letters, and original accounts of life in the Southwest, 1860-1960.* Boulder, CO: Johnson Books

Wheelwright Museum of the American Indian http://www.wheelwright.org/about.html

Whitehill. W.M. (1962). *Independent historical societies: An enquiry into their research and publication functions and their financial future.* Boston: Boston Athaneum.

Los Luceros

Sze, C.P. (2000). *History of the Los Luceros Ranch.* Santa Fe, NM: Research Services of Santa Fe.

Undated real estate sales brochure from "The Road Runner Agency, Santa Fe. This is apparently from the time that Mr. and Mrs. Charles Collier owned the estate.

"Los Luceros Restored Wheelwright Property alive with layers of history," by Carmella Padilla in *New Mexico Magazine,* April, 2005.

"Historic Los Luceros" informational handouts from the Los Luceros Foundation, n.d. but acquired at Los Luceros, August, 2004.

"Los Luceros New Tourist Destination" in *Ultimate Guide to Rio Arriba County,* Summer 2004, pp. 4-5.

"Daytripping through northern New Mexico: A trip to Los Luceros and the surrounding area..." by Michelle Pentz Glave in *Santa Fe New Mexican,* August 18, 2004, p. C1-2.

Hosteen Klah

Jacobs, S., Thomas, W., and Lang S. (Eds.) (1997). *Two-Spirit people: Native American gender identity, sexuality, and spirituality.* Urbana and Chicago, IL: University of Illinois Press.

Newcomb, F.J. (1989). *Hosteen Klah: Navaho medicine man and sand painter.* Norman and London: University of Oklahoma Press.

Roscoe, W. (2000). *Changing ones: Third and fourth genders in native North America.* NY: St. Martins Griffin.

Roscoe, W. (1991). *Zuni Man-Woman.* Albuquerque, NM: University of New Mexico Press.

Williams, W. L. (1992). *Spirit and the flesh: Sexual diversity in American Indian culture.* Boston, MA: Beacon Press.

Henrietta Schmerler

Schmerler, H. (1931). Trickster marries his daughter. *Journal of American Folklore*, Volume 44, pp. 196-207

Spyra, Jen (n.d., but it was on the internet on 11/04/06. It no longer comes up on a Google search). "True tales that will have you sleeping with the lights on: Indian burial ground." *Columbia Spectator.* The Eye. Note: This is a brief but highly detailed and sensationalized account of Schmerler and what she did in Arizona. The author claims she found the information in boxes of old clippings, letters, and notebooks in Columbia's Low Library.

There are many contemporary newspaper articles about Shmerler's murder, including the New York Times, Los Angeles Times, Washington Post, and many regional newspapers. Many are easily available on line. Here are some of the most substantial articles:

"Girl Student Slain in Arizona Canyon, NY Times" AP (1857-Current file). July 25, 1931. Proquest Historical Newspapers. (The New York Times 1851-2001.) p. 1.

"Apache gets life for slaying girl," NY Times (1857-Current file). March 22, 1932. Proquest Historical Newspapers. (The New York Times 1851-2001.) p. 24.

"Agent solves cruel murder by Indian." (November 18, 1934). The Washington Post (1877-1954) Proquest Historical Newspapers The Washington Post (1887-1988).

"Cherokee princess offers to serve Apache's life term." AP. By the New York Times. March 31, 1932, Proquest Historical Newspapers The New York Times (1851-2001).

"El Asesinato de Henrietta Schmerler" in "Detectives y bandidos" Primera edicion Ano: 1937, Paginas: 194. I have never seen this item, but it turns up in a Google search and I can't help but include it. This is a Mexican pulp comic book, "Detectives y bandidos" from 1937. This issue also has a long article about John Dillinger. The only current internet reference to it is on http://spiderreturns.com/reprints/bandidos.html.

San Gabriel Dude Ranch

"The call of the Southwest" (advertising brochure for San Gabriel Ranch.) (ND). Woodcuts by Gustave Bauman. Santa Fe, NM: Santa Fe New Mexican Publishing Corporation.

Poling-Kempes, L. (1997). *Valley of shining stone: The story of Abiquiu.* Tucson, AZ: University of Arizona Press.

National Geographic photo of women at San Gabriel in "The Santa Fe Trail, Path to Empire," *The Nationai Geographic Magazine*, Vol. 56, No. 2, (Aug, 1929), 213-252, 213-214.

New Mexico State University "Brief history of the Sustainable Agriculture Science Center Alcalde, NM." One-page handout. ND

Photos by Edward A. Kemp and T. Harmon Parkhurst in the Photo Archives of the Palace of the Governor, http://www.palaceofthegovernors.org/photoarchives.html, with digitized collections at http://econtent.unm.edu/cdm4/indexpg.php

"San Gabriel Ranch Alcalde, New Mexico near Old Santa Fe." (advertising brochure) ND

Columbia and Anthropologists

Deacon, D. (1999). *Elsie Clews Parson: Inventing modern life.* Chicago, IL: University of Chicago Press.

Fowler, D.D. (2000). *A Laboratory for anthropology: Science and romanticism in the American Southwest, 1846-1930.* Albuquerque: University of New Mexico Press.

Goldfrank, E.S. (1977). *Notes on an undirected life: As one anthropologist tells it.* Queens College Publications in Anthropology. No. 3, 1977.

Parezo, N.J. (1993). *Hidden scholars: Women anthropologists and the Native American Southwest.* Albuquerque: University of New Mexico Press.

Stocking, G.W. (1992). *Ethnographer's magic and other essays in the history of anthropology.* Madison, WI: University of Wisconsin Press.

Frank Hamilton Cushing

Green, J., Ed. (1979). *Zuni: Selected writings of Frank Hamilton Cushing.* Lincoln and London: University of Nebraska Press.

Hinsley, C.M. (2002). *The lost itinerary of Frank Hamilton Cushing.* Tucson, AZ: University of Arizona Press.

Hinsley, C.M. and Wilcox, D.R., Eds. (1996). *The Southwest in the American imagination: The writings of Sylvester Baxter, 1881-1889.* Tucson, AZ: University of Arizona Press.

Hughte, F. (1994). *A Zuni artist looks at Frank Hamilton Cushing.* Zuni, NM: Zuni A:shiwi Publishing.

McFeeley, E. (2001). *Zuni and the American imagination.* New York: Hill and Wang, a division of Farrar, Straus, and Giroux.

Acknowledgements

Building writing communities and supporting other people's creativity has been as important to me as my own writing, because without the many people who have been part of my formal and informal writing communities as writers, teachers, role models, cheerleaders, readers, and most of all friends, I would not have written my novel. Many generous organizations provided resources and educational presentations which built my writing skills and helped my research. "Thank you" just begins to say how much I appreciate your ideas and support.

Thanks to the Lambda Literary Foundation, New Mexico Book Association, the Arizona Book Publishing Association, the Golden Crown Literary Society, the Arch and Bruce Brown Foundation, and the Astraea Foundation for awarding recognition to my earlier novel *Land Beyond Maps* and inspiring me to continue writing.

Thanks to the many organizations that provided instruction and support and a time and place to believe in myself as a writer and creative person: the Lesbian and Gay Men's Literary Circle of Bloomington, Indiana, 1976 -1980; Cambridge Center for Adult Education; Cummington Community for the Arts; Vermont Studio Center; the OutWrite Conferences of Bromfield Street Educational Foundation; *Gay Community News*; the William Joiner Center for the Study of War and Its Social Consequences Writers' Workshop; National Writers Union Boston Local; Society of the Muse of the Southwest (SOMOS); Haystack Mountain School of Crafts, and the Feminist Womens Writing Workshop.

Thanks for research materials and librarian help at the Southwest Research Center in Taos; Santa Fe Public Library; Taos Public Library; Tozzer Library at Harvard University and especially Gregory Finnegan; Albuquerque Public Library; the Bostonian Society; Boston Public Library; and the Palace of the Governors Photo Archives. Thanks to the

Historical Society of New Mexico for supporting all of us who write to preserve and honor New Mexico history. Thanks to the Somerville Public Library and the Minuteman Library System. Thanks to all the "Friends of the Library" for the book sales at so many libraries.

Thanks for their encouragement and for preserving lesbian history to Barbara Grier, Ann Bannon, Marie Kuda, Tracy Baim, and Joanne Passet. Thanks to all the people who write, produce, and sell books.

Thanks to so many wonderful writing groups and classes, especially the Harvard Square Scriptwriters from 1988–1993, and our facilitator, Laura Bernieri. Thanks to all the inspiring teachers: Toni Rea, Vincent Tampio, Tim O'Brien, Larry Heinemann, Jill Bloom, Erika Dreifus, Arthur Gold, Joan Larkin, Nadine Gordimer, David Farmer, Linda Sonna, Rachel Guido deVries, Leslea Newman, Lucille Clifton, Alexis DeVeaux, Summer Wood, Yani Batteau, Judah LeBlang, Toni Amato, and so many more wonderful writers who presented at conferences and workshops.

Thanks to Josephine Ross, Heidi Friedman, and Chris Guilfoy for thorough readings and copy editing. Thanks to Robin Cohen for her meticulous near-final reading and for the suggestion that led to the title.

Thanks to Susan Ressler for her online course "Women Artists of the American West" which was crucial to the research and writing of this novel and to my understanding of the history it covers. See the excellent publicly available course site on the internet at http://www.cla.purdue.edu/WAAW/. Thanks to Lesley University for its wonderful course *"The Traditions and Cultures of the Southwest: Teaching and Learning in Santa Fe, New Mexico"* taught by Sharlene Voogd Cochrane and Kristina Lamour Sansone, and to all the wonderful women with whom I spent an unforgettable week of travelling and learning about New Mexico in July, 2008. Thanks to Cathy Knott for our invaluable visit to the Los Luceros estate before it was renovated. Thanks to Marie Markesteyn for her help with Los

Luceros research during its brief time as a house museum.
Thanks to the clerk at Nahas Leather, 65 Charles Street,
Boston, who let me get a good look at the 1925 site of Mary
Cabot Wheelwright's "Carry-On Shop." Thanks to the Rose
Nichols House Museum on Beacon Hill.

Thanks to Mary Walker and Jenny Slick, the teachers for
the Navajo weaving and sightseeing class I took in Window
Rock, Arizona, in September, 2000.

Thanks to the historians who researched and wrote of
the crucial roles that women, lesbians, gay men, Native
Americans, Hispanics, and other previously overlooked
groups performed in the building of the American West.

Thanks to Ellen Larson and Thomas Hubschman for
all the help to make it happen, and for their inspiring writing
careers.

Thanks to everyone at Cambridge College for giving
me the stability and income to achieve my dreams while
helping others achieve theirs.

Thanks to my Tilchen family, especially my sister Cindy
Rogers and brother Carl Tilchen.

Thanks to all my friends in New Mexico for their
hospitality and friendship, especially Leora Zeitlin, Stuart
Kelter, Carol March, Molly McLaughlin, John Chester, Mary
Winslow, Jerry Richardson, Cynthia Homire, Jean-Vi Lenthe,
Barbara Shepherd, Abbie Conant, William Osborne, Daphne
Kutzer, Jean Smith, Kate O'Neill, Susan Ressler, Miriam
Sagan, Summer Wood, Veronica Slade, Lisa Schultz, and so
many more.

Thanks to all my friends in Massachusetts and
elsewhere: Carrie Dearborn, Maida E. Solomon, Helen
Meldrum, Eric Buck, Betti Brewer, Michael Beach, Lenni
Armstrong, Myrna Greenfield, Chris Guilfoy, Josephine Ross,
Heidi Friedman, Lynn Tibbets, Erica Brotschi, Duncan
Mitchel, Catherine Seo, Berni Zisserson, Robin Cohen, Alix
Dobkin, Joanne Passet, Hilary Koski, and so many others.
Thanks to Marsha White for accompanying me on so many
of the travels to places that are settings in this novel. Still

writing, talking, eating, rubberstamping, collaging, sewing, potlucking, rummaging, and walking to the beach since 1993, there are no thanks too many to the Swampscott writing group over our many years: Anne Sears, Dianne Jenkins, Irene Baker, Janet Dephoure, Lee Lewis, Sue Anne Willis, Sharon Rogolsky, and Laura de la Torre Bueno. Thanks to David Jenkins for being, listening, and so much more.

To all of these friends and so many more, I am so grateful. I dedicate this book to all my friends for listening to my dreams and plans. I can only hope to be there for you as you have been there for me.

About the Author

Maida Tilchen writes primarily to preserve and/or dramatize lesbian history. A lifetime book collector, she co-wrote the first "second wave" article on lesbian pulp novels, published in Margins magazine in 1975. Her writing has been published in *Gay Community News; Sojourner; Body Politic;* and books including *Nice Jewish Girls: A Lesbian Anthology; Lavender Culture; Women-Identified Women; Feminist Frameworks; Gay Press, Gay Power: The Growth of LGBT Community Newspapers in America,* and includes the foreword to the bibliography *The Lesbian in Literature.* She served as a VISTA volunteer in southern Indiana, was promotions manager for *Gay Community News* (Boston), and has had many research and writing jobs in the educational field. Currently, she is a library administrator and research skills instructor for a college serving primarily older minority women and immigrants. She has visited New Mexico often since 1993. After her first trip there, wanting to continue to live in the library-rich Boston area but to keep one foot in the "land of enchantment," she started writing fiction set in New Mexico.

Maida Tilchen's first novel *Land Beyond Maps*, won the following awards:

Finalist, 2010 Lambda Literary Foundation, Lesbian Debut Fiction

Winner, 2009 New Mexico Book Award, Gay/Lesbian

Finalist, 2009 New Mexico Book Award, Historical Fiction

Winner, 2010 Arizona Book Publishing Award, Gay/Lesbian

Finalist, 2010 Arizona Book Publishing Award, Multicultural

Finalist, 2010 Golden Crown Literary Society, Dramatic/General Fiction

Winner, 2000 Arch and Bruce Brown Foundation Full-Length Lesbian/Gay Historical Fiction Competition

Maida Tilchen also won:

Honorable Mention, 2007, Astraea Foundation Lesbian Writers Award, Fiction

Maida Tilchen can be contacted at maida@savvypress.com

Learn more about *Land Beyond Maps* and *She's Gone Santa Fe* at

http://landbeyondmaps.typepad.com/land_beyond_maps/

and

http://www.savvypress.com